THE CALLING OF HIGHBROOK

JO PRIESTLEY

*Copyright © 2023 Jo Priestley
All rights reserved*

Dedication

Many special people have shared my book-writing experience with me, and I would like to thank them sincerely.

Thank you to my readers who provided invaluable feedback, some anonymously but the ones I know, in alphabetical order are Ann, James, Lisa, Lynne, Martin and Tracey.

Thank you to Andrew for his superb editing skills; and to my family for their support and encouragement, without which, little old Jo would never have believed in herself enough to pursue 'The Calling of Highbrook'. She will always be grateful.

4

William
Chapter 1

I've watched your hazy outline approaching for so long, and when you finally emerge from the veil shrouding the moors the sight is ethereal.

Eyes round, a curl escapes your bonnet—a real curl, not a preened one grown lank from the damp like mama's, like Lottie's; you look like a startled child.

"Oh," you say, caught unawares. "I don't often see anyone out here in the back of beyond."

Your cheery tone is a pleasant contrast to the dismal day. Our eyes catch and hold.

"William, erm Will," I say, hastily trying to soften the formality, "Hudson," I continue. "I tend to walk a couple of miles every morning before work if time permits."

How disappointing, William, I think. Such uninspiring words will never encourage you to discover more about me, will never make you think of me again after this brief interlude.

"I fear I will grow fat now I own a car."

Your burst of laughter makes me smile then drop my eyes to the heather at our feet. I want to stay right where I am, but I also want to bolt like a deer, the strange conflict striking me mute.

"Helena Beaumont," you say, "But most people call me Nell. So nice to meet you."

Your steady gaze makes me think you know something I don't. I'd like to ask where you've come from, where you're going to, but I only muster a cursory smile and nod in response.

Now the silence swamps us leaving you with no alternative but to restart your walk. Raising my hat, I am compelled to simply watch you go.

"Perhaps I may see you tomorrow then, William erm Will," you say, throwing a warm smile at me over your shoulder.

I feel like a dear friend.

"Her smile was like sunshine," the epitaph grandpa chose for grandma's headstone suddenly springs to mind. I've never come across a better one.

Step by step you're leaving me; will you ever return? You look over your shoulder one last time before vanishing again into the fog. I turn away, my face hot at being caught in the act of staring at you.

Yet you did the very same.

Blowing out my cheeks I've already begun a mental countdown to tomorrow morning. I swear to myself that come hail or shine I shall be here.

The imprint of you walks in rhythm by my side as I glance at the low sky. A hole has been scorched through the mist.

Oh, how lovely, the sun has come out.

I am blinded.

*

The fifteenth day of September is circled and marked in bold type on the calendar. It is the second anniversary of the establishment of *Hudson & Carr* and we've made quite a splash in Yorkshire and beyond in that short space of time.

The Yorkshire Post wrote about us in their latest edition with a two-page article about our "fine establishment" and the local Chamber of Commerce has proposed a gala dinner in our honour such has been our success. So, we thought the best pat on the back for our staff would be to give them the afternoon off. They scurried off like mice at twelve o'clock on the dot for drinks at the Feathers in the Market Square before heading home for the weekend. For me, the call of home is never strong so I'm in no hurry to head off.

I look up as Harry bobs his head around the door on his way out.

"Come on, Hudson, I know that desk is made from the oak of the Spanish Armada or something along those lines, but it can't be so enthralling surely," he says, "Time to head off and live that little thing called a life."

Wearing his new-season suit without the jacket he's just returned from his latest trip to his parent's home on the East Coast. His hair is blonder from the sun and his white teeth popping out from his tanned face with each smile startle me every time.

"It was an English ship which fought the Armada if you must know. I'll be done in a minute," I say, "Enjoy your weekend of decadence."

"Enjoy your weekend of servitude," he calls, already on his way home to his wife, Catherine.

She's much older than him and they don't have any children because Harry told me once he couldn't possibly stand the competition. It may well have been just an excuse because they're unable to have them. I wouldn't know. We're very much just friendly business partners and doing rather well out of it. Jumping ship from *Thornton Black & Associates* was the best thing for us in the end, though we're both now persona non grata. This bothers me though far more than Harry.

Working on the plans for a particular house called Highbrook is taking up far too much of my time of late. I'm in two minds whether to buy it, and the owner has become a friend over the months which is fuelling the obsession. Business is undoubtedly good, but I sank most of my savings into it, so I'll need some additional funding. If I'm not drawing the plans, I'm thinking about them.

Since that day I met you, our paths haven't crossed again though it isn't for the want of trying. I've been tramping the moors, driving around the area, even popping into shops I've never been in and generally just mooching around town just to try and spot you. I pray in vain as I turn each corner that this time you will be there, but each time I head home with the bitter taste of defeat. I should relent but somehow, I just can't.

Slumping back in my chair, I drop my pen and rub my eyes between my thumb and forefinger. I can't fathom why I would be so unsettled by one encounter. How can I still be recovering from the loss of something I never had?

I grab my things and lock the door, juggling my umbrella as the rain is coming down like stair rods. Everyone in the world looks like they've left to go somewhere else, and the quietness of the street makes me think of the emptiness of home. I can't face it.

My eyes still scour the roads as I drive, yet I know it's fruitless in this weather. Spotting a sign for Highbrook Falls I make a split-second decision to take a detour. Far better to be lonely there than within four walls. I head to my special parking spot which isn't necessary today, but I found it years ago to protect the privacy and solitude I have always craved. These days walkers appear like a swarm on the few hot days a year, but they haven't stumbled on the forest track bearing off behind the gorse bushes. I used to walk it, but my Austin is up to the job.

The track eventually peters out at the tree line, and I hear the roar of the Falls as I pull on my boots and tie the laces with wet fingers. This place has seen me in every weather, every season and I can hear it calling me now that I'm nearby. I can see the recent rain has made the stream a torrent as I scramble down the banking to get to my little piece of paradise. Always waiting, this place is solid, dependable.

I perch on my rock and stare at the water rolling by as day wanes. The sound of the water is a meditation though I try to ignore the damp seeping into my bones.

But my thoughts are not peaceful today because I know I've reached a dead end in my search. Who knew you were just passing through? I could be driving around here the rest of my life to no avail, the saddest most sickening of thoughts.

Breathing the fresh moist air, I tap the rain from my hat.

As I drop my hand, I cock my ear. Is that a voice? Surely, it can't be.

"Hello, William Will," it says again, this time as clear as a bell above the babble of the river.

Turning sharply around, I need to focus a second or two through the curtain of rain. But now I'm certain who it is from those curls spilling out from her hat and draping over one shoulder.

Lifting her skirts and heading down the banking towards me I see mud splattered on the bottom of her coat and boots and I'm standing up to wait. I'm too impatient, taking a step forward to meet her as she reaches the bottom.

So here you are, Nell. Here you are, appearing from nowhere yet again. Where on earth did you go? I shrug the question off because I don't care as you're right here, right now and I'm looking at you. You have a half-smile on your lips the same as our first meeting, your intense expression intoxicating.

This could only be a chance meeting, so I hold my breath and play the waiting game. The hammering of the rain on my coat is getting louder and I'm perspiring.

You peep at me from under the brim of your hat, and I can only stare at you and cross my fingers you will say the right thing.

An almost theatrical sigh escapes you, making me raise my eyebrows.

"So, what on earth does a girl have to do around these parts to speak to you, Mr Hudson? I'd prefer not to have to trudge up hill and down dale to get your attention."

I'm laughing now because you said the right thing in the end. The release is so powerful I must seem like a mad man, but the sound is bouncing around us and I can't stop it.

Jumping, you smile quickly so I know everything is fine, I haven't scared you away.

Just a few, long wonderfully tortuous weeks ago you came out of the mist like an hallucination, and I've lived a lifetime in my head since. Now suddenly my world has shifted; once a rough stone my world has been polished to perfection when I didn't see it happening.

My eyes roam across your face and somehow, I sense you want me to kiss you, but I don't. Your face is taut, and you seem uncertain, and I don't like that expression. I offer a grin to reassure you and you smile back with eyes darting quickly between my own.

I can't help reaching down to touch one of the contrary little curls at the side of your ear under your hat. The softness makes it seem like it isn't really there.

"I thought you were never going to ask," I whisper.

Laughing together now my neck relaxes freed of all the horrible tension. I feel poised to start the rest of my life; to start my life even.

Suddenly from nowhere I shudder. I have a sensation like someone is walking over my grave. My blood pressure pounds in my ears but I'm careful to fix my smile in place.

Why I should be thinking it I don't know but how dreadful it would be if one day this memory soured.

I'd hate this moment to turn into some kind of living hell that I'm desperate to erase from my mind.

Chapter 2

We must decamp.

Casting my eyes upwards the rain is showing no sign of abating, but where to go? Horton is out of the question for so many reasons, but I frequent a little local inn occasionally and although women rarely venture in, they're not forbidden. I'm not keen on the alternative of us sitting dripping wet in my car.

This simple little inn is set to become the centre of the universe. A few die-hard locals huddled around the bar are in their own little regular pub world where everyone sees each other every day but knows nothing of consequence about one another. They haven't a clue they're now the supporting cast in our little drama.

We brave the stony silence which fills the air and exactly eight pairs of eyes if you include the landlord, slowly travel up and then down us. As expected, we raise a few eyebrows, less because of the state of us and more because of you. They're sizing us up and making no bones about it.

I don't smile or nod a greeting as this would be inappropriate. Now, as if by unseen choreography, conversation resumes because they've decided we're no threat to their cosy little evening. We are now invisible. I expect this type of behaviour around these parts.

The Yew Tree is a basic inn, well-worn stone-flagged floors, and wooden settles. It's quiet most of the time and especially in bad weather. I don't care about the lack of creature comforts as all we really need is the warmth of a fire.

Removing your coat for you I place it alongside my own on the coatrack. Your dress is simple, you're not a lady in the literal sense but a lady is exactly what you are. Sitting across the table from me that knowing expression reappears and if I'm not mistaken, you're enjoying yourself toying with me. The raw appeal of you has me shifting in my chair as your eyes stare directly into mine then drop seductively as you speak. I think you may know the affect you're having on me, and I think you may just like it.

"Well now, here we are," I say, "I confess to being a little confused about your whereabouts, I thought I would run into you again."

You look at me coyly.

"It was painful watching your awkward behaviour that morning," you say, sliding your tiny fingers distractingly up and down your sherry schooner, fully aware now of the effect this is having on me. You laugh, your eyes full of mischief.

"I can't believe how uncomfortable I made you. It was so charming, utterly endearing."

If only you knew how I feel about you. My feelings are powerful and I'm still trying to make sense of them, but I've finally realised I have absolutely no choice in the matter.

You interrupt my mental wandering.

"When I happened on you earlier it was a surprise. I watched you a while and then I saw it as a sign."

As our eyes lock, I clear my throat You raise your eyebrows and grin like a little imp, so a low laugh escapes me.

"I only thought you wouldn't entertain a man like me for many reasons."

I smile ruefully as I say it, but you shake your head. I've always had a quiet self-confidence for the most part, a comfort in my own skin, but this has apparently lessened over the weeks.

"You do yourself an injustice, sir, you need to see yourself from where I'm sitting."

Tilting your head back you narrow your eyes. I'm thrown from such bare-faced seduction. I blush but I don't want to come over as a bumbling bag of inexperience because I'm certainly not that.

I just can't help myself.

"It was as though you disappeared, Nell."

I haven't said your name out loud before. I've carried that unsettling name in my mind for so long it sounds odd to hear it coming from my lips.

Your wistful expression makes me want to swallow the words and you stare at the fire for a long second.

"I'm staying at my grandmother's cottage. It's not too far from here. There's a path up to the Falls from the back of the cottage which I used when I visited as a child. Perhaps you know it. That's how I came across your car. I knew it was yours, there aren't many in the area. Granny left the cottage and a little money to me and my brother, but it needs some love and attention. It deserves some to be honest."

You take a small sip of sherry.

"I'm fine financially at least for a while, so I thought I'd take the opportunity."

Somehow, I can't help thinking there's far more to it. The thought is fleeting as I'm too engrossed in just looking at you, listening to you. Your chestnut curls frizzed from the rain; your skin pale but not sallow I'm overcome by the natural perfection of you.

"Shall we go?" you ask.

I nod and swig the last of my beer. So, I must take you home, but I don't want to leave you. Holding out my hand to lift you from your seat you wrap your fingers around mine, holding fast briefly before I help you on with your coat. We leave to walk to my car sharing my umbrella and our shoulders touching make me think it might be the most erotic contact I've ever had. The realisation saddens me.

Once settled in the passenger seat you offer the first of many directions to your cottage as I set off, wipers squeaking inadequately across the windscreen.

"I've seen *Hudson & Carr* in town. Your premises on The Crescent are very impressive," you say, "What's Mr Carr like?"

I really don't want to make polite small talk as its wasting precious time, but I know I must for the time being at least.

"Mr Carr and I complete each other in business terms. What I lack, he doesn't and vice versa. We've known each other a long time and we wouldn't be doing so well without him because I'm not very good at promotion and pushing myself forward."

"No, I'd say you're more one of life's observers."

The comment isn't said unkindly. You've been thinking about me more than I could ever have hoped.

I'm intrigued about where you live and the fact you live alone, I find it highly irregular. I know women are becoming far more independent after holding the fort in the war, and who can blame them, but you certainly don't seem like an old maid.

Emerging from the lane which leads to the Falls we turn right and follow the main road for a few minutes before you point to a track between hawthorn hedges which ends at two stone pillars. They stand forlorn, custodians of an empty space, the gate having long since departed. I can feel a wry smile break at the thought of just how close you were all along. I keep my headlights on as it's so dark with the rain, and the white render of the tiny cottage shines my way. The perfect location, the place is isolated but not remote. Civilisation is still nearby.

My nerves are returning. I'm finding it hard to look at you again as I jump out of the car and grab the umbrella. I think how I should behave as I make my way to open your door.

Stepping out elegantly you stand with me under the shelter. We look at each other in silence with only the rain battering the umbrella as background acoustic. This time I manage to hold your gaze but I'm painfully out of my depth here.

I take a silent deep breath. The next part needs to be perfect so I can think about it forever.

"Thank you," is all I can muster but your eyes tell me you know the meaning behind the words when you close them. Startled by the invitation I recover to edge my face nearer to yours. Though it's a terribly big step I'm ready and I bow my head to give you just the lightest of kisses. Your lips are trembling; I hope it isn't just from the cold. My throat constricts realising I've been waiting too long for a kiss like this.

I want more. Restraint is now a challenge as my body is responding as it should, but I must find it. We must proceed with the greatest of caution and a second kiss will have to keep.

You don't ask me to see inside your cottage and I'm happy and sad in equal measure. I don't want to go home, not without you, but I must, and I do.

We make plans to have a walk on the moors in two days' time, but all the way home I think once you find out more about me, you will no doubt disappear once more.

Chapter 3

My unbuttoning has begun.

The waiting game is finally over, and we walk on the moors when I finish work, but I haven't any time to catch my breath. Life with you is a whirling tornado of a ride and if I didn't know already, I soon have rubber-stamped confirmation you are unlike anyone I've ever met before. Our conversations are fluid, uninhibited and those hidden depths appear quickly exposing my stupidity in thinking I could ever, would ever see them all.

You're unconventional but so much more. You can be irrational, almost childish sometimes during our animated conversations, but then you can be sweet, loving, tender when I kiss you and I kiss you often. You can be entirely yourself with me, you say, and I'm delighted to hear this. Discovering so many sides to your character is a joy.

"Which Nellie will be making a special guest appearance this afternoon I wonder?"

"If only I knew in advance, I would be sure to give you notice," you say as we set off again on another moorland adventure. They are an adventure, never a dull moment.

In truth I love meeting the petulant Nell, the vivacious Nell, and the elusive Nell. They all put me under your spell in equal measure. I'm playing catch up all the time, trying to keep pace with you and your myriad of emotions.

It's a huge step for me and will be a huge shock for my mother, but I suggest a visit. Though a little hasty, her birthday falls at the weekend and I'm keen to get the formality of the first meeting out of the way. I know what I want and I'm not getting any younger, so I must pursue it. I'd dearly love to meet your family, but they live some distance away you tell me.

Before he retired, your father was the village doctor in Wrenbridge where you lived as a child and your mother left the cottage to live with him there when they married. She enjoyed the simple life of a doctor's wife.

You're taken aback when I mention meeting my mother and naturally, I understand, so I leave the burning question hanging in the air. However, the following day I'm reassured when you ask what time we will be visiting and if you should arrange a posy for her birthday.

I pick you up Saturday morning with more than a little trepidation about the next few hours. Visiting my mother has always been more out of duty than love for many reasons. She still lives in the lodge she bought with my father when they were first married but has help to keep it immaculate, never an item out of place.

She's taken extra care with her hair specially for the occasion, but it isn't long into the visit before it's obvious to me that she has her reservations about you. It's no surprise; I know her, and I know why. She prefers straightforward women, with a straightforward approach to life; someone who won't rock the boat, much like herself and like my late wife, Charlotte. She's disappointed and I'm disappointed in her for not allowing herself the opportunity to get to know you, especially when you are being so perfectly charming.

"I've heard so much about you," she says disingenuously, a sickly smile accompanying one of her limp ladylike handshakes.

I'm glad I've never been on the receiving end of one of those handshakes, it would wither me, but you seem unfazed. This lie falls casually from my mother's lips because observing the niceties at all costs is at the core of her. She's betrayed by her body language and in this I am well versed, due to conversation being in short supply in our household. I catch the brief sideward glance your way, the slightly disdainful look on her face which would go unnoticed to the untrained eye.

"So, you haven't known each other long from what I understand?" she asks, the faintest note of hope in her voice that you're just a flash in the pan.

I look at you, wearing what I'm certain is your best dress, strewn with tiny blue roses and ending just above your best boots. I'm utterly bewitched, beguiled.

"No, Mrs Hudson, not long," you say, "but I almost feel like I've known William all my life. I appreciate this might sound strange."

Your cheeks are aglow and my heart leaps and pirouettes as much as my mother's must be sinking. She smooths the hair at the back of her head and coughs her irritation away, disguising this with an elegant hand over her mouth. I know what she's thinking or at least the gist of it. She's thinking what fairy tale drivel; the girl needs to get a hold of herself. It cements her conviction we'll fold at the first sign of real life.

I talk more than usual to compensate for the awkwardness, and this too irritates my mother. She'll be worried you will lead me a merry dance and she's probably right, but I'm chomping at the bit for the challenge. Not before time I'm with someone who is almost like part of me. I'm keen to fix things if you're unhappy, I want to make it all better so I can be fixed and better too. You're so lost and insecure at times in contrast to my pragmatic ways but I find your take on life captivating. You make me see things differently, like from a child's eye.

Freshly made Victoria sponge cake by Mrs Franks and copious amounts of tea help the time pass bearably enough. My mother watches me intently as we head out of the drawing room and into the hall to make our goodbyes and seems like she wants to say something. I hesitate in the doorway, but after a pregnant pause she just offers a feigned, cheery, "Thank you for coming William," and with a delayed, "Look after yourself."

Back in the car you turn your wide eyes on me.

"Do you think it went well?"

Oh, what a question. I really don't want to lie to you, so I choose my words very carefully.

"As well as it could go with my mother," I say, "She's not one to wear her heart on her sleeve."

You nod, and I'm not sure what you're thinking but then you change the subject.

"You know, William, I've been wondering when you plan to invite me to your home."

I've had the very same thought for weeks little do you know.

"Well, as you mention it there's no time like the present. What do you say?"

Lifting your shoulders, you smile my way.

"Oh, I'm so relieved. I was beginning to worry you were ashamed of me."

Your laughter sounds nervous.

I turn quickly towards you placing my hand on your arm. I don't even care my mother might be looking out of the window though I doubt it.

"Let me make myself clear, Miss Beaumont I could never be ashamed of you, quite the opposite in fact. I'm nothing if not gallant and I want to take our… relationship at your pace."

Your eyes glistening, I see I have made my point well.

I don't have a team of staff like my mother. I have a housekeeper, Mrs Charles who lives in Horton with her family and I'm very happy with the arrangement. We did have staff when Charlotte was alive but when she died, I found after a while I wasn't in need of their services. Has it really been fifteen years?

My Victorian terrace is on four floors, and I'm lucky to live in an extremely coveted area on the outskirts of town.

Mrs Charles opens the door in her coat when we arrive. I could sense the twitching of curtains as we walked up the front pathway.

"Mr Hudson, I was just on my way home," she glances over my shoulder at you, blushing, "How do you do, miss," she says with a small curtsey which I always find mildly embarrassing.

"Please Mrs Charles there's really no n...," I start but before I can finish your warm smile has put her at ease.

"I'm very well, thank you, Mrs Charles. Mr Hudson tells me he doesn't know what he would do without you."

Dropping her head her mouth twitches and she stands back to allow us to enter.

"Thank you kindly, miss. There's a pie at the top of the cellar to warm, sir but if you like I can stay to make tea before I leave as you've got company."

"That's alright, Mrs Charles I would hate to interfere with your Saturday afternoon plans."

"Righto, well see you on Monday sir and nice to meet you, miss," she says, donning her hat without looking in the mirror so it sits comically askew.

Dear old Mrs Charles, I think as she heads to the gate, if I go ahead with my plans, she would be a sad loss.

Showing you around the ground floor is strange. There hasn't been anyone here since Charlotte though not really through choice, only circumstance. I watch you as you take in the impressive original features, including the grand fireplaces in the sitting and dining room. The décor was Charlotte's choice, very opulent in keeping with the house.

"I'll make the tea," you say, "I'm sure I can locate everything I need. Go sit in the front room and stoke the fire into action," adding, "Please," then laughing.

Shaking my head I beam at the sight of you at work in my kitchen, I can't quite take in the ordinary yet extraordinary scene. You're making tea for me, for us, in my kitchen and you look so at home.

"This is how I like my women, shackled to the stove. Any man who tells you differently is a complete and utter liar, enlightened times or not," I say.

I try to keep my face straight as I wait for my ears to have a boxing.

"Enlightened times indeed, didn't I tell you that I eat arrogant men for pudding?" you bat back, glancing over your shoulder and raising an eyebrow in a threatening but so, so seductive way.

I have no doubt about it. I shake my head thinking there are worse ways to go.

I rarely use my room nowadays as I much prefer to sit in my study. After retreating there during my marriage, I just never got out of the habit.

There is a charge in the atmosphere as I look at the way your dress skims your figure. I've always found it difficult not to let my eyes stray to your curves. Big but not too big, your dress is straining ever so slightly at the buttons. You wouldn't notice unless you were looking but I can tell you're taking great pleasure in watching me watching them.

"I really think I ought to be getting you home," I say after only about an hour.

This situation is unbearable, a gentleman I may be, but I am still a man. I've been picturing myself tearing the buttons of your dress to open it wide and bury my head in the pale mounds.

"Do you really want to take me home?" you ask.

I don't see any sign of a smile about your lips and at first, I'm not sure of the meaning behind your words.

"No," I say deciding honesty is always best when it comes to us.

"Then don't."

As I stare at you, I'm finding it difficult to control the passion which is threatening to be revealed.

"I think it might be best, Nell. I've been alone for many years and the effect you have on me is somewhat distracting."

You sigh but still no hint of humour appears in your eyes. I'm out of my depth, drowning in intoxication and losing control.

"I could ease your loneliness. I see it within you, and I would dearly like to ease it."

"What are you saying to me? I don't want your pity; I couldn't bear it."

"Pity is far from what I feel for you, my love."

Standing, you walk towards me and bend to kiss me. You kiss me so softly, so tenderly it almost breaks me.

I lift your hand to put it to my lips and you stroke my face, your sweet expression talking to me. Pulling me gently by the hand we make our way to the foot of the stairs.

"Nell, I must tell you I'm not the sort of man to take advantage of a lady," I say, my willpower fading with every step.

"I know," you say, pulling some more, "And I will never be a lady to be taken advantage of."

At the top of the stairs, I guide you to my bedroom, but I don't draw the curtains so as not to arouse suspicion - the nets will have to suffice as camouflage. To think I would ever consider drawing my curtains in the middle of the afternoon.

I'm almost dizzy as we fall onto the bed. Stroking your hair, I look down into those eyes which entrance me so much and I can see all my passion staring back at me. You reach up and pull my face down to yours, kissing me and then I'm surprised when your tongue slips into my mouth in the French way. We're breathless with lust, long-awaited yearning. I fumble with the tiny buttons of your dress, heavens they are so tiny, but then I finally get the chance to see what had been teasing me all night and feel the blood flow furiously. You know how to swiftly undo my trousers making me think fleetingly if you might have done this before. I quash the thought quickly because I must quash that thought. Exposing me and my desire in all its proud glory I pull up your dress to reveal a glimpse of milky skin. I unwrap another layer to see a darkness at the top of your thighs. I'm pulsating, eager to have you.

"I need you, Nell, I need to be inside you. Don't make me wait any longer," I say, using words I could never have imagined, only desperate to be part of you.

"Come get me," you whisper.

Your legs come up around my back as you moan and bite my shoulder when I enter you. You are somewhere else, somewhere which clearly gives you overwhelming pleasure. I'm doing this to you, and you are doing something new to me. I'm left in no doubt you are ready as the fervour is so intense, and I think I lose my mind for a while.

I would have been forever satisfied with that one time if this is how it had turned out for us, Nell, it would have been impossible for me to predict, imagine even.

I've smashed through the glass ceiling of expectation. You have spoiled me, the shards that stick in my being for all time are the most painful of pleasures.

You lose yourself in me and the feeling is all-consuming, making me wonder what was happening before you and all those lost years.

Our unexpected first time together takes me far, far away from my comfort zone. I'm so glad to see the back of comfort.

I lay panting, staring at the ceiling, still recovering from the shock.

"Did you love your wife?" you ask.

The directness of your question takes even more of my breath away. We've barely spoken of Charlotte before, and I still want so much to be honest but I'm afraid it might make me sound hollow.

"Would you think less of me if I said that I'm not certain."

Taking my hand you stroke it, staring at it lost in your thoughts. It looks like the hand of a child in comparison to mine.

"No," is all you say.

A sudden flicker of something new appears in the pit of my stomach. Trying in the silence to put my finger on what it could be I finally recognise it as a gall of guilt. I close my eyes and shiver.

Oh, Charlotte, how I wronged you. Please forgive me, I didn't know better.

How can a man tell his wife he loves her when he does not feel it in his heart?

Chapter 4

I know I've little to draw on to impress you. I don't have a stock of funny anecdotes from a life well lived, no riveting adventures to recount. I can't do anything about my past, my future is what matters now.

"So, your parents separated when you were ten, that must have been quite a scandal," you say, taking a bite of your sandwich.

We're nestling in blankets on our rock by the Falls and Mrs Charles has provided us with a little picnic. The weather's much more clement than the last time we came but the cold wind is never far away here.

"I suppose it might have been for my mother," I say, "But we were financially secure. The only thing I hated was the well-meaning pity bestowed on us. Before he left us, my father was a busy man making his money in textiles in the West Riding until we moved to the countryside."

"Did you see him ever after he left?"

Your face if full of concern but there's really no need.

"Not once. You don't need to look so upset because he was a remote figure even before I went to boarding school. I can picture my mother listening to him waxing lyrical about the minutia of the textile industry at the end of each day, gin and tonic in hand. He didn't notice the bored glaze of her eyes. I was just a boy and I noticed."

Patting my hand, you stop eating to give me your full attention.

"I think you might have been a lonely little boy. I can't imagine your mother filled the void."

You laugh to take the sting from your words, but you're spot on.

"During the school holidays she was always busy dabbling in the latest fad, be it watercolours, needlepoint, piano lessons, and she was never far away, at least in body, if not in mind."

Chuckling together, I pour some lemonade and hand you a tin cup.

"I was completely unaware of it then of course, but I've always felt disconnected from my mother. We speak in the third person, never discussing the happenings of our lives or what we really believe in any great depth or any depth at all in fact. I often think of life back then as one long play I was watching from a back row seat and had no part in."

"I'd no idea you were so poetic, William," you say.

You lean forward and touch your lips to my cheek. How can such a small gesture stir the very core of me?

"I still struggle to comprehend why someone would decide to have a child then almost pretend they didn't exist. It may be too late for me but I've no intention of repeating their mistakes," I say.

But you're not my mother, you're not Charlotte who was sickly I realised soon after we married. Sadly, we never conceived a child but now I know it was for the best as she simply wouldn't have been strong enough.

Your previous life and loves remain a mystery, and one I find myself burning to solve. This unknown past makes me jealous and insecure, traits which are proving difficult to hide. I'm amazed how irrational it can make my thoughts. I must take great care.

By the end of our picnic the question is choking me.

If you did have a previous love, it clearly didn't work out. Perhaps they tried to change you, that might be why. I make a secret vow now to never ask anything from you I'm not certain you want to give. You're poised to be my love, at least I pray it so, but it may be like trying to hold dry sand in your hand. How I hope not.

"Charlotte and I met when we went to visit my mother's cousin from Nuneaton one summer. She was a friend of her daughter. I find it odd how one moment a person is a stranger, the next you're planning a wedding. Were you ever tempted?"

A little clumsy but needs must, I fear. I hold my breath.

Turning your head you stare at the waterfall, your mouth set in a line.

"There was one person," you say.

The silence is unsettling me, yet I can't risk not discovering more so I sit tight.

"In the end, we were just at different phases in our lives."

Are we at different phases? I don't think we are, but he may not have thought so either.

"How long were you together?"

I'm pleased you're facing away otherwise my face, tense and pensive, would have betrayed my attempt to adopt a nonchalant tone of voice.

"It must have been around a year, a little longer perhaps."

I'm unable to gauge if your heart was broken because you're far away in a place I don't know. I must find out if you liked it there, so I cover your hand to bring you back to me. When you turn your head, I can you're still affected by it, and I really wish I hadn't been so inquisitive.

"Sorry," you say, though I'm unsure exactly what it is you're apologising for, "His name was Mark, and it simply didn't work out but now I'm so very pleased it didn't."

I beam at you, thinking this is exactly what I need to hear. I don't feel the need to ask any more questions... and risk getting answers I wouldn't like.

As I'm considering how to put the afternoon back on track you break the silence suddenly, a smile emerging and lighting up your face.

"That's all in the past now, what matters is us, here and now," you say.

So, that's that I see. I can't help but play out my own bleak images about your time together over and over in my mind, torturing myself with sickening thoughts of you stealing secret kisses, sharing special moments. The sheer arrogance of these emotions makes me ashamed, so I feel small, and possessive. You're a grown woman, why shouldn't you have loved before, had a life before me?

But it's still a horrible little twist of the gut.

*

I must learn from past mistakes. Something Charlotte once told me sticks in my mind.

"My dearest wish would be for you to let me in, William," she said.

She'd nipped into the study, to tell me she was retiring early that evening. Her cough had been steadily worsening, but it wasn't uncommon for her to experience bouts of pleurisy every few months and confine herself to the house or even to bed. I'd almost become inured to the sound though this pains me now.

I looked up from my drawings, to see an odd expression on her face.

"I'm sorry, my dear," I said, "I thought you were engrossed in your book."

I wasn't keen to continue the conversation, but she clearly was. She sighed, looking terribly weary and I wondered if she was tired of constantly being ill, or tired of me.

"You show me so little of yourself, it sometimes just isn't enough. I would be glad if we could spend more time in each other's company."

My wife made a fair point. I'm not entirely sure why we lived separate lives, but it was just our way. I didn't hold back on purpose, I only assumed she felt the same, but she must have decided at some stage she wanted more.

She leaned and kissed my cheek from behind and I patted her hand on my shoulder, craning my neck to look at her.

"You look tired, Lottie, I'm sorry you're feeling neglected. We'll talk about it more in the morning."

She shook her head, but didn't appear irritated saying, "Yes, tomorrow it is then."

I watched her walking from the room in her elegant velvet gown, one of many, her pretty, fair hair looking as perfect at the end of the day as it did at the beginning. She was never without a lace handkerchief in her hand.

I wonder now if she had a sixth sense because for Charlotte and I tomorrow never came.

The following morning, Derby, her ladies' maid came flying down the corridor to my room to inform me Mrs Hudson had left this life.

Then she left me to my dark thoughts, thoughts I was to endure for years to come.

I can safely say it wasn't pleasant.

*

Now I know precisely what Charlotte meant. You should want to be connected to your love and I'm troubled because I really can't picture a life without you. The realisation is like an exposed jugular; exposed, ripe and ready for the kill.

"I know you say you think I'm the most special person you've ever met, Will, but please don't put me on a pedestal. It makes me uneasy; I can never live up to such high expectation."

I think I catch a glimpse of your own insecurities, but I shrug your words off.

"Never fear, I know what I'm getting myself into. I'm growing to know every side to you," I smile raising my eyebrows, "Well, I'd certainly like to."

You laugh a low laugh, one which unsettles me in the best way. Our conversations are my most treasured part about us. We're free to say what's on our mind.

"Don't worry, my darling, life has never been or felt more real. You don't need to be perfect to sit on my pedestal, believe me. I've done everyone else's idea of perfection; it wasn't for me."

You look away waving your hand.

"Oh, words come easily, time will tell," you say.

"Oh, so flippant. Well, I will take the greatest of pleasure in proving you wrong."

An idea has been germinating which will let me prove how much I love you, and I won't let you down if that was what happened before.

And my plan puts Highbrook centre stage.

I have only one more person I need to convince before I can be sure everything is finally in place, and I can be happy forever:

Frances.

Chapter 5

Perhaps the important people in our lives don't need time to grow on us. They're the ones who make an instant impact and this may be the whole point. We don't have to try.

Mrs Frances Cundall is a very important person to me.

It was mid-July when we first met. She needed help she told me as country estates are costly and although she had more money than most due to her late husband's shrewd investments it was still insufficient to maintain a grand old property. She considered the possibility of selling but was astute enough to know however that either way the house or grounds needed some work. I could tell that despite being on her own, she wasn't keen to turn her back on the Victorian splendour of the house. I knew because she never once mentioned during our meeting where she might go if she was to leave. Frances fascinated me from the start: confident, composed, a trailblazer, she's still an attractive woman despite being in what I suspect is her late fifties. Marrying Benjamin, Ben as she refers to him, transformed Frances from a woman of humble beginnings to a woman of substance. Ben had died and their son, Joshua left home soon after, so she was left to "rattle around the old place," as she put it. It was obvious though that the thought of locking the door for the very last time and walking away clearly left her cold.

"When you see Highbrook you'll know why I'm here," she told me, "My mother-in-law had to go into a home because she lost her mind. This was the only way she was going to leave the estate behind before she died. I completely understand."

I was surprised she confided in me so quickly, but perhaps loneliness makes one a little more trusting. I've never discovered why she came to a smaller company such as ours, and not one of the more established firms but she said my enthusiasm sealed our partnership. I'm keen to help bring her ideas to life because her enthusiasm is infectious.

"I can suggest some remodelling on the house, but it will certainly be a huge life change for you," I told her.

"I'm ready for change," she said.

We were on the same page.

My whole life has taken an about turn since my first visit I think on the drive over. If I'd known my world could alter so quickly, I wouldn't have thought I'd be ready. But, like Frances I am ready. The itchy sensation of discontentment has scattered to the winds.

Nerves are making me nauseous as I approach the familiar outline. Highbrook has taken on a different hue in the weaker light of another season, the dark clouds creating shadows and textures which weren't there the first time I came. The gardens have shed the exotic colours of summer for the more subtle tones of autumn.

I stop in the driveway and wind down the car window. Though a little past its former glory the house is stunning nevertheless—a fine example of Victorian gothic revival. My eyes scan the asymmetrical towers and turrets and I know it's right to leave the outside untouched.

Frances is sitting on a bench to the right of the portico entrance, cup and saucer in hand. In her cream cotton dress, she looks the epitome of elegance. I bend to give her a peck on the cheek, and she touches my face briefly, making sure I'm left in no doubt about how pleased she is to see me. Over the weeks we've moved swiftly beyond a purely professional relationship.

"Good morning, William, how lovely to see you. Come inside and Crawford can make us some fresh tea."

I follow on her heels along the patterned tiles of the hallway, turning and craning my neck to scour the architecture. She pulls the cord at the side of the fireplace and Crawford appears from the scullery, face puce from the heat of the range.

"Good morning, sir. Yes, madam?" she asks.

"Tea for two and some of your fresh scones if you will please, Crawford."

Crawford gives a small curtsey, bowing her head and I smile at her. I wish Frances had more staff and I have an idea Crawford might too. Frances told me her butler died in the war, and she found she managed perfectly well in his absence with just Crawford. She must cut costs she said if she was to survive financially here for the rest of her life. And at least for now she has a gardener to help with the grounds.

I find myself rehearsing my speech as I take my seat to have tea, only half-listening to her telling me what the gardener needs to do with the grounds before winter.

I'm uncomfortable under her gaze for once and clear my throat as her brows knit.

"I can only apologise for the suspense. I have an idea, but not one you will have been expecting. It could be the answer to your prayers and a little selfishly to mine too."

I sound odd even to my own ears, as though I'm reading aloud a proclamation.

After a pause she places her cup on the low table saying, "I see. In that case I'm all ears."

Oh, if only you knew, Frances you have the power to determine my destiny.

The room is quiet, apart from the spit of the fire. Her parlour has the feel of a thousand lives having passed through it such is the character. It's crammed full of heirlooms and treasures, but not too many as clutter is a sign of a life out of control. Frances is firmly in the driving seat of her own life.

"Well, my proposition today is that I create a self-contained apartment on the upper floors of Highbrook … and live there. Of course, this will mean you're still able to live here on the ground floor."

I watch a flurry of thoughts behind her eyes, but she doesn't respond. I must push harder to convince her it seems.

"I'm not rushing into it," I say, "I've thought of little else for weeks and if I will be able to afford the refurbishment. But I understand if you have other opportunities now because I realise that I may have been dithering too long."

She rolls her eyes, raising her palm.

"Stop!" she says, "Breathe, William. I can't listen to you anymore."

Her expressionless face is giving nothing away. There's a metallic taste in my mouth and a terrible hollow sensation in my legs like I'm standing on the edge of a precipice.

"What is it? I'm sorry if I've upset you or presumed too much," I say noticing her eyes glistening in the stream of morning sunlight.

She pulls a lace handkerchief from the pocket of her dress and dabs daintily at the corners. Her hair once blonde has a smattering of grey, but you wouldn't notice unless you were paying very close attention. Ordinarily she has a soothing aura, but this isn't the case today and I'm unable to read her.

She takes a deep breath now, saying, "Oh, William you'll never know how many times I've wanted you to tell me you'd like to live here, but you had to come to the decision alone, on your own terms. You understand the bones of the place. I've secretly pictured you living here."

She leans to place her hand on my arm. I'm taken aback by such depth of sentiment as I'd no idea she'd given it so much thought sitting here all alone. I lean across to pat her hand gently.

"I've prepared the plans, but I think it will be easier if I show you how I see it working. Shall we go, Miss Havisham?" I say, bowing then pulling her to her feet.

She laughs at our little joke. One night when I called unexpectedly, she was sitting in candlelight in the parlour wearing a long white house coat.

She stands with her hands in mine, and I grin, attempting to lighten the mood.

"Mrs," she says.

"Dear me, bang goes that book then!"

She laughs freely and I join her, so thankful of the release.

The chilly temperature upstairs contrasts with her snug parlour but I'm not cold long because I'm too busy paying close attention to matters today. Frances has already taught me so much about life and love and I like to hear her talk about her marriage; I aspire to a relationship like the one she had with Ben. How I would love to create a similar home for Nell and me.

"Love is never only one thing but endless untold things," she told me once.

The description struck a chord and I've come to think this is the definition of home. I've never had one. I've never had any of those endless tiny things which blend seamlessly together to make one. My mother could never create the omnipresent sensation of home for me or my father. Her dissatisfaction with life pervaded the atmosphere, sucking out the sensation to leave a vacuum. I could never imagine my mother passing on any advice, even of a practical nature.

But then I mustn't blame her because how can she know? She's never had such a love.

*

Every inch of Highbrook reeks of the wealth of bygone days, but it simply makes me happy. Nothing more contrived or convoluted than this.

"I've lost you, William?"

Frances looks concerned, perhaps thinks I'm having second thoughts. She touches my shoulder and turns to make her way back downstairs, intuitively knowing to leave me alone. How I admire her sensitivity.

As I climb the stairs to the very top floor, the evocative smells and sounds of time make me recall my grandparents' rambling house. They lived there all their married life and I stayed with them most weekends in the holidays. I looked forward to the chance of freedom. The huge garden, the moors all gave me a break from a stifling routine.

I glance into the rooms on my way down the corridor and go into the one with the glass case. It houses hundreds of tiny hand-painted soldiers in regimental colours, placed carefully in battle scenes or on parade. They're only some of the many that Ben painted in boyhood and beyond. It's like a museum dedicated to his memory, a fitting tribute from Frances.

In the last room, I sit on a small bed I imagine might once have been Joshua's. The door to a walk-in wardrobe is ajar and I see a few coats which may have been Ben's or his father's. So, now I am the one who gets to hang my coat here. I will become part of the fabric of Highbrook.

Back in the corridor I stare through the glass doors at the end and see the red, shiny cherry of the house. There is a terrace with a stone balcony overlooking the estate and moorland beyond. I stand rooted for some time, wondering if you'll ever agree to marry and live here with me. I can wait for as long as you need me to; just need me to, is all I ask.

I join Frances in the parlour eventually. She's settled in her wingback chair by the hearth, waiting for me. My mind's racing ahead and I'm thinking how to set the wheels in motion so I can make a start. The room is dark but not gloomy, a lamp in the corner and the fire the only light. We sit in companiable silence for a while, staring into the flames.

"What made you decide you wanted to live here after all this time?" she asks.

I'm not really in the mood for talking; I'm drifting in and out of my own world, unable to take my eyes from the fire.

"To be perfectly honest, I've been considering the idea since the first time I came. It didn't take long to see how perfect this place would be as a home for Nell and me one day … if she'll agree."

I look up and smile over at her, seeing my reflection in her eyes. I expect her to smile back but instead, she sits looking at me for a while. I grow tense, the reassuring crackle of the fire suddenly deafening me. I don't understand why her face is so serious.

"William, I don't want you doing this for Nell. You must do it for yourself because she may not always be in the picture. You haven't known her for very long after all."

Where have these words come from? She sounds just like my mother.

She tries to sweeten her direct approach with an unconvincing smile now, realising too late the effect it's had on me. I'm not sure how to respond.

So, Frances has no idea how I feel after all, even though I've spoken of you several times on my visits.

I take a deep breath.

"Much like Highbrook, Nell's become important to me, but I would want to live here with or without her. I didn't think I would need to convince you of all people, Frances."

My voice is polite but my tone chillier, more than I wanted.

Nodding, she continues smiling her vacant smile and looks back into the fire. I can't guess what's going on in her mind. She's taken the wind from my sails, leaving me confused and out of some invisible loop she's fashioned.

I'm shaken. I thought that Frances, after all our chats, would be the one to understand how lonely I was until I met you. I thought she would understand how you've become my central character. Just like Ben was hers.

Chapter 6

I've been so eager to share the news with you all day.

I imagined I would slip it in very casually after I drove you home from our walk. I pull up outside your cottage but keep the engine running to avoid any prelude to the big news.

"So, I'm buying the apartment," I say, "Frances is in agreement, and all the legalities should be finalised before Christmas."

I watch your eyes sparkle.

"Thank goodness you came to your senses before you missed the boat. You're such a slow burner, William but this is just one of the many things I've come to love about you."

Oh. I don't know how to react, so I pretend I didn't hear.

"Would you be good enough to take a look at Highbrook with me, Miss Beaumont to give it the royal seal of approval?" I ask.

I smile at you, my stomach flipping. This is no time or place to respond to your sudden proclamation. You almost said it as an aside and saying I love you too for the first time now would appear glib. Glib is far from what I'm feeling.

I've never said those words before and meant them. A sense of unease springs from nowhere. I should be ecstatic to find out you want to move our relationship up the ladder but am I up to the mark? So, this is how being in love really feels, all-consuming with your destiny dangling by a gossamer thread.

"Yes, of course, if you want me to. It would be lovely to see it."

That was easy.

Driving away, I'm far too preoccupied to ponder why you've never invited me into your cottage.

*

Today is the day for pushing boundaries and showing you, our future. There isn't a ta dah moment in the offing to scare you away, only a whisper of what we could have together; a gentle whisper to sow a seed.

The journey to Highbrook is part of the joy. The loneliness of the moors frees my mind and eases me into a steadier rhythm. I watch real life fade further away in my rear-view mirror with each mile. I find peace. I'm thinking of it less as Frances's house nowadays and beginning to think of it as ours. One day I hope to think of it as our home.

I can see you're impressed as Highbrook comes into view. You've been quiet the whole journey and now you're picking imaginary pieces of fluff from your pristine clothes. This is your tell-tale sign of anxiety.

"Perhaps I'm being over-sensitive, but I'm worried Frances won't like me. I know you've become the best of friends, so it's important she does. No doubt we'll be seeing quite a lot of each other when I visit."

You smooth down your dress, satisfied now that it's sufficiently de-fluffed. I presume this is because you have confessed what was on your mind. How quickly we notice behaviour traits when we bother to pay attention.

I've come to know how important it is to you to be liked by someone. I secretly nicknamed it your 'need to be loved' affectation. This shows a lack of self-esteem which you manage to hide impressively well. It can be misleading.

"Frances will be eating out of your hand ... just like me," I say.

I open the car door for you, and you put your arm in mine, smiling my way. All is well in my world again.

Crawford takes our coats and my hat, then shows us into the parlour, announcing our arrival.

I kiss Frances's cheek swiftly before turning proudly to Nell.

"Hello, Frances, this is Miss Helena Beaumont whom I've mentioned. Nell, to her friends."

Frances inclines her head, and you do the same.

"How do you do, Miss Beaumont," Frances says.

"How do you do. I'd be very pleased if you would call me Nell."

"Indeed, and I would prefer it if you called me Frances. You're not a servant after all, one day we may be neighbours.

I wince, thinking Frances may be giving too much away before the time is right. I watch you both carefully. Your smiles seem genuine, your manners the same. Oh, I'm worrying unnecessarily.

Over high tea, I start to settle and enjoy the conversation.

"I certainly admire you, Frances," you say, "I'm sure it will have been a very difficult decision for you to make to share your home."

She nods thoughtfully.

"Needs must if I want to stay here. I need some help, but I would have had my work cut out finding someone like William. It's a huge relief after all the soul searching and sleepless nights."

She smiles affectionately my way. I smile back.

You're nervous, talking at a pace and fidgeting. It occurs to me now that you and I can go for a long time without talking when we're alone, whilst other times we don't come up for air. I've never been one for banal chatter and our conversations could never be described as such.

I'm eager to go upstairs and for us to be alone and Frances reads the signs and stands up, showing her sensitivity yet again.

"Off you go you two, I'll see you shortly."

So much is at stake with this visit. I'm awaiting the verdict with all the trepidation of a man on trial for his life. You share some thoughts as you walk from room to room saying the stove should be moved to the alcove, the bed under the eaves to look over the grounds, a bedroom would make a good library you tell me. I make a mental note.

I can sense you steadily retreating into your own world on the way to the top of the house. Staring at the soldiers frozen in time and waiting for inspection, you don't comment or ask questions. I study your face through the glass of the cabinet and want to step into your mind, but I must wait for you to allow me.

This time, Frances has requested the key from Crawford so we can go through the glass doors to the terrace outside. Opening both doors with a huge push, they scrape across the black and white stone tiles; damp weather having made the wood swell. We wander over to the outer wall, the hillside rearing up in front of us. The chilling silence is disturbing me. I can see the wind blowing the trees, but we're so sheltered I can't hear it or even feel it on the terrace. Either I can't hear a sound or there isn't any sound to hear, the sensation is otherworldly. Time stops as we take in the view together, shoulder to shoulder much like that first night under the umbrella.

I turn to you, holding one hand in both of mine unable to stand it any longer.

"Nell, I can't lie, I really would want you to be here with me in the future. All in good time of course."

I pray you're not about to shatter my fragile dreams, so I don't speak. I don't want to blunder in and say the wrong thing, break the spell. I sense the mounting tension, but my eyes stay firmly fixed on your face.

Turning your head to look at me, your voice is a whisper, so quiet I need to push my face closer to yours to hear you.

"We're going to be very happy here, William," you say.

You don't add any ifs or buts to tarnish my joy.

Oh, joy, I smile my relief.

I believe you.

Chapter 7

With Christmas fast approaching the apartment legally belongs to me.

The new era seems like the right time for me to think about cementing our bond. We're getting along nicely with the transformation and as a couple, so I build myself up to ask you to join me at Highbrook for a little celebration.

You readily agree. This is good news, but now I need to make it a night to remember. I pool some ideas from Frances.

"I'll ask Crawford to light a fire and some candles and prepare a little supper. It will be lovely and cosy and of course, conducive to romance."

I blush but she's right, the weather's cold now, so we'll need the fire. You can see your breath in the rest of the house, making it like an outdoor adventure.

"Shall I pick Nell up?" she asks.

Frances caused quite a stir as she's taken to driving around in Ben's old car, insisting that as it was going to wrack and ruin in the garage, it seemed only sensible. Ben showed her how to drive when he bought it before the war. Unfortunately, she rarely has anywhere to venture now.

"Yes, thank you for the kind offer," I say, pleased she's keen to be involved.

Friday arrives and Crawford sets the scene beautifully as per Frances's instructions. We'd agreed four o'clock, and Frances set off in plenty of time, but the time has ticked slowly around to fifteen minutes past the hour. What is the appropriate length of lateness for these matters?

By half-past four my nerves have taken hold and I can't sit down. My mind drifts to what could have happened; Frances isn't that confident and could have had an accident or somehow just as bad, that you might have changed your mind. Real fear gets a grip, and I take my watch in and out of my pocket like a madman.

I head downstairs to stand outside on the steps not even bothered that I'm cold without an overcoat. I can hear Crawford in the scullery but there's still no sign of you. I blow out a cloud of icy air—I must set off to find you both.

As my foot touches the first step, I spot Frances's car over the hedge, and I'm overcome with relief.

Stepping out of the car alone and straightening her hat, Frances walks briskly towards the steps, shooing me inside. Crawford appears at the top of the cellar steps, but Frances tells her she doesn't require her services at present, so she scuttles off.

"Where is she, Frances?" I ask, whilst she's removing her things.

Striding into the parlour she sits down heavily in her chair.

"I'm afraid your plans have been somewhat waylaid, William. Nell is not feeling herself, so she won't be coming this afternoon."

My brows knit saying, "Not feeling herself, what do you mean, Frances?"

She warms her hands at the fire.

"She's a little tired, so she thought it best if she stayed at the cottage. She sends her apologies and hopes you understand."

I don't understand. It would take more than a little fatigue to stop you coming here today. I'm irritable with Frances and know I shan't rest until I've seen you. She must know it too.

Swinging around abruptly, I ignore her startled expression.

"I'm sorry, Frances but I simply must pay her a visit, I'm sure you understand. I'd be obliged if you could ask Crawford to keep an eye on the fire and candles."

My tone was a little too sharp. I glance at Frances who has the strangest expression on her face. I hesitate briefly, but she doesn't say a word. Frances isn't my main priority at present, so I hurry out of the front door slamming it behind me.

Frances is staring from the window and waves once. How oddly she's behaving. But I still wave back, cursing for once that I'm a slave to politeness.

I don't want to drive too fast and must fight the urge. The roads are narrow and windy, and it would risk life and limb. How I'd like to flick a switch to turn off my irrational thoughts at this moment.

The black outline of the trees to the rear of the cottage swamps the tiny building in a dark cloak. The rooms are in total darkness, and my fear and confusion mount as I walk up your path. I wish you had a means of outside light like most people. This is the first time I've wanted you to be like most people I realise. Lighting isn't necessary, you told me as you know the way to your front door blindfolded.

I knock on the door and wait but you don't answer. I knock again and wait, forcing myself to be calm. I don't like the sensation one jot.

You really aren't at home it seems, but where would you have gone in such a short space of time? I'm stuck what to do. I push my face to the window in desperation, putting my hand over my eyes to get a better view through the glass. Nothing.

So, what to do now? I drop my hand and look to see if there's a way to go around the back. I spot a gap at the side of the house and head towards it. I have newly found hope.

The turning of a door handle behind me makes me jump. Heading back to the door you open it just far enough for me to see your face in shadow.

Hope turns immediately to relief, but in the blueish black of the early evening darkness, I can just make out that your eyes are swollen. You've been crying.

"What on earth is going on, Nell? Please open the door."

My patience is wearing thin, its evaporating too quickly.

Finally, you step back from the doorway to allow my entry, and I stride over the threshold.

I'm a stranger inside your cottage, so I must quickly get my bearings in the semi-gloom. I close the door behind me to walk across the tiny room, as you perch on the edge of the settee. Sliding my suit jacket off I sit by your side so I can be near you. I've never seen you cry before, and I need you to tell me why you're crying so I can make it stop. I look at your beautiful face half-hidden by your hair which you've left undone for once. Placing my hand over yours I need to try in some small way to ease your obvious distress.

"Just tell me what's happened, my love."

You turn your head to stare through me as I swallow an impatient sigh.

"I'm sorry I made you worry," you say, "I simply couldn't come. I want to be with you, Will, far more than you know, but things are progressing too fast. I'm sure you'll have gone to so much trouble today and I feel terrible."

I see the quiver of your bottom lip, but I'm not convinced. Life is never too fast for you, I know you.

"Don't worry about today, there's plenty of time," I say trying to keep my voice on an even keel.

You're looking away from me and I pause to pick my words wisely.

"Are you telling me the whole story, Nell? I don't know why but I sense there's something you're not telling me."

Your mouth opens slightly as though to speak but you don't, instead you sit back on the sofa and sigh, pushing your hair from your face.

"I had a conversation with Frances when she came," you say quietly, "She knows how you feel about me, and she wanted to know if I feel the same. I don't think she believes I do."

I shake my head. What on God's green earth would possess Frances to do such a thing? This isn't Frances; not the Frances I love, at least. She'd know you would tell me about the conversation surely and yet she didn't say a word about it when I left. Nothing is making sense. It's as though I've stepped for the first time into your home and into an alternate universe.

45

As you walk over to the window, I realise the room is still in darkness. You light two candles on the windowsill so I can see your reflection in the darkness of the glass. You're staring beyond it into the nothingness, the outline of your face taut, your back tauter. I sigh in silence.

"Frances had no business to do that, Nell and I'm sorry, truly I am. I'll speak to her about it tomorrow."

How disappointed I am in you Frances.

You don't turn around, so I walk across to stand beside you and try to pull you towards me. I want to try and extinguish the pain etched on your face, but you move to one side. Dropping my arms, your rejection cuts me.

"Frances is right to be wary. I don't wish to be blasé about your feelings, but I must confess I find it hard to commit. I know you're in deep; too deep perhaps for your own good, William," you say.

I think of the carefully prepared romantic scene I've set in the apartment. This was not how tonight was meant to be. I'd planned to tell you I loved you, that I wanted to marry you and I wanted the romance, not because of convention but because of the way you make me feel—loving, passionate. I brush the thought aside and reach for you again. This time you don't pull away, so I have a glimmer of reassurance.

Cupping my hand against your cheek, my thumb tilts your chin upward to stare down into your huge eyes. You look so small, so fearful.

"I love you, Nell," I whisper, "In fact, I wouldn't be going too far to say I've never felt this way about anyone or anything before."

I bob down on one knee, remembering that the ring I'd taken all day to choose from the best jeweller in York is waiting at Highbrook. I realise it really doesn't matter under the circumstances.

"Please will you do the honour of marrying me?"

Tears are burning my eyes. I've rehearsed what I was going to say in my mind tonight, but in the end it simply isn't necessary. It fires straight and true from my heart.

You're studying my face as if for the very first time as you wrap your arms around my neck then drop your face onto my chest so I can't read your expression. Your hair tickles my chin and I smell the scent of your shampoo. You're silent for a while, not raising your head.

Nell, you must know that I'm waiting, I think. I'm waiting for you to speak next, and I can't anticipate your response, I never can.

I hear a peculiar noise like a laugh. The sound doesn't fill me with joy.

"We will see, we will see," you say.

I have a creeping sensation up the back of my neck.

What the hell is that supposed to mean?

Chapter 8

Shamelessly, I end up staying the night at your cottage.

I can't tolerate gossip, though nobody would gossip other than Crawford who is a trusted, loyal servant, and I certainly don't have anyone to answer to including Frances.

My priority is you, and I wanted to stay so I have.

We lay side by side in your bed which is far too small for a good night's sleep. Sleep eludes me anyway with you lying so close to me and so filled with sadness. Cocooned in your personal space I'm not an intruder amongst the trinkets – a porcelain doll, looking a little worse for wear in a tatty dress, a small wooden jewellery box inlaid with pearl or ivory, and family portraits of a child called Nell. I know so much about you yet nothing at all.

You're such a troubled soul, but I can be the one to give you stability, I can make you feel loved for being entirely yourself, perhaps for the first time. I twirl a lock of your hair around and around my finger, soothed by the repetition as you snuggle closer to me in your sleep. I know I make you feel safe. I hope this will be enough to set me apart from the one who loved and lost you.

I remember how I thought I'd lost you when I didn't even have you. I never want to wake to such a sense of desolation again.

What on earth was Frances's thinking going behind my back on such a special day? I can't believe she could be so deceitful and underhand.

She is however worried, and I know she has concerns, the same as my mother. You're certainly no ordinary woman and she's protective of me, but this … a line has been crossed. Now, I have no choice but to tackle Frances about it, so I'll need to be a man and confront this whole situation head on. You need a man.

Sleep comes slowly and I awake after an early morning catnap to see you resting on your hand, smiling down at me.

"So, you say you love me, and you'd like to make an honest woman of me, would you?" Your playful grin is unexpected and such a sight for sore eyes, "I think you may have to prove it to me, I'm not entirely convinced."

I laugh and whip you over so I can push myself against you. My arousal makes you squeal with surprise and delight. You turn your head around now to kiss me. I want some delight all for myself, so I push your stomach towards me, and you feel my hardness. You moan your pleasure. We have reached a far deeper connection between us, making our lovemaking tentative and gentle. Here is another side of you to know and to love. I have never been closer to you …to anyone.

"You're one crazy fool, William, to fall for me. Soon, you'll be wanting that quiet life of yours back."

"Never," I say, kissing your shoulder.

I'm quiet at breakfast knowing the time to head off and face the music is looming. I notice a black and white photograph of you, and who I imagine is your grandmother as you look so alike. I somehow can sense the affection even within the context of a formal pose.

The cottage is beautifully basic, and I doubt it will have changed much over the years aside from a few home comforts and your decorative touches here and there. I know you don't worry about it being so remote because your grandma always felt safe as houses here so why wouldn't you?

It's almost time to leave you but not yet. Pulling you towards me I give you a kiss which reignites the spark in the pit of my stomach, the one which is never far away.

As I turn to leave you touch my arm, stopping me in my tracks.

"William, I'd rather you didn't mention any of this to Frances. I was over-reacting. I've had time to think, and I know she was only taking care of you, ensuring my intentions are honourable."

I nod slowly and think what to say to ease the tension.

"Not too honourable, I hope."

You smile weakly, but you're not fooling me as the tautness of your jaw has returned. Your red eyes raise another tinge of anger at Frances as I search your face.

"If you're sure," I say after a moment, "I'm disappointed in Frances but I know her heart is in the right place. I suppose we're all going to be living in each other's pockets more in future and we need to rub along."

"I'll just have to prove her wrong," you say.

As I head down the path to my car I turn around and catch my breath. I've never looked at the cottage in detail as I've been distracted by our farewells. Swamped by the forest at the rear the sunlight is a perfect backdrop to the trees. You're waiting at the door to wave to me and you raise your hand. I wave back and catch my throat. You must never sell this cottage; you must always have it. I see now this house is part of you in the way Frances spoke about her home that day in my office.

Arriving at Highbrook I remain seated in the car a moment or two. I must compose myself as my annoyance has grown during the drive over.

I don't knock and wait for Crawford as was the custom up until today, instead I let myself in with my key as it's my home too now after all. Frances is sitting in the front room looking fresh as a daisy and reading the paper without a care in the world. She looks up, slightly startled I imagine because I've appeared from nowhere. Smiling at me she drops her paper to the floor and takes off her glasses. She's acting as though nothing has happened. Why would that be; why would she be so certain you wouldn't tell me about the conversation?

"William, I can't tell you how relieved I am to see you," she says, "I've been quite worried during the night."

I let out a small laugh which sounds too hollow.

"No need to worry, you're not my mother, Frances," I tell her, "No news is always good news with me."

She looks fleetingly put out by my choice of words but ignores them.

"How is Nell?" she asks.

I look directly at her and see genuine concern.

"Oh, she's fine this morning after a good night's sleep."

It's as though we're playing a game and it's not one that I care for. I submit.

"I apologise for worrying you," I say, "I'll see to one or two things upstairs, then I'll head back home. I have lots to do."

Staring at her it's as though I'm standing on quicksand.

She nods and smiles warmly before putting her glasses back on to continue reading the paper. Her head bent I stare at the lovely golden hair on top of my dear friend and I'm suddenly on edge.

I wish I knew what was going on, but I can't quite grasp what it is as she's dangling it just out of my reach.

But then I remember her favourite saying of the many she has stored away for every occasion. She tells me that one should be cautious about what one wishes for in life just in case it happens to come true.

My eyes never leave her face, but she doesn't look up as I head to the door. My palms are wet.

I have an uncomfortable feeling this saying might befit the occasion perfectly.

*

Building work has been put on hold for the Christmas period and I've been so caught up with everything I've almost forgotten about the strange events of that night. All seems well between the two of you.

Frances continues to be my constant, quiet support that I wonder how I ever survived without, and she clearly has my best interests at heart, as do you. I consider myself a very lucky man.

Frances visits Joshua over the Christmas break giving us chance to have some blissful uninterrupted time together as

Crawford takes the opportunity to visit her sister. I find it all so exciting and illicit, adding to the thrill.

It lives up to anyone's expectations of what Christmas should be and it's the first time I've truly felt yuletide spirit. I know this time next year we'll be married, all legal and above board. I'll miss these covert times, but I'll be so much more settled when you're my wife.

We place the tree in the window of our front room, with me pulling out all the stops to ensure the decorating is finished in time. I worry that no Christmas in the future can ever live up to this one. I see peace and contentment written all over your face, making me determined to enjoy the ride and swallow any doubt about our future. I must not spoil today for tomorrow.

This is the first time I notice you don't seem to want to go far. You don't go out much at all in fact, not even to the cottage. I admit that I love it, feeling happy as a sandboy.

"When we marry, I'll be known to the villagers as the madman on the moors who keeps his woman locked up if this goes on."

"Who cares?" you say, "I think we both know I'll only be someone's woman if I want to be, don't you?"

"Oh, yes," I say, with mock disdain.

We laugh together. It just so happens to be your most desirable yet unnerving trait.

You've written to your parents to ask them to come after Christmas as you have news, and we will meet them at the train station. I'm then going to play the game of asking your father for your hand in marriage. Everything in my world is now considerably topsy turvy.

On Christmas Day evening with the tree lights twinkling and the fire crackling away, we're sitting opposite each other in our two new chairs. The curtains are drawn to the snowy world and I'm enjoying myself reliving the day. The pleasure of waking up beside you on Christmas morning is already a cherished memory.

"You're such a perfect little Christmas box," I said, tracing a finger down your neck and below, cupping your breasts.

You gasped with pleasure when I pulled you on top of me. My lovemaking is far less predictable and more instinctive nowadays. The covers slipped so I had the pleasure of seeing the curves which always drive me to distraction. Bending down to kiss me your tongue lingered making me ache. You arched your back as I entered you and started to move in the way only a woman knows how. I watched your breasts swaying enticingly and reached up to play with them making me almost lose myself with longing. Our eyes locked, brimming with all the passion we both shared. I knew it, I felt it. The slow rise and fall of your body made me climax after you, leaving us hot and overcome.

I held you close muttering into your hair, "Don't ever leave me, Nell, I would be nothing without you now."

Oh, how I meant it.

"You've got it all wrong, my love," you said stroking my hair out of my eyes, "The bubble will burst, and you'll see me for what I really am, a whole barrow full of trouble."

I laughed then kissed you. We made a champagne breakfast together and opened our stockings in bed and you were giddy; that little child keeps making an appearance.

Now you look across at me, your eyes sparkling with tears.

"I can't tell you how special today has been, my darling. This has been my best Christmas ever," you say.

I bask in such high praise and think you must be reading my mind. We're in a lovely little bubble and I suddenly realise I have everything I will ever need in this one room. Nothing will burst it, not for me at least.

It should scare me to death, but it doesn't.

Chapter 9

The train pulls in and I hang back, hat in hand, whilst you greet each other.

You turn towards me, saying, "Mother, father, this is Mr William Hudson, I spoke about him in my letter. We've been friends for some time."

Your proud smile stirs my heart.

"I'm so very pleased to make everyone's acquaintance," I say.

Your father steps forward offering his hand.

"I've been waiting for some daft so and so to take this one off our hands," he says.

He turns to you and tweaks your nose, then grinning as you kiss his cheek.

"So, you're the one who's captured our Nell's heart," your mother says, laughing.

I'm charmed by these down to earth people. You warned me about your father using humour as an outlet for affection but also to help him deal with the taxing life of a village doctor.

I somehow had the idea you and Daniel were close, but you appear almost standoffish with each other, only cordial. Your parents appear not to notice, so perhaps I'm wrong.

We're going to my house—Mrs Charles is on standby but we're planning to call in at Highbrook on the way so they can see the progress on the apartment. I asked Frances not to go to any trouble with tea as we wouldn't be stopping long. She said she'd make herself scarce on this occasion but would look forward to meeting them in the future.

We have a plan. After showing them around the house, I'm to take a stroll around the gardens with each of them to get to know them a little better.

Your father is first on the list because I'm desperate to ask him the all-important question. As we stop at the rose garden, I take the opportunity and watch as the question sinks in.

He looks delighted saying, "Well, I can't lie, William I had my doubts when I saw the age difference, but I can see Nell couldn't be more content. I was sorry to hear you're a widower, it must have been difficult at such a young age."

Shaking his head at the thought his eyes are showing his sympathy at the situation.

"Yes, it was at the time, but we must get on with life the best we can." I pause, "And I can't lie either, I love your daughter very much."

The declaration seems woefully inadequate.

"I see it, I see it, old man," he laughs, slapping me on the back.

Somewhat crushed by his general term of endearment I shake it off, then swear him to secrecy until later in the day.

Daniel sits between you and I in age. I would say around mid-thirties. He's a pleasant fellow in looks and temperament.

"We lived in each other's pockets growing up, but not so much of course nowadays," he tells me, "I hope it might be different going forward. She tends to be a little emotional, I'm not sure if you've noticed," cocking his head he raises his eyebrows good naturedly, "but she has goodness running through her like a stick of rock. I think she scares herself sometimes."

So, he has the measure of you like me. I must make my intentions clear without giving the game away.

"I was married before but the way I feel about your sister is quite different. I was treading water until she rescued me though I know this sounds dramatic. It's taken a long forty-three years for me to find her, but she's been worth the wait."

He grins at me, the wind blowing his black hair around, so he looks youthful.

"I'm glad Nell's found you. She needs someone steady. I do know that feeling, a hand-in-glove sensation which is impossible to ignore."

He has someone dear to him it seems, but he doesn't elaborate, and I would never pry.

I find out later from you that your parents adopted Daniel before you were born. I'm not sure why you haven't mentioned this before.

"I've got something to tell you." you say, "I'd rather we didn't have any secrets.

Your face darkens and my heart plummets. Do I want to know the secrets; am I ready? My stomach muscles tense waiting for the punch.

"Daniel was in contact with his birth mother," you close your eyes, "but our mother is completely unaware. He was in touch with her but also her family regularly from his late teens."

You sit sullenly in your chair by the fire.

How unfair of him to draw you into his deception, he should have carried the burden alone. No wonder your relationship has cooled.

"Her name was Molly," you say.

I don't understand the past tense, but he may not see her now.

"She became a big part of his life, but she died a few years ago. She was in a violent relationship when she had Daniel and his father had even been in prison. She thought it would be best if a family adopted him so he could have some stability. She went on to marry a nice chap, but Molly told Daniel she had no idea where his birth father was."

The haunted look on your face is torture. I'm right, the burden has been heavy on you.

"He explained to Molly time and time again he understood why she had him adopted, but although she battled with the guilt, she never overcame it. Daniel said she was a sweet, kind person who always encouraged him to speak to mother and father about their connection. She even offered to speak to them with him if it would help. He did almost tell them on more than a few occasions, but he was simply unable to find the right words."

I put myself in his shoes. It's easier said than done to drop a grenade in someone's lap and I'm not certain they would have understood.

"I tried to persuade him our parents would be able to cope with the situation if he told them - rather that, than deception - but there was no convincing him."

I beg to differ here.

"If I'm honest, I think they would be upset. I can understand his thoughts on the subject." I say, "They would feel like they weren't enough, and you can flower it up all you like, but they clearly weren't."

"This doesn't excuse the lie. It will be better if they don't find out now, the deceit has gone on far too long."

You're annoyed with him still.

"How did he find her, I wonder?"

"He overheard mother and granny talking about it when he was a boy. He gleaned a name and a village from the conversation, and as soon as he was old enough, he started drinking at the village pub and began making tentative enquiries over many months. He knew he had to tread carefully."

"Life must be hard for you both tiptoeing through the deception," I say.

I'm starting to wish you hadn't drawn me into it, but I see you need me to at least carry some of the burden and I agree, I'd much prefer we didn't have secrets.

"I confess I was sometimes jealous of his 'other life.' I was firmly on the outside looking in. Growing up, Daniel and I were always together; in fact, we were inseparable, and I wasn't prepared to be put in a position where I had to share him. He was always, popular with his tall, dark, and brooding looks, but he spent his time with me. I looked up to him; I adored my big brother. But the situation with his mother changed everything. I couldn't possibly get involved as it would be a step too far for our parents to cope with if they ever found out. Stuck between a rock and a hard place, I couldn't be part of his new life and I just … just couldn't bear it."

I hear raw pain in your voice as you tell me the tale, and you're clearly far from over his betrayal of your parents. The distance between you might be a good thing.

I pull you into my arms.

"You're not being selfish to feel this way, it's completely natural."

Your arms tighten around me.

I can't help yet again admiring your honesty.

*

Your mother and I are last to take a stroll around the grounds together. By now, I would like to have the cat out of the bag if I'm honest.

"I must say, I can't believe this is to be your home, William," she says, her eyes roaming the grounds.

"Frances is struggling to live here alone," I tell her, "Times are changing in so many ways."

I show her the shed tucked away in the trees which is the perfect bolt hole.

"This is every man's dream by the look of it."

"I know, I imagine I will get up to all sorts in here."

"I bet," she laughs.

She looks at me.

"Nell has really taken a shine to you, and I can see why: you're the solid, calming influence I think she needs. She can allow her mind to work itself up into a frenzy sometimes."

She snorts softly, saying, "I remember when she was about eight and her friend at school lost her grandmother. It was the first time the finality of death had registered obviously, because she spent a day curled up in her bed, sobbing periodically. She didn't want me to die, her father, Daniel, her grandmother, she was overwrought. I know death is a brutal concept, hard to grasp at that age, but I can't imagine any other child would deal with it in such an extreme manner.

I can picture the scene well, and I'm not as dismissive as your mother. I'm upset by the thought of it.

"You seem to understand her," I say, "I'm sure it would have helped."

Coming to a halt suddenly she looks into my eyes, as though she's about to confess something. Startled by the sudden change of mood I steel myself.

"I'm more accepting than understanding, I think. I had a mother who was away with the pixies, so this behaviour wasn't unusual to me. Nell has always been fragile, just like my mother was. They were as thick as thieves, so much so that it could make me feel like a third wheel sometimes. They seemed to communicate without words, it was always the same. All that concern about the meaning of life, it must be exhausting. I take after my father, dealing with what life presents to me each day without question. I had my doubts she would ever settle with anyone. If I'm honest, we just hoped she would find someone who could cope with her idiosyncrasies."

We share a laugh together; I like the term and the release of tension more.

"I can cope with them," I tell her, "That's not to say the road isn't without bumps, but then I had a smooth ride for long enough. Regardless, she's lumbered now. I intend to cling on to the woman of my dreams."

The slightly theatrical turn of phrase makes me laugh to lessen the impact. So, when she turns my way without a hint of humour behind her eyes, I'm awkward under the spotlight.

"I believe you, you're clearly dotty about her," she says, "Just don't let her swallow you up, William. Your feelings matter too, and it does a person good to not have their own way all the time."

I note a flicker of irritation float across her face. I might have missed it if I hadn't been paying close attention.

My tight smile hides my exasperation.

For god's sake, what is it about the women in our life, do they resent what we have or simply not understand it? I'm finding it utterly bewildering.

But either way, I pity them.

Chapter 10

Oddly, it's as though I'm marrying for the first time.

We've only waited a month which included three weeks for the vicar to read the wedding banns in church. I can't possibly wait any longer; I just can't risk you changing your mind. We dutifully attended church each Sunday, and I acquainted myself with your childhood village and the people who have always been part of your life.

The wedding breakfast is to be at Highbrook, Frances's idea and your parents agreed. They've been saving all your life for your wedding, but I suspect funding will still be limited so I tread carefully.

I've arranged a surprise with your parents so some of the villagers can come on a bus to help us celebrate. Hired staff are on hand to help, and Frances arranged for Highbrook to have garlands of fresh foliage strewn gayly on the stair post and around the fireplaces. In terms of family, there's only an aunt—your father's sister—your uncle and two cousins, one being a bridesmaid. My mother's cousin, Fran's friend, declined due to ill health, but it would be a difficult day for her regardless. Daniel is my best man as the only alternative was Harry, so I chose family.

Our wedding day is a crisp January day, full of sunshine, full of happiness.

As I stand at the altar with Daniel, I can't quite take in the sight of you gliding down the aisle towards me. Your dress is exquisite; you are exquisite. Your beaming smile matches your father's as I wait for you to be by my side not just at the altar but in our new life.

Why can't I remember Charlotte's dress, Charlotte's flowers? I just can't picture them for some reason as I spent much of the day feeling like a guest.

I'm overcome as we say our vows, listening to every single word, watching every single nuance. I see a tear fall and

I almost follow with one of my own but somehow manage to hold my composure.

You know though. You just know.

*

The mundane matters of life are nothing short of magical to me.

You haven't any time for staff watching your every move you tell me, having more in common with Crawford than Frances. You want to cook for your husband, keep house for your husband as your mother managed with minimal help, and you want to be alone with me. This is surprisingly unconventional, but music to my ears.

I look forward to the weekends the most with the slower pace of domestic bliss. Frances comes for tea on occasion, and I pop down most days to see her but she's keen to stick to her pledge of giving us our privacy.

Even your teasing about my foibles is amusing.

"So, let me get this straight, William, having three coats cluttering the coatrack is acceptable when one will suffice?" you ask.

"Yes, I'm so pleased you understand," I say with a twinkle in my eye.

You roll your eyes as I tell you I'm a very lucky man to have found a wife who's not only beautiful, clever and humorous, but also understands me so well.

You laugh and then I pin you playfully to the wall by the cluttered coatrack and you stop laughing. You push your head forward to kiss me and put your tongue in my mouth, and I have that feeling. The feeling which makes me want to touch you in all the places you like me to touch you. We're suddenly frantic. I lift your dress and pull your underwear down to the floor and lift you up. Your legs are wide open, your back against the wall. You push me deeper inside with your legs and I like it. Faster and faster, we go, panting, groaning.

"Oh, my love," you moan into my hair, on your way to euphoria.

I race to join you there myself as I press my face into your neck and savour the pleasure that you're giving me. Lifting my head, I see and savour the pleasure I'm giving you. I feel manly, empowered by you.

The memory stays with us. You never mention me leaving three coats by the door again because we enjoy the memory. I know we do.

I admit it won't be the same life we're living as every other couple of our standing. You still run back to your cottage most weeks to check all is well and our conversation is possibly a little livelier, but I wallow in my newfound happiness for a little while.

The renovations have gone well and the last task on the list is the best: the terrace. No structural work was necessary, but the nook has become a little unkempt in the winter. I offer to help, and we're wrapped up against the cold but I'm loving just being outside in the place we've been waiting to enjoy. You look sweet with your little red nose and wild curls as you sweep. I wish I could kiss you. I would settle for talk to you because you've become progressively quieter over the last few days. I'm hoping this task will be just the thing to bring you out of yourself.

It's a small space to avoid each other but I'm not fool enough to ask why you're quiet. You'll only tell me when you're ready.

The suspense is torturous and the sooner you tell me what's bothering you, the sooner we can resume the status quo. Letting things blow over is never an option. Any issues must be vocalised and dealt with accordingly. Most would consider this a healthy approach but tackling problems head on scares the living daylights out of me.

By teatime we're almost finished, and I put aside a fine bottle of champagne for this occasion, so I pop inside to get it. I find myself stalling to go back upstairs. I can sense things are coming to a head and I have a knot in my stomach at the thought of what I may done or said to put you in such a strange mood.

I try to catch your eye as I go through the open glass doors, but you're steadfastly avoiding eye contact. I delay the uncorking of the celebratory champagne due to the lack of festive atmosphere, but I see you spot it as I sit down on one of the iron chairs. A toast to the new terrace is not an option I see. I watch you begin picking imaginary pieces of fluff from your coat. I am now sufficiently on edge.

As I sit with my eyes closed to the watery sunshine, I can't help a tinge of disappointment, but it will be a cold day in hell for me to break this silence.

"I'm pregnant."

My eyes are on stalks. I'd thought of a list of items which may need to be discussed; but this most definitely wasn't on it.

I couldn't speak even if I wanted to, and I don't. I take a moment and sit very still as I'm prone to do when thinking. Slowly, disbelief gives way to joy. The joy mounts but, I know I must quash it. It doesn't take a genius to know joy isn't pulsing through your veins. You briefly flick your eyes my way and I'm sure you will be reading a diluted version of what you anticipated on my face. Why aren't you happy, I want you to be happy.

"It's complicated, William."

You tuck your hair behind your ear and settle back into your chair. It looks as though you're about to tell me a story but I'm not sure I want to hear it.

We've never spoken about having a family and it may have just been an assumption of mine. I didn't think it was a discussion to be had as it either happened or otherwise, or so I thought.

"When is the baby due?" I ask the obvious question.

"Around June, July."

"Have you seen the doctor?"

"Not yet, I wanted to tell you first, but I will need to see one soon.

"So, when did you know?"

You sigh.

"I had my suspicions before Christmas."

Christmas? What a gift that would have been but then it was only a suspicion, and you might not have wanted to disappoint me. Still, I don't understand why you've waited so long to tell me the news.

I have a sickening thought suddenly the baby I've fallen in love with already may not be mine. I'm trying to push the devastating thought away.

"I'm still getting used to the situation myself," you say.

A long pause is hanging between us.

"The truth of the matter is I've always had this niggling worry I wasn't meant to be a mother. I needed time to think about the situation."

Is that all? Lord, relief floods me and I let out an enormous, dizzying breath which alarms you slightly.

How do you want me to respond to this statement because it seems the burden is weighing heavily on you? I take my time to piece my sentence together carefully without it sounding trite and dismissive.

"I think it must be natural to feel this way amongst so many other worries of a first-time mother," I say, "This is the biggest change of your life, I'm sure it's perfectly normal to have concerns."

Oh no, my words are trite and dismissive I think, as you heave another sigh.

"I understand what you're saying, but I'm not sure I think like most women. I have trouble looking after myself, let alone another person, who will be totally reliant on me."

"Us," I correct you.

"Oh, William," you snap, "you say this but you're at work. A baby will change my life beyond recognition, not yours."

I don't like your harsh words, I've longed for a child, and I nearly say so, but think better of it.

Ideas flutter around my mind about how to get you on board, I must think quickly. Can I sell my half of the business and be at home more? I'm tempted but then get a dose of reality when I realise that we won't be able to afford to live here if I do.

I'm so reluctant to speak and add fuel to the blazing fire but I must try to reassure you.

"Nell, I know we're surprised, and it's happened far quicker than expected, but I've always dreamed of becoming a father and I for one think you will be a wonderful mother. We wouldn't be human if we didn't worry but most married couples have children if they're lucky and they seem happy. This isn't considered unusual."

I try a small smile and use the 'we' to make you feel better. The unity of our thoughts on the matter is a platitude and you're fully aware of it. It doesn't inspire you. It doesn't make you alter your obvious deep-seated doubts on the subject. I know you far too well already.

My memory of being told I was to become a father is tarnished but I'm far more concerned about you. All women long to be mothers surely.

But then you're not all women and that's precisely why I love you as I do.

You're standing at edge of the terrace with your back to me. I've run out of words of wisdom. I know you're not looking at anything at all; you just can't bring yourself to look at me, to face my suppressed elation.

I should be finally living the dream; a dream wife, dream job, dream house, dream neighbour, and now I'm going to be a father! Why is life going off kilter yet again? Expect the unexpected must be my mantra.

I approach warily. Although I don't know what to expect, I must always be brave.

You swing around now so suddenly it startles the life out of me. I stop dead in my tracks to wait for your next move.

The brightest smile is splitting your face.

"I'm sorry to spoil it for you, my love, you're right of course, I'm sure it's natural to be a little apprehensive. I suppose I haven't had you in my life up until now and I just know you were put on this earth to be a father."

You speak at a rate of knots, and I race over to take you in my arms. You let me. This is better, the world spins as my neck and shoulders relax.

I pull away to look down and study what's going on behind your eyes. My face falls and you look away quickly. The beaming smile I was so euphoric to see just doesn't quite reach those eyes. I'm staring at a mask. You're embracing me too tightly almost like you're clinging on to me. It all seems so terribly wrong.

It preys on my mind too many a time afterwards. It haunts me. I should have taken you seriously instead of expecting convention.

Expecting what every other man expects.

Chapter 11

Frances is the first person I tell the good news.

If she's surprised at the speed at which it happened, she tactfully doesn't show it.

"I know you'll be employing the services of a nanny, but I'll be around to lend a hand. I need something to fill my time, life can get dreary around here nowadays," she says, "But never fear, I shan't interfere."

I know she won't, and it will be comforting to know she's nearby when I'm at work.

My mother's reaction surprises me. Frances's influence may be having an effect. She appears quite often on the pretext of popping to see us, but not long afterwards she heads downstairs to see Frances. She's finally found a friend and I couldn't be happier for her.

"You'll make an excellent father, William," she tells me, "Some people are just born to be parents."

I glance across the table to see you smiling my way oblivious. How I hope so; the comment is perfectly innocuous, yet I can't help but wish my mother hadn't made such a pointed remark. But I may be reading too much into it.

Your parents' reaction doesn't surprise me in the least. I expected them to be over the moon and they are.

We're enjoying a pre-dinner drink on the terrace whilst you cook. You have a new recipe to try you tell us, insisting you don't need any help. It's only been days since our conversation up here, but you do seem lighter now you've spoken of your concerns.

I enjoy your mother's company. We soon get to the nitty gritty, both having little patience for small talk.

"Daniel shows no signs of getting married never mind having children and Nell has always seemed a little indifferent towards babies and children in general," she tells me. "I've loved every moment of being a mother. Having a family was all I ever really wanted in life."

The expression on her face is beautiful. Daniel may have made the right decision in shielding her from the truth. I wouldn't want to be the one to ruin such an expression of pure motherly love.

"But you know, William, when Nell holds that tiny baby in her arms, she'll be content. She's cut from the same cloth after all and until a baby arrives, one couldn't possibly understand."

I nod along, pleasantly as she speaks.

Oh, Ann, how I pray you will be right.

*

You do seem to blossom and as the months roll by, I give myself permission to become a little excited.

I mention interviewing for the position of nanny and even a wet nurse, but you tell me we have plenty of time. I know little of such things, only having Frances to advise me of the correct protocol.

Time is ticking. The baby is due at the end of July and the apartment looks spectacular. This is a place to raise a family.

The nursery is my favourite room.

This is the room I would never have predicted during the late nights I spent drawing the plans. The smell of fresh paint and new rugs, all done in anticipation of another human being, makes me grounded, secure.

"It's exactly the way I pictured it," you say.

Frances has given us the little wooden cot Joshua used and Ben before him. We have it on long-term loan, and we've placed it under the window. The pale lemon wallpaper with sweet little grey and white bunny rabbits is the perfect choice, you tell me.

"I think you planned this all along, William," you say with a genuine smile.

I look at your contented little face. Who would blame me?

I've waited a long time to be a father and I will make sure I throw myself into the whole sham-bang and be the rock both of you need me to be.

I catch you looking a little wistful from time to time, but it's clear to me now that you're looking forward to becoming a mother.

My ducks were in line like Ben's little soldiers.

Life was good then.

I could breathe.

Nell
Chapter 12

Oh, the nightmare that was last autumn. I relive it constantly and the memory still hits me on waking.

Excitement isn't a word I'd ever thought of before, never mind felt the effects. Life with my parents in Wrenbridge was mundane though I wasn't aware of it at the time.

I know I'm a born worrier and many believe I court drama but really, I only ever want a quiet life. Peace equals happiness is my philosophy. Yet, I know I would never have found peace with Mark.

I doubt anyone would think it unusual to find a man like Mark attractive. Tall and broad, he was a man's man who knew how to treat a lady. He thrived on a challenge, never allowing the dust to settle. But love he told me had eluded him, so he's paid a price for his independence. Or he may have paid no price at all, life is all about perception.

After granny died, I walked to and from her cottage constantly—six miles there, six miles back. I felt close to her and eventually began staying the night and returning the following day. Mother knew some of the grief I felt, so she left me alone to deal with it my own way. I was grateful to her because we're not alike in any way, but she made herself understand the intensity of my grief. I love her for trying.

Mark had seen me walking many times. He said the freedom of the moors, the fresh air had done more for him than any of the quacks at the military hospital in Harrogate. He was a platoon commander in the Duke of Cornwall's Light Infantry but offered me only fragments of the horror he must have experienced. He told me he had suffered serious shrapnel injuries to his back in the final weeks of the Somme offensive. Although sufficiently recovered to now be allowed out of the ward, he said he was destined to spend the rest of the war stationed at a training camp in Ripon, preparing more boys for the front. I still shudder at the thought of what lay ahead for those boys.

He told me he spotted me one day, then a week later he spotted me again but after that didn't see me for months. During that time however, he said each leave day he would walk the moors and nearby villages to look for me. But to no avail.

Then one snowy winter's day in 1917 he found me.

He said he waited until I was off the path and followed me away from prying eyes but not for too long as he didn't want to startle me. He's quite right, meeting a stranger out of the blue in the isolation of the moors is always unsettling.

I heard his crunching footsteps in the snow and turned. Raising his hat, he bid me good day with a smile. A bedazzling smile from a handsome stranger was a new experience for me.

And oh, how he knew it.

"Good day, sir," I said, assuming he would pass me by.

My eyes widened as he joined me to step in time by my side.

"Now, where on earth would a young lady like yourself be heading in such weather? Surely you should be curled up by the fire with a good book."

I laughed and he joined me. It was the right thing to do to put me instantly at ease.

He didn't sound entirely like a gentleman, but he had on a long, smart woollen coat with heavy boots, and he spoke well. I liked the sound of his pleasant voice.

"I'll read my book when I get to my granny's cottage some six miles away."

"Six miles in snow!" he exclaimed, "It will feel more like twelve. Won't you let me accompany you as I'm out for a walk?"

I looked around and he read my mind.

"Do you think we will see another person on the way?"

I gave a little smile, knowing we would be alone and not likely to be the talk of the village.

"That's better," he said, "Such a lovely face should never be without a smile."

His manner charmed me, and I couldn't help a blush starting from my chest to creep steadily upwards. I felt my face on fire.

He laughed, asking if I'd never received a compliment. I said of course, but I didn't tell him I'd never been handed one by such a confident gentleman. When he helped me up and over the stiles of the drystone walls, I could somehow feel the touch of his hand through our gloves.

By the time we'd reached granny's cottage, I found out he was in the army even before the war but stationed down south close to his parents' home in Bournemouth. He lived with his mother and father before then, and had one younger sister, Amelia.

As we looked down from the hill, he saw the cottage in the distance and told me it was simply breath-taking nestled in the fold of the snowy woodland. I followed his gaze, so proud it now belonged to me.

How long could I avoid it, how long could I last before I looked his way? I bit my bottom lip as it tends to quiver when I'm nervous and swallowed rapidly. I had to pull myself together somehow, but the sensation of him watching me wasn't doing anything to help my nerves. The air was thick with intensity. It had been a long walk and we'd never stopped talking.

He took control of the situation. He reached across to boldly lift my chin, so I had no alternative but to look at him. He was grinning madly away, enjoying the effect he was having on me. I'm sure he was used to it.

"I have a confession; I've been trying to locate you for months, since the first time I saw you walking the moors."

Our breath was flying in clouds around our faces as I let out a small gasp. His laugh was low.

"Dear Nell, you have no idea how hard it was to find you but more, how hard it was to think of never finding you again. I fear you're going to get me into serious trouble and army life might need to be a thing of the past after the war."

I smiled through my blush, thrown but at the same time pleased to have made such an impact on a gentleman who could clearly have his pick of the ladies. The silence wrapped around us as I searched for a suitably ladylike response.

"Well, thank you for the stimulating company," I said, shyly, looking down at the wetness of my coat which had seeped through to my dress, "I hope to meet you again out walking one day."

I didn't want to leave him to go inside but the light was fading, and he still had a long walk back.

"I'm on leave until Monday. Would you care to meet me tomorrow for your return trip?"

Deep blue pools of intrigue were staring at me when I finally raised my head. I quickly looked away from the danger—such sensations were new and intoxicating.

But how I wanted to see him again.

"I usually set off around one o'clock this time of year. I could meet you here," I said, braving a small peek at his handsome face.

"It's a date," he said, lifting his hat and bowing my way.

The excitement came flooding back. It didn't go away again for a long, long time.

Chapter 13

Suddenly, I found myself swept along, living from one spell of leave to the next, much the same as Mark.

He was twelve years older than me, and I found his worldliness and experience of life was fascinating. He was like a comforting blanket providing me with security, protection yet he had the risky combination of good looks and charisma. He captivated me with tale after tale of travels and camaraderie he brought to vivid life.

Sometimes his C.O. cancelled his leave at short notice, and there was no way of letting me know, so I always set off after lunch at one o'clock each weekend day, so he knew a definite schedule. I worked the land all week, gruelling hours which went on endlessly between breaktimes and lunchtimes and home times. The war seemed so far away, and life went on, cruelly punctuated by the constant stream of grim telegrams and injured men returning home changed forever, to remind us life could be far worse.

One day I set off and walked around two miles before Mark joined me. I heard him shouting across the gorse land and my heart stopped for a beat.

"Nell, Nell!" is all I heard but it was the most poetic sound, and the most overwhelming sight, seeing him trampling over the heather at speed, in a rush to see little old me.

I often caught him staring at me, not even bothering to look away when I noticed. He was enjoying himself far too much playing his little game.

Of course, I never invited him into the cottage as this would have been far too dangerous. In the warmer weather, we sat and talked on an old fallen tree trunk in the woods, because I always struggled to say goodbye.

It would have been the easiest thing in the world to just say lightly, "Would you care for a cup of tea before you head home?"

Yet I never did.

I knew he'd cast a spell, but I tried not to fall under it completely. I'm a firm believer in fate and I do ponder how differently my life would have turned out if Mark hadn't walked into my life that day. A chance encounter veered me off track to a place where I was out of control, with repercussions beyond my imagination.

I should have kept my wits about me.

*

The war was over.

We celebrated all day and night in the streets whilst wondering what life would be like the next day.

The pub served free beer, cider and tea in quantity all day long, and my father managed to join us for a time between calls.

Such a bitter-sweet period. Women had been the glue of the country and then they were suddenly surplus to requirements.

I'd imagined how it would feel many times to be free of the war. I imagined waking to help mother with some chores, perhaps running to the shop, then returning for lunch and then a walk to granny's house. I could take the walk every day for a while until I thought about getting a little job. We could live our lives knowing we lived in peace and the constant knot we all carried around with us miraculously unravelled and left us for good.

Yet, life didn't return to normality, at least not the normality we all knew. We replaced one knot with another as we adjusted to life with the memory of war etched permanently in our minds. There were constant reminders, and some had memories far worse than others, but they were never ever spoken about.

And all the while I waited for Mark to come and sweep me off my feet.

Chapter 14

The weekend after the celebrations came but then went with no sign of Mark.

Perhaps he'd gone home to visit. Yes, that was why, I'd possibly see him the next weekend or even the one after, depending on the amount of leave he had. But it was strange he left no word.

Four weekends became six, then eight and it was only then I finally knew that I had to get on with post-war life. I spoke to my parents who were slightly concerned for my welfare by then, though I tried to hide my heartbreak. I told them I'd like to stay at the cottage and think about taking a job.

"Are you sure, sweetheart?" my father asked, "There's no necessity for you to work and the cottage can be a lonely, isolated place."

We'd finished supper and were sitting at the table in the dining room. I'd taken the opportunity to open the discussion as father didn't often join us for supper and I knew I must take action to stop myself from declining further.

"It can be lonely for some or a retreat for others," my mother said, handing my father a cup of tea, "Mother certainly didn't feel that way living there, and I somehow doubt Nell will either. Goodness, she's spent plenty of time at the cottage to know."

They all laughed, and Daniel saw it as an opportunity to tell us he was going out. My parents never questioned where he was going but he avoided eye contact as he left the table. His predicament had taken a back seat for a while.

My mother searched my face for clues a moment then patted my hand.

"I think it will be a very good idea. Some people need space to breathe, others manage just fine in the middle of a crowd."

I mustered a smile, my heart bursting with love for her.

I took a short secretarial course at the evening institute in Harrogate, and it didn't take me long to secure a job in Horton.

I could walk into town in pleasant weather or just walk in general, especially through the forest at the back of my cottage. I loved taking the little path into the woodland up onto the open moor. I always stopped and took in the sight of the moorland stretching endlessly to the horizon. Like Mark, I was free, anonymous and I never tired of it.

It was the last place I expected to meet anyone, but that morning I met you Will. It would have been a straightforward decision to walk the same route the following morning, but as Mark was still firmly entrenched in my mind—though I didn't care to admit it—I checked myself. There was a little voice inside whispering, "Give yourself time to heal, Nell."

In the end fate intervened and took the decision out of my hands. I'd thought about you often after that first encounter and somewhere in my soul knew there was something bigger, more powerful than the two us and I had to take my heaven-sent opportunity by the Falls. The way you searched for me reminded me of Mark but you're very different to him. Although you're mature in years you have an innocence about you, the same sense of unworthiness I seem to lug around with me until my knees buckle. Your uncomplicated ways are such a contrast to Mark with his deeper side. You have no idea how attractive you are, which is a breath of fresh air. Your dark hair flops constantly into your gentle blue eyes, your build is strong, and you turn heads but you're completely unaware. Mark is too aware of the hold he has over women.

In the end, despite the scar of how it ended with Mark, I didn't even have to try to fall in love with you, William.

*

I had finally stopped waiting for Mark to come and sweep me off my feet.

Life often has a way of demonstrating how little control we have over events, as much as we like to think we do. The very morning after meeting you I was busying myself with some chores, finally feeling like I was on the right path, or at least on a path when there was a knock at the door.

Visitors were practically non-existent at the cottage, but I opened the door, unable to help a wide smile for no real reason other than my light mood.

Then my cheeks dropped, the smile running away like I'd been given some terrible news.

It was Mark, it was Mark looking magnificent in his uniform and now promoted to captain to boot. Once upon a time I knew nothing of uniforms and ranks but by then everyone knew them all.

I couldn't really take it in at first. Was this really my Mark I thought, my undisguised shock glaringly obvious. Cool as a cucumber, he removed his cap, smoothing his hair before tucking the cap under his arm. His face was drawn, his expression earnest.

"I know I've no right to ask, Nell, but please will you let me explain?"

I held tightly to the door handle suddenly feeling nauseous. For two pins I could have fainted and thankfully he noticed, ushering me towards the settee. He threw his hat on the side table and hunted for a glass in my tiny kitchen to fetch me some water which I took gladly. I sipped slowly to control my nervous reaction to the shock.

He sat in the chair by the fire opposite me, his mouth set, unsure what to do next. I understood then how much he genuinely cared for me.

Dropping my head back on the settee, I asked, "Why have you come? Why today and not last week, the week before?"

He strode the few steps to sit beside me and take my hands. Startled, I pulled them away quickly.

"Please, Nell. You're all I've thought about since I left. I returned home and … everything had changed."

Sighing, he loosened his tie and stared at me.

"I knew real life loomed. I had to go face it sooner or later, so I chose sooner to spare us even more pain. I've felt terrible since and couldn't stay away any longer."

I count the medal ribbons on his chest and think about the horrors he'd witnessed "I thought you were a simple soldier, from a humble background," I said, a tightness appearing at the back of my throat. The shock was too much, I thought he'd left me, never to return.

"You would never have been yourself if you knew I was a lieutenant, I would only have had the fake you, the nervous you, when there was so much more to be had."

He leaned forward and touched my lips with his own. I instinctively closed my eyes and sunk into it, forgetting who I was, where I was completely. He was still the same magnetic man, a rank in the army made no difference to me.

Pulling away, I was fearful of letting go of too much of myself.

"Are you hungry?" I asked him, "You must be, you've travelled a long way."

Smiling, he stood to take off his jacket and hung it on the coat stand. It looked odd in the homely surroundings. As he rolled up his sleeves, I stared with fascination at his forearms. The brown skin, the dark hairs were the embodiment of manliness. Manly is the perfect description for Mark.

I went into the kitchen and cut some bread to make a doorstep sandwich for my starving man. As I buttered the bread, sliced the cheese, I suddenly thought of you. Why would that be I wondered as I returned to the parlour to watch Mark eat his food.

He talked all afternoon about the future. We should be together; we could make it work. He could buy himself out of the army and he could come and live at the cottage. I missed him; I couldn't deny it.

The darkness descended and I realised it would be impossible in so many ways for him to leave that night. I should have sent him on his way hours before, but I was clinging to every word just the same as before. He added wood to the fire periodically as though he lived in the cottage with me already.

It was getting late. As I collected his plate and teacup from the table, he put his hand lightly on my arm and I almost threw them back down. He pulled me into his embrace and kissed me with a passion igniting something fresh and new within. It was powerful, it made me feel powerful that he wanted me so badly and not just for a while. I forgot everything and everyone and fell into the sensation. Still kissing, we climbed the stairs to my room, tripping, falling over each other. It was wanton but it wasn't my reality; it wasn't me even.

Opening the buttons of my dress, his hands were trembling, and I realised he was just as nervous as me.

"I want to get it right, Nell. I want your first time to be wonderful. You're a darling, beautiful girl and I need you so badly. I don't know how I've managed to stay away for so long."

He undressed me layer by layer, then laid me in the cold sheets. I watched him take off his clothes then climb in beside me, folding the bedclothes snugly around us for a moment. I'd lit a fire earlier thinking at the time it would just be me tucked up in bed for the night.

When he kissed my neck, then my breasts and moved lower I gave a bolt from surprise which made him moan. He took my hand to push against his hardness and I knew I had done this to him. Climbing on top of me, he entered me so slowly, so gently. I foolishly thought I knew what to expect from my father's anatomy books and girlish discussions.

Except I didn't know what to expect at all it transpired. How could they prepare you for the sensation of lovemaking? I could never have expected such pain, such pleasure. He thrust a little harder, a little faster and I moaned, instinctively moving in time to the rhythm of his body.

"Oh, my darling, I love you," he almost yelled, as we entered another world together.

Shuddering, we clung to each other, and he held me in his arms until our breathing slowed.

Raising his head he asked, "Do you love me, my little Nell?"

He stroked his hair from my face, looking for the answer in my eyes.

"Yes," I whispered.

But I knew it to be a lie. Mark was not the man for me I'd found out too late.

I woke in the night many times and could barely bring myself to look at the person sleeping peacefully by my side.

And each time I woke I had the same thought:

I have lost too much myself, and worse still I've lost a part I can never get back.

Chapter 14

What a terrible mess.

By morning it's as though I'm hovering above my little home, parting the steam to peek at my own strange torrid love life. Of lying in a bed with a man who isn't my husband, an unthinkable thought only hours ago. I feel changed, sullied, and not just because of last night.

I have betrayed you. We're not together, I know nothing about you, yet this is exactly how I feel.

Mark wakens with a lazy smile to reach for me. I try not to show my horror in the cold light of day, but I'm up and dressed in two shakes of a lamb's tail.

"I'll make us some breakfast," I tell him, hoping to detract from my odd behaviour.

I keep my back to him but feel his eyes upon me the entire time while my skin crawls with a new sensation.

His voice telling me he's found the perfect woman sounds so far away, no louder than a whisper.

As I comb my hair and wash downstairs, I pinpoint the sensation. Making love to Mark, the supposedly heady pinnacle of our relationship now carries the price tag of disgust with myself.

There is nothing permanent or solid here. My permanence lies in someone else's hands and not Mark's. My path is as clear now as a babbling stream.

By the time he's bounced down the stairs, the range is blazing, the table set and I'm pouring steaming tea into cups. I can't look at him, but he doesn't notice.

He tells me he's famished as he tucks heartily into the eggs and bacon. I can only push my food around my plate.

How I want him to go.

"You're not hungry?" he asks.

Sighing, I carefully refold my napkin to stall for time. I'm startled when his knife and fork clatter on his plate as he's clearly seen something in my expression for a panic to widen his face.

"What is it, what's wrong, my love?"

I look at his army jacket hanging on the coat rack and start to cry. I wanted him to come back so badly for so long and now I only want him to leave.

"I'm so sorry, please believe me, Mark. Yesterday had an almost mystical aura to it, surreal may be a better word."

His face is set but his eyes are telling me a story.

I look down as a teardrop splatters my dress and watch the stain splay into the fabric. Swallowing manically, I search for words to minimise the damage, but I must restore reality however stark.

As it does so often of late, your dear face rolls to the front of my mind and the expression in your eyes as you spoke so few words to me the morning on the moors. This gives me the resolve I need. With you, without you, Mark is not my man.

And all the while Mark stares at me.

"I … I'm sorry, this isn't right," I say, my voice breaking.

His eyes are still burning me as he slumps backwards, but a chill descends on the warm, snug room.

Scraping his chair on the flagstones as he stands, he snaps his braces onto his shoulders. He walks over to the fire to lean against the mantle, forehead on forearm.

"I've left it too long. I should have come sooner, I knew it, I know it."

The sadness of his small voice makes a sob escape me to bring him rushing to my side.

"What of last night, Nell? That was real. I know it was."

I settle my eyes on him, so he can see the sincerity of my words.

"It meant everything." I say flatly.

The past tense hangs around us, haunting us already.

"It's because I abandoned you. I'm so sorry about how I handled the situation, more than you could ever understand. You were right the first time; mystical is the perfect description of our time together during the war. But it gave it an almost unreal sensation, dreamlike and so removed from real life. I think I was battling to take it all in for so long."

He drops to my feet and grasps my hands as though drowning and only I have the power to save him, nobody else. The irony is choking me – this is all I ever wanted only yesterday.

It seems a stranger I thought I knew and a stranger I don't know the first thing about have given me clarity in a few short hours.

"Forgive me, Mark, this is far from how I imagined I would feel this morning."

I remove my hands from his to search for a handkerchief. I can't look at his face, but I sense he knows my mind is made up.

He's defeated, I've defeated him, and this makes me feel cruel. He can't understand what I'm trying to tell him because he's so certain I'm his future. He does love me in this alternate universe we've created, where reality is on the other side of the front door, yet another world away.

Love is one thing, but Mark will never need me. At least, not in the way I would like to feel needed. Somehow, I'm certain of so much and I'm not second guessing. As granny once told me, when you know, you know… it's as simple as that.

I try to compose myself as I look at Mark still on his knees, staring at the floor. He looks bereft, as though he's kneeling at my grave after I've left him forever. In his mind I may as well have.

I'm not equipped to deal with his wounded expression. I hesitate before laying my hand on his hair and he turns swiftly into my skirts to hide his face.

The sound of his soft tears almost breaks me, and I lean my body to rest my cheek on his head to try and bring him comfort.

I must end this torture for both of us.

"I wish you only happiness," I say, stroking his back gently.

A solid lump in my throat breaks my voice.

But it's the trigger he needs to stop his tears. Removing his face from my skirts he rises to crumple in the chair. It seems an age before he speaks as if he has nothing to say yet he knows he must respond.

"Your wish will be some consolation one day I know, Nell but not today," he says, the words flat and small, doing their best not to leave his mouth.

I go to sit in the chair by the fire, shivering from cold and far more.

Eventually he makes his way upstairs and I listen to him moving around, no doubt trying to prepare himself practically and mentally to leave me forever.

My stomach whirls as I hear his loud slow footsteps on the stairs and I'm suddenly uncertain how to deal with the very last part of our story.

When I see his distressed face, I want to pull him to me, and tell him everything will be all right, that he'll find the right love and I'll fade from his memory day by day.

Yet, I can't get up as he puts on his coat and cap, restoring himself to the perfect army gentleman.

I search for words as he looks around my pretty little parlour for the last time. I press my handkerchief to my mouth and feel as though the ground is falling away beneath my feet. But the tears do not come. The remorse is accompanied by the slightest flicker of relief I've finally made the decision and more importantly, I've found the strength to carry it through.

A part of Mark will stay with me until the day I die, but we could never have survived the harsh realities of life; I'd only ever shown him one side of me. He would never have been able to understand all of me.

Mark had done a great deal of thinking in the short time he was upstairs. He was a proud man; a proud soldier and he had displayed his vulnerable side to a woman who in the end did not want him.

I tell myself now he needed to restore equilibrium in his mind, so he could restore dignity and self-respect. It allowed him to cast the final damnation which shattered me, the cracks visible for all time.

His hand on the door, he looked through me, unable to meet my eyes as he inflicted his damage yet knowing all the while he must do it to save himself.

I'm glad in the end I was sitting down as he left me with his parting shot.

"And to think I was set to leave my wife and children in Bournemouth ... and for a little harlot like you."

Chapter 15

Spending time with you I have the chance to finally experience what I thought existed only in the mind of poets. Yet I know now you can only write convincingly about something you have felt to your core.

True love is the purest of emotions.

I stood by helplessly watching you falling deeper and deeper seemingly never to stop. You say for you it was love at first sight. My feelings were slower burning but nevertheless become just as strong.

You obsess about losing me though you try to hide it, so you don't appear weak and vulnerable. It might surprise you that I have the same worry. You treat me with such tenderness, such sensitivity, other women would want the adulation you have for me for themselves given the opportunity. Few are lucky enough to find it.

But I am lucky.

Demons lurk deep inside me since Mark, and if they become out of control, they can drain the life from me or make me bare my teeth.

When you're late back from work one evening I'm pacing the floor, the anger spitting and bubbling within. I'm waiting for you, and it takes you completely unawares.

My suspicious mind has gripped me. I know you're not Mark and I want to trust you, but I keep you at bay with one foot over the threshold to run should I need to.

I pounce before you have chance to take off your coat.

"Where the hell have you been?" is my greeting, "I'd thank you not to think for one moment I intend to spend my life like your mother waiting for you to grace me with your presence. We know how her story ended; the best years of her life gone to a man who made work his god."

Your usual 'happy to be home' expression slips then drops right from your face. I may as well have spat at you; the reaction would be the same. You look bemused, then horrified but at this moment I really don't care. I will never give you the chance to make a fool out of me, William.

I flounce past you on route to our bedroom and slam the door, revelling briefly in the sense of satisfaction it gives me. Mother once said I've been known to do a fine line in flouncing on occasion, especially as a young girl. I'm determined not to let the look on your face seep into my mind. I doubt you will have witnessed such a display with Charlotte, never mind been the victim of it. That was the first time the disturbing image flashed into my head. It was akin to throwing your doting puppy out into the snow and slamming the door.

When I think about it rationally, I can imagine your eagerness to get home to see me. I can hear you asking Harry to stop talking and wind up the meeting. Harry would have grinned boyishly and done just that. He seems like a man who needs a stopper.

Rationale is sometimes elusive. I'm unable shake off the knowledge you met me out of the blue, I met Mark out of the blue. You can meet someone in such a way any second of any day and it might happen again. But then there's the voice whispering I must remember you are not Mark.

You wait a moment or two, I'm unsure whether this is through wisdom or self-preservation, then I hear the creak of the door. I lay clutching the eiderdown, my mind spinning out of control.

The bed sags as you perch beside me. How reassured I am suddenly to know all is well; that I haven't toppled off my pedestal. You gently touch my arm, the lightest of touches because you will be afraid of me pushing you away. But you are brave, and you are strong.

"Nell, you mustn't worry so, you must know there's nowhere I would rather be than here at home with you."

Your level tone is comforting; patience has always been your virtue.

I turn my head to search your face and see you peeping at me from under your fringe which refuses to behave. You're like a small boy seeking my approval, all wide-eyed and earnest and hopeful.

How can I stay angry?

Sighing, I reach to move your fringe from your eyes with my forefinger. You bend to kiss me—a completely disarming butterfly kiss fuelling my remorse as the intensity increases.

You pull away, your eyes twinkling when you open them.

"I know you have a darkness lurking in that mind of yours but relax, I promise you have me forever. You don't fool me; this is the Libran balance you tell me of in the sun signs of your magazine. I've read the traits and it's such a shame you were born on the cusp, so you swing to extremes, this way, that way, and the other. I realise it all balances out in the end though."

I look at you agog. Who else would think to say this and not to patronise, but to smooth my feathers with humour? You don't miss a trick.

"Come on woman, I'm ready for my tea!" you say, in your best Yorkshire accent.

I push you so hard and quickly off the bed you land with a clatter. Shocked, you laugh the loudest I've ever heard you, even louder than when I went to see you by the Falls that day. I throw my head back and join in at the sound of it.

You're late having your tea tonight. Tea is the last thing on your mind for quite some time.

So, you've evaluated me to a tee and understand I use attack as my first point of defence. It's difficult to accept as I've never shown anyone every complex side of me except Daniel. Apparently, I've finally found someone mature enough to love the traits which terrify me.

It appears so. But Nell, you must never lose sight of your wits.

*

Highbrook looks like the fairy tale castles in my books with its mock turrets and crenulations, and when you showed me around, I loved the house more because of how much you loved it. My wish came true when you bought it before it was too late.

But the sensation I had that Saturday was profound and unexpected, the pull on me extraordinary. It was the thought of building a life together there with you; more, of sharing our life there.

The house envelopes me in the same way as my childhood home. You never understand the feeling until you've left it behind and it's gone and then you get it back if you're very lucky. I know now I had to love you to feel it beyond the skeleton of Highbrook. As beautiful as the house is, it could never be enough without our love. The two go hand in hand.

It's you, William, I understand now that you are my home.

Frances was waiting for us outside on the bench placed there long ago to take in the spectacular view. She fitted your description to the letter.

My own first impressions of Frances were very favourable. She has a kindly face, warmth radiating from her eyes, and she was smiling broadly at both of us as we approached.

She has a classic beauty, taller than me and slim, almost patrician with her blue eyes and angular features. Her hair and clothes are in keeping with the latest trends, her blondish greying hair cut radically to her chin. Such a brave move which I've been unable to make, and I think I would break your heart if I did. I hope people think so favourably of me at Frances's age as she's obviously discovered the secret of how to stay vibrant beyond middle age. It was obvious why you'd grown to care about her so much, why your face had a softness to it when you spoke about her, and you spoke about her often.

Sadly, things turned out differently for Frances and me. After our first encounter, she never found it in herself to smile at me in such a way again.

I quickly became the pesky little fly in her ointment.

Chapter 16

Forever is an unsettling word.

However, the thought of forever as your wife does nothing to scare me. After we marry, everything is far from perfect. We expect perfection in the early days, and we invariably achieve it, much as I did with Mark. We want to bend and twist to agree with each other, to stifle our true selves.

We are imperfect. I try to push you away, but you stand steadfast, going nowhere as promised.

My cottage will always be there, so I'm never cast adrift.

You tell me you don't know if you're coming or going but I never deliberately keep you on your toes; this is the way I've become because of the cracks. Fear makes me uncertain; uncertainty makes me insular, a lone wolf.

With Mark I thought I was a conformist, but how wrong I turned out to be You never expect convention from me, loving me more because of the lack of it.

Frances and your mother are conventional in terms of marriage. They think I'm difficult because I don't fit a mould but I'm sure in your mother's eyes Charlotte was a match made in heaven.

They think I have you wrapped around my little finger, and I manipulate you, but you wouldn't love me as you do if this was the case. They really don't give you enough credit.

How strange when my upbringing couldn't have been more traditional. My parents loved the bones of one another and us, tucking us up safely in a nest full of love. My father worked long hours as a doctor, but that didn't matter because we had fun when we saw him. Mother, Daniel and I were never happier than when we were together. We were quite the team. Tennis tournaments on the back lawn in the summer holidays, mother refereeing, keeping score, picnics, sledging, painting all the usual pastimes you assume everyone does. Then after an idyllic childhood, you find out life beyond often throws you to the wolves and never lives up to the same standard again.

Daniel was my big brother, but he was also my best friend, and it would be fair to say I idolised him. He was always a protective arm around my shoulders. We were happy playing together and didn't mix much with the other children in the village. I didn't feel we missed out then, but now I think it might have been better not to put all my eggs in that one basket.

But all this was a long time ago. Now I think I would have benefitted from the healthy competition of a sister.

It would have done me good.

*

We've always had fish and chips from Annie's on Fridays as a nice little prelude to the weekend as mother calls it.

I peer through the raindrops on the window and see no sign of her, so drop the curtain to join Daniel by the fire in the parlour. How cosy the room is in winter, and I think of granny by the fire in her cottage. We're going tomorrow. We go every other Saturday to take her some shopping because she lives in the back of beyond as father describes it. Mother worries about her on her own now she's getting older, but granny said she has enough people calling on her and sometimes she wishes she could have more time on her own.

She wasn't talking about us; I knew she meant Brian who keeps turning up unannounced and then every so often asks her to marry him. She told me he's after her money, but mother said she was joking, she doesn't have very much money, but this is plenty for her. Mother says Brian has been in love with granny for years, but she says she only ever wanted to marry one man. She likes being on her own with her thoughts and her memories. They're entertainment enough she tells me. I'll understand one day because I'm a lot like her, she says.

She lives in a teeny tiny cottage that was an old woodsman's cottage because granddad was a woodsman. Mother said her dada would take her to school on his horse and cart because it was too far to walk to the village and all her friends would wait to give Hector an apple even in the rain.

Granny had a little dog when I was younger called Branwell after the brother of the Bronte sisters, because he was a boy, otherwise it would have been Emily. I loved Branwell so much that when he died, I said I wanted to stay with granny. We put up the little wooden bed mother had slept in, and I laid in it for three days on the trot while granny sat in her chair by the fire. I only got up to go to the outside toilet and wash my hands and face in the sink or eat the bread and stew she cooked on the black range. We didn't talk much, and she didn't tell me any stories. She didn't want to, and I didn't want her to. We stared into the fire a lot and granny sometimes read one of her special books she had if she was sad. We cried a lot about Branwell at first and then not as much. On the third night there were gale force winds which shook the house and woke me up. Granny was sitting by the fire, and she told me not to be scared because the cottage had been standing for over three hundred years and nothing had ever happened to it. She said the forest protected us from everything. The sound of the wind lulled me back to sleep and now the sound of the wind is one of my favourite sounds. The following morning, we heard mother coming down the path on the horse and carriage. I jumped out of bed, pulled up the covers and combed my hair quickly to sit in the chair opposite granny. We smiled at each other.

When mother came in, she looked at us and said she should have listened to the voice in her head telling her to come sooner because she knew we would be driving each other to madness. I wasn't sure what she meant, I thought we looked fine.

When granny tells a story, it sounds like she's reading it from a book. She says this is because she's living them so she can feel what's happening and some of the stories are true but she's not going to tell us which ones because that would spoil it.

"Nell, I have to talk to you before mother gets back," Daniel says, cutting into my memories.

"Why?" I ask, not really paying attention because I'm thinking of Branwell and if I could persuade mother to let us have a dog.

"This isn't something I've just thought about believe me, I've been mulling it over for months," he says.

He pauses and watches my face. He now has more of my attention and I'm starting to be uncomfortable. I want him to just say what he needs to say.

"I've decided to try and find my birth mother."

Now, I regret my impatience.

How blissfully unaware I was that everything was about to change, that I'm sure I will never be able to eat fish and chips again without thinking of this moment.

I try to digest this new piece of information and I notice he doesn't say real mother. It's odd I should notice.

The information is slowly digesting but laying heavy. Now my world is spinning, and Daniel has taken control. I decide I don't like feeling out of control.

I hear the children playing in the street, and I wish I was little again, and Daniel and I were laughing because he was chasing me after I accused him of cheating in a game of tennis.

I'm not sure how to respond, how he'd like me to respond, so I don't speak for a while. I think about mother and father and then I start to panic.

"When are you going to tell our parents?" I blurt out.

They really won't like hearing this news I'm thinking. Mother will say that it's fine, but it won't be really. The weekend is not looking so appealing any longer.

"I'm not. Well, not yet anyway. I may not even be able to find her. If I do, I'll tell them then."

I'm so relieved. The weekend is looking rosy once more.

But I can't stop thinking about it. Why has he told me this; why is he upsetting the apple cart when no good will come of it? I start to feel a little sickly.

We have such a lovely life I suddenly realise. I don't understand why he would want to go to the trouble of finding someone who didn't want him.

We do, we want him.

I hate that he's drawn me into his lie which will spoil everything.

It takes months before he finds out where the woman lives. Then it takes another two months before he plucks up the courage to go and see her. I've been hoping he'll get tired of looking and change his mind, but no such luck.

The first time he goes to see her I try to fake excitement for him, but he knows me too well. I'm feeling pushed out, so I'm behaving strangely.

He picks a night when he knows my parents will be at a dinner party. This seems very devious to me. He comes back before they get back, which also seems devious.

I go to bed. I don't want to be in bed, but I don't want to talk about it. I'm peevish, I'm jealous.

I picture them together all night in a cosy little scene. Will they embrace; will Daniel see her again? All I know is her name is Molly.

He tells me all about her the next day. He doesn't ask if I want to hear all about it because he's in his own world and this is a world where I have no place.

Granny says you need to walk a mile in someone's shoes before passing judgement. I try to remember this when the resentment gets too much. When I have thoughts about my brother which I'm not proud of.

Daniel grows to love his real mother and oh, how it hurts. He's so happy, and I'm ashamed because I love him, and I should be happy for him.

It's all too much to come to terms with and over the years I keep him at arm's length. I start to run away from him and discover I'm more of a 'flightier' than a fighter when times are difficult. He tries his best to justify his deception, but he just wants it all. He just wants too much.

As time goes by, I remind myself everyone has a skeleton in the cupboard but his has turned putrid for me because he lacks any sign of guilt.

The irony is our mother never has any idea the safe, secure little world she built with love and care was smashed to smithereens by her beloved son.

Of course, I will always love him, and I'll continue seeing him for mother and father's sake, and all those unavoidable occurrences which crop up in life. I intend to always make nice.

His betrayal, Mark's betrayal, they cut me to the quick.

Is it any wonder I'm difficult?

Chapter 17

Some days you never forget.

The usual milestones and the more unusual. Your first and last day at school; riding a bicycle instead of a tricycle; your first kiss; your first house; the day you find your first chap in an alleyway doing ungallant things to another girl, which was a big day; the day you find yourself staring at the calendar realising nearly two months have gone by without a period.

I want to cry. Tears of fear, of shame and self-pity. Oh, Nell. This isn't right, I don't want to be pregnant; I'm a single woman and the scandal will break me, and my parents. But a darker cloud is quickly forming in my mind. I try to calculate the time again, to try and be certain but it's impossible.

Oh no, no, no. What am I to do?

I could never talk to you about Mark. I was still recovering from the trauma of his sudden reappearance, and it would have been too upsetting and disconcerting for you.

I needed to tell you something about my past which wasn't a lie, so I simply played the whole thing down. It was for the best.

But this is different. I'm caught in a web of my own making, damned if I tell you and damned if I don't.

I thought it was too soon but that day at your house something carnal came over me. Being alone with you in your home made me almost desperate to love you, love you as a woman. I couldn't wait any longer to show you that love and take the doubt from your eyes. It was an ache.

I never gave what happened with Mark a second thought, so, I really shouldn't be surprised with how things turned out.

I perch on a fallen trunk at the edge of the woods behind the cottage; its cold and damp and the brooding, slate sky bears down on me, I have a moment of weakness and consider the unforgiveable.

I am having a baby and every instinct is telling me this baby is yours, William.

I don't only feel it in my bones, I feel it in my soul.

*

The wedding gifts are barely unwrapped before everyone is focused on the baby. We had to tell everyone and quickly and they are united in joy.

I wish I could be too, but I can't help but think I'm missing a piece inside; the all-important 'survival-of-the-human-race' craving people seem to have. You think you understand, but you really don't and you're not alone.

I've lost count of the babies who were brought to the house over the years. They came in a steady stream to show off their little bundles and bestow gifts on my father for helping with their safe arrival. Mother and I cooed and fawned and told them just how perfect they were, how they looked like their mother or had their father's eyes. They were, they did. I was usually the first of us to hold them or even feed them, mother often insisting. I could admire their adorable little faces, but I didn't look down at any of them and imagine having one just like them. Not even for a second.

My mother is loving and nurturing, she solved the mystery surrounding motherhood easily. She is a natural.

When I finally voiced my concerns to you, you weren't listening to me. I tried to explain but you were hearing my words, not listening to the meaning behind them, the implications. You were thinking about your own joy at the news. The joy was brimming over, and you were trying your best not to display it, but you failed. And I had to look at it.

Everyone has doubts and insecurities about parenthood, you were thinking. I'm certain you will have your own but at a more acceptable level, a level which is understandable. I should have tried harder to explain, even been a little more forceful.

Regardless, it was impossible to alter the outcome.

I often articulate my worries to myself to see if I can find a solution, and sometimes I can. I thought about not having the patience or focus of my mother. I have a 'butterfly mind' as you call it, flitting from one thought to another, easily distracted. Mother was more than happy to make us the centre of her world and on this we agree, a child deserves nothing less. I'm prepared to put my heart and soul into motherhood to reach for nothing less.

I'd love to be as certain as you and I know I must stop myself thinking about it so much. The biggest challenge is sitting on a roundabout of thoughts, unable to stop the perpetual motion, but it could be like trying to change the colour of my eyes.

Initially your delight lifts me and carries me along. All you've ever wished for is just within your grasp and I refuse to be the person to stand in the way. This is quite simply your calling in life and you long to be everything to a child your own father wasn't.

You want me to lean on you, you want me to need you. This is the only way for you to feel secure in our marriage as you live in fear I'll bolt from convention.

Mother has plenty of wise words to offer.

"You'll come to realise that having a child brings about change but in a good way. It shifts your whole outlook on life, it is after all the meaning of life. You're lucky to have William; he'll be your rock. Not many women are lucky enough to have such solid support."

Her judgement sits heavily because I know she's always had concerns, which was why the babies were foisted on me as a ploy. You can't hide from your own mother. She has a point of course, however my rock will be home two days a week, so I have worries about the other five. I spend my days tramping the moors in all weathers, reading, writing, pontificating, emoting, analysing; all of which will be of little help to a baby.

"It will be difficult to live up to my own expectations. You're a hard act to follow, mother."

She's earned her smug little smile.

"I had to learn the same as everyone else, Nell."

She's fast losing interest—a glaze sets her eyes and I hear a note of agitation in her voice. I must give up yet somehow, I'm desperate enough to make one last attempt, resigned to not bringing up the subject again.

"You're a natural born mother, I'm unsure if I am, is all."

"I admit to not giving it as much thought as you appear to be," she says, "but this is your trouble, you analyse everything to death Nell, make life far too hard for yourself. You're so like your grandmother. You won't have any time for all this nonsense when the baby's here and this can only be a good thing. You feel differently about your own child. Just have a little faith."

She's annoyed with me now so this is the last I will say on the matter. I feel worse than when we started the conversation and concede another defeat.

How I wish I could talk to granny. She was such a good mother, but she may have had her doubts at first. I could have explained, and she would have listened without judgement whether she understood or not.

My fears ebb and flow during pregnancy but with everyone excited for the arrival of the baby it's easy to join in. The doctor explained a surge in hormones, and they are certainly helping. You're so attentive and caring, I'm sure it will all be just fine.

You stroke my stomach one morning after making love, always the perfect gentleman. The thought crosses my mind I've become your own little pot doll to play with then carefully place back in my box. You're undeniably sweet, but it gives me another reason to not feel myself. I don't want to be handled with care; I perhaps shamefully want to be handled with unrestrained lust, to be thrown down on the bed in careless abandon like before.

I can sense you incessantly making plans in your mind for when we become a family.

"We're in this together, Nell, I'm not going to sit in the background like most men if this is what you're worrying about," you tell me.

I have no doubt about it and I'm truly the luckiest girl in the world.

So, I decide to take slow, deep breaths and keep putting one foot in front of the other until one day surely, I will make it to the other side.

Chapter 18

My period of confinement has begun.

I look like any other mother-to-be, and Miss Crawford is on hand for the time being. I can't bring myself to call her Crawford unless Frances is the vicinity.

I shan't be using the services of a nanny, let alone a wetnurse. Frances will think I'm being awkward, whereas you will just be anxious. Ordering staff around would make *me* anxious and them watching my every move, well, it would set my nerves on edge.

So, I conclude in the meantime if I pretend that I feel happy, I will become happy.

I'm dangerously good at the pretence.

On only the third day of confinement an unmistakable pain grips me as I'm reading the new Agatha Christie mystery which my mother brought to occupy my time.

The pain soon stops, and I hold onto my swollen stomach waiting for the next wave.

Am I ready? Yes, I think I might be practically speaking, because after what the doctor termed 'nesting', I gave the apartment a good spruce just before I was confined to my room. You have come to an arrangement with Miss Crawford with cooking and housework whilst I'm indisposed.

Being friendly with her doesn't put her at ease and she's uncomfortable around me because she doesn't have her proper place in the hierarchy.

I ring the bell, and she appears, immediately panic-stricken by the look on my face. Neither of us have any experience in this area and the doctor came only hours ago to say it would be at least a few more days.

"I'm off to get the mistress," she splutters, before I have time to respond.

She flees the room as though it's on fire.

Frances knocks before entering the room briskly. I'm rotating between pacing the room and rolling on the bed.

"Crawford," she says, without turning her head, "Go fetch the doctor and then ask him to arrange for Mr Hudson to be informed the birth is imminent."

Miss Crawford has already left to carry out her instructions.

The date is July 23rd, and we have a heatwave outside though you wouldn't know it in here. The pain, I wonder could anyone prepare you for it, is steadily increasing with me clawing the bedclothes, barely registering Frances in the room for once.

"It would be best to lie on your side with a pillow to crush against your stomach to control the pain. I found it helped when I was having Joshua."

I do as she suggests, thankful for her presence, but at the same time wishing she was my mother.

An hour passes, then two with no sign of the doctor. Frances is a little ruffled and out of place, treading a path to and from the window to return to sit on the chair by my dressing table.

"Frances," I yell suddenly, I think the baby's coming!"

She jumps to attention.

"Hold on, I don't think they will be much longer," she almost pleads.

Letting out a howl I've been holding inside for hours, the noise is so disturbing it brings Frances rushing to my bedside.

Her voice telling me to push harder travels into the distance and with two huge pushing movements the baby is here. I see Frances holding the baby's tiny body in her hands before I faint.

I only discovered what happened next retrospectively.

Miss Crawford apparently arrived with the doctor fifteen minutes later and Frances had the baby wrapped in a blanket in her arms, with the cord still attached. Dr Ratcliffe had been tending a dying patient and so was unable to leave at once. You arrived a little later, insisting the doctor allow you into our bedroom. He told you this was completely inappropriate and refused you entry until he had things under control. Unfortunately, Dr Ratcliffe was unable to gain control, and in the end, I had to go to hospital by ambulance for a blood transfusion. I understand I'm very lucky to be here.

Our beautiful son, Albert William Hudson was born on 23rd July 1920, with me not laying eyes on him again until 7th August, some fifteen days later.

You almost lived at the hospital staying by my side the whole time.

And all the while Frances had sole charge of our boy.

Chapter 19

How I love Albert.

As I look at his tiny face, his dark mop of hair, I feel it, I feel the love. I'm surprised but more importantly relieved. It's over, thank God.

"I'm so proud of you both," you tell me, visibly choked, "What did I tell you, I knew you'd be happy once he arrived. Now he's a real, living person."

Your tear-filled smile melts my heart. It really is over, and mother was right. All the fretting will be something for us to discuss in years to come. Do you remember when I was sick with worry about motherhood, I'll ask you.

We'll both laugh.

In hospital and on the road to recovery, I reflect on our new life ahead. I prepare myself to be the best mother; to become my mother.

Once I'm home and convalescing, you keep your promise, and your support is unwavering. You take it all in your stride as though you've done it all before.

Frances arranged a nurse and a wetnurse in my absence and I'm so grateful for her support.

She sits with Albert in her arms in the very same chair she sat in on the day he was born. She stares at him, mesmerised by his beautiful little face. She stares at him like I stare at him …with awe, with wonder.

I am now invisible.

"You've made a perfect baby," she tells you, as though I played no part in Albert's creation.

You laugh and tell her she's mistaken, as he has my incredible genes. She throws a smile graciously my way without meeting my eyes.

Your smile does its best to thaw the chill a little.

The nanny, the wetnurse, Frances; they unite to become your guardian angels. Looking on, I watch them all doing what I find myself longing to do. I look on from afar, from some distant land.

Yet, I don't speak a word of it.

*

Routine gives me peace. Miss Crawford is busy, as is Miss Glover the nanny, as is Mrs Miller the wetnurse, so after you return to work, I start housekeeping.

"Mrs Hudson, what are you doing?" Miss Crawford asks, horrified the first time she sees me with a duster in my hand, "The mistress will have my guts for garters if she knows I'm not keeping up with jobs here."

"I shan't tell the mistress if you don't. Let it be our little secret, I'm sure you've plenty to keep you busy and I must have something to do, some distraction or … or …."

The words elude me, I want to cry.

"Don't upset yourself, now," she says.

She reaches to touch my shoulder, then quickly pulls her hand back remembering her place. The place I really don't want her to be in. We're of a similar age, we could be friends, yet you can't force a friendship and she would consider it improper. Unnatural.

By mid-afternoon Albert has just gone down for his nap. Miss Glover took him away and rocked him to sleep. I wanted to ask if I could do it, but her matronly manner intimidates me. We've yet to have a proper conversation and yet she and Mrs Miller live in the attic. Mrs Miller has a family of her own, but she lost her third baby to measles in infancy shortly before Albert was born. Poor woman, she haunts the place. Her grief follows us around constantly, and she's moved in for three months until Albert is weaned.

So many people, so many staff. I miss my tiny cottage, the isolation, the vastness of the moors. I can't breathe.

Something new appears—just the merest flicker and I'm unable to pinpoint it to begin with as I've never felt it before.

It takes a while before I realise what the feeling is but when I do I try and deny it until I can't any longer.

I feel alone. A house full of people, a loving husband, an adorable baby yet I feel alone, lonely even.

To begin with I brush it aside but steadily it grows. I decide to establish a routine of my own, something to use as a base to build on.

When my mother visits she's just returned from a city break to Bath with my father to take the waters. She describes the city in detail—so cultured and sophisticated, William would be in awe of the architecture. On and on she goes but it's as though she's talking to me through a glass window.

I'm not interested in hearing about it because I've so much to get done and every second counts towards achieving my daily target. A mental list of tasks has appeared, and the list gets longer every day. The tasks need to be done; they're of utmost importance and my day is devoted to them. My mind drifts in perpetuity between the jobs on my endless list.

I continue to follow the instructions the midwife gave me to the letter. Albert's environment should be as clean as a whistle, and this is a must as I'm unable to risk him becoming unwell because of my laziness. I scrub his cot lining each morning when Miss Glover takes him out for his morning walk. I scrub so hard it loses its beautiful sailboat pattern.

"Go easy there, my love," you say, laughing, "I know you said you wanted to resume some light housekeeping, but really Nell, you must focus on the word 'light'."

I laugh too but carry on the next day, the pattern has long gone anyway. I know I'm exhausted but hide it well and avoid afternoon naps as I have too much to do. I dread night times. My mind in turmoil, they bring horrifying dreams about unspeakable things befalling Albert. If the dreams aren't about Albert, they're about you. I dream of you leaving me in one disjointed illusory way or another and I wake up breathless to reach for you in the darkness. Oh, the relief when you're still there.

And all the while the wind howls as a backdrop to the terror they instil in me.

Or does it? I can't be certain anymore.

I try my best not to wake you but sometimes the breath escaping me is too loud in the stillness of the house. You wake up with a start and hold me to you.

"It's alright, it's alright, I'm right here, my darling," you whisper, stroking my back, my hair, trying your utmost to soothe me.

"You and your strange dreams, Nell, those psychologist chaps would have a field-day with them. What was it about this time?"

You make light of the situation; I need you to make light of the situation.

"I dreamt I woke up and you were gone but I had no idea where to look for you," I lie.

The nightmare was too disturbing to vocalise.

I'm lost in the fog. Once upon a time I would have talked to my mother, but I don't know where to begin to explain. Even if I could, she would be unable to process the meaning. I'm avoiding her and have many excuses prepared not to see her.

However, she must have caught an expression on my face because she asks me one morning how I'm feeling.

"I'm just a little tired; I'm sure you remember what it's like."

Nodding, she fixes her eyes on me.

"This is perfectly normal, dear you're just adapting to a new life. Give it time. Have a little cry when you're alone, I find it helps."

She pats my hand; convinced time and a little cry is all it will take and perhaps it will. I have hope.

I ask Miss Glover if I can have an hour or two alone to play with my son. Her grey uniform and white hat make her look austere, and I'm hesitant to ask, but I miss him.

"Well, if you're sure, madam," she says, her expression the same as if I've made an obscene remark.

Her disapproval withers me briefly but my longing for Albert overrides it.

She's left a cosy little scene to go to her room. Albert on the rug by the fire, me shaking his silver rattle to amuse him. If only she knew a sense of hopelessness my life is now to be like this forever spoils the scene and I must request to spend time with my son. When Miss Glover returns from her walk, I know she calls in to drop Albert with Frances and then joins Miss Crawford in the scullery. The hopelessness smothers me, and I think how mother was mistaken when she said there would be no time for this. But mother didn't have a team of staff to tend to her every whim so time would have been in short supply.

I jump when I hear Frances's familiar knock, so unused to her calling unless you're at home. I hesitate to answer but she knows I'm in, as where else would I be? She sweeps into the apartment, and I think how much Albert has enriched her life.

Walking towards me, she directs her gaze toward my son. When we're alone there's no need to bother with her usual dead smile and hollow pleasantries.

"William is concerned about you. He asked me to keep an eye on you so here I am."

Oh, Will, you're always looking for ways to make it all better for me. It might help to talk to Frances, she has been in my situation after all.

"I can't lie, Frances I'm struggling a little."

Her head tilts as she considers my confession.

"You know, I think it would help if you allowed yourself to succumb to the natural order of things. You must accept your life is vastly different to before. You are mistress of your home, and your staff are here to make your life better for you. They will not be comfortable with any peculiar arrangement."

I have a flutter of hope. Frances wants to help me. She's always cordial but more so when you're around. She would hate to raise any alarm bells with you.

We have the common ground of being mothers now.

I look down lovingly at Albert. He's gurgling, content in his little world.

"How did you fill your time with Joshua?" I ask.

She's staring at Albert, her silence making me think she's deep in recollection.

"I spent the days resting to have time with him in the evening. As he became older, I had a hand in his education before he went to boarding school. I could do the same for Albert."

Her eyes never stray from my son.

You could indeed, Frances, but I must get through the rest of the today before I can think about years from now.

However, her kindness is encouraging, and I hope we may have turned a corner because the days are long without you and an occasional chat would be just the tonic.

Picking Albert up from the rug I lay him in the crook of my arm and stroke the downy skin of his cheek. I thank Frances warmly for coming to see me.

I watch as her eyes slowly come back to life.

"No problem at all," is her brisk response, "You could ask Glover to bring Albert downstairs so you can take a little nap or read. I'm happy to do this daily if you're agreeable."

Such a lovely gesture, I can't help being touched by her thoughtfulness. What a pity she can't bring herself to look at me.

Later, when Glover comes downstairs not a second later than the specified time, she fulfils Frances's request.

I then sit in the chair looking out onto our beautiful garden. The dark clouds beyond create a dramatic landscape which once would have taken my breath away. I yearn to be part of the landscape, part of my soothing familiar home.

My throat constricting, I try to swallow, then I try again. I feel as though I'm going to cry. I think I'm going to cry huge great rasping sobs, the likes of which I've never cried before.
And I do.

Chapter 20

How to fill my time is now the least of my problems.

The apartment is a millstone around my neck in keeping it pristine but then what else would I do with my days? This has become the burning question.

I consider walking the moors but then Frances's disapproval is the perfect deterrent. I can no longer see the beauty of my home, only a list of duties, unable to settle even to read a book. I'm on edge if one item is out of its carefully chosen position but try to hide my new-found compulsion from you. The deception is another layer of pressure.

Mrs Miller has returned to the comfort of her family, so this at least is one less person to worry about watching my every move.

You must give your heart and soul to looking after your children and I would give them gladly, but Frances and Mrs Glover have my son's wellbeing in hand. Instead, you and I have an allotted one-hour slot before he's whisked away for his bedtime routine and his nursery in the attic.

The tranquillity of a home has disappeared, I can only see chaos. I want to go out, but I can't leave the house because there are too many tasks on my list. I haven't even any time to go outside into the grounds. If I did, I would feel the windows of the house watching me, or the people stood hiding behind them.

Do you ever wonder where the other sides to me have gone? You must, yet nothing seems to have changed for you. The lovelight still burns brightly. I watch closely for signs it might be otherwise but apparently one piece of me is more than enough.

There is still one time of year however when I feel part of the old me still exists: Christmas. I count the days down to get there from as early as September.

Mother was the magic-maker, and I want to take up the mantle. I have memories of a time when all you had to do was sit tight and wait for the magic to happen, for someone to present it to you on a platter. I want to create magic for Albert, for you too.

On our second year as parents, you arranged a trip to the east coast on Boxing Day as a way of extending the festivities. We've done it every year since, creating a tradition. We stay in the huge attic of an old guesthouse, with a tree lit with candles and the rooflights open to the stars. It's a truly magical place.

We do the same things every year. We walk on the beach, collect shells, drink hot milk in bed, read Christmas ghost stories, all of us slipping easily into the routine. How wonderful it is not to have a member of staff in sight as we eat out in restaurants and cafés by the sands.

Although I'm away from the comforting routine at home, I force myself to overcome it as I know how much you look forward to the trip. I hope you think of it as a compromise as a longer holiday would be a step too far. By the end of the second day, my thoughts are back home. Though not the welcome of home.

I do have the reassurance at least the house will be just the way I left it when I return.

So, then I can pick up exactly where I left off.

*

Frances has Albert taken downstairs every afternoon.

I've spotted her walking in the garden with his pram, tucking the blanket she crocheted under his chin, her face soft. She's engrossed in the action.

"I'm glad Frances has Albert for a while each day. She looks forward to it and you need the rest."

I smile brightly and nod in agreement as ever.

Often, you too will go downstairs to join them and give me time to myself. I have an endless supply of time to myself. I lay on the sofa with a book and play the game, then spring into action the second you leave. You've no idea I'm using it as an opportunity to clean. I go around and around in manic circles, lost in my regime. It calms me, I'm in control.

I have a little word with myself and decide to take a walk outside with Albert like Frances. I turn my back on Highbrook to stare at the moors, my son's chattering the backdrop to my thoughts. The next day, I'm donning my hat and coat when my chest tightens, so I forgo our walk. The day after is worse and I find it difficult to get my breath as the time draws nearer to leave the house, so I seize the excuse to stay indoors.

Frances keeps any observations she has to herself. This means she can spend more time with Albert and in turn more time with you. You all live happily together in your own charming little world only a short flight of steps away.

Mother played with Daniel and I every afternoon when we were children. I consider asking Frances if Albert can stay and play with me every other day as a compromise. I rehearse the request in my mind, but the words loiter on the tip of my tongue and never see the light of day.

I try to simply stop what I'm doing and sit down. I sit a moment in the silence until my heart beats faster. Then a voice starts whispering inside my head. It whispers I must keep going with what I need to do, and if I ignore the whispering it turns to a monotone drone so this is all I can hear.

Albert has all the practical care he needs. He's clean, well-fed, loved, embraced, has a story in the evening. I must remember I'm getting it right as a mother within the constraints of my peculiar standing in society.

You look forward to our time alone together when Miss Glover has retired to her room. Sitting side by side on the settee, we are a picture of togetherness. We read, we hold hands occasionally, and share the odd comment like millions of other couples; except I'm unable to feel the togetherness, I stare straight through the pages. Your contented expression tells me all your plans have come together; all your dreams have come true.

"I must say you make it look easy, everything is always shipshape and Bristol fashion when I get home. To think now how I worried you might not take to married life," you say one night.

"One tries. In any case, how could I outsmart your meticulous manoeuvres to make me your wife?"

I mimic the sound and expression of a laugh and thankfully you have other things on your mind to notice the facade.

Turning your head to look at me, I can see what's going on behind your eyes. Our love making is still a freeing, wonderful experience for us, at least for a while and I want so much to please you.

"The way to a man's heart isn't really through his stomach, you know," mother once shamelessly told me after too may sherries one Christmas.

My father had just left the room to go to bed and she watched him leave, giggling girlishly and forgetting who she was talking to.

I didn't want to hear such advice from her, so I pretended I hadn't heard. Your own mother should be beyond such things, but it fixed in my mind. I can't risk your head being turned by a pretty face. Is it absurd to have such concerns? I suspect you would be horrified to find out.

Now you pull me from my seat to go to our bedroom. Closing the door you stand with your back to it, almost smouldering my way. Undressing me slowly, carefully you carry me to our bed then take off your own clothes. You lay beside me, your breath warm against my neck. Stroking the top of my thighs and higher, I tremble – this always does something to you, I feel it. Closing my eyes, I can sense you're in no hurry. You take your time to look at every secret place and I'm left in no doubt you want me as much as ever. You take one of my nipples in your mouth, flick your tongue and bite it gently. Moaning, I reach for your hardness, rolling my hands up and down the way I know you like it. I apply the tried and tested, perfect amount of pressure. You turn me over to enter me, arching your back to savour the sensation. You are such a special lover, so attentive and present.

Our lovemaking is so free and natural, and our own little world of pleasure beckons us in ... for a while.

"I love you so much, Nell," you say, twirling a strand of my hair as always, "I think if you knew just how much, it would scare the living daylights out of you."

I do. It does.

"I love you too," I say, and this is the one honest thing which has fallen from my lips since Albert was born.

Too soon my distraction is over. The harsh realities of life are back doing their best to swallow me whole.

I have only one option left to me now the way I see it. I must bear my own cross in silence with a beaming smile.

Some people have a beam of light within. Now I realise the beam has dimmed so steadily, so slowly I'm left with only a dense blackness.

Chapter 21

My life has become like a runaway train and it's only a matter of time before I hurtle off the tracks.

Living hell, living nightmare, I conclude they're both the same. They're possibly the best way to describe how my bleak, twisted thoughts have made everyday life for me after six years and nine months. Day by day, month by month, I've lost control of the situation and a few carefully placed smiles aren't convincing any longer. My smoke screen is clearing, the mirrors are shattering.

You go down to see Frances most evenings for a little chat. You told me Albert had said his bedroom in the attic was unsettling, in fact, scary was the word he'd used, and he asked if he could stay with Frances. You asked me if I thought it might be nice from time to time. Miss Glover would be on hand, staying in Joshua's old nanny's room next door. I was hesitant of the strange arrangement at first, but it soon became clear I was in the minority.

Albert is tucked up safe and sound in his own bed tonight and although I don't like the thought of him being scared so I've asked Miss Glover to a leave his small pirate boat lamp on in the corner. I asked you to ask the question as I'm still as uncomfortable around her as the first time I met her. I want to be free of a nanny but then I wouldn't have any time to clean and regardless, you wouldn't hear of it for my sake. We need to have a discussion.

Pirates are Albert's current obsession. This stems from the Peter Pan book he's been reading with Frances of late. The thought nudges a memory.

I almost lost control not so long ago with Frances when she clearly overstepped the mark. Albert fell from a chair in her apartment and hurt his arm and without a second thought for me, she bundled him into her car to go to the doctors. He needed an x-ray at the infirmary in Harrogate and instead of

120

returning for me she called for you in Horton on the way. I was livid, it was a step too far.

When Albert returned with a splint on his arm after I'd been worried to distraction for hours, I couldn't hold my tongue for once.

"You should have called for me, Frances, I would have come with you to the doctors and to the hospital. Glover and I were searching everywhere for you when she raised the alarm. Crawford told me she'd seen you drive away in the car.

My voice was level, but it was far from how I was feeling. You swung your face in my direction with an expression of horror.

"Yes, I realise now I should have done," Frances said benignly, "I apologise but my only concern at that moment was for Albert's welfare, and I thought you might be napping. I panicked a little when the doctor thought he may have broken his arm and realised Hudson and Carr was on the way to the infirmary. I didn't even think to take Glover with me. I feel perfectly awful about it now."

You look at me for the right thing to say and I buckle. I may have been picking and choosing when I needed Frances's support. Perhaps I was being oversensitive.

"All's well that ends well," I say, wanting the awkward moment to end.

The fire had left the pit of my belly.

How I like having you out of the way for a while nowadays. I can drop the pretence, and this is such a sweet relief.

I'm listening at the bottom of the stairs whilst Albert is in bed. You think I'm in bed too and I always ensure I am by the time you return.

Your conversations with Frances are open and free.

"You can catch up on some sleep," you tell me, "Frances and I may as well keep each other company. She can get lonely down there on her own sometimes. We've been playing chess a lately. She's incredibly good at it."

You snort awkwardly, avoiding eye contact.

I don't think chess has been on the agenda for quite some time. I think I may have become your entertainment for the evening.

Sleep is still eluding me, and the cracks are now gaping holes, my obsessive patterns of behaviour more apparent. To be fair to her, Frances has been doing her best to persuade you to seek help for me.

"If not for Nell's sake, then for Albert's," she says.

You had been steadfastly in denial embracing our strange way of life as a new normality, but I know you've started to notice. I have become a problem which is becoming increasingly difficult to ignore.

For me, the struggle to get out of bed each morning by now is draining, I'm tired before I even start the day. Once up, I wash, and dress then begin the laborious cycle of chores which no longer give me any comfort. This has been the case for years now. I'm compelled to do them in a certain order and in a certain way. You've both noticed.

At the bottom of the stairs, I'm eavesdropping on your conversation, and I don't like the direction it's taking. Curiosity is killing me.

Albert is with Frances longer on an afternoon and she's become his tutor until he goes to boarding school. I don't want him to go because he's slipping through my fingers day by day and living away will only widen the distance between us.

I take myself up to the roof terrace every day even in bad weather for the peace and privacy. This is where I feel safe, somewhere I can be myself without anyone watching.

I listened one day to Albert playing in the garden. Frances joined you and his laughter validated my sadness; he sounded happy, carefree. I wasn't around, and that was the main reason why. Your easy, loving relationship could make me jealous but if I can't make my son happy then I'm just thankful somebody can.

I yearned to be the one he rushed his breakfast down for, the one he couldn't bear to be apart from. I'm his mother and this honour should be for me.

But I've come to a sickening resignation of late: Albert does his utmost to avoid me all day long.

At the stone wall of the terrace, I stared down at the gravel drive far below. I did this often. The ground came up to meet me, making it out of focus to swim before my eyes, each tiny nut of gravel blending into a carpet.

I had a beautiful sensation of calm. Catching my breath, the pleasure I felt shocked me. So many years had gone by since I'd felt such pleasure, such peace—too many years.

You came in from the garden, taking me unawares. The first sign of your presence was your voice.

"Nell," is all you said.

It was a whisper in the silence.

How long had you been there? Startled, I spun around and smiled as quickly as I could manage. I worried my face betrayed what was racing through my mind but I'm still not entirely sure what that was. Hesitating for the briefest of seconds you strode quickly over to bundle me into your arms like a sick child.

A jumble of thoughts was spinning around my head, crossing wires, and tying itself in knots. What on earth was happening to me, what was I doing? I needed to stop shaking in your arms. I needed to pull myself together. Oh, how I wanted life to be different for all of us.

"What is it?" you asked, bobbing down and lifting my face gently to read my expression.

I tried my best to make it a good read, not one which would disturb you, terrify you even because you know me so well. The pain in your eyes made me look away.

"I'm sorry, William, I didn't hear you. I was just listening to Albert playing. It made me a little sad for a moment because I never find the time somehow.

I prayed my voice sounded different to you than it did to me.

"There's always time. I know you like to do everything yourself but if you'll let me employ somebody to help, I will. It would do you good to put aside some more time to rest or play with Albert. I'm forever telling you this."

You drew me tighter towards you and I could feel your heart beating as fast as my own.

"I know, darling, you're right. I need to find a way to take a step back. I promise I'll try and take it easier."

I beamed at you, but I knew already I would never be able to break the cycle of my routine. The mere thought of relinquishing a task to anyone else made my heart nearly stop dead. They would have no idea how to do it to my standard, nobody would.

We held hands and headed downstairs to have tiffin together before tea. The gin and tonic helped calm me.

You hid the key to the terrace. You didn't mention it, the key just wasn't there anymore. You needn't have bothered because I've scared you and myself enough to stay away. Later, I came across it by chance, glued to the underside of a draw in the bathroom. It was a good hiding place, just not good enough.

Sitting on the step now in the dark, I can hear Frances getting agitated and not for the first time in recent weeks. The tension is mounting between you both and any subtle inference is fading.

I'm so cold. Shivering, I wrap the old shawl I've taken to wearing to eaves drop tighter around me.

"For pity's sake, William, he needs to know his mother loves him, surely you can understand how important this is!"

She almost hisses the words as she can't risk raising her voice. Standing up I move my ear closer to the door. I'm shaken by her tone because I've never heard her speak to you in such a manner. She's been trying to reason with you more than a few times recently and she's becoming exasperated. I hold my breath, terrified where the conversation might go.

"You force my hand, Frances," you say, "with all due respect you have never liked Nell, and she hasn't done anything to you other than try to get you on side since the day you met. Honestly, you're as bad as my mother, don't think I don't notice. She doesn't deserve it. If we're laying our cards on the table, I'm starting to think you're partly the reason why she feels like she does."

You raised your voice ever so slightly. This is a low blow William, but I see you've been paying attention after all.

I would dearly love to run away upstairs out of earshot, but I'm fixed to the spot, and I put a hand over my mouth to avoid any sound escaping.

I can't believe how you spoke to Frances, and it demonstrates the amount of pressure I'm putting you under.

Something is brewing in there; I can sense it. Frances will be struggling to take in your outburst the same as me. My legs begin to tremble, and I push a hand to the wall to steady myself.

"Doesn't deserve it," she mocks, "do you really think so? You've no idea, my boy. It's about time you saw your dear, perfect Nell for who she really is—a deceitful little liar!"

She scoffs to nail home the point.

Please, Frances, please don't. I want to burst into the room, but I can't move.

"What do you mean by that remark?" you ask.

You're both stripping away the pretence layer by layer like old paint. I picture you standing there, defenceless to what I now know is afoot.

I realise I'm still holding my breath, praying Frances will find some self-control.

"I should have told you this a long time ago and I've wanted to so many times, believe me. The reason why I'm not as taken with your poor little Nell as you'd like me to be is this: not long before you were happily preparing to propose, I sat and watched her walk into an … an … establishment of ill repute!"

The words seem melodramatic but resonate around the entire house, ricocheting off the walls.

Silence returns.

"What the hell are you talking about?"

You spit the sentence out like a bad taste, part question, part expletive. I imagine your brain trying to catch and process the meaning behind the words which can never be unsaid.

But this time, I run upstairs.

Chapter 22

How could she do it, how could she tell you something which will destroy you?

I replay the words over and over in my mind.

You pushed her too hard, William, you pushed her up against a wall, so she had no alternative but to attack.

I often wondered why Frances just happened to be in that area on that day. There were so many things I needed to explain or even talk to her about, but I never found the courage. She's an authority figure as so many are to me, but the main reason was that I knew whatever I told Frances she would never understand. And she still wouldn't like me.

I needed to pick my face up from the floor when I answered the door to her that day. It was like the day Mark reappeared all over again, I even briefly thought the very same.

I hadn't known her very long and I didn't think she knew where I lived. Her expression told me there was trouble afoot, just not the scale of it.

Sitting down she ignored any pleasantries, shooting straight from the hip.

"I know what you did," she said.

The simple statement still stings when I think of it. The thought of her telling you terrified me, but more for the pain it would cause you than myself. She thought she knew my secret.

Oh, how distraught I was, and I had an inkling you were going to propose at Highbrook later that week.

I busied myself on the day washing my hair, calling for provisions in the village but Frances's visit still haunted me. Once back at the cottage I dropped my bags and burst into tears.

As I paced the floor in the darkness, I knew Frances was due to collect me to take me to Highbrook, but I just couldn't stem the flow. She told me to stay home in the end thinking her excuse would be adequate.

I knew differently; I knew you would come to the cottage. I needed an explanation and quickly.

So, in the end I gave you a diluted version of the truth and that night I thought it would be better for everyone if I stopped seeing you.

Yet it turned out losing you was unthinkable because I had completely, utterly fallen in love. There could be no turning back.

At first, I thought Frances might disclose what she discovered to your mother, but I don't think she would want to hurt her. Frances is one of the kindest, most thoughtful of people I have ever met, and it upsets me that I can't call her a friend. She has kept the secret for seven years but the dread of you finding out has been torment. I've spent the years walking on broken glass, being punished.

So, I've created one almighty mess for all of us to live in and I'm standing in the way of Albert's happiness, I know it, she knows it, and so does he. There's only one person who doesn't know it yet …you.

Now as I lay in bed in the dark, I'm shivering uncontrollably from shock.

I'm afraid. I'm afraid as I have no control over what is about to unfold and I'm completely in your hands. You won't look at me the same way—I've broken the spell.

My ears are pricked for you coming upstairs as I lay frozen for the longest time fear crushing my chest.

Eventually I hear the creak of the door to our apartment then you pad quietly up to the attic to Albert's room to check on him. You do this every single night but tonight you stay longer. You assume as always that I'm asleep so I will be blissfully unaware the tide has turned. Oh, William please don't wake me to challenge me about my version of events. I have no strength for confrontation.

You climb into bed and my cold body relaxes into the warmth of yours just for a second and I bite my pillow to stop the tears.

What are you thinking, laying there in the darkness? You're thinking I didn't want your baby, that's the reality you're wrestling with.

Oh, Will my darling, my love, forgive me.

As though you sense my plea you wrap your arms tighter around me.

We are all living a lie and I'm at the core of it. The lump in my throat is choking me but I can't move. I can't run the risk of you thinking I'm awake.

I have a sickening thought as we lay secretly awake and troubled in the blackness of the bedroom. I remember something mother said to me more than once in a throwaway, light-hearted manner.

"That man would forgive you every one of the seven deadly sins," she said.

How right she has turned out to be.

It's a pyrrhic victory.

Chapter 23

The strain between you and Frances is showing.

You're both doing your best to hide it from me, and to be fair I wouldn't be aware had I not been eavesdropping.

I know you have plans. I don't know what they are, but I know they are coming. You took so long to return upstairs after Frances's revelation, and I imagined you both picking over the bones of my wrongdoings but from hugely different perspectives.

You have your own demons. I'd warned you of my worries about becoming a mother, but you ignored them, not deliberately, but you did. At the very least you didn't take them seriously. We were both as naive as each other in thinking it would all turn out wonderfully for us if we buried our head in the sand.

Frances and I continue in much the same vein except she has the added resentment of being backed in a corner enough to tell you what she uncovered. She's broken your heart and I am the one to blame, so I've managed to refuel her resentment.

But we all know only too well the reason we must move on. We must move on because we need each other. We need each other for one very important reason: Albert.

It takes a little while for you to build up to broaching your plan of action. I can see you've been struggling to find the correct approach but eventually you suggest seeing the doctor.

I sense your agitation before you start the conversation. You've been pretending to read the paper for half an hour and now you're folding it neatly. I hear you take a breath, knowing you're only a heartbeat away from setting the wheels of your secret plan in motion.

"You know, you seem much more tired than usual, Nell. I wonder if it would be worth seeing Dr Ratcliffe to rule out something quite simple. I understand anaemia for instance can cause extreme fatigue. What do you think?"

Your voice sounds as though you're reading a cue card. I can imagine you rehearsing the words in your mind or even aloud for days. Opening such a conversation is especially hard for you and you're out of your depth.

I'm searching for a suitable response. I can't find one so stay silent, staring into the dregs of my teacup.

"It's worth a chat at least," you say.

Your tenacity is impressive, but this is serious. A broken mind is serious, and it can have immeasurable consequences when doctors are involved.

I'm just too weak to argue, so now I'm resigned and compliant. My mind is racing ahead to the next step. Highbrook may have become a high class prison cell, yet the thought of the doctor sending me away is distressing.

But I only nod, unable to raise even a fake smile for once.

You strike whilst the iron is hot, and Dr Ratcliffe appears the following afternoon. He strides in as your guardian angel whereas I see him as my devil incarnate.

You're not giving me the opportunity to have a change of heart.

We sit around the table under the window, and I steal the odd glance at the familiar face of the doctor who has the power to determine the next part of my destiny. I try to be clever. I play with the truth with my answers to his questions and keep my wits about me. You chirrup in the odd comment but only when prompted because you promised me that I would be firmly in the driving seat.

"So, Mrs Hudson, you tell me you're not sleeping and you're unable to concentrate and focus. Added to this you're constantly cleaning and avoiding going out of the house. You say all this has been building up since the birth of Albert," he looks down at his notes, "Who's now six years old? My, where does the time go?"

His kindly eyes peer at me over his half-moon glasses.

"Yes, this is how I've been feeling in a nutshell," I say, watching him write down more notes, unable to see what they're saying about me.

I choose not to tell him about my blacker than black thoughts. I forget to mention my disturbing dreams I've given up telling you about.

There's mention of a private psychiatrist's name. You're adamant you want me to be seen as quickly as possible, so there isn't any time to catch my breath.

"I'm confident we can get you back to your old self, in fact I'm sure of it. Leave it with me, you'll have an appointment soon, tomorrow if I can arrange it. You've done the right thing in speaking to me, I only wish you'd done it before now."

"That's possibly my fault," you say.

I put my hand on top of yours. No, I've been a master of deception. Now my demons finally have me firmly in a headlock with my arm up my back you can see the real me.

"I'm proud of you, my love," you say as we close the door to Dr Ratcliffe. You fold me into your arms, resting your chin on the top of my head.

"That can't have been easy, but the doctor's right we'll have you sorted before you know it. Have faith."

You smile down at me, your dear face pale and drawn with worry.

As you head downstairs to get Albert, I think if sheer love could fix me, I would be home and dry.

*

There is no part of me that wants to explain to a stranger how I'm feeling when I can't even explain it to the person I care about the most.

Nell, you must remember you're fortunate to have the option as not so many years ago you would have been whisked away to an asylum for treatment, I think. The realisation makes my heart race.

I know the consensus is I have a touch of melancholia or depression, but you're all wrong. I'm a square peg which has been bashed into a round hole for years. By now my mind has become misshapen, unrecognisable. I have no end in sight, in fact there is no end. I've become powerless, desperate.

The problem isn't a house I don't like, an unhappy marriage, instead my own mind is the problem, and I can't see how you can make my mind go away without taking me with it.

Dr Haigh, a psychiatrist in Leeds, schedules our weekly sessions for Friday afternoons. I wonder what you told Harry about your Friday absences. More than likely, you didn't tell him anything at all.

On the first Friday, my 'things to do' list is beckoning. I must get up early and try and get ahead of schedule before my first session. You see this as a positive sign I must be keen to start the process.

The familiar panic mounts as the deadline to leave the house draws near but the familiarity does nothing to ease the sensation. My list of chores isn't completed.

I want to cry.

So, I have no alternative but to remind myself I'm going along with these measures for you, and for Albert.

Dr Haigh's consultation room is a rather pleasant drawing room, as peaceful and tranquil as one would imagine. Two leather button-back wing chairs separate a coffee table on which stands a bronze statue of a woman arching backwards whilst holding a ball. I imagine this is meant to convey a calming atmosphere. The walls are sage green, and each has a painting of a picturesque view, except for the wall behind a large mahogany desk. This wall has an array of mounted certificates with Dr Alexander Haigh italicised on each one.

The peace and tranquillity elude me even though someone has gone to a great deal of trouble to create the perfect atmosphere. Someone wanted to put me at ease so I can disclose all my deepest darkest secrets in the most comfortable of surroundings.

Dr Haigh's rates are extortionate, I saw the indent of the hourly rate on your pad, but you've decided only the best will do and you're hoping to fix me quickly so we can resume the rest of our lives. You will think it money well spent, and in any case, we can afford it, the business is doing extraordinarily well.

We should by rights be living the dream.

Dr Haigh has a tried and tested plan. He wants to start by building a mental picture of my life he says. There's no quick route to the heart of the problem he tells me.

"I need detail. I need a good grasp of your personality traits. It will take time to go over your previous life and your current day to day life. Remember, detail is the watchword, Mrs Hudson. Please don't fall into the trap of thinking only the big events matter. The smallest, insignificant detail may help us."

He likes to make regular eye contact which only intensifies my discomfort.

"Not every problem starts because of a difficult childhood. If your childhood is too perfect, for example, you can find yourself having unrealistic expectations with relationships in trying to replicate it. You only see a part of your parents' relationship. Even if it appears perfect, this isn't a true reflection of all the hard work involved."

This makes sense but I've found the perfect husband, so how can this be explained away? I'm guarded, determined to tread very carefully.

His manner never fails to intimidate me, and Fridays are now looming. By the end of the third session, he has set me some exercises to do at home.

"I want you to leave just one glass out on the top after clearing up, so you become used to it being out of place. Make sure you do this every night. It won't happen immediately but over the course of a few weeks you'll come to realise nothing bad will happen because of it."

I have my doubts about such an approach. If he thinks for one second, I can stare at a glass staring back and taunting me night after night, then he's sadly mistaken.

I nod serenely.

"I'm not sure yet if your obsessive behaviour is a separate issue or just a symptom of a more deep-seated depression. We need more time, but we have plenty of time."

I think about how I can describe my feelings towards my homework all week. It was impossible to leave the glass out the first night, I say. The second and third night I left it out for a timed minute and then put it away as you suggested. I left the room on the fourth night, but then I had to put it away. The task is getting easier, but I still can't keep the glass out for very long just yet, I say. All lies; I'm far too conditioned to consider this exercise. It would be like repeatedly slapping myself in the face, expecting to carry on with my life as normal.

I've been prescribed medication, one small pill each day to piece my mind back together. He tells me the pill may need to be changed if it isn't the right one for me. There are many side effects including loss of libido, loss of concentration, loss of sleep, and others on a disturbingly long list. I decide after three nights it might be best to stop taking them mainly because they're keeping me awake and I crave the sweet relief of any small amount of sleep I can manage. I tell Dr Haigh I'm coping with the side effects and throw one pill a day down the toilet, so you will never suspect.

"How was it?" you ask, each week when you pick me up.

"The session seemed to go well. It really does help to talk to a neutral party."

Oh, how easily I can deceive now. Now my liberty is at stake.

"Dr Haigh says he's sure he can get to the bottom of it. He's had several similar cases before to deal with."

I smile to reassure you, convince you. Are you convinced?

Chugging along together day by day, the thought of Friday is becoming an additional burden.

Then my luck comes in if this is the correct term.

I don't need to carry the burden of my sessions for very long.

Chapter 24

I'm sitting with Dr Haigh in what I now consider familiar surroundings on the grimmest, gloomiest day of winter so far.

It's mid-December and under different circumstances, it would be a pleasant setting, almost cosy. As I stare out of the huge window which overlooks a small, neat square tucked away in the city centre, I'm thinking we must put the tree up at home. The one in this office is beautifully decorated in three colours, bronze, gold, and copper, so tasteful.

As usual, Frances had her tree delivered and decorated on the very first day of December especially for Albert. I imagined her looking on lovingly as he and Miss Crawford trimmed it together and filled it with all the Christmas baubles he's made over the years. She even has some Joshua made when he was a child.

Then Frances invites us to go down for a sherry and a piece of cake made early November with Wensleydale cheese atop. As is tradition, he and Frances will have stirred the mixture with the wooden spoon and made a wish. Her front room is nothing short of spectacular this time of year, much like stepping into a Christmas card.

I bring my mind back to Dr Haigh's room. His hands are linked neatly in his lap and he's giving nothing away as he waits patiently with his steady gaze upon me.

He always dresses immaculately in his dark grey tailor-made suit accompanying a selection of matching cravats and pocket squares. A tie would make him appear too austere, so we wouldn't be put at ease. His salt and pepper hair surrounds a slightly younger than middle aged face, his mouth permanently set with the gentlest of smiles. I wonder if they teach you the perfect facial expression to adopt at psychiatry school. I wonder if he has children, if he has any idea at all what it is to be a parent, to love a person so much you would risk everything.

I am sitting here and risking everything.

Christmas is just around the corner. This is our last session and you're breaking for the festivities, taking extra time away from work this year to keep an unspoken watchful eye on me. I'm trapped here, I'm trapped at home. You have completely ensnared me, William.

Dr Haigh is still waiting as I clear my throat.

"I'm not certain what you mean," I say, playing for time so I can continue to think very carefully about my answer. I want to work out exactly the pitch of my voice, my correct body language.

"I beg to differ, Nell, but I think you do know what I mean."

I can wait forever because I'm frozen, staring into the abyss.

His brow furrows ever so slightly knowing he's beaten.

"When are you going to start being honest with me?" he asks, his voice sounding a touch higher than usual.

I look down at my feet. I don't speak but the heat has risen in my cheeks to incriminate me. The silence is scaring me to death, but I know when I speak, I will change everything.

"I can't seem to do it," I tell him eventually. "I'm worried about what will happen if I do."

"What exactly is it you're worried about? There's nothing you can tell me which would come as a shock. Think of your worst thought and trust me when I say, someone else has already confessed it right here. They too were convinced they were the first one to think it, that they would be the first one to shock me. If you can't be honest with me, then we're wasting our time here. You're wasting your husband's money here."

"How did you know?" I ask, warily.

"I've had a few years of practice, don't forget."

He smiles warmly, but it doesn't make me feel any better. I smile back; I've had years of practice at this.

"Have you done any of the things I asked you to do?"

I still don't answer, the end of the session is within my grasp. He leans forward in his chair.

"In the New Year, I want us to start afresh. Do you think we can?"

My panic increases. There is now a deadline. My top lip is beginning to perspire and not from the heat of the fire. I fake a cough so I can wipe the evidence away unnoticed. I nod another lie.

He stares at me for more than a few seconds, his eyes moving around my face, his smile waning signalling I'm proving to be a challenge.

"Before we finish, I would like to ask you two questions," he says, "They are the most important questions I have asked you so far. You must answer me truthfully. I hope you can be brave enough to be honest."

I swallow. I ponder the horrors inside the alphabetically ordered files on his shelves. I would rather think about those instead because I know what is coming. I've been expecting it since the first session, before even.

Hold on tight, Nell, here we go. I fight the urge to close my eyes.

"Have you ever thought about harming Albert in any way?"

I was right, but this one is easy.

"Never," I say without even a flash of hesitation.

It is the absolute truth, and I can tell I don't need to convince him any further. He is convinced.

The next question is obvious, but he says it aloud anyway. He has no alternative.

"Alright then. So, the next thing I would like to ask you is, have you ever thought about harming yourself in any way?"

Such a deep, dark question, one which has the capability to blow your life into the water if you give an incorrect answer.

He has now hung me out on the washing line to flap about in the wind. What is the correct answer to offer a redeemed psychiatrist, one who cannot be lied to?

139

If I say no, he'll spot the tell-tale signs of a liar. If I say yes, he may well take all decisions out of my hands, claiming this is for my own safety.

But answer I must.

I purse my lips for a second. When I begin speaking my voice is oddly controlled as I mustn't risk tripping myself up. I'm so close to the finish line.

"I have thought about it," I say, "Only once, and it's the reason I'm here. I can't lie, I do sometimes believe Albert would be better off without me in his life, but I'm here to overcome it. I don't want to believe it."

There is enough truth in this answer I hope to pacify him.

He allows the words to digest for a few seconds before speaking.

"Thank you for your honesty," he says, inclining his head slightly, "When we resume, we can start to make progress. It won't come overnight, but we'll get there together, Mrs Hudson, have faith."

He smiles. The knot lessens; I've passed the test, thank the lord above. I may have been whisked away to an institution for my own safety if he hadn't known you were at home for the Christmas break. I had carefully and deliberately woven this detail into the conversation.

"Your obsessive behaviour is part of the problem, but I believe you have what my colleagues and I refer to as circumstantial depression, a depression brought about by your circumstances. There is an emerging school of thought that this is caused by, or exacerbated by childbirth but I'm sceptical given the time that has elapsed. This is difficult to treat with medication as we need of course to tackle the circumstances, but together we will be able to work on those changes steadily yet effectively.

I try and force myself to listen as he goes on, but I only catch snippets. Running out of this stifling office is all that is on my mind.

"The heart of the problem is you're a person who likes to please others and you believe the responsibility for other people's happiness rests with you. The worst thing for you is if you think someone doesn't like you."

I think of Frances, and he must have spotted something on my face.

"Don't worry, this is a common trait, especially in women who are keener to please others. I promise you, now you're prepared to be honest with me, we can work on the problem – acceptance is a crucial factor to recovery. Please remember, you are not on your own in this situation."

He genuinely thinks he understands me. Nodding in all the right places as he speaks, I've retreated into my shell. I've retreated because a cold, harsh realisation is dawning on me. I realise my circumstances will never change and not just at Highbrook. They will never change no matter what I do, where I run. I'm destined to have the dull ache of failure forever more.

It is an undeniable and devastating conclusion.

Mercifully for him, he will always remain blissfully unaware he was the one who hammered home the final nail.

Chapter 25

For a layperson, my predictions are remarkably accurate.

As I lie awake beside you, I doubt I will ever find the peace of mind to sleep soundly again.

There will be no going back to see Dr Haigh in the New Year, of this I am certain. This is frankly a hopeless waste of time and money. I must find a way to deal with the nagging pain in my head and I know now I'm alone in this challenge. I've worked out I am the only one with the power to change our lives.

In the days running up to Christmas I find a rare moment of solace in making my plans. I'm not terrified of my future any longer, but the solace soon gives way to being terrified for yours.

Something is lurking on the horizon, and you sense it.

"Nell, you know you can talk to me, don't you? You mustn't slip backwards, I couldn't bear it, and more to the point, nor could you."

The grim situation has forced you to say this because you much prefer to pretend all is well. This is how you cope with the trials of life.

"I'm just feeling a little cast adrift; I don't have Dr Haigh to talk to for a while, is all. Please try not to worry, January isn't far away."

I smile your way, but you don't fall for a smile any longer. My ability to fool you is long gone.

As soon as my head leaves the pillow on a morning, the slog of the day ahead begins. I drop my head back, close my eyes and breathe deeply as though preparing for battle.

Now I've lost the sanctuary of the terrace to be alone, I can only go into the bathroom on the pretext of taking long, hot baths to relax me. This is now the one and only place I can be on my own.

I'm so trapped, cornered even that Christmas itself is unable to register. You're in the house all day, watching my every move but trying to disguise it. I'm increasingly on edge.

Spade after spade, you're slowly burying me alive.

*

I've somehow made it through the forced festivities. I managed to put on my best dress yesterday and join everyone to open Albert's gifts.

"You look a Bobby Dazzler," you told me, coining my father's favourite expression when I came down the stairs, hair up and freshly bathed.

You gave me a feather-light kiss, trying your best to catch my eye afterwards, but I was carefully watching the scene in the living room from the hallway. You had lit the fire first thing and it was blazing away, our mothers and Frances huddled around it discussing the latest board games for children. My father was trying to construct Albert's new tin car with his help. Oh, how I wish I could join in the banal discussion.

But then my eyes strayed to the wrapping paper strewn gayly around the room. I swallowed, forcing myself to look at the stunning tree in the window and remembered Daniel was due to join us later. He never came and I found myself disappointed and delighted in equal measure. You laid the ground days before and told everyone I had a chill, so we could have lunch alone.

"You look pale, Nell," mother told me as Miss Crawford was helping her shrug on her coat to leave, "You need to get out in the fresh air more."

I swear I saw your mother and Frances glance at each other.

"Leave her alone," my father said, "She's always been an English rose, haven't you, sweetheart?"

I smiled, looking at the ground, hoping it would swallow me up. I had never been more appreciative of his ability to lighten a mood and we all said our Christmas wishes in turn, some longer, some briefer than others.

By evening, the solitude of the bathroom beckoned, my face aching from a painted smile.

Boxing Day finally upon us, Albert wanders into the kitchen with his hair on end. He got himself ready as Miss Glover goes home to see her family whilst we're away.

"Tatty Ed," you call him, ruffling his hair, then laughing.

He joins you at the table to look at the map you're studying. I watch you with your heads pushed together and feel like I'm not in the room.

As you pack the car with an excited Albert, I'm inside the house manically getting through my chores.

I almost gave the game away last night. I just couldn't get out of bed quick enough to hide the rasping sob escaping me. You rolled over in bed to draw me into your arms and stroke my back, soothing me with loving words. I told you I'd had a nightmare and you believed me, trusted me.

You deserve more than the person I've become. I've tried so hard for you both, William.

From the corner of my eye, I can see you glancing my way more than you should on the journey, but I'm determined not to fall at the last hurdle. I turn my head and force a smile from time to time, making the odd comment to try and reassure you.

Albert is chattering away in the back, playing with his new tin car, and delighted to be spending time with his papa. I'm still struggling to justify what's ahead to myself. It must be here, it must be now, because you will never guess.

I owe you an explanation. I have given you one and I only hope I can make you understand. I've left no stone unturned. You'll come to know this is going to make everything better and you will forgive me. The letter I've written to you is honest and raw as you must never doubt how much you are loved. I know you know but this overwhelming need is for me.

The letter, folded many times to fit, is in the bottom of my small handbag. I'm certain it's there, but I still curl my fingers around it from time to time during the journey.

I've written it in the bathroom over many nights and carried the papers to and from the room within the pages of an innocent-looking homemaking magazine. It denied the horror within, like the files in Dr Haigh's office.

I'm doing the right thing. I've reached the place where nothing and nobody will change my mind, not even Albert, not even you. It has become so right. Unable to drag myself through each day any longer, I know now without a shred of doubt there can be no escape for me.

We've had our walk on the beach, and you promised Albert he could have a tiny wooden pirate figure tomorrow from the shop on the end of the cobbled street, which was closed today. We've had our fish and chips and hot cocoa. At bedtime I read to Albert and stroke his hair until he falls asleep. I play with his soft, dark hair and close my eyes.

I need to keep reminding myself he's still young enough for it not to take over his life. I've always been such a remote figure to him. You and Frances are at the centre of his world, and you will always be the centre of his world.

I can't allow my mind to wander to you. I simply cannot.

I sit and cry in the small water closet at the top of the stairs, splashing cold water on my face afterwards to hide the evidence.

When I return, if you notice, you never say a word.

Chapter 26

I am alone. I know my timing must be precise.

Fifteen minutes past two is the perfect time. St Mary's Church clock chimes on the hour, so, at five minutes past two, when I'm satisfied that you're still sleeping soundly, I set my plan in motion.

I'd laid awake until then listening to your steady breathing. I was numb. Tuning in to each breath had eventually lulled me into a false sense of calmness. My clothes from last night are waiting at the side of the bed in a tidy pile. I pick them up silently and open the door which I'd pretended to lock when we went to bed. I have mentally worked through my exit plan over and over to pinpoint any obstacle. I can leave nothing to chance. I cannot make the slightest noise.

I watch you both sleeping, numbness giving way to sorrow. I allow it to wash over me, and the first hot tear runs down my cheek. I must pull myself together, I'm wasting time. I pinch a tiny piece of skin on my wrist. I'd read it helps to stop you crying and I'm relieved now to discover it works.

Before I leave the room, I place the envelope under the one small lamp, positioned carefully so the spotlight will shine on it as soon as you switch it on. I had toyed with a thousand ways to address the note, but I settled on simplicity in the end, writing the words 'To My William' on the folded note. I wish now I'd gone for something more poetic, but I'm too late. Tiptoeing with the utmost care from the room, I ensure I keep going out of the door.

I dress in the cramped water closet, then grab my shawl which I left at the bottom of the pile of clothes. Tentatively, I make my way down the two familiar flights of stairs to the outer door, avoiding the creak on step six of the first flight and steps three and four of the second. Another unlocked door makes it easy to slip out unheard into the freezing night.

I have no time now to dwell on what I'm about to do, there can be no going back. If you wake, I know that blind panic would drive you to do the unthinkable and leave Albert alone to run after me. But there must be a note.

Walking quickly now, almost running, I'm desperate to get to the pier, taking huge gulps of air, the icy cold burning my chest. I frantically look over my shoulder to check I'm still alone, slipping on the wet, mossy planks of wood.

There isn't a soul to be seen. This is one of the many reasons this time and this place are so right. But right on this occasion is a terribly wrong word.

The gates are closed and padlocked at the end of the pier at night—but they're quite easy to climb over even in a dress. I know this. The waves are crashing up and over the sides of the walls, the spray and wind gluing my wild, uncombed hair across my checks. My breathing is laboured, my face distorted from crying. I must run faster, faster.

I run as though my life depends on it until there is nowhere left to run. The inky nothingness beyond is beckoning. The wind whips my shawl from around my shoulders and I watch it disappear forever.

Oh, the bittersweet relief of that being me, of finally extinguishing the torment in my mind, of a true, peaceful sleep.

Forgive me, my darling, I thought I could be what you wanted, how I've tried, but I can't. I just can't.

I close my eyes to the grief coursing through me.

You will come to know I've been left with no choice, my love. The free-spinning coin which is my mind must now stop spinning out of control.

It must rest in its chosen place.

And for good.

Frances
Chapter 27

The ear-splitting sound of someone banging on the front door startles me. It's a terrifying sound in the dead of night.

I steel myself as I walk across the hall, shivering, cursing the fact Crawford goes home after Christmas. The house is freezing.

I put a thick woollen overcoat over my housecoat, certain I will be looking a frightful sight to greet the person on the other side of the door.

I turn the huge key and pull open the door, considering my expression.

A police constable is on the steps, looking decidedly young and uncomfortable.

"Mrs Cundall?"

"Indeed," I confirm.

"My name is PC Bentley. May I come in for a moment?"

"Certainly," I say quietly, my hands suddenly starting to shake and my stomach rolling. I glance at the grandfather clock in the hall. Twenty-seven minutes past five, hardly the middle of the night but not an hour usually reserved for house calls.

We head to the parlour and then the constable suggests I might want to sit down. I immediately oblige whilst he stands, towering above me.

"I'm very sorry to startle you at this hour, Mrs Cundall," he says, "but there has been an accident, erm, an incident involving your neighbour, Mrs Hudson."

He carries on talking but my mind is already miles ahead and far away, wondering about the correct reaction to such news. As I place a hand to my mouth Constable Bentley, who appears increasingly agitated, explains Mr Hudson wishes me to accompany him in the police car to Whitby.

"He needs you to come as a matter of urgency, if you wouldn't mind."

PC Bentley looks as though he's the one who needs to sit down, and I ask him to do so as I rush to my bedroom to get ready. I decide to tidy my hair in the car. I've never left the house in such disarray but then needs must.

The turmoil in my mind reaches a crescendo, waves of panic surging through me as I ride in the police car to the coast. I know too well the stench of trauma; I've smelt it enough times.

I don't enjoy long car journeys as a passenger, they make me nauseous at the best of times, but we finally arrive at the guesthouse, and I see you sitting outside on a bench with two other police officers. You have your head in your hands. The freezing temperature makes the scene look almost otherworldly in the sea fret.

You don't hear the slam of the car doors as we get out, so I must gently touch your shoulder. You visibly jump and look up at me with a haunted expression in the pale light. I will find it impossible to forget the expression.

"I tried to get to her, Frances but she'd been gone too long. They're starting the search at first light. It's all my fault."

You drop your head in your hands again.

"You're not making sense, William. Where's Albert, what's going on?"

But you're somewhere only you know. One of the police officers explains what has happened whilst the other tries to reason with you to stay still. You are having none of it, pacing like a man who has lost his mind.

I'm trying to listen carefully to what the police officer is telling me, but I'm unable to focus. I decide to pretend I'm listening.

I must get to Albert, but I must keep you safe as I don't want you to bolt. I can't risk you doing anything reckless.

I run down the path and try to get a hold of you. You pull free from my grasp, foul words coming out of your mouth the like of which I have never heard you say before. You've suddenly become a stranger and I pray this detachment will only be temporary. Albert is beckoning me the whole time.

So, I give up. I stand watching you for a moment before I head off in search of my boy. I look on at you with the worst pain of all: helplessness.

You're unreachable for the time being so I make my way up to be with Albert.

He needs me.

I need him.

*

You had perfect timing William, appearing in my life like an angel of mercy.

Unexpected loneliness plagued me for some years due to being made involuntarily redundant by my son, Joshua. He loves me dearly but couldn't wait to leave home. I miss him terribly.

Highbrook is undeniably beautiful, but this house can be like a gilded cage. The town too had its limitations. People need people, or at least I do, and I made a concerted effort to get out into the world after my beloved husband, Ben died. I dabbled with a whole array of diverse ways to fill my life, clutching at straws to occupy my time with anything from flower pressing to decoupage. They didn't last long. Forced fun activities never really appeal.

Boredom for any length of time can be a problem, I found out. I suffered my bleakest of times after being widowed, limping through life, and struggling to find my calling for years afterwards.

Then the war came, and I faced life with gusto once more, chairing the local fundraising committee for the war effort and organising volunteers. I brought Ben's car out of retirement and used it to get around easily. Nobody batted an eye – it seems anything goes in a war. I stepped up to the mark, the whole town did. Like being a wife, a mother, it gave me my reason to jump out of bed on a morning. But then the war ended, but I couldn't revert entirely and be cooped up at Highbrook, so I continued to hop in the car as I saw fit. It doesn't worry me being the talk of the town, at least I'm not invisible.

Even before the war I'd found myself with a life my poor mother could only dream of. It was by no means unusual in those times and in our town, but she suffered terribly at the hands of my father whereas I was the apple of his eye. He was top dog at the mill where he worked but we didn't see the money.

"Salt of the earth is Michael, a real gent, he'd give you the shirt off his back."

Just some of the many favourable descriptions I'd heard of my father.

But I hated him.

I had an older sister Lily who we liked to think of as childlike. My mother and I adored her, but my father pretended she wasn't there. We cherished and coddled her like a doll, combing her hair and dressing her in pretty clothes neighbours often donated. It became harder for mother to manage with Lily at home as she got older. I helped as best I could, but perhaps not enough by then. Youth can be a selfish beast.

"It's time, Frances," mother told me one night.

We were washing up together. It was our time of day, the time when we shared our news, our worries. We could never talk at the table as my father forbad it and told us mealtimes were for eating not for chatting. We had to concentrate on the flavour of each mouthful of food and be thankful for it.

I knew what mother was referring to. It was obvious it was coming.

"You've done your best, more. Please don't feel bad, we can visit all the time."

She laid her head on my shoulder and I slid my arm around her back. The wetness of her tears seeped through my dress and the slight shake of her body broke my heart. She released the torment only a mother would have at the thought she was abandoning the beloved child she had tended to morning, noon, and night for the whole of their life.

It took over a year to find a home which could cope with Lily's needs. Mother was being a little particular but had resigned herself to placing Lily in someone else's hands as I was married to Ben by then and wouldn't be there to help out.

We lived three bus rides away but would visit her every Saturday without fail, mother in her best dress and coat, her one and only hat. I was her companion, most of the time and I ached to see Lily in between each visit, only imagining how my mother must have felt. I can imagine more now.

She was in a corridor with five other women. It wasn't a bad home, and it could have been far worse I suspected. The smell of the place distressed me. The stench of bodily fluids and cooking odours pervaded Lily, making it seem as though I was kissing a stranger. Mother didn't seem to notice or at least she never mentioned it.

Lily didn't look like my Lily any longer.

However, fate had other plans for Lily, and she died less than eight months later.

More than a little piece of my mother died with her.

*

I had my ambitions, some may think them small, but with my experience looking after Lily, I imagined myself as a nurse, looking after the sick and the frail.

However, mother needed me to bring home some money, not train to be a nurse. She didn't say so, but she did. That door was closed to me as even if I didn't want to help mother, my father would have thought I had ideas above my station. He pulled a few strings to get me a job at the mill, and the decision was cut and dried before I knew it.

I spent hour after hour on my feet, wearing hairnets and earmuffs, spitting out fibres of wool. It was a far cry from the rewarding career choice I had in mind.

I had only one event on the calendar to look forward to each year.

Life in a small village can be rather drab, so the annual August Feast was a chance to escape our humdrum lives. Much like the rest of the girls at the mill, my friend Dorothy and I wouldn't have missed the event for the world. The hustle and bustle, the dazzling carnival colours at dusk and beyond, they were a mesmerising sight for sore eyes.

We'd put on our best frocks, secretly apply a bit of make up once we were out of our parents' gaze and head to the feast ground in Horton. It had fairground rides and stalls, a cabinet of curiosities and circus acts like Hercules, the world's strongest man. My favourite was riding the Shamrock until I felt dizzy and sick and then we'd eat cinder toffee and Stockbridge's Lemonade.

That year, as we waited in line for the hall of mirrors I just happened to glance idly over Dorothy's shoulder.

And there he was. I double-took and stopped talking as I saw him looking at me. He didn't look away and I quickly found out my eyes weren't going anywhere.

Dorothy followed my gaze, then turning back she winked moving slightly to one side. He seized his chance to step forward leaving Dorothy to make stilted conversation with his friend. I had no time to feel sorry for her, I knew this was one of those moments in life.

"I like your dress," he told me, "It matches your eyes.

I smiled, basking in the glow of his compliment. I chose it for that very reason.

"Ben," he said holding out his hand.

"Frances," I said taking his hand, trying to make it appear as though I did such things all the time.

He raised my hand to his lips and gently kissed the back of it. I'd never had my hand kissed before and it was hard not to positively swoon.

Afterwards he told me the way I blushed was the clincher. His confidence without a hint of arrogance was mine. Quick-thinking and stimulating company, Ben and I were on an even playing field when it came to our outlook on life. He liked my mischievous sense of humour, and I liked his blue/black hair and strong features which made women all a dither when they met him. I struggled to see what he saw in me when he could have had his pick.

"You have a dangerous combination of beauty and brains," he told me when I happened to mention it once, "This is rarer than one might think."

My father wasn't impressed because he thought anyone with money was full of themselves. He thought Ben an upstart but when he asked for my hand in marriage he readily agreed because he was no fool. His daughter marrying a wealthy lawyer gave him something to brag about.

I didn't need to borrow a dress for our wedding, Ben told me he would be honoured to pay for it and anything else I might need. Life had truly blessed me.

We compromised and had a wedding which wasn't too fancy because I wouldn't have wanted my mother to be uncomfortable.

On our wedding night, I was nervous. I so wanted to impress Ben and be the wife he always dreamed of. I had a new white cotton nightdress with tiny roses on the collar and cuffs which I bought with my wedding allowance. I looked at myself in the mirror, raising my chin to try and prick my confidence. The nightdress made me look sweet, virginal. I liked what I saw, I can't lie. Lifting my dress, I reached to touch the small, raised scar at the back of my thigh. Barely visible by then it didn't spoil me.

Ben opened the door to the bedroom and stopped in his tracks. His eyes were full of love as he stared at me, his gaze dropping to admire the view. Somehow, I wasn't shy, instead I felt heady.

He raced towards me, and we fell on the bed, arms, and legs around each other, kissing with more passion than I was used to. I wanted more.

He pinned my arms above my head and looked down at me.

I gazed into his eyes.

"I like it hard and rough," he told me, waiting for a response before he went any further. A true gentleman.

I gave him a wry smile.

"So do I," I told him.

Chapter 28

I admired Ben for wanting to make his own way in the world even though his family was incredibly wealthy.

I finished work the week before our wedding and settled down to the joy of looking after my husband and home. We had a full team of staff to cater for our every whim and I liked to see him off to work ensuring he was immaculately turned out as he waved to me on his way to the car. He looked every inch the dashing lawyer; how proud I was of him.

I liked to please my husband. I dashed upstairs to comb my hair and pinch my cheeks before he got home because if I didn't take care of myself, I'd find myself on a slippery slope. There were a few ladies waiting in line for my place at Highbrook, I'd seen their predatory glances in Ben's direction. I knew their game before they begun to play it.

I pinched myself sometimes. I'd come from nothing but moving to Highbrook was like I was living a fairy tale life in a fairy tale castle. But Ben and I were just as content with the simple pleasures of family life. You enjoy the ups more when you have the downs and the lows, as mother often said.

She thought I'd found the 'catch of the century' and fawned over Ben like a God. He lapped it up but always with a twinkle in his eye.

"By, you've dropped on your feet with that one, lass, you'll never want for nothing now," she said.

I laughed. She was sitting in her favourite spot by the fire with her swollen feet up on a footstool.

"I know but the money isn't important, mam. He's just so good to me."

"Aye but it helps, there's no denying it."

Living hand to mouth most of her life, it would naturally have been a priority for her. It was hard watching her cobble a meal together for years on pennies. She was right, money doesn't do any harm.

Joshua coming along made my little Highbrook fairy tale complete and I threw myself into looking after my boys.

I'm thankful even more that despite a meteoric rise through the legal ranks—Ben was called to the Bar at just thirty-three—he didn't really enjoy the 'hob-knobbing' which goes with a life in Chambers. That suited me because I'd find it so hollow and tedious. We had the odd essential function to attend but I could relax into my role as his wife and Joshua's mother. In time, I balanced out the splendour to give Highbrook the gentler feel of home.

It upset me Joshua didn't like the house. His imagination ran away with him as it can for children, and I understand huge old houses are eerie for overactive minds. He never liked his bedroom, often creeping into our bed during the night when he was small. Ben often told me I should lock the door to stop him, but I couldn't. He would whisper he'd had a nightmare, but I never told Ben about his overactive imagination. He never would have understood because Highbrook was all he'd known. He would have thought him silly.

Ben thought I pampered him, and I think I might have.

But we are bestowed the honour of children to pamper them.

*

The top floor was home to Ben's very unusual hobby. He spent hours holed up there painstakingly painting his little soldiers. There were thousands of them laid out in battle scenes or lined meticulously on shelves. He started the hobby with his brother when they were young boys, and it was his way to unwind.

His job could drain the life out of him, I understood his need.

The night times are of course the worst after Ben dies, and my lonely future taunts me in the blackness. I regress to childhood and sleep with a candle burning. When I return from visiting Joshua, I close and lock the door, turn around and listen to the silence. It screams at me, and I feel lost. I never thought I would say it but overseeing Highbrook has become a millstone. The staff left and couldn't be replaced, or they weren't up to speed and dismissed. Eventually I only have the Godsend she is, Crawford and Stanley the gardener.

Nowadays, I spend most of my time on the ground floor, where I'm safe and secure because you need the cocoon of a small space when you're alone. It's not good for you to look at too much emptiness. I've created a bedroom of my own now because our bedroom holds painful memories. Memories of us, our life as Frances and Ben, and our private alter egos which gave each other such pleasure.

Moving away is simply not an option as Highbrook is the bones of me. Joshua thinks I should buy somewhere smaller, but I can't imagine myself living anywhere else, not ever.

Life trundles along for all of us in much the same way for years. The comings and goings of daily life bring a reassurance you assume will always be there. I learn the hard way this a foolish mistake to make. It's foolish because in the end it only took one second of time to shatter my fairy tale forever.

My Ben, the person who lit up a room just by entering, who made every woman look when he walked past, my Ben was gone. My Ben is gone.

It all happened so quickly the memory is blurred around the edges. The coroner's report said my husband had died an accidental death after a fall from the terrace broke his neck.

The contorted expression on his face when he was lying on the ground haunts me still.

After that, Joshua couldn't wait to leave home.

It didn't surprise me when he never came back.

Chapter 29

Highbrook is an idyllic haven and a bottomless pit of expense in equal measure.

Taxes, a few debts to be cleared and Ben's insurance money was all but gone. Highbrook became my only asset and so, after going back and forth in my mind, I had decided I must sell.

But then I met you.

You played the starring role in getting back on my feet. I enjoyed the whole process of the renovation and that my opinion mattered once more. You gave me back my sense of purpose, a new reason to get up on a morning.

Before choosing Hudson and Carr, I had approached another company about my plans for Highbrook. They were unexceptional.

When I met with you in your office that summer day, I knew my search was over and I'd found you. The work you'd done on your office conversion was advertisement enough, but you, personally took me unawares. You obviously have a gift for creating the right look, it has a distinct air of class about it. No wonder you have clients beating a path to your door.

It's important not to ruin the spirit of Highbrook, you said, so I don't regret making the decision. You invested yourself the same as I did, which took me by surprise.

More to the point, you understood perfectly how fundamental my home is to me. You listened to all my ideas without brushing them aside as the yearnings of an old widow, obsessed with the memories of her dead husband. It had been a long time since someone had listened to me.

On your first visit you walked from room to room, soaking up every detail. The house enthralled you as it did me when Ben showed me around the very first time all those years before. He was blasé about it as one is with one's childhood home. You wash your face every day in the same bowl, you comb your hair at the same mirror, it's just home, unremarkable.

You returned time after time to take notes, make sketches, engross yourself in the house, I could see the cogs of your mind turning and you were brimming with ideas. I'd not only found the right person for the job, but I'd also found a kindred spirit.

"An opportunity like this doesn't come your way very often," you said with obvious delight, "I bless the day you walked into my office, Frances, I really do."

Oh, how my heart sang with pride.

We spent weeks discussing the renovation. Your visits became increasingly important to me, and I looked forward to them more each time. You called regularly at the end of the day before going home and often we ate our evening meal together. I appreciated the simple pleasure of eating a meal with someone else; far preferable to eating alone in silence. We would sit talking for hours afterwards by the fire with a glass of port or brandy. In time we didn't just talk about the renovations.

We simply enjoyed each other's company. You started to stay over in Joshua's old room on occasion, having breakfast together before you headed off to town. I became a much-needed confidante. I knew you weren't particularly close to your family, and you didn't appear to have friends to talk to, but I still find it hard to understand why you're such a loner.

You have so much to offer.

*

Since getting to know you, William I've also discovered secrets about your mother.

Everyone has a history of course. You meet a person at a certain point in their story but you've no idea what happened in the chapters before, mother once said.

There are things you should know, but it's not my place to tell.

Like you, your mother can talk to me. I listen, I empathise. She's lonely, much the same as I was, but she tells me she's unable to talk to you about it.

We became friends almost at once and having similar backgrounds was common ground. Neither of us was born with a silver spoon in our mouths.

"I wasn't always like I am, Frances," she says one day in the garden, "I was popular once, believe it or not."

How very unexpected.

I don't speak, I don't move as she sits back in the garden chair and takes a sip of her second gin and tonic then swirls the ice and lemon around the long glass. I don't respond in any way; I hope she'll forget I'm here.

"Things were different when I was a teenager," she says, staring into her drink, "I grew up in a small village like you as you know, Frances and I went to school with a boy called Samuel, though everyone called him Sam because it suited him better. He'd pass me notes and bring me gifts; little things like a flower or a bag of sweets and in our childish way we always said we'd marry. He was the class clown who made everyone laugh and he certainly made me laugh. My stomach would hurt, my eyes run, you know, Frances, that rare kind of laughter. It wasn't quite so rare then.

We left school at fourteen and Sam proposed on my sixteenth birthday with plans to move in with my mother and father until we could save enough to rent a home of our own.

We waited until we were eighteen, but then we couldn't wait any longer. We booked the church, hired the hall, and mother and I decided to do the flowers and fuddle ourselves to save money. It was the same for every wedding. I had my mother's wedding dress altered because I would have worn it regardless. It was beautiful and I still have it.

Sam had his stag party a week before the wedding to err on the side of caution and he did this for me so I wouldn't worry. The night before, he was going fishing on the lake with his father and two brothers. It sounded very civilised, and it put my mind at rest he wouldn't be getting drunk and doing silly things he wouldn't normally do.

Our wedding day was in June, and it turned out to be a beautiful sunny day like today.

My mother threw back the curtains early in the morning, telling me, "The sun shines on the righteous, Sylvia."

I always think of that. She washed and rolled my hair while we chatted. My dress and veil were hanging on the wardrobe door ready for our big day. She was as excited as I was.

Around ten o'clock there was a knock on the front door, and I heard my father speaking to someone. I recognised the voice.

My father came upstairs after a while and appeared around the door. I knew at once by his expression it was … unpleasant news."

Sylvia takes a long sip of her drink and swallows noisily.

"The police pulled Sam's body out of the lake that morning. They'd been drinking and one thing led to another, and he fell in. They couldn't find him. It took the police and the water bailiff to pull him out the following morning. His father was in shock, so his brothers raised the alarm.

I never wore my wedding dress, not that day, not ever.

The whole village mourned him, putting us on the map for good as the village where that boy drowned the night before his wedding.

But I had another worry.

I had found out I was pregnant not long before the wedding and I was going to surprise Sam on our wedding night with the news. Of course, sex before marriage is unacceptable.

I burst into tears one day talking to Sam's best friend, Jeffrey. He was the polar opposite of Sam, but he stepped up when I told him the news and asked me to marry him. It was very good of him.

So, two months later I was his wife. I wore a borrowed dress because I couldn't bear to wear my mother's and we toasted the day with a glass of fizz back at home. Jeffrey had his own cottage and was destined for good things as one day he would be taking over his father's business. Then William was late being born, but the villagers wouldn't have put two and two together even if he hadn't been. They thought I'd married on the rebound, and they felt sorry for us. I had. This however *was* acceptable.

I was miserable on the day of the wedding, and it continued throughout our married life. I didn't show it though because I was grateful to Jeffrey, and he saved me from ruin. Devoid of emotion I made a vow to do my duty until duty no longer served him well enough.

I don't miss Sam and what might have been because I don't allow myself to think about it. I live in a state of numbness.

Loneliness wasn't new to me after Jeffrey left.

I've been lonely since I was eighteen years old."

Oh, Sylvia, how trite you make your sad story sound, how insignificant. "Unpleasant news"; "Very good of him", it's as though you're retelling someone else's tragedy.

You and your mother are peas in a pod, both needing me to lend an ear. I've asked her to tell you the tale because I know you would understand, and it would explain your distant relationship. She's spoken of it once, so surely it would be far easier next time.

She says a new kind of relationship with you would seem forced after so long and you're both too far down the path to turn back. But the main reason is she would have to let go of the numbness and begin to feel again. Telling me is different she says because I'm a neutral party.

Why doesn't she want to make you feel better like a mother should? I wonder if she blames you, resents you even for the life she's had. I'd like to make it better for you, but this isn't my secret to tell. So, I decide to look after you both and snuggle you down under my empty wings.

You are indeed a little boy lost, asking me to like you, to love you and it's so easy. You need me and nobody has needed me in so very long.

I'm having my own floor renovated too. I pour over housekeeping books and magazines and I've even started a scrapbook, finding it all so engrossing and satisfying. I finally understand how Ben must have felt about his hobby. I have a cosy routine, and I have so many distractions, there are never enough hours in the day again. I now know I thrive being busy and needed. The remodelling of Highbrook is exceeding my expectations and everything is panning out nicely.

I couldn't possibly be more fulfilled.

Panning out nicely indeed until that day. The day that crafty little madam appears from nowhere.

She manages to whip the rug from right under me.

Chapter 30

When you tell me about the girl on the moors it appears no more than an aside and I can honestly say I don't give her a second thought. So, I'm thrown when you say you'd found her when I didn't even know you'd lost her. Gradually, you disclose your feelings to me. You're besotted with her; she's all you ever talk about.

"She's so different from anyone else I've ever met. It's the way she makes me feel, like nobody before. You'll understand when you get to know her, Frances," you say excitedly.

And then a few short weeks later, she appears here at Highbrook. True, she's very pretty, very natural, she even has a certain wildness about her, but I'm not sure I understand what all the fuss is about, and it isn't long before I realise that I don't like her.

There is something a little off with her which I can't quite put my finger on. Is she chasing your money? I can't be sure as she doesn't seem to spend frivolously, if at all.

I know I have to swallow my less than favourable opinion for your sake. You'll surely see through her before too long or she'll tire of you.

Deluded, that's what you are, William. She's self-absorbed and weak. I see right through her, and so does your mother, I thought to myself.

"There's no point trying to change his mind, Frances, she has him wrapped around her little finger. He won't listen I fear, so he will just have to learn the hard way," your mother says.

Her prediction turned out to be spot on.

After her arrival on the scene, gone are our cosy nights by the fire, our lingering chats. Instead, we snatch ten minutes here and there. You're always preoccupied, and I never have your full attention anymore. I'm cast aside, and it hurts.

You fall so deeply, so quickly. I can't shake off the niggling doubt that she is not all she appears to be. Yes, she's charming and respectful of me and your mother but a little too good to be true.

Serious doubts begin to creep in. To start with, your stories don't always tally.

"I thought you were at your mother's last Thursday," I say to her as innocently as I can muster.

I watch her carefully certain I catch sight of a blush.

"Yes, that's right. I thought you said Friday. I can't keep up of late, Frances, I apologise."

Do I make her nervous or is she hiding something? I saw her folding her napkin over and over, fussing with it until she'd made a perfect fan shape. I looked at the top of her bent head and the ringlets which hang in coils were so defined you could put your finger in each one. It looked like dolls hair. Watching you, watching her, she's like your little doll. Lily was my doll, but Lily was different, special.

She's lying. I know all about lies; her body language tells me she's a liar.

You ask me if she can join us for tea. As if I would or could refuse. I want to and I'm somewhat miffed at you for asking. I'm not enough anymore.

Maybe I'm a little envious, but I can't bear the thought of you being taken for a fool, or me.

I admit things got a little out of hand. The tip-tapping on my mind had been building over a couple of weeks. I was on my own more, so I was festering, but I still didn't know exactly what about. I find her creeping around my thoughts far more than she should. I can't shake it off, she is living inside my head, my first thought when I wake up, when trying to read, getting dressed, even when I climb into bed after a draining day of festering about her. The tip-tapping has become incessant.

I have to be careful. I'm becoming obsessive and know this could upset the apple cart for me and for you. I have too much at stake.

If I'm going to prevent these poisonous thoughts from ruining our relationship I need to act, and I convince myself I am only doing what anyone else would do to protect someone who is dear to them.

So, one morning I simply decide to follow her. What I think I will find I really have no idea but what I do know is somehow it doesn't feel wrong. I can easily justify it because I owe it to you to find out if she is pulling the wool over your eyes. You're gullible enough to be taken in by her wiles. When it comes to women, naïve is the word. You just can't read us.

Call it women's intuition, but I'm sure she will slip up sometime. I'm certain she's up to no good.

I watch her for a few days and am quite enjoying myself in perhaps a slightly twisted way. She isn't with you all the time, so I can easily take a stroll to see where she goes. I'm quite good at following her, quite the little private detective. It gives me a thrill and I have an excuse prepared in case she spotted me.

I resent her. A more dramatic person would go further and say I have come to loathe her. It shocks me when I think about it.

Loathing: the definition is powerful. I look it up.

'Noun: An intense dislike or disgust, hatred.'

Oh, Frances, you really must get to the bottom things.

This morning she nips to the village shop and then to the post office. I'm rather bored, my mind wandering, but I know it might take time to catch her out.

My interest pricks when I see her walk in the opposite direction of the village. This is new, we were heading much further afield than usual. I follow at a distance for about a mile or so, keeping to the other side of the hedgerows. We reach Woodlesfield and I wonder if she is visiting a relative. It's a tiny hamlet with only six or seven houses. Walking further still, she suddenly stops and leans against a lamppost, dropping her head. I pause half hidden behind a wall and watch her carefully. She seems to be thinking, and for quite some time.

I see her disappear down a dirt track and I can just see signs of a chimney twirling smoke around the treetops. I decide to wait and not risk following her further and in any case the clouds are darkening. I doubt I'll find out where she's disappeared to, so I resolve to head home and return in the car the following day to add the next piece to my jigsaw.

After an unsettled night's sleep, I ask Crawford to make a little picnic telling her I fancy a walk on the moors.

I find a secluded area to park, away from Woodlesfield and retrace Nell's footsteps from the previous day to a perfect viewing spot in the middle of the trees. Laying my old blanket on the grass I sit down as though at the theatre, waiting for the performance to start. I have all day, I'm in no hurry knowing I can always return the next day, if necessary.

After about an hour I see a young girl leave the house looking a little unsteady on her feet. She looks as if she might be drunk, but then I realise she looks unwell. It's all very peculiar. I watch the girl disappear and am thoroughly intrigued now. Is it a den of iniquity I wonder. Surely to God Nell isn't a lady of the night.

The girl disappears down a winding path through the woods and I read my book, but nothing more happens. I have no choice but to return later.

The following day I inform Crawford that I'm going to see William's mother so as not raise suspicion. After settling myself in the same spot I wait for over two hours, then I see a different young girl from yesterday walking up the trail to knock on the back door. It opens but I can't see by whom as the entrance is in the shadow of darkness. The door closes and I wait, and I wait until finally the door reopens. Worryingly, this girl looks as pale as death, and I notice another girl then waiting at the end of the track. She puts her arm around her shoulders as she approaches, and the girl bursts into tears. Why would this be, I wonder as they disappear into the distance. Must I return a third time?

I gather my things then drop the blanket to put both hands to my cheeks. Oh, Frances, how dim-witted you are, I suddenly realise, you're being positively stupid.

It is indeed a den of iniquity but not the to the one I had in mind. Nell is no lady of the night.

How naive of me, how incredibly gullible. I remembered whisperings about Maisie Walton at the mill needing to come to Woodlesfield, but of course I'd no idea where exactly. I liked Maisie and I certainly wouldn't have wanted her to get into trouble.

But there is no jubilation at finding out the depths Nell has plummeted in my estimation. In that moment I am completely… devastated.

Returning forlornly to the car, I shed a tear or two for you, William. You are so trusting, and she clearly doesn't such a trust. She is toying with you, and I will not allow her to get away with it.

I make my way home to contemplate my next step, my hands gripping the wheel tightly to stop them from shaking.

Then only a day or two later you drop your bombshell: you are to propose. I decide I must try and forestall the moment and give her the opportunity to do the right thing. I feel reassured she won't tell you I've been to see her as she risks giving the game away.

I know the way to the cottage like the back of my hand although I've never dared get too close. The area is far more isolated than the surrounding villages, so I would be a sitting duck.

I consider the extent of her betrayal and picture your open, trusting face and it fuels my annoyance. It will be satisfying to wipe that smile off her face, I think. I've waited long enough and now at least I have justification for the way I feel. When she opens the door to me, my eyes travel straight to her face. I notice the paleness of her skin, almost translucent in the daylight. It startles me. Her red eyes blink in the light, and she gives me a hesitant smile. She doesn't look ready to leave for Highbrook, her hair is down, her dress slightly worn.

"Are you quite well?" I ask, from devilment.

I watch her lips tremble as she pulls back the door further for me to enter.

"You've caught me feeling a little under the weather, I'm afraid, Frances."

Oh, a little under the weather indeed.

I have no great plan about how to open the confrontation, I only want her to be left in no doubt I've discovered she was a liar. How I've been craving the gratification.

Her forlorn expression is pitiful, I can see how she arouses your protective instinct.

The room is the smallest room I've ever been in, but homely. The fire is blazing, and there are candles on the mantle. I notice a shawl bundled on a chair where she'd left it to answer the door. She has unusual taste in décor. Nothing matches but everything fits together somehow. The atmosphere of the cottage is welcoming, I can see why she's so taken with it, as was her grandmother before apparently.

She makes a small motion with her head, and I sit down in a chair opposite her, by the fire. Perching on the edge, my hands carefully folded in my lap, I wait for her to move the shawl, so she can join me. She too perched, as though she is getting ready to run out of the door.

"Can I get you a cup of tea?" she asks, with a painful attempt at a smile. She can't meet my eyes.

"No thank you."

My chilly tone startles her. Her eyes almost fill her face, so she looks like a cornered deer. Pulling her lower lip between her teeth she can't speak.

"I saw you go to the cottage."

She looks quickly down at her feet, the classic look of shame. Her bottom lip frees itself then begins to quiver again, one big tear falling to the bottom of her chin and plopping onto her lap. Stop the crocodile tears, Nell, I think. You've been found out now face it.

"How could you do that to him? It pains me to think how crushed he would be if he found out. You must know how much you mean to him. He, of all people just doesn't deserve it."

This was clearly the last conversation she was expecting to be having.

"Oh, Frances, it's not what you think. I'm so sorry I would never want to hurt William, intentionally or otherwise. You must believe me," she says.

She gulps then sniffs, looking at me dolefully.

"I've been tortured, I beg you not to tell him."

She's pleading now, her teary eyes wide with panic. She doesn't need to worry because I have no intention of telling you. I'm not going to be the one to break your heart, William.

But I'm not going to tell her that. She can have a few restless nights wondering.

It will do her good.

Chapter 31

She and I have a moment alone a day or two later. Tiptoeing around me all morning she's been getting on my nerves.

I grab the opportunity to ask her the burning question. Is she still intent on marrying you? Part of me wishes she would disappear for good somewhere, but I know you would spend the rest of your life looking for her.

"Yes, despite what you may think, I love him, and I couldn't be without him."

Oh, poor, poor Nell. Couldn't be without him, so, you want the penny and the bun. She has a knack for saying the wrong thing.

"I hope to god for his sake he never finds out what you did," is my bitter response.

She shoots me a look of a wounded dog. It might work with you, but it doesn't work with me. Playing the victim is her forte and you so love a lame duck, you thought I was one once. A soft touch you may be, but she has blotted her copybook forever with me.

The wedding soon comes around and for your sake William I put on my best outfit and best smile even though it makes me sick to the stomach to watch her exchange vows with you.

So, you can imagine how shocked I am when you tell me the news.

You call in to see me after work, and I am irritated that, once again, you're in a rush. No time for cake even. I have to just settle for crumbs while she gets the cake.

"Frances, we haven't told anyone yet, you're the first to know."

I look at you expectantly, my face set in a smile.

"Nell is expecting a baby."

A baby?

"I haven't known long but I can't contain myself. I don't like keeping things from you, Frances, and I'm sorry I had to tell a white lie about why the doctor had called," you say.

"I know everything has happened so quickly but if I'm truthful, I didn't want to wait too long to marry for many reasons. But a baby, well..."

Your eyes mist over, and I manage to pull myself together at the speed of light.

"Oh, William I'm so happy for you."

How I mean it; I'm surprised just how much I mean it.

So, she didn't go through with it after all. Does this let her off the hook? No, it's bad enough for her just to have considered it.

But a baby; this house needs a baby, Highbrook needs a baby; it's been too long. I get up from the chair and meet him halfway for a heartfelt embrace. I can feel his heart beating madly with excitement. It's infectious.

I can't help myself planning ahead and I have a new focus. I'm genuinely happy for you and wholeheartedly share your anticipation.

You've longed to be a father, telling me often you would want to do it differently to your own father. You would show your love for child you might have. I thought of Jeffrey, determined to talk any your mother again about enlightening you.

"The most important gifts you can give a child are your time and attention," you say.

How true, William, how true.

You're overly attentive towards Nell though and it makes me very uncomfortable. You moon at her like a doe-eyed teenager completely blinded by love. It rankles when so much had been going on behind your back.

I've taken to sitting at the bottom of the stairs to your apartment on an evening when Crawford has gone to bed. I like to just listen to your voices and hear you going about your life together. You never seem to argue, and I find this odd. Ben and

I could go at it hammer and tongs sometimes, it keeps the sparkle.

So, I become increasingly invisible each day. I have no choice but to watch on as you are increasingly wrapped up in each other, your new home, your new life.

All that's left for me to do is stomach it.

That is until Albert arrives.

Then suddenly you need me.

Chapter 32

Albert is born early and my involvement in his birth is fate I'm inclined to think.

Still, we're more than ready for his arrival. At least you and I are.

It doesn't take long to see what's happening with Nell. She's sinking but not steadily, she's sinking like a stone. I swoop to her rescue, spending time with Albert as I can't bear him living in such a miserable environment.

Now he is my sense of purpose.

Oh, she may appear composed, but the truth is she's living a shell of a life. That life is somewhere far, far away and in her head. She might be fooling you, or you might be choosing to ignore it, but what a dangerous game you're playing.

She's a smiler. I find it an annoying trait to grin inanely like a half-wit, but those smiles have become scarily unconvincing. You're in denial, William. You are always in denial.

Now though, I'm the one you all turn to, and I have become instrumental in all your lives. I have all the answers … and all the power.

My sweet little boy is part of my big boy and somehow, he feels part of me. It might be because he was born at Highbrook, and I was there at his birth. I've been granted a second chance, a second wish. Simple pleasures are wonderful again, better; walking for hours around the grounds, reading him stories, staring into his eyes as he sits contentedly in my arms, they all stop nothing short of wondrous.

I watch you with your son as he grows. You're true to your word and give him your gift of time and attention, spending hours playing and even working on the grounds together. He follows you like a little duckling in his tiny little boots. You two are inseparable. If you wrote a storybook about you both it would be a fairy tale—not the Grimm ones people remember the most because of the darkness. You don't have any dark parts. There is enough darkness from the cloud his mother casts.

Nell's so lucky you have her back. She's lucky I have your back, and Albert's back; lucky, lucky Nell.

"I don't know what all the fuss is about, you would think she was the first woman to have a child," your mother says, "It doesn't make sense, especially as Albert's no trouble and William is involved so much. I never had the luxury, and I doubt you did either."

Yes, it would certainly have been nice to have a husband who was so involved. Men can be so dogmatic in turning a blind eye to what's going on right under their nose. If they ignore it, it isn't happening, which is generally their preferred approach.

I can see it as plain as day. Nell is living her life on autopilot, smiling, smiling, smiling to try and lighten the burden of life.

Some days I wonder if they will take her away and all our problems will be solved in one fell swoop. Albert would be happier and surely even you would have to admit that now.

But then I must remember you wouldn't be happier. I must remember you would live in this god-awful situation for the rest of your life if you had to. I know you'd be prepared to do it because you could make sure Albert was happy and you still had the love of your life.

My apartment is Albert's sanctuary, I made sure of it, allowing me to spend more time with him. His mother's bizarre traits mean he can't wait to get out of his own home. I can't wait for him to get out.

I should let her lean on me and how I try for your sake.
I dig deep, but somehow, I just can't find it in me.

*

How was I to know her plan?

I'm left to watch the life drain from you ... and her poor, poor mother.

It torments me, has me lying awake at night, terrified you might contemplate joining her and I'm powerless to stop you if you want to. Nobody has the power except Albert, and then I can't help but think only to a point.

In and amongst the trauma Albert and I carry on with our routine in the same vein for the most part, even though we're terribly worried about you. I can tell Albert is worried by his constant questions.

I knew Nell was suffering but I never really stopped to think to what extent. I was too busy going about my life, absorbed in the everyday and the everyday was Albert and you. She was always frail of mind, so that was nothing new. My thoughts about her were peripheral by then. I wasn't prepared.

I must stop my mind from spiralling in the wrong direction. I had a part to play but I can't risk my guilt dragging me under because you need me. You both need me.

This dreadful situation is painful to watch and isn't for the faint of heart. It is raw. There are too many emotions to slog through I know now, far more than if a person you love dies, leaves you forever in the usual way. That's hard enough. The greyness of your face becomes a permanent feature, fading but never quite disappearing for good.

But time doesn't stop for anything.

After a few months I suggest one night I teach you how to play chess, like Ben taught me. He taught me so many things. I want to take the first step to restoring some normality and how happy it makes me to see you absorbed in something so trivial. At least I hope you're absorbed.

You yawn and stretch at the end of the game. I take it as my cue to go back downstairs as I'm always very careful not to outstay my welcome.

"I don't know how we would have got back here without you, Frances," you say, "Albert, but me too. I feel like I've been to war."

You look like you've been to war. It plays my heart strings.

I push your fringe out of your eyes.

"You need a haircut," I say.

You smile a sad smile, telling me to not be so cheeky then draw me into your arms so I can't read your face. I know your little game.

As for Albert, we agreed we needed to get him used to the idea of his mother not being around any longer, so we came up with the story of her being in hospital between us.

That fateful day, I took him out when you'd left to go to the police station. It was surreal, walking on a deserted beach with him, pretending to be scarecrows bobbing about in the wind, singing his favourite song at the top of our voices, calling at Harriet's for afternoon tea. I was numb.

When I got back with him, it hit me she was gone for good. Shamefully, like magic, the house took on a different atmosphere. It was like I'd gone back in time years to when I lived here as a young woman. The dark cloud had gone and there was no chance of it ever returning.

When Albert and I are having dinner together one evening in the dining room, curiosity gets the better of me. I ask the question which has been preying on my mind for a long, long time.

"Do you miss your mother, Albert?"

He stops eating and puts down his knife and fork. I hold my breath, my eyes pinned to his face.

"Can I tell you a secret?" he asks finally.

My stomach clenches.

"Of course … always."

"I don't think about mama very often and it makes me feel mean. I heard you and grandma talking about her once. I should have talked to her a bit more and then she might have known I liked her. I think sometimes it was because of me."

His voice is a whisper, as if his papa might hear but you are at work. I can tell he didn't want to hear himself say the words.

"What was it you heard?" I ask, my throat knotting tightly.

He tilts his eyes my way, his face expressionless.

"That she was never happy."

I hear a small sound escape me, clearing my throat to cover it. I did say that, but it was meant in a bitter, peevish way that he wouldn't understand. I think carefully how to proceed because I may make a terrible situation worse. What would be the correct response to such a bombshell; of a little boy thinking his mother was unhappy because he didn't talk to her enough, because he preferred to be with me. How can I give any words of comfort, reassurance? The words elude me.

I watch him pick up his knife and fork again and start eating his tea, carefully cutting a potato, and squashing some peas against it on his fork the way he likes, though I would not have been pleased if Joshua had done it.

He looks calm, safe in the knowledge his secret will go no further, and relieved to have unburdened himself of the confession. He isn't expecting a response. My breathing settles as I realise that I've been handed a reprieve.

That day the tide turned. It was the day I first noticed the ever-increasing circle called remorse. I've had a voice in my head for some time. I must face it now because it won't go away, and I've tried to make it go away many times. I must ask myself a very painful question. Did I steal her son's heart, or did he give it to me willingly, unquestioningly?

Should I admit to it, should I admit I did steal it? I don't think it could make me feel better to do so and regardless, she can never again be his mother.

Inadvertently, I have now become the biggest part of Albert's life. But he had a mother, and she should have had that place in his heart, as I did for Joshua.

Time may not stop but it is the healer of most things. Eventually I can bask in the warmth of Albert's love with only a niggling doubt of her in the very depths of my mind to taint it. He breathes life into me in so many ways.

I have only one insurmountable problem which I can never overcome, and I must accept it, William.

It's true you can never feel the same way about me as I do about you, but I can't help but think this is such a shame.

With her gone, I did wonder sometimes but I would never have been able to sway you. Of course, I'm not her, but I could have helped heal you more as a woman and not just as a companion.

It's quite obvious to me at least that we would have made a perfect little family.

Joshua
Chapter 33

I was such a lucky boy you told me at every opportunity.

I was lucky to attend a private school, even though the fees for a term would have fed a family for a year in your day. I was lucky to live in an historic home like Highbrook, to have money, breeding. The list went on.

Boarding school would have been a better option. I suspect my father would have preferred me to go because he was a boarder, and he loved the life. I'm sure he thought it would have done me good. But you were having none of it and he didn't push. You got your own way.

"I wish we lived in a normal house on a normal street," I complained once.

"You do sound spoiled sometimes, Joshua. I would have given my eyeteeth for what you have. You should never take things for granted because you can lose them any time. You'd do well to remember that."

My grandma on my father's side lived with us for a time. Her name was Victoria, but everyone called her Tora. Vicky would be too common, you said. She was old, far too old to have a life. There was a black and white picture of her with grandpa at the side of her bed. Grandpa was in a soldier's uniform with a sword hanging from his belt. I looked at the picture and I looked at my grandma and I didn't think it was the same person. She was beautiful but now it looked as though someone had drawn all over her face with a black crayon. The only part of her which was the same on the photograph was her hands. They were white as snow.

Grandma watched from the attic window when my friends came to play cricket in the summertime. She looks like a ghost they said, and I wanted them to come in and meet her, but they wouldn't. If they had met her, they would have felt differently about her because she was a proper lady.

Grandma and grandpa had plenty of staff, but you said you didn't need so many. You were always fond of Stanley our gardener the most who went home each evening.

*

Today is a sad day for me as Stanley is retiring and he's worked for us all my life. I can talk to him about anything. We've talked about role models at school and when my teacher described one, Stanley popped into my mind straight away. I don't see much of my father because he works so much but that seems to be the same for everybody.

I can watch Stanley working for hours and he tells me all about nature. He has a bird book we check if we see a different bird in the garden and the illustrations are just beautiful.

I like watching Stanley's hands as I have a thing about hands, I notice them all the time. He has old, crooked hands and he calls them careworn. He says they tell a story of a man who enjoyed his work so much he never worked a day in his life.

I nag him to play tennis, but he'll only play after he's finished for the day. He rolls up his shirt sleeves and ties some twine between two holly bushes for a net and we play to the best of three matches. Five if I push him. He doesn't need to rush home because his mother has died, and he lived alone with her until he was old. I ask him if he feels lonely.

"Sometimes," he says, "but then you can still feel lonely when you don't live alone."

He doesn't believe in letting me win. He calls himself a hard taskmaster, because a win only counts if you've earned it.

"It's character building; sport sets you up for life. The teamwork, friendship, the highs, the lows, the passion. What would be the point of a fake win?" he asks me.

I try to understand.

We sit in his little shed at the back of the garage and have tea which, "you can stand your spoon up in." That's how he likes it, nice and strong. I'm not sure I like it, but I want to. We do this at exactly eleven o'clock and three o'clock every weekday in the holidays. I often sit on the steps in the hall and watch the minute hand tick by on the grandfather clock until it stops at the top because I'm so bored. Everything in Highbrook runs like clockwork and Stanley says a large house needs to run like that. The trick is to make it look like everything happens as if by magic and you don't see it happening.

"I'm going to be a gardener like you, Stan when I grow up," I tell him.

He laughs, throwing his head back and patting my hand when he sits up. I'm not sure why he finds it so funny.

I like Stanley and he likes me too; I know he does. He puts his hand in his pocket now and takes out his watch. It looks as though he might be handing it to me, but I don't reach for it as I'm not sure what to do.

"I won't be needing this anymore," he says, pressing the watch into my hand which I've seen him pull out and tell the time with all my life.

I look at the back. It says, "To Stanley, Love Mother."

I know this is a special present and I don't speak for a while.

I can't take it because it seems too important to Stanley for me to have it. I tell him but he says it will make him happy if he knows I have it and I'm the best person to look after it.

"I never want to check the time again," he says, "Now that's proper retirement."

I sleep with the pocket watch under my pillow every night. Before that I have it in my bedside drawer and I study it a long time before I put it under my pillow.

Stanley visits us every now and again, but I can tell the awkwardness of the situation puts him off. He never thinks it proper to use the front door, despite mother and father telling him he must. I don't think it helps when Crawford makes fun of him for becoming all high and mighty. She makes me cross when she says it because Stanley could never be that.

He sits with his flat cap in his hand, like he's waiting for the right amount of time to elapse so as not to appear rude when he makes a move.

I called in to see him at his cottage after he became ill. My father ensured he had all he needed in retirement, and for me it was only part-payment for all the sagacity he bestowed to carry along with me in life.

I still look at his pocket watch every single night and think of Stanley.

I hope he's proud of me.

Chapter 34

My grandma was quick-witted, quietly ruling the roost. You called her a kindly force to be reckoned with, running a country house and town house with ease before she sold the town house. She was ahead of her time and didn't fuss when my father brought you home. It was all about what prospective in-laws could bring to the table then, but dowries weren't important to her. She believed in true love.

She'd been acting out of character for a long time before her problem was diagnosed but other than wandering around the house in the night sometimes, we were managing with some help from Crawford.

Then one day we couldn't find her. We ran from room to room to check but we couldn't find her anywhere. I started feeling sick and panicking then set off on my bicycle to scour the country roads but went back without her. My mother sent for my father, and we called the police. I decided to take myself off to the moors even though you said she would never be strong enough to walk so far. I couldn't sit still so I just had to try something. After twenty minutes or so I found her. She was heading back down the hill, climbing over the heather in her house shoes, her white hair knotted and matted to her head from the wind. She looked like a mad woman. I started to cry. I knew she would be leaving us then. I knew it.

I missed her. I missed her more as time went by.

I'd listen with envy when my friends told me about their weekends. Some had been fishing or camping with their fathers. The challenge of being a lawyer drained my own father, leaving nothing for me. He didn't need to work but he loved the cut and thrust of a challenge.

"He has a low boredom threshold," you told me, "I love this about him."

I noticed you loved it less as the years went by and I grew older, demanding less of your time. You started to feel more like I did, that we were getting further and further down his list.

You loved Highbrook more because you came from nothing. My nana could never be "nothing," she was a wonder. She had a saying for every occasion, the wisest person I've ever met. She and Stanley would have been a match made in heaven. Her life had been misery until the day she was set free which was the day my grandfather died.

You and my aunt made life bearable she said, and nana talked about my aunt so much I felt like I knew her. She painted me a picture.

"Your Aunt Lily was too good for this world," she told me.

My grandfather was a nasty piece of work. He was physically cruel, but she always said his mental cruelty was the worst. Be it keeping her short of money whilst spending it down at the inn or telling her to recook his tea after he got home because it wasn't hot enough, she had too many stories.

"Your mam was once playing in the street and her friends came running to tell me she'd got her leg stuck on an iron railing. I'd told her a million times to not jump off the top steps, but she wouldn't listen. I thought her friends meant she had caught her leg between an iron railing not that she had impaled it. I almost fainted when I saw it. In my panic I ran for your grandfather who was washing in the kitchen sink. He wouldn't come out and I shouldn't have bothered wasting my time. So, I ran back, pulled your mam's leg from the railing, wrapped my pinny tightly around it and carried her a mile across town to the infirmary. It was all I could do."

I felt sick when she told me the story. She would sit by the fire waiting for my grandfather to come home, you said. You said you could never forget the look on her face when she heard his key in the lock.

My selfless nana nursed him to his last breath, something I contemplate often. How could one be selfless enough to nurse a person you surely hated and had wronged you so badly? I wished she had found the strength to leave him, but you eventually realise life is never so straight forward.

There was just nowhere for them to go.

Chapter 35

People assumed I had a charmed life.

We often make sweeping judgements about other people and their lives. There are unwritten criteria for happiness such as how attractive a person is, what they do for a living, what kind of house they have. The most significant is how much money they have. If you have pots of money, you must be happy.

I used to make sweeping judgements too, this is only human nature.

I rarely talk about my childhood now because if I'm perfectly honest, it really doesn't help. But I must keep trying.

My friends often tell me they think you're beautiful. You have that 'je ne sais quoi' as my grandma, who was fluent in French, told me. 'That indefinable something' was the translation, she said. You look at least ten years younger than you are, which of course helps. Impeccably turned out, you take great pride in your appearance. Accommodating of everyone, you always make time to help a person in need and this makes you very popular. You consider it important to be popular.

You never go to functions very often but if you have no choice but to attend some work gala or other with my father, I can't help but be impressed. You look like a film star couple on their way to a glittering red-carpet event. My father tall and striking in his dinner suit, you in a shimmering gown, you certainly cut a dash between you.

Stooping to give me a kiss you say, "Good night, my darling. Grandma is only next door, so no need to be scared."

You sweep out of the room to join my father. The eyrie sound of grandma shuffling about her room does nothing to help me sleep.

My nana always says my father looks as though he doesn't belong in the real world. He looks and acts as though fabricated, although this wasn't the word she used. I know what she means. She reveres him because he looks after her and she deserves it.

My father loves his hobby. It's a disturbing sight in that room, all those thousands of soldier eyes seemingly watching your every move. The silence doesn't help. Highbrook is an impressive place to live but I can't imagine living my adult life here, raising a family. Highbrook doesn't feel like home.

My nana's little two up, two down in the village is where I'm happiest. I'm so at ease there, I never need to be asked twice to stop over though I don't do anything to write home about. I only lay in bed later, have breakfast when I feel like it, read, eat to excess, play out on the street, chat or not, go to bed when I want. There's not a routine in sight. I love that. The structure of my days at home and at school can be oppressive. I know there are those who thrive on routine, but not me. I find it suffocating.

"I know what you mean about Highbrook," my nana confesses to me, "Your mam's done her best, but I always feel on edge. It's too grand for my taste. Don't tell her though, will you?"

"Never. What goes on at nana's house, stays at nana's house."

I wink at her, and she laughs, reaching to pat my hand playfully.

"You're such a good lad, Joshie."

My home life though was less easy breezy.

"You spoil that boy," my father said, "You need to give him chance to become a man."

Ready for work with his hair brushed back from his face, he adjusted his cufflinks and straightened his tie. I remembered the conversation with my nana.

I was sitting at the breakfast table, and he was cross you told me I could go outside to help Stanley before you'd finished.

"You're not here enough to know enough," you said dismissively.

I could understand why he would think you spoilt me because he only saw what he saw. He only saw what you wanted him to see.

Unbeknown to him you had lined up your own unique way of dealing with my 'behaviour' which suited you and didn't cause a scene with Crawford.

You locked me in the attic and left me alone for hours on end up there.

It was so much more distressing when you knew full well the terror the attic held for me.

I learned my lesson young.

Chapter 36

You have a terrible flaw.

This flaw stopped you from being the wife and mother everyone thought you were or even who you wanted to be. I can only describe it as the most horrifying mood swings. You simply had no control.

I missed out on the childhood I deserved because of it. The hysterical highs were as alarming as the disquieting lows and your mood could change fast. My nana called it 'turning on a sixpence.' It was the perfect description when I heard it, but she wasn't referring to you, she was referring to my grandfather. She didn't know about your traits then. Watching the constant swinging of the pendulum made me a nervous wreck. I've heard enough about my grandfather to think his own reign of terror may well have been passed down. Patterns often repeat themselves, or so I'm told.

I'm never free of the nagging sense of foreboding.

I have no way of pre-empting a mood and you don't have any consistency. I'm very careful to tiptoe around the eggshells but sometimes you're just looking for an excuse. You must release the devil. You need to. He will only go away when he's burnt himself out.

I carry the fear alone.

The isolation we live in isn't helping me and I miss my grandma, I miss Stanley. It dawns on me they had been my inadvertent protectors all those years.

You can behave normally, particularly when my father and Crawford are around. Normality can sometimes lull me into the briefest sense of security.

Sprawling on the rug in the parlour, I'm playing Solitaire, like Stanley showed me. It's Crawford's afternoon off, and you said you were going for a lie down, so I took the opportunity to relax a little.

I hear you coming down the stairs. Automatically sitting upright, my hands are still in perpetual motion with the cards—I've become quite the expert. The urgent strides you're making across the hallway means a knot appear because something is wrong, I sense it.

Glancing over my shoulder I see Stanley's pocket watch in your hand.

"What is this?" you ask. There is a quiet threatening edge to your voice.

I didn't tell you about his gift. Partly because I thought you would tell me to give it back but mainly because I wanted it to be our secret; something for only Stan and I to share. She must have been rummaging through my top drawer because I made sure it wasn't easy to find.

"He gave me it when he retired because he said it would make him happy and he didn't need to know the time in retirement."

I can tell my honest answer is falling on deaf ears. You're not interested in the truth because you're in one of your moods and you just want someone to take it out on. You've purposely been looking for a reason, more than likely because Crawford is out of the house.

"Liar, you took it didn't you. You stole it. I wondered why you were always so keen to visit him."

"It's the truth, mother, you can't ask him, I know but it is. I wanted to visit him because he was my friend."

I want to go outside. I don't want to be in her vicinity, so I head across the room to make my escape.

"No, you don't, my boy," you say.

I am too slow. Your tone has already risen to the next level but I've nowhere to turn now, I know the drill. Grabbing my arm, you spin me around, your face a shade of crimson.

"You're a deceitful little brat, I know that much. It's no wonder you bring out the worst in me. Your father's right, I've indulged you too much."

I try to pull my arm, but you grip tighter and managing to break free, means you fall backwards. I gasp, waiting with the delay of a stubbed toe for the pain to start. For the devil to rear his petrifying head.

I see him.

"I'll go out in the garden, please just let me go," I'm pleading now.

This time you have a hold of me by my elbow and fury is giving you the power of the strongest man. I know where I'm heading, and I don't want to go. I lash out with my other arm in a blind panic, and my nail scratches the tip of your chin. I can tell by your shocked expression you think I've deliberately hit you.

"I didn't do it on purpose. I panicked, I'm sorry, don't send me upstairs mother, please!"

I'm babbling and start to cry. Alarm is pounding through my heart. You haven't heard one word of my pleading. You've now arrived at your place of no return.

I trip and stumble backwards and fall against the sideboard in my hurry to make an escape. I bite my tongue so hard on impact I immediately feel the blood pooling into my mouth. The warmth slips down my throat. I begin to choke but you just don't care. You're pushing me roughly out of the room, across the hall and up the stairs. I'm making it easier for you by now. Fear has made me compliant.

I sob, the mix of phlegm and blood making me feel sick, or its fear having the same effect. You continue your barrage of abuse, your relentless pushing and shoving of me.

"If you'd done as you were told, there'd be no need for any of this. It's your own fault."

A droplet of spit lands next to the corner of my eyebrow as you hiss the words.

You unlock the door with your free hand and give me one last vicious shove over the threshold. I crash against the stairs, your strength in a temper insurmountable.

"Don't leave me up here again, mother. Please!"

The door slams.

As the key is turning, I'm frantically pulling the handle and yelling, "No mother, please, no."

There's no hope for me now. There will be no way out for me for hours.

I could have forgiven you anything else, but I just can't forgive you for that.

Chapter 37

I find the silence the most disturbing.

The silence of the attic at Highbrook is difficult to explain. It's like being in a coffin, buried deep in the ground. There's no other living sound. No voices, weather, birdsong, just stillness, but not the reassuring kind.

I know a pattern of cruel behaviour. I knew it before a professional explained it to me because it was my own pattern. First there is the build-up, next the cruelty, then the regret.

The regret part is what I think of the most. I've lived through the menacing threat of what is to come, or maybe the shock of it coming from nowhere, the horror of the act itself, but then I must contend with the guilt which engulfs you making you weep and plead for my forgiveness. I'm just so relieved the tirade is over for the time being nothing else matters. This is the truth of it.

You left me for hours, sometimes day turning to night if my father was working late. Crawford never came into the attic except to clean so it was a safe enough place to detain me until dinner. You were downstairs but I knew you weren't alone. The devil himself was cajoling you, justifying your actions. He deserves it, he needs it, he should be taught a lesson, it's for his own good. Your nasty little companion could stay a long time.

I worked out a coping mechanism for being up there alone amongst the silence.

I try to do it now. As I flick on the light, I climb the stairs, and go into the first room on the right, the one which has a guest bed. Yet we never have guests, never mind the kind who sleep over.

The door to the room with my father's tiny soldiers isn't open, but the soldier's eyes still watch me.

I always make a running jump to the bed to slink down as far as possible under the covers, pulling them up and over my head. The bedding smells foisty, even in summer because the room is always slightly damp. It feels cold and this is another reason I hate it, but this isn't why I get into bed. I get in because I feel safe under the covers. Cold and fear is a distressing combination.

I'm unable to make my way immediately to my safe place this time as I have blood all down me, all over my clothes so I go into the bathroom first to wash my hands and face and take off my shirt. In a daze, I watch the water turn red as it pours over my hands. I don't feel part of the situation, as if nothing even happened.

A noise startles me. The sound is becoming louder than the running tap, so I turn it off to hear. My father's voice is accompanying yours and your voices are increasing in volume. This means you're getting nearer.

With alarm I try to get to the door to lock it because for some reason I don't want my father to see me looking like this. I'm not sure if this is to protect you or if I'm avoiding the necessity to explain.

I'm too slow. The door is heading in my direction. I jump back out of the way and watch it bash against the wall and bounce off again, the sound echoing down the corridor. I take another step backwards into the room. My father stands in the doorway and stares. I see revulsion slowly creep over his face as he takes in the sight of me before him.

"What have you done?" he asks.

His gaze never leaves my face, but I know he isn't talking to me.

I flick my eyes to look at you and I can see you carefully choosing your next words, your face wan. I watch your throat moving up and down, swallowing.

"It's not as bad as it looks. I think he must have bitten his lip or his tongue or something. He stole Stanley's pocket watch, I tell you. It's hard for me here without his father, trying to deal with his behaviour, his moods. You've no idea."

I'm thinking about my behaviour and my moods. I don't have the luxury of being a moody, sulky adolescent.

My father's still looking at me. I notice the whiteness of his shirt, the top button undone, his tie hanging just below. He's still wearing his new charcoal suit.

"I heard it, or enough of it. I could hear you walking from the car, but I was too late to stop you."

Shame passes across your face. Your shoulders slumping, you lean against the wall. He knows ... finally he knows.

Tears hurtle down your cheeks. You've been caught in the act, found out. You are in disgrace.

My father walks towards me, his handsome face ashen. I try to move my head away, but his large hand comes out to gently cup my cheek and I can see the glassiness of his eyes. Tears spring from nowhere to my own.

"I'm sorry, son," he says, "I've failed you, I should have been here. Has this happened before?"

I open and close my mouth but can't find the right answer. This gives him the answer he already knew. He drops his head and sits down on the edge of the bath.

I glance at the doorway, but you're nowhere in sight. My stomach rolls and I run to the toilet to wretch. I bring up all the blood, tears and anguish as though cleansing my body of its backed-up turmoil. My father pats my back softly, squatting down beside me.

Worn out, I sit with my back against the bath. I watch as he gets up to fill a bowl with hot water and grab a flannel and towel. He takes off his suit jacket and hangs it over the doorknob. It falls off, he doesn't notice.

He sits himself down opposite me, cross-legged and wipes my hands. Then he moves to my face with the warm flannel. The act is so soothing, so calming. I can see his mind processing, his eyes telling me a story with each passing emotion.

"I haven't been fair to you Josh, forgive me. I was jealous of the way I thought your mother spoilt you. I've been leaving you to it for far too long."

He's talking as though I'm not here, using my childhood name. It warms me, settles me so my heartbeat slowly returns to normal.

"She's always had a temper. I admit I liked it a little at first. I found it exciting, almost thrilling but I never thought for one moment she would be losing her temper like this with you. I thought she idolised you and you could do no wrong. It drove me to distraction if I'm being completely honest."

I want to lessen his obvious guilt, to do anything to make him feel better.

"This is the worst. It's never been as bad as this, father, honestly. I've been sent up here, and she's been rough with me, but she didn't hit me, I fell against the dresser. She thinks I stole Stanley's watch, but he gave it to me, I promise. It's because she thought I hit her when I scratched her face pushing her hand away. I hate it up here.

I'm finding it difficult to talk, my tongue is sore, and a flap of skin is grazing my teeth as I speak. I fail to convince him.

"I promise, father, she hasn't."

A weak smile turns his mouth but he's still deep in concentration, intently wiping the blood meticulously from my face.

"There are many ways to be cruel to someone, Josh and I know you would never steal anything, least of all from Stanley. He told me he gave it to you when I checked he hadn't lost it. I noticed because I always admired the watch as he showed it to me after his mother gave him it for his birthday. Proud as punch he was with the engraving, so much love in such a simple message. Your mother knows you didn't steal it too, she wanted an excuse. I know how she can be. Things are going to be different around here, son from now on. I've been as cruel to you as your mother in my own way. I apologise for my self-absorbed behaviour. I've been off the hook for some time in bearing the brunt of her moods, but I see now why this is. What a blind, stupid idiot I've been."

I think back to their arguments when I was younger. They were in another part of the house so they thought nobody would hear, or that was their intention. They could get heated, and I remember thinking I would never want to get on the wrong side of my mother. I always try my best not to.

"I think you should stay with your nana for a while. Your mother needs help, and she will not argue with me over this. Even if she does, she won't win this time, believe me."

I watch his jaw set with determination.

My spirits lifting, my heart soars. Staying with my nana, now this is just music to my ears, though a pity about the circumstances. Will my father explain them to her? I hope not, I only want my nana to be happy.

"When I'm satisfied that we have things under control, you can move back home, and we'll be a proper family. I promise I'll be around much more, and we can start doing things together, just the two of us. Your mother's not an evil person, I just think she's not herself for many reasons. I'm not entirely blameless."

My stomach muscles relax a little. The future looks bright, and everything is going to be better for all of us. I can feel it.

My father stands and goes to the bath to turn on the taps. The water eventually comes steaming out and he adds some *Epsom* salts which I've never even noticed before.

"You can have a soak whilst I explain my plan to your mother."

He leaves and returns a moment later with a cricket pullover of his own which he must have found in one of the wardrobes.

"You need to get out of those clothes. I'll burn them; I don't want to see them again."

He forces a smile before he leaves the room. How out of place he looks; fabricated as ever in his pristine, white shirt and immaculate dark hair. His teeth shine brightly. There is only one, minute drop of my blood on his cuff, otherwise he is complete perfection.

"I don't want you to worry about a thing anymore, son. It's all going to work out, I promise. In the meantime, you and your nana can have fun together at her house. You'll both love it."

I smile back at him as he closes the door behind him.

Climbing into the bath I slip slowly down into the reassuring warmth of the water.

Chapter 38

I wake to the sound of raised voices. I must have drifted off to sleep. Oh no, please, not again.

The water has turned tepid. Immediately the fear kick-starts as I sit up and grab a towel. I climb out of the water and dry myself furiously, tugging my father's pullover on for it to fall to my knees. I put my ear to the door to hear more.

"It's not happening. No way in hell is he leaving here, not temporarily, not even for a day. You can forget it!" you shout.

"You need a break, and your mother will love having him. We can't ignore what's happening anymore, Frances. The decision is not yours to make any longer."

"How dare you," you spit, "How dare you leave me to it all these years and then sweep in like some poor excuse of a knight in shining armour to sort everything out!"

Your voices are getting fainter, telling me you're both making your way downstairs again. I must know what you're saying, so I open the door and risk sticking my head out of the bathroom door.

I catch a glimpse of my father, opening one of the doors to the terrace at the very end of the corridor, so I can't hear what you're saying. He closes it behind you and he's guiding you to a chair to sit down. He is always a gentleman, he told me every man should always be a gentleman. You won't sit down. I see the fury on your face as you swing around to face him. You push him, so he falls back but springs up with the agility of a much younger man.

I'm now out in the corridor, creeping forward to try and keep my view but side on to the wall to limit the chance of you seeing me. You're both too close to the edge but I can't shout out. My father reaches again for you, but you're too quick.

"You dare!" you yell, "You bloody dare try and come between me and my son!"

I hear the silence once more but his time the silence sickens me.

I know what the silence means. I know it's going to change our lives irrevocably in untold ways. I know that silence will haunt me to my very last breath.

You pushed him. I'm sure you pushed him.

My mouth drops, aghast and I find my voice.

"Father, no! Father, father!" I shout as I run down the corridor. I trip over my own feet but manage to somehow to keep running.

You turn, startled by what has just happened and by my sudden appearance. Instinct makes you block my way, some protective instinct which was always there but came too late. You start talking fast, jabbering.

"Joshua, it was an accident, he got too close to the edge and fell over the balustrade. Believe me, please believe me," you plead, trying, and failing to pull me into your embrace.

Is this the truth? I'm already unsure about what I saw.

For once I find the strength of mind and body to knock your arm away. I stand looking down at my poor, poor father. He's lying on the ground, his body twisted in such a way I know immediately that he's dead. His blinding light has already left him.

My saviour is gone, the one who was going to make it all better. He is gone.

I drop to the floor, and you drop with me, flinging your arms around my neck.

"It will be alright, it will be alright," you say, over and over.

You rock me back and forth, but I'm certain it won't be alright, not ever again.

We sit together like this for a while, my mind spiralling. I grow unaware of your embrace or even your presence. When I come back to reality, I squirm away from the nearness of you and remove your arms from around my neck. Rising from the floor I walk back through the glass doors as if in a trance.

The corridor is long, longer than I remember. It takes time to get to the bathroom. I take in the scene, my bloodstained clothes, the red water in the bowl, the last of the bubbles still in the cold bathwater and I'm overwhelmed. I slump to the floor sobbing with my back to the door. I don't want you to come in. I don't want you to come anywhere near me.

I must get out of Highbrook. I need to get out of this terrible house which has demons lurking in the walls. I take the long walk back to you, still in my father's damp pullover.

"I would like to go to my nana's house now," I say.

It's a polite demand. I don't know it or want it but, I have become the one with all the power.

You're standing still, staring down at my father. My voice shakes you from your stupor and your expression tells me you now realise the enormity of the situation. I have snapped your brain into action and awoken you to what you must do.

I trail behind you on the way to the bathroom and sit on the floor in the corridor, staring at the wall, listening to you clattering about. You're carefully cleaning away the evidence. Evidence of what I wonder. How I wish I could be sure.

You reappear eventually with my clothes in your hand, touching my hair as you walk past me and disappear downstairs. I shudder. I'm not sure if this is from the chilly temperature or the touch of your hand. My safe place beckons so I get into bed and pull the covers right over my head. My damp hair is unpleasant.

Disturbing images of my poor father are flashing in and out of my mind. My shivering becomes uncontrollable, but I cannot cry.

You are gone quite some time. I imagine you burning my clothes on the living room fire like father wanted to do, watching them go up in flames piece by piece.

I hear your footsteps in the bedroom. When you pull back the covers, you stare down at me, but I have no fear. My angry mother is nowhere in sight, and you've brought me some warm clothes to change into. By the time I've dressed and combed my hair I've become another person.

When I make my way downstairs, I want to go outside and be with my father for the very last time. As I go down the front steps of Highbrook I'm glad to watch you disappear in the car so my father and I can be alone. I force myself to look at my father's perfect features and carefully place his jacket over him, so he isn't cold. I wouldn't like him to be cold.

When you arrive back at the house you're accompanied by an ambulance, and you tell me to go in the front room by the fire, so I'll be warmer. The ambulance men express their condolences and ask if there is anyone who can look after me. They also inform you that due to the circumstances they must involve the police.

I'm sitting on the settee, staring straight ahead at the fire. You come in from time to time to poke it with the barley-twist black iron poker my granddad made. They will think you're making sure I'm warm enough, but I know you want to be sure all you are worried about is gone forever.

The policeman who doesn't have a uniform, talks with you for over an hour in the dining room around the table, whilst another policeman sits with me and tries to distract me by talking about whether I like football or rugby. The other policeman who looks far more serious, eventually joins us to ask me questions. I tell him I didn't see or hear anything because I was in the bath, my father had fallen from the balcony when I was in the bath. You took a chance, you didn't ask me to say this, I just want it all to go away. I want to go to my nana's.

You agree I should go and stay with my nana for a time so you can sort out the funeral arrangements. Other people from the police have arrived and are taking measurements and dusting walls. It takes them an age and all this time father is still lying there. Finally, a dark van arrives and two men in long dark coats come in. It reminds me of that scary story nana used to tell me under the covers … "There was a dark, dark house."

Shuddering, I am suddenly very lonely, and think of Stanley.

I feel the two police officers watching us as we say goodbye. You don't risk trying to draw me into your embrace, so instead you put your arm around me from the side and kiss my cheek. I stare straight ahead but this doesn't look odd as they know I'm in shock. You tell me you'll see me later and you love me. I nod and head out of the door, hearing it close behind me for the very last time.

As we drive down the driveway, Crawford appears, and she stands watching the scene with her mouth open. So much has changed in the few hours since she left. I wave and she waves back, her mouth still open.

The policemen kindly drop me at nana's house on their way back to the police station, wanting to help you out in your hour of need. They gently explain to my poor, bewildered nana, what happened to my father.

I watch her expression of disbelief. She wants to see you to make it all right again like mothers need to do. What most mothers need to do.

She rocks me in her arms, and it brings me comfort. She wants to stay, she wants to go, I know it, so I make the decision for her, telling her I'm going to bed. She studies my face and I try out a weak smile because I don't want her to worry.

There isn't any visible evidence to contradict your story, but nana must know more than she discloses because she never asks me why I don't want to see you. But she never says a bad word against you because we are all she has, and we are all she needs. Questions are far too much of a risk.

I live happily with my beloved nana for five years, even continuing at my same school. She visits you often.

"Your mam sends her love," she always says on return.

I always smile when she says it. This is a little game we play.

I see you briefly from a distance at my nana's funeral. You look lost, but I have no desire to speak to you because we have nothing to say. There is nothing we can say.

I've been told since it's rare to hate a person who is cruel to you. In my case this is true, as this would be far too simplistic. You are my mother. You treated me well in between each bout of cruelty and could often be a wonderful mother. The trouble was I never knew for certain one moment to the next which version of yourself you would serve up.

So, at least twice a year you make the journey to see me and my family. You no doubt want to convince me you have changed and want to make amends but I've no doubt the devil still resides within. I can't imagine otherwise, but I'm sure you are living with untold guilt and regret which may help to keep them at bay.

I have no secrets from my wife, and she knows everything there is to know about me and about you. She agrees if we happen to be in when we see you sitting on the railway banking at the end of the garden, we will go into the front room with our son and daughter, play games and wait it out. I saw you by chance one day and now I look out constantly to where you sit just out of view. Only I know you are there, but you will know I sense your presence as mightily as ever. You are calling me back home.

I don't hate you, but I think it essential for me and my family to keep you at bay.

I need to ensure the devil stays firmly in her rightful place:

Safely on the other side of my very own locked door.

William
Chapter 39

Of all the times for you to pick, I just never thought it would be then.

That trip was so special to us all and I could never have predicted what lay ahead, but of course, this was the whole point. Now I must find the strength to keep going, and busy myself each day looking for a way out of it all because there is Albert.

The police are understandably sceptical and initially appear to treat me with suspicion, but I take it on the chin. I don't have to be questioned at a police station and I'm thankful for small mercies. A young policeman and his colleague come to Highbrook, apologising for intruding at such a trying time.

"You say your wife was seeing a psychiatrist for depression, but you don't have a formal diagnosis?" he asks.

His older colleague is keeping a watchful eye on proceedings. They told me their names, but I forgot them instantly. They both study every twitch of my face intently, as though they have a murderer's handbook to refer to. I picture them thumbing through it back at the station to assess my innocence. I wonder if there is set criteria for a murderer, and if I meet it.

They questioned me first, then they talked to your mother, your father your brother, Frances, and Dr Haigh. I've been thinking of Dr Haigh of late because he knows things about you I don't. He gave evidence at the inquest as did I, Frances, and Daniel.

The police described their investigation and they read out every terrible word of your note while we sat and listened … and listened. It was galling and my only comfort was Albert was too young, and so spared the pain.

Dr Haigh was very convincing in describing your vulnerable mental state as he termed it, and the coroner recorded a verdict of suicide. It was at least an end to a painful chapter, if there ever could be such an end for you and me, Nell. I'd been warned that without a body, it could be an open verdict, but the coroner was satisfied all the evidence pointed to a clear suicide. Although unlawful, of course, there was no trial. Just the social stigma, though I didn't really give two hoots about what anyone else thought, I just wanted you back with me.

Finally, after several weeks, I started to hold my head up. I'm left to get on with my life but a life I don't want to live, one which is surely too painful to live.

I know I'm not coping very well. Trying to put on a brave face is draining. I have a real fear of the future. The torment takes me to breaking point in the months that follow.

But there is Albert.

"I can't do it, Frances, I can't keep going!"

I'm sobbing. I have never sobbed.

She holds me tightly and rocks me like a child. She tries hard to stitch my gaping wound together, all the time knowing nothing she says or does will be enough. I try to fathom a way forward, but it seems unimaginable. Even Frances can't help me see a way out of the dark.

I learn to live in the dark, like you did, Nell.

"I know something about the agony of loss," she tells me.

She genuinely thinks she does.

But I have a secret and one I can't bring myself to tell Frances because I'm ashamed.

I'm strong but I'm not made of stone. I sensed a shift in me before that night, something which wasn't quite right, something which didn't make sense. The doctor prescribed me a little something to help. I hadn't wanted to start down such a dangerous path, but I was buckling, and you needed me.

I looked at the ominous glass bottle for days and willed myself not to start taking the pills. I could try and do without them, but I knew I was floundering. I couldn't allow myself the luxury of a deep sleep just in case you needed me in the night. So, I decided to take only half a tablet each night, pulling them out from the bottom of my wash bag from inside a painkiller bottle. It took me a while to find the correct receptacle, the correct disguise and I thought it was perfect – if you came across the pills, you would think nothing of it.

That tiny pinhead of tablet was a lifesaver. It threw me a long overdue lifebuoy and an ability to cope, so I decided to continue taking them after the dread turned into reality. I took a whole tablet or even two if I could or I dared, making the pain on the right side of bearable.

Because there is Albert.

I have so many complex emotions. I'm so overwhelmed at you Nell for putting us through this, especially the toll on your poor mother. She aged overnight.

"I should have seen it. I'm her mother for crying out loud. If she couldn't talk to me then who could she talk to?"

An icy hand gripped my heart.

"Listen to me, Ann," I plead, grabbing her face between my palms, giving her no choice but to look into my eyes.

"Nell didn't want us to know how bad it was for her, so she was trying to navigate herself through the pain. How could we help her if a professional couldn't help her? She didn't know how to carry the responsibility of being a mother, it was as cut and dried as that. Please don't blame yourself."

I love this woman, she's a part of my Nell. We cling on tightly to each other, wracked with guilt but for different reasons. She makes a kind of life for herself eventually because she needs to be there for Daniel, like I do for Albert. She too is forever grateful she has Albert to keep her going through the daily grind. We all are.

I wish Daniel would just tell his parents his suffocating secret. Surely it doesn't matter anymore on the scale of things.

"There's no chance, Will," he tells me, "The boat has well and truly sailed on that discussion, for me if there was ever a boat. My poor mother, one child gone and the other lying to her for half his life. No, I think it more important than ever to keep my secret. She's had enough bombshells to deal with."

I bumped into Daniel in Horton a few months ago and he was with a girl who he introduced as Ava. Was this the love he talked about when we first met? They certainly looked in love, even without holding hands or touching in any way, it was easy to see by reading his expression. I hope he's found happiness.

As for Albert and Frances, I'm still their focus outside of each other. They don't miss you Nell, not in a way that would be fitting and proper. Their bond must have been painful to see, adding to your sense of inadequacy, your despair. Yes, I know you were living in your own head for a long time, but I also know you couldn't help it and I understand. I understand everything about you.

I chose many years ago to swallow down any thoughts I have on Frances's involvement. You were never going to be right for me in her eyes. She couldn't comprehend your way of viewing the world and your self-destructive personality traits. Frances views life in a rudimentary way. She can't grasp that I wouldn't have changed anything about you, that I loved you more for all your complexities.

I'm so thankful Albert never found out the true story. He was young enough to accept a new way of life. We talked about you from time to time, but I took his lead, and I could tell his memories were getting hazier by the day. I tried to be everything he needed, and Frances made up for any shortfall. We are his family.

He would never say he has an unhappy childhood, which most would consider strange under the circumstances.

We're sitting together in our cosy parlour, having battened down the hatches for the evening. We're on the brink of change and a change for all of us. He's laid on the settee and I'm sitting in my favourite chair by the fireside. I have drawn the curtains and the fire is blazing merrily away. I should have everything I want in this room.

But I don't.

"Will you be alright when I leave, papa?" he asks, "I know you didn't really want me to go to boarding school. If you feel lonely and you ever want to find a new friend, it might be just what you need. I think mama would want you to be happy."

I know she wants me to be happy.

His words take me unawares and I'm glad to be facing the fire. Such wisdom for one so young. I don't turn my head, but I can picture him laid there, so like you to look at. He has your quick smile. Oh, how I hope nothing happens to him to dampen that smile.

He's waiting expectantly for a response, but it won't be the one he wants to hear.

"I am happy, although I might not say it. I can't help that I'm a one-woman man. You should know by now surely, Bertie."

"Bear," he finishes with a chuckle.

"I'd feel better about going away if you weren't on your own."

"I'm never alone, I have Frances," I say. "Will you miss us when you go?"

"Mmm … I'll miss Frances," he teases.

I purse my lips, shaking my head.

"Seriously though, I think boarding will be the right thing for you. St Edmund's is too good an opportunity to miss."

"Well, there are plenty of holidays when I'll be home. If you want to live like a hermit in between, then so be it."

He's young. He doesn't understand I can never live my life with someone else. My wife, my son and Highbrook were all I ever wanted.

You are simply irreplaceable.

211

Chapter 40

Twilight is always my favourite time of day whatever the season. I suppose darkness would be too startling if it instantly followed the daylight, so one needs the steady wind down from day to night. It slows the pace, smelling and feeling different to the other hours.

Frances and I have just returned from taking Albert to St Edmunds. We left Highbrook early in the morning to get a head start, travelling in the same car and using mock joviality to mask the pensiveness we all had. I was nostalgic, remembering what Frances had said about being redundant.

We lingered more than he'd wanted after chatting with his new teachers and settling him into his dorm. There was no denying, life would be unrecognisable for both of us without him around every day. I sensed his growing impatience for us to leave, but he was hiding it well.

"I think you should head off now," he told us, laughing, "or I might just change my mind."

So, we left him to join his new friends for their first of their evening meals together.

"He's ready for his new life, Frances but you'll always have a special place in his heart, you know that. Regardless, the Christmas break will be upon us before we know it."

Smiling unconvincingly through tears, suddenly looking older, I could see it was cold comfort for her. He had always been with us at some point every single day up until now.

Back at Highbrook, we stand together and look up at our beautiful home which has given us both so much pleasure and so much pain. After all the happenings within those walls, I never regret moving here.

Crawford opens the door to us and takes our coats, the quiet mainstay of this house.

"Well, I think I'll climb into bed and have myself a good cry now, William," Frances says.

Her weak smile is unsuccessful in hiding the fact she means every word.

Looking up at me, she studies my face. I must look weary, older too.

"What are your plans tonight?" she asks.

"I have some drawings to work on, so I can get my teeth into those," I say.

She notices something in my expression she isn't happy with, I know it because her gaze lingers. She's no fool. I hold her gaze.

"Are you sure you're going to be alright? If you don't want to be on your own, we could have supper together, have a drink by the fire. You know, like the good old days."

They may be her good old days, but they aren't mine. That's unfair, they were at the time. They were very different from the life I had before.

"Perhaps we could do that tomorrow instead," I say.

She's trying to second-guess what's going on in my mind but I'm keeping my thoughts as still as I can manage. I would just like her to leave me alone.

"Sounds like a plan," she says.

I can still sense her watching me as I climb the stairs, but I don't turn around.

Inside our apartment, I lean against the door and look about. Years ago, Frances and I talked about what will happen with Highbrook after she dies. She's stipulated in her will that I should be the one to buy her apartment. She says she's spoken to Joshua about it, and he agrees as he has no intention of living here himself. He really must not like the house because he never visits Frances with his family, but I suppose Albert isn't the biggest fan either.

I give in to the urge to head up to the terrace. The key has been in its original position for years and I unlock the door to go upstairs, listening to the familiar creaks underfoot, the familiar sound of home which used to ground me.

Making my way down the corridor to the room at the end, I peer into the other rooms and see the toy soldiers in their glass case. I hope they will live there forever as they're in their rightful place as far as Frances and I are concerned. I can always picture Ben painting them as Frances has one or two framed photographs of him. I particularly like the one of them on their wedding day. They look happy; they were a beautiful, happy couple. I don't give enough thought to how she must miss him.

This is such a painful room to visit but I'm often compelled still to come here. I look at the scenery beyond from the windows, vistas I've seen a thousand times before. I think of it as a world within a world in this bedroom and not one I care to remember. But tonight, I can't help it.

The memory of that awful day I discovered you up here descends to haunt me. Were you going to end it all at that moment? I have replayed the scenario in my head too many times to mention. I don't think you would have done it because we were all in the garden that day and you wouldn't have wanted us to find you on the gravel. Or the thought may never have entered your broken mind.

I go through the glass doors then walk over to the edge of the terrace feeling the chill of the evening. I need to block out the day, compose myself but it's a struggle. I look far down below, taking a deep breath through my nose. Just one second of panic and all the pain will be gone for good… forever. This is what would have been running through your head.

I'm dizzy, unable to focus my eyes as tears burn them. I look up at the darkening sky, turning my neck this way and that to try and release the knots of tension which are always there. I picture Albert.

I must get out.

I spin around and make my way down the old servants' staircase. As I walk down the garden, the night is silent, the darkness a blank canvas for the stars.

I quicken my pace and crane to see if Frances is at the window. If she hears the car she'll come outside, and I just want to be alone. I can't take a chance as she might follow me, so with the driver door open I push the car until I'm well out of earshot. I'm thankful for the cover of darkness.

On the road I start the engine. Picking up speed as I twist and turn down the country roads, I'm lost in thought, ignoring the familiar sights as I drive.

I come to a stop and sit for a moment holding the steering wheel. As I stare through the windscreen into the emptiness of the night, I think I'm back to being Frances's whole world again. I don't want to have to sneak out every time, so she doesn't ask any questions.

It isn't a long journey, but this is one I could drive with my eyes closed. I step from the car to make my way up the path, stopping at the back door. I notice my hands are blue as I reach for the doorknob and they're shaking, but not from the chilly evening. The door's stuck so I press my shoulder hard against it to try and open it. I try again. It opens. I never got around to doing that job, amongst too many others.

The kitchen is in darkness. This is often the case when I go in and I hate it. Through the gloom I can see light in the tiny parlour as I enter, the warmth from the fire burning through the cold reality of my life.

My eyes settle straight upon you. You are sitting in your chair by the crackling flames. I look down into those warm brown eyes reflected by the candlelight. The gentlest of smiles plays about your lips and I know you can sense how hard it has been for me to leave Albert. You of all people know.

Your smile, your pure uncompromised smile is gone never to return. I've had to make peace with the sacrifice, but this is still enough for the blinding sun to come out for me again as it always did, as it always does.

You've been waiting as patiently as ever for me to be with you again. How lucky I am.

How lucky I am to still have my best friend, my world, my love.

My Nell.

Chapter 41

I confess I find it all so hard to reconcile.

Nell paid the ultimate price and I always try to remember.

But then I think of the question which haunts me still and will haunt me until the day I die: how can we live with ourselves allowing our son to believe he has lost his mother forever?

The twisted question gives me nightmares and makes my heart race. Sometimes I sit bolt upright in bed after waking in a cold sweat.

Nell had thought it all carefully through for the both of us and her disturbing prediction is now real. She was always convinced he would in the end, have a better life without her. The absolute truth is that Frances is his mother; a mother in the truest sense, the mother I wished I'd had.

My mother didn't know what a mother should be. Nell did, Nell knew. So how cruel is it that Frances is the one who lights our son's life, who makes him feel safe, who makes him laugh, is the one he runs to in times of need.

This is just too much for Nell, for any mother. She could not look at the truth any longer. I understand, I don't want her to.

Frances didn't intend to hurt Nell. Albert and Frances have no control over the way they feel about each other. Nobody has any control over their gut feelings.

It would be impossible for someone to understand how I can love Nell knowing what she did to our son, our boy, but I've slowly come to realise she hasn't done anything to Albert; she has made the ultimate sacrifice for him.

It's the bitterest pill. I want to believe he loved his mother, but the brutal truth is he didn't like being around her, or at least that version of her. I had to face the harsh reality that he's happier without her in his life.

The guilt Nell's mother had was the pain which nearly broke me but how could we turn back? I had no choice but to go along with the elaborate plans Nell had made. She handed me a fate accomplis.

This way Nell has been able to be near Albert and in the most bizarre of ways, still in touch with his life. This is a completely surreal existence but one I have now become accustomed to. One tends to do this when faced with no alternative.

It will be different now Albert has moved away, and we know he's still happy even if it isn't living with us. Many families live happily apart and surely happiness is what every parent wants for their child. Especially Nell.

She is a shell. I can't deny it, though I try to. She needed to continue with professional help but of course it was impossible. She was silent with guilt for too long, guilt for what she had done to me, of handing me this jail sentence. But jail is somewhere you don't want to be. No, she isn't the Nell of old, but she's still my Nell and at least I have her. I will always thank God for that.

She wrote a second letter just for me. That long, long letter was waiting for me on my side of the bed, under the cover on top of my pillow. It was the last thing she did at Highbrook. She had given the plan so much thought and covered everything, not shying away from the truth.

The reality is hard, harder than she could have imagined.

I picture her writing the letter. I feel the hope she had when writing it that she had a way out. I thought she was in the bath, but she couldn't have been because the paper it was written on was pristine. I wonder often if it was the original draft or if she'd done many before and burned them.

That letter. It was my heaven, yet also my hell in revealing my Nell was alive. How unbridled my euphoria was, but it left quickly. A web of lies had begun spinning, spinning around us both, binding us together in a cruel deceit which we must hide at all costs now for good.

What had she done?

I pleaded with her it was not too late, we could explain it was a mistake, and she was unwell. Everything could go back to normal.

Then she told me what I knew already. She said if I made her do that, she really would take her own life. She told me she could not look into her child's eyes and see what she saw any longer.

She had beaten me.

Because I know what she saw—I saw it too.

She sat there, freezing, and terrified, unable to talk to me or let me hold her for days. I had to try and figure out the best course of action. Except there wasn't one.

I couldn't possibly be with her all the time, of course, she knew this. I had to wait for the fake search to finally be over, the possibility of newspapers reporting a fake death. Worse still, I had to wait for the fake funeral, and they found no body. How could they?

The only piece I could find was a brief paragraph in the *North Yorkshire Star*, but that was all. I looked; I looked very carefully but one small paragraph was all her life amounted to. People must throw themselves in the sea regularly, it must happen so often it becomes unnewsworthy. Her family were relieved, not wanting the intrusion, but I was on full alert, certain we would have to come clean. Fortunately, the few people we knew were too concerned about Albert and me to think about anything else.

I spent a long time living in fear she really would end it all because the new reality was too grotesque. I was certain someone would find us out at any moment.

As for Nell's plan, I followed it verbatim, paying obsessive attention to her every detail. I read the words over and over, day after day for weeks on end until I knew them parrot-fashion. It was a focus, and I had the consolation of hearing her say the words to me to keep me going when we were apart. I drove Albert past her cottage most days on the way to and from school, the park, the shops, his grandparents, anywhere I could think of so she could see but nobody could see her. She could wait patiently for a glimpse because this was her solace, her enchanted solace. She knew it was impossible for me to be there every day, but I call in most days and I'm agitated within if I can't. I feel her waiting but I've learned to live with it.

She no longer has the urge to clean or anything else, just to hear me talk about the tiny details of our lives. This is what she lives for. She lives for me.

Sad as I am Albert has left home, life will be easier. I have plans for us now, huge plans. I want to make her well and now I will have the opportunity. This has kept me going throughout my despair. What else would I want to do?

All in good time, the here and now is what matters.

She has stood up to greet me and I reach out to hold her, longing for the feel of her tiny, bird-like body close to mine and press her head into my chest. I breathe in her evocative scent and, closing my eyes, allow the nearness of her to wash over me. How can another person make you a whole person?

If only life could have stayed that way forever, living the moment on endless repeat. If only I could have kept my eyes tightly closed and never opened them again because when I do, I want to clamp them shut instantly but I'm too late.

My stomach churning, I squint past Nell's shoulder, unable to see properly what I'm looking at but sensing that I don't want to know. My eyes grow wider with fear, fear in its purest form, terror and I tense in her arms, trying frantically not to reveal my alarm.

I've been careless, reckless. I have been stupid.

In the shadow-light of the candle, I can see someone watching us through the mottled panes in the window. Our worst fears surely are now becoming a reality after all these years.

The look of horror on their faces is ghastly from the distortion of the filthy glass. I start to sweat, my body shaking and the piercing, dazing, whistling adrenaline in my ears is overriding even the sound of Nell's breathing.

The faces disappear momentarily but now I hear them trying the door and I realise I should have locked it. It sticks. This should have been my opportunity to try and hide Nell, but my legs are clamped and think of it too late.

Now they are stepping into our world. They are an intruder in our world, and I want them to step back over the threshold, to step back in time and leave us alone.

They hold the door in their hand and stand looking at me.

"What on earth is going on, William?"

They have found out our terrible lie, and now it will tear us apart, make our families hate us.

Our boy's expression of incredulity when he finds out flashes in my mind as it has too many times before in my waking hours and in my hazy, pill-fuelled nightmares.

Nell shifts in my arms and I pull her tighter into my chest, to protect her. This isn't her fault because she couldn't help it. She's unwell, we couldn't help it. We did it for Albert, for our son to be happy. I am desperate to convince them, make them see sense. I need them to keep quiet, keep it to themselves for his sake, not for ours.

"I'm sorry," I say. I know it's not enough, but my thoughts are locked, and I don't have the key.

They stand staring at me ashen faced, questions pouring out of their eyes, but they do not speak. I don't think they have any idea what to say.

They close the door behind them and walk the few steps through the kitchen towards us.

"Sit down," they eventually say, pointing to the settee by the fire, the one Nell and I sat on all those moons ago on that game-changing night. We still share it now.

My arms drop in defeat. We are well and truly snared, and my main concern now shifts to limiting the fall out. I can try and convince them to never speak of it to another living person. I don't know if I will be able to.

Nell has realised what is happening to us. She reads my thoughts and the anguish on her poor face is surely now reflecting my own. I pull her gently by the hand to sit down and let me face the music.

Her cold hand tightens around mine seeking reassurance.

"It's okay darling," I whisper, wrapping my fingers around hers.

"Can you explain what is going on, William?"

I don't know how to begin. I sit and study their faces for the longest time. Their gaze never leaves mine. Their expressions exclaim their shock and confusion.

I cannot speak. I glance at Nell's seat next to mine and stare, a sudden emptiness and aloneness enveloping me. It's starting to scare me. The room is suddenly colder, darker. It begins spinning, spinning, spinning, whipping up speed around and around me like a hideous carnival ride.

I gaze back into their eyes, still fixed on my own, my lack of focus smudging the edges of their faces. Their faces disfigured, they're unrecognisable.

A silent scream is building, the stark realisation punching me mercilessly between the eyes.

Nell is no more. Nell is no more. My Nell is no more…

I feel the comforting grip of Nell's fingers slipping through my own as I plunge my way headlong to the floor.

Frances
Chapter 42

We simply had to know.

You were managing of course but managing too well. Albert was leaving home and you were fine about it, fine and dandy. Did you think we were born yesterday, William?

I had an awful worry you were thinking about joining her that night. The look in your eyes told me something was terribly wrong, and I was anxious you'd been planning a way to reunite with Nell.

Your mother and I had plenty of discussions about life for you after Albert left Highbrook and it didn't sit well. I had installed a telephone and when Sylvia followed suit, we took to ringing each other every evening. After we returned from dropping Albert, I was expressing my concerns to your mother, when I noticed you pushing the car down the drive. If I hadn't been sitting down by the window, I might easily have missed you and I was immediately troubled by the ominous sight. You clearly had a plan and you'd wasted no time in setting the wheels in motion.

"Sylvia, I'm very concerned about William," I interrupted her telling me we really should visit more often, "He appears to be sneaking out of the house, but I haven't a clue where he might be going."

There's a long pause during which I'd already made up my mind to follow you, even though you had a head start.

"The cottage! What about the cottage?"

I hadn't thought about Nell's cottage in so long. I assumed it was out of the picture, but it made sense. Where else would you head to be truly on your own?

I flew out of the house, not even telling Crawford I was leaving, and started the car, cursing that picking your mother up meant a slight detour. Almost running down the lane in our desperation to be with you, we had no idea what we would be walking into. Surely you wouldn't leave Albert, I thought. I wished for a moment you couldn't bring yourself to leave me.

The memories came flooding back when I walked up the path. Sylvia was right, you had parked your car at the front of the gate, but the still darkness of the house was unsettling. I wanted to get inside, needed to get inside but we didn't want to risk startling you and not finding out the truth. I gestured to your mother with my hand for us to go around the back of the cottage.

I'm still unsure exactly what we discovered. What we witnessed peering into the blackness of that room was like a scene from one of those dreadful gothic horror books Ben loved so much.

You were sitting on the sofa, and seemed as if you were talking, and you were smiling. In profile you were smiling that old William smile of yours which had lit up my life like a sunbeam. But when you spotted us at the window your expression became like a wounded, cornered animal. The vivid contrast was disturbing.

Once inside the situation worsened. You were unreceptive and we were both at a loss about the world we'd walked into. Then when you crumpled to the floor, the look of pain and terror on your face was accompanied by something else. Desolation, I think would describe it best and I wondered then if you'd finally realised Albert, your reason for living, had left. We picked you up and tried to calm you, but you were clearly in distress, apologising and not making one iota of sense.

We had no idea how to tackle the situation. The cold, damp room, so different from the last time I'd been there, made me shudder.

You wouldn't leave the cottage, and knowing something positively dreadful had occurred, I eventually left your mother in charge—this was my first mistake—and drove off into the night in search of Dr Ratcliffe.

A long few hours later the doctor admitted you to a private clinic in Leeds for assessment.

You were in so much pain William, we could see it, but we had no power to ease it.

We are not the masters of your universe.

*

The sanctuary of Highbrook is no more.

The sense of home has disappeared and I'm not sure how it can be restored.

I haven't been able to see you since that night. I'm the one who can talk to you, give you the comfort you need if anyone can, but I'm not allowed near you. I think again for the umpteenth time how life can take an about turn overnight.

Albert didn't come home for October half-term because he was invited skiing with a friend and his family. He thought I already knew from his letter. It's Oscar this and Oscar that nowadays.

"What about skis, what about salopettes, jackets?" I ask Albert when he telephones from school, but this is all in hand.

Who has it in hand I wonder.

He tells me he's enjoying school and he doesn't want me to worry, but he only has me to worry about him.

I miss him like an ache, but at least it allows me time to get life at Highbrook back on track for his return at Christmas.

The days are stretching ahead like an empty road again. Where on earth is your mother? Albert and I couldn't be rid of her once upon a time. If I didn't know better, I'd think she was avoiding me, and I've given up calling the house because she's never at home. She's keeping me at arm's length, and it diminishes me.

Finally, she pays me a visit, and I'm unable to conceal my delight in seeing her after so long when Crawford announces her arrival. But by then, I would have been delighted to see anyone.

"How lovely to see you, Sylvia," I say, inclining my head towards her usual chair by the fire, then asking Crawford to provide refreshments.

I notice she doesn't look her immaculate self; nearly, but not quite I would say.

"I've been so worried about you both," I tell her, "I tried to get hold of you in the hope of being able to visit William."

"I know, and I'm so terribly sorry, Frances, "The situation is dire, they're struggling to get to the bottom of it," she explains, her taut face expressing her anxiety.

So, your mother is your only visitor. After all the things you've both said about each other in this house, I find it incomprehensible. I have a twinge of something; I am uncomfortable.

"Have you any idea yet about what has been going on? I'm obviously keen to resolve the situation before Albert comes home for the Christmas break," I tell her.

"That's what I came to discuss, Frances. I can't imagine a resolution will be reached by then, there's so much still up in the air and they haven't made anywhere near enough progress. I've told Albert his father has to come to stay to look after me for a while because I'm unwell. It was all I could think to do under the circumstances. I've been writing to him on his father's behalf, almost acting like a little go-between. I've even written the same to St Edmond's."

She offers me a conspiratorial half-smile.

Well really, the Hudson's have become nice and cosy. What about me, did anyone think to have a discussion with me before they sent the letters? How very presumptuous of you, Sylvia.

My mind goes to Albert. She's right, he needs to be shielded from the predicament we find ourselves in. At least I will be able to have him all to myself for a whole month. Life has suddenly taken a welcome turn for the better.

"William is in a terrible state," she continues, "The limited conversation we've had, well they're not really

226

conversations at all, just fragments which don't really add up, but they all seem to be focused on Nell and the early days before Albert. It's all so distressing.

A thought occurs to me now.

"What about the business?"

"Harry is holding the fort for the time being. I never heard William talk about him much, if at all to be honest, but he's been quite concerned for his welfare. At first, I thought it was concern for the business, but I genuinely don't think this is the case any longer.

Harry? A name from the past I'd almost forgotten about. William did say they were like chalk and cheese but that was about the sum of it.

"Well, we can't let it go on indefinitely," I say, "We need to have a plan for the New Year."

"I know, I'm speaking to the doctors again next week."

"He just needs to talk to someone," I say to press the matter.

"He does have someone, he has me, but I doubt this will be for some time. Often things need time as we know, Frances."

As she stares into the fire her mind is far away, with you. You're both in cahoots, I just know it.

"I'm struggling to comprehend how he can leave Albert with me at Christmas time and not arrange to join us for a little while at least, even just the day itself. This isn't like him."

She lets out the barest hint of a sigh as though she's irritable with me.

"I really can't stress enough that he's really not himself. I don't think he cares its Christmas, and I don't think he even realises it's just around the corner. Whatever happened has affected him very deeply, and I'm not one for theatrics Frances as you know, but the words breakdown and delusion have been mentioned."

Her hands flutter to her neck and her expression is one of disbelief that any son of hers would be in such a situation.

"All I ask is you keep in the picture. I've been losing my mind sitting here," I say, somewhat sullenly.

"Of course, I'm sorry," she concedes, "I've thought a great deal about you lately and how good you've been to William and Albert, but also to me. I've decided to do what you would do, what I should have done a long time ago, and make him my priority. I've been lacking in this area as you know and I'm grateful to you for unwittingly showing me the error of my ways."

She smiles across at me with misted eyes.

Her priority? Her priority! I think it might be a little late for that. He might not have become besotted with some broken little doll who wore her heart on her sleeve if it hadn't been so new, so exciting when someone actually showed some raw love and affection. Well, someone other than me.

Your mother's the last person you'd talk to, I know that much. I just need to get you to start talking to me and the floodgates will open, I'm sure of it. I can pull the right strings, so you allow me access to your thoughts, your mind, I've always been able to do it. I just need a visit, that's all I need, but I can't make it happen naturally this time. I'll just have to bide my time.

Oh, William, I just want you to come home.

I pull the cord for Crawford as Sylvia stands up to leave, promising she'll ring me regularly over the Christmas break. I have no alternative but to believe her, I can't rock the boat. But I'm now as delighted to watch her leave as I was to see her arrive.

By the Saturday before Christmas, I've been waiting ten whole days after he broke up for the holidays for Albert to put in an appearance. I know where he is because Sylvia rang two weeks ago with his revised itinerary.

"I've had a letter from Oscar's father. They're having a Christmas party and then they've said they're going to their lodge in the Lake District for a few days. He hoped Albert could join them. Oscar's father will go with them in the car to return home the Saturday before Christmas if this is acceptable, Frances? I'm sorry, the trip has been dropped on me a little too, but he so wants to go."

"Of course," I say flatly, "I hope he has a pleasant time."

I wait for her to hang up and then slam the telephone back down in its cradle, startling Crawford so much she drops and smashes the plate she's clearing from the side table.

Chapter 43

What to do now?

I watch the yule log on the fire. I watch as the flames lick the sides, a thought appearing suddenly, a dangerous one which knocks me sideways with surprise for a second or two. I must wait a day though until Crawford's afternoon off, and this is precisely what I do.

It's a long time since I've been upstairs alone, a very long time.

I still have my keys from the pre-drama days in the top drawer of the dresser, and I've been told in no uncertain terms that I'm to be side-lined for the time being. No chance of interruption, just me and the four walls to explore this afternoon and explore I must. For the sake of you and your state of mind, I simply must.

Taking the keys from the drawer I sit down at the dining table, staring at them. I shouldn't have them by rights, I'm no longer the owner of upstairs, not even the landlady, but nobody asked for them, and I never offered them.

I go upstairs and put the key in the door. I hesitate then drop my head back. For you, William, I remind myself as I turn the key.

My coat doesn't offer much protection from the cold as I cross the boundary into your territory. It's the damp miserable kind of cold which slowly chills one's bones.

A slightly heady sense of purpose flows through me now though. I've missed it. I consider myself to be a detective on a mission to seek the truth although I can't imagine what the truth could be. If I did find it, would I be able to cope with it? I recall how I played detective once before.

The rooms have the sour smell of neglect.

I sit on the chair by the front room window, gazing out at the bleak scene of the winter gardens. Resting my head on the chilliness of the chair back, I realise I've been thinking all this time you would be home to share Christmas with us, that you would at least take a break from your decline. How ignorant of me to think a person would be able do that.

I don't like being upstairs on my own. It makes me think about Ben and the day of his accident. Staring at the door to the attic stairs, I think of the terrace, unable to prevent myself replaying the moment he left us forever. I've never stepped foot on it since. My throat tightens. It was an accident, a simple step backwards and perhaps a lean in the wrong trajectory. One simple step backwards in the madness of the moment.

I will keep trying as long as I have breath in my body to convince Joshua. People change, mellow with age and experience, and one day I know he'll be unable to resist heading down his garden to have a discussion with me. I'm his mother and one day he'll relent and listen to what he knows I'm so desperate to tell him. I know him too well. I'm his mother.

Pulling my mind from the mire, I remember my mission. Heaving a breath of the stale atmosphere, I cast my eyes around the room, considering the best place to start the search.

From one corner of the kitchen, I steadily check each drawer and cupboard for 'evidence.' I'm in no rush, nobody is waiting for me downstairs to have tea, or sit down to play a game of chess. There's nobody even to have a chat with about our day. I told Crawford not to rush back as I was going to William's mothers. She will take advantage of it, so I have all the time in the world to explore the apartment, inch by inch.

So much of Nell is still here. Everywhere I search I find her. She's haunting me from every document, photograph, book. In the bathroom a small drawer is dedicated to her shampoos and other paraphernalia, all meticulously ordered. It looks peculiar. I draw a blank in every room so there's only one place left.

I hesitate at your bedroom door. This is surely too personal a space for even me in my frame of mind to consider entering. Your private world lies just over the threshold.

However, I realise if there are clues anywhere, the likeliest place would be your bedroom, away from Albert and prying eyes. Turning the handle, I push the door and peer around the barrier from communal to sacrosanct.

By now darkness has descended and I still have upstairs to search. I light another candle and carry it with me into your room. It's a woman's room, I suspect untouched since Nell ... died. My suspicions are confirmed when I open the wardrobe next to the window.

I smell her.

Her scent clings to every item of clothing. It clings to the shoes and the handbags, and I think it a beautiful smell, a pleasant break from the smell of the rest of the apartment.

I stumble backwards to sit on the bed, the scent making me overcome with cloying memories. Not good memories. Not the comforting kind you will have. I imagine you enjoying her smell, finding solace from it each night. I imagine you putting your nose to her clothes like I want to do now so badly.

A tear drops and watch it fall onto my lap. Then another and another until a loud wail escapes me. The guilt distorts my throat so I'm now struggling for breath. I lie back on the silky flowers of the bedcover and take great gulps of air as though fighting for my life in some melodrama.

I stare so long at the ceiling the candle burns out.

I'm wrung out, weak because I've had so much to contend with recently. I want to go back downstairs but I have a compulsion to finish my search of this room, so I never need to enter it again.

With the moonlight as my only guide, I find another candle and place it on top of the bookcase. You have meticulously lined the books, the size and shape of each one a carefully considered placement. You like order, structure.

My eyes meander the rows until they rest on the final book on the very bottom right of the rectangle. My mind is already heading to the next place to hunt in this room, the bedside table, but it swiftly whips back to the book when I spot it. Tilted slightly, I scan the book's equivalent on the row above and then go higher to the top. They're all perfectly aligned. I'm thankful then for the luxury of time to allow my search to be so thorough. I note the title, *Little Sunbeams*, Albert's favourite for a time. It makes sense to me now why it should be out of alignment.

I pluck it from the shelf and run my hand over the front cover. I've seen the artist's interpretation of the barefoot boy and girl making sandcastles on the beach many times over the years, and I picture you taking it from the shelf to relive the memory of reading it to Albert. This is a room crammed full of memories, far more so than the main house.

Flipping through the pages of the book, I spot something between the back cover and the very last page. I recognise the writing immediately and this alone makes me catch my breath.

It's a letter. A very thick letter by the look of it.

I hesitate. Should I read it? A letter is like a diary, it's intended for the owner's eyes only. As I wipe a tear, I know the answer to the question already.

I must settle myself to read it. I leave the bedroom and walk with the candle to the settee of the parlour, the one which overlooks the moors but it's too dark to have their comfort tonight. I feel sick with adrenaline and something else. Fear, I conclude. I'm going to unlock Pandora's Box in the next few moments, I just know it.

I smooth my skirts, and place a blanket over my knees, then carefully fold out the well-thumbed pages of the letter. A letter from Nell to you.

"My Will," it begins.

Less profound an opener than I expected. I expected a "My Darling," or a "To my Love," at least.

I breathe deeply twice before going on.

"Today I know I will have taken you to hell.

I have no excuse for it and this guilt is added to the sea of it that I try to keep my head above every day. I can't do it any longer, not even for you. I can't save us now, but I can save Albert and I must, for you and for him."

The next part makes me sit up and forward in my seat, dropping the letter to the floor as though it's burning my fingers.

This is sick, this is exactly what it is. Pages and pages of twisted sickness staring up at me written by a twisted, sick woman. On and on it goes about me being Albert's true mother, about how he doesn't love her which is worse than him hating her. How he would be happier without her.

All this is bad enough without the next words which are just too dreadful to even comprehend. I read page after page of a detailed plan to allow them to lead a life together without her blighting their son's life. The words swim after a while so I can't digest them. I don't want to digest them.

So, that's what's going on. You've been living the life she carefully mapped out for you. But you've been living it all with one significant difference. You're doing it with a ghost. A ghost which does not exist except in your poor, broken mind.

I now know one thing for certain and it makes me wail and shake to my very core; my life as I knew it has gone forever. I've lost you for good because you will never come back to me or to Highbrook. Even if they make you well, even if you don't end your own life, you will live in that cottage until the end of time now you realise Nell has truly left you, never to return.

Her plan went awry. She may have intended to try and live that incomprehensible life with you, but she couldn't in the end.

*

I don't often think of that Christmas. Like losing Ben, I push it far away, to the back of my mind, so I don't send myself to stark staring madness.

You were all ready to go on your trip to the coast whilst I was thinking about being without Albert for three days. I should have been looking forward to time on my own, but this never sits with me.

Nell was still seeing the psychiatrist but if I think back, she was behaving stranger than ever, if this was possible. You were concerned you told me, but thankfully the sessions were due to restart in only one week.

I embraced you then Albert before you got in the car. Nell was dragging behind, and I watched her intently for once as she walked towards me. She was thin and pale, a waiflike pathetic figure as she approached. We played the game for you boys and kissed each other on the cheek. It was a well-practiced ritual which we barely noticed any longer. At least I didn't.

She startled me when afterwards she looked directly into my eyes. That hadn't happened since the first time we'd met, and I held my breath waiting to see what would happen next. I noticed the oddest smile pass her lips as she wrapped her arms fleetingly around me. It was awkward and uncomfortable as she held me in her arms, and I almost squirmed away.

She got in the car and my usual cheery wave followed you all until you were out of sight.

The interaction shook me, disturbed even.

Something was looming.

Chapter 44

My day didn't improve.

Crawford had always gone home on Christmas night for three days even before you moved in. She didn't see her family very often, so it was almost seen as an additional little Christmas box.

I planned to use the time to start my new books but as it happens, I didn't read a single page.

Instead, I spent the day trying to stop my thoughts careering from a cliff. What was on the horizon? What did that last encounter with Nell mean? Am I just bored and restless, so reading too much into the situation?

We were all separated for the next two days, there was nothing I could do about it except wait it out, I decided by the time I went to bed. You would be with her every waking hour, so I couldn't understand why I was unable to shake the sense of foreboding.

I couldn't sleep and I gave up trying in the early hours. Then at precisely eighteen minutes past four I sat bolt upright and switched on the bedside lamp.

I thought about William being on watch every waking hour. So, if she had a plan, she would need to execute it at night.

Was I already too late to pre-empt a catastrophe of some description?

Time was of the essence, so I grabbed my robe and hurried down the corridor to take the keys to your apartment from the dresser. As I climbed the stairs, I knew I was right to follow my instinct as it had never let me down before. Rushing from room to room I was on the hunt for something unknown. But unlike today, after opening the first drawer I closed it again, knowing it was all a waste of time. Nell was many things, but she wasn't stupid.

Sighing, I lifted the kitchen bin lid and peered inside. It was empty aside from a homemaking magazine staring up at me from the blackness of an empty bin. The sight of it somehow unsettled me. Why would you think to place a magazine in a newly emptied bin when you were rushing to leave for a holiday and your family was waiting in the car? I wasn't sure what it meant but I knew that magazine and the peculiar embrace had hidden meaning.

By teatime I'd worked myself into a state, unsure how to proceed. I couldn't burst into the guesthouse on some whim, I had to be much more astute than that. I asked myself what a person of unsound mind would do in the middle of the night. That's it, I thought foolishly now, she was going to run away, I knew it. She was going to run away, and she was going to take Albert with her.

This was the seed which grew into a tangled forest in a few short hours. I knew she'd given me a farewell embrace, I felt it. If for any reason I was wrong, so be it. I had nothing to lose and everything to save.

It was windy and bitterly cold that day and the drive to the coast was well over an hour. Nothing to lose, everything to save I reminded myself. What else had I planned on my evening schedule?

As I filled a vacuum flask, thoughts of you and Albert hounded me. Of course, I was doing the right thing because I was your protector. You always needed my protection.

I hauled a spare blanket from the wardrobe not wanting anyone to find me dead in the morning from hyperthermia. After cutting a great slab of Christmas cake and cheese to take along, the last thing I did was grab a book. This completed the tools I needed for my expedition.

My body itching with adrenaline, I tried to drive slowly and carefully but failed on occasion. I spoke to myself to try and calm the manic sensation so I would arrive in one piece.

It was slightly later than I wanted, but just before nine o'clock I found a spot at the end of the cobbled street of the guesthouse. I joined the end of the other parked cars by the deserted pier. I had a clear view of the street and if a taxi were to be part of the plan, here was the only place it could stop.

I turned the lights off and huddled under the blanket, unable to stop my whole body from shaking. Why did I even entertain the idea of refreshments and a ludicrous book? I could have a long wait ahead until first light, but I knew it would be impossible to indulge myself with any of them.

A group of men passed the car, but I was relieved to discover I was invisible in the darkness. With my mind in turmoil the time passed quicker than expected, surprised then when I saw it was two o'clock.

When the church clock struck the hour, I started to think I was overreacting. The rhythmic sound of the thunderous waves and the rain on the roof had soothed me, brought me to my senses. Nell would never leave you, let alone take Albert away from you. Spending time alone always sent me a little mad.

My eyes getting heavy, the sound of boots on cobbles threw me into full consciousness. It was loud as it passed the rear of my car and I threw my arms out of the blanket, to sit up on full alert.

It was her.

She was a blur but there was no mistaking it was her by the silhouette of her hair. But she was alone.

By the time I'd processed the scene and jumped from the car she was already at the end of the pier. I stopped dead when I saw her shawl fly from her shoulder into the stormy night.

She was perilously close to the edge, but I didn't think about startling her in that second. I didn't think about anything at all surprisingly other than stopping her from jumping into the depths of the freezing sea.

I did the thing I now know you should never do, and I knew it then if I'd had time to think about it. I called out her name at the top of my voice.

Running full pelt towards her, skirts lifted high above my ankles, I paid no heed to the treacherous wet planks of wood beneath me.

Pure horror is the only way I could describe the look on her face as she turned. As I tried to reach her, she did exactly what I was trying desperately to avoid at all costs. She took a faltering step back in shock and surprise and then disappeared into the black void beyond. There was no dramatic confrontation, no time for explanations, she was just simply…gone.

Desperate, I ran to the end of the pier calling her name, but the wind swallowed the sound, and she was nowhere to be seen. My eyes scanned the water for a sighting, but as I know now, it was to be in vain.

I stood with the rain and wind lashing my face, wondering what to do next. Should I run to get you, should I run to a police station? Both would be best and without delay I thought.

Then, running back down the pier I thought about it some more.

She was gone. She was gone from our lives. I thought she had planned to run away with Albert but oh, how wrong I was. I thought of Ben's accident and the inquest. The police would pick over the bones of my past and think they were putting two and two together. There were no witnesses as far as they were concerned then, and there are no witnesses now. They would be wrong on both counts but who would believe I was not involved in a second accident, a second coincidence.

What if Joshua read about it and came forward? Now I needed to protect myself, for your sake, but also for Alberts.

My stomach churning, my body lacking basic coordination from fear, I knew there was only one possibility open to me.

I had to get home. I had to get home immediately.

Chapter 45

Four years have passed since that fateful night and here I am at Christmas time again. This time I'm waiting for the arrival of his lordship.

I've had the tree delivered and lined up the baubles so we can both reminisce over the fun we had making them. I woke early to ensure everything was perfect with Crawford and now I'm giddy as a schoolgirl. It's been too long since September.

I'm watching from the window as the car approaches early in the afternoon. Albert clatters out of the car when the chauffer opens the door. A chauffer, now here's a sight to stir memories of another time.

Albert and Oscar are chatting animatedly and his father, tall and moustachioed, follows them to the steps, cane swinging in hand. I resume my place by the fireside. Three months is a long time in a boy's life. He looks different, grown.

I think it might snow by the look of the heavy sky. What a wonderful Christmas homecoming snow would be.

"Thank you but we must make tracks," the father says in response to Crawford's offer of taking his coat.

They appear one by one around the door of the parlour, ruddy faced from the cold.

"Hello, Frances," Albert says, kissing my cheek briefly then stepping aside as though he saw me only yesterday, "This is Oscar, and this is his father, Mr Broughton."

He speaks with familiarity, with confidence.

"Jonathan, please," his father says, accepting my extended hand.

Oscar steps forward and I take his hand. His greased fair hair doesn't suit his round face but he's smiling broadly. His suit looks as though it's cut from the same fabric as his father's. Penny-pinching is how the rich get richer.

I offer our visitors tea to be polite though I know already they are keen to be on their way.

Jonathan tells me they must prepare for the festivities, but another time they would love to revisit our stunning home and meet Albert's father, if this would be acceptable.

"You have a fine boy, Mrs Cundall," he says, smiling affectionately at Albert who has his hand on my chair back.

I look up at my boy and glow with pride.

I'm relieved they won't be stopping. I'd like to start our own preparations and I don't wish to be held up unnecessarily. After wishing them greetings of the festive season they finally leave us, and we are alone.

Standing before me, I look him up and down.

"Well, my boy," I say, "welcome home to you, finally."

He comes into my arms but only a second later he's pulling away. I'm a little wrong-footed at how different he seems, and I heave a deep breath suddenly wondering what to say.

"I'm sorry about the situation with your papa and grandma. He's disappointed because you know how he loves Christmas."

He shrugs.

"I know. He says we'll have Christmas again at Easter to make up for it. He's potty."

I presume this charming message came from your mother. I hadn't heard from her again until last week when she informed me light was on the horizon. I'm getting a little tired of being Albert's unappreciated guardian and I've decided to have a quiet word with her when he goes back to school.

"Right, so hot chocolate first I think to warm you and then we can make a start decking the halls."

He's gathering his belongings together. The beautiful, old leather suitcase of Ben's he so desperately wanted to take with him looks battered and dented. So much for his promise to treasure it.

"I'm a bit tired to be honest, Frances," he yawns, almost forgetting to cover his mouth, then remembering where he is, "Would it be alright if I had a nap first?"

"Of course," I say.

He reappears at half past seven to have his evening meal leaving the tree dejected and forgotten. Much the same as me, I can't help thinking.

The following morning, I'm up even earlier knowing Crawford is going home to deliver her Christmas gifts before she returns to her family on Boxing Day. Albert saunters down at nine o'clock and heads to the scullery to ask Crawford for breakfast. She's getting ready to leave, just plating some lunch for us beforehand. He mooches into the parlour.

"Good sleep?" I ask sarcastically.

"Yes thanks, I needed it. We don't get to sleep until late at Eddie's, even though it's lights out at nine."

"I'd like to be a fly on the wall in your dorm. I'm glad you've settled in and made friends though, darling, it stops me worrying about you so much. Shall we make a start when Crawford leaves?"

Right on cue she appears in her coat, delivering the tray for Albert and informing us she has lunch prepared and waiting.

"Thank you, Crawford," I say, watching Albert help himself to the porridge.

"Yes, thanks very much," he says with his mouth full.

We bid her farewell as she leaves basket in hand for the long walk ahead.

"What do you think?" I ask yet again, joining him at the table.

"Would you mind if we do it later, Frances, there's plenty of time don't you think. Oscar isn't doing his tree until Monday."

Damn and blast that Oscar. If I hear his name one more time I'll scream, just see if I don't.

"I was looking forward to it though, Albert. We always have such fun looking at all your old handmade decorations, Joshua's too."

My head whips in his direction when he snorts.

"We might have had fun when I was six," he says.

242

Once, I would have thought this comment charmingly cheeky. I tense; he's cocksure, so full of himself. What the hell happened to him in three months? St Edmond's isn't all it's cracked up to be then if they don't teach them respect and manners. Even his basic table manners seem to have gone awry. They're undoing all our hard work by the look of it.

I notice the snow begin to fall with what should be perfect timing. We would ordinarily watch it with the curtains open and the tree lights twinkling in the darkness of early evening. I've played the scenario out in my mind with festive anticipation many times over the last few days waiting for him to come home.

I'm beginning to doubt there will be any sparkle this year.

"Oh, I forget to mention," Albert says eventually, "Oscar's parents are having a New Year's Eve party at their house, and they'd like me to go. You don't mind do you, Frances? We don't usually do anything."

My lips pinch tightly together. No, we don't usually do anything, Albert except batten down the hatches, read our favourite Christmas book, the one we save until last because it really is the best one, have a snowball to drink by the fire, and watch the finest display of stars in the world in the blackness of the moors at midnight. No, nothing to write home about there. We haven't even had Christmas and he's backing out the door already. I want my Albert back; I want my William back.

I want it to be last Christmas.

"You've only just got here, and I thought we would be spending New Year's Eve together as always. I was thinking we should still go to Whitby for a walk on the beach on Boxing Day."

"I told Oscar you wouldn't mind. They're having a band and dancing. I've told him now, so he will think I'm rude if I don't go. I didn't think you would expect me to be holed up here for three weeks."

Holed up here; what an expression! He's dismissed my thoughts on the subject, it seems. He has an air of arrogance now which makes me think he doesn't take after you after all. Perhaps he's more like his mother than I thought.

It appears I'm not exciting enough to spend New Year's with any longer. I see his dark head bowed as he looks down at his favourite porridge with fruit and nuts. I stare at his perfect little swirl of a crown and have a sudden urge to swipe the bowl off the dining table. I have an urge to see it smash against the dresser and watch the look of horror on his face as he witnesses the scene.

I'm trying my best not to rise to his bait.

He looks up and pushes a spoonful of porridge into his mouth. I watch him crunch noisily down on the nuts, then up again, then down again. The sullied food spins around in between each mouthful.

Irritation rises like bile to burn the back of my throat.

I simply cannot help myself.

"You do sound spoilt sometimes, Albert William," I tell him. "Sadly, your dear mother had the same affectation. It might be better if you didn't force me to go into detail about how life turned out for her because of it."

The look on his face is satisfaction enough for now.

PART II

THE BINDING OF HIGHBROOK

Albert
Chapter 46

One could never refer to her as bookish.

She looked out of place in the family-owned bookshop on the cobbled lanes of Oxford when I saw her. I had the sense she was just biding her time until life presented her with a better opportunity.

I'm glad to be in Oxford instead of Cambridge to study medicine. Medical studies were put on hold for some time due to excessive bombing in Cambridge, so I made the right decision. I had my year in a small room overlooking Exeter's beautiful quad, then rented a room above a bookshop in the High Street. This is how I met Elise, who ironically is their daughter.

Her boredom threshold is set low, and I did hear someone in class once describe her as the 'flighty type.' She also isn't opposed to the odd swear word, which makes me think of Frances's disapproving expression every time.

I don't live above the bookshop any longer. It was becoming too dangerous a game trying to fight off Elise's advances when Mr & Mrs Marwood were sleeping on the other side of the wall. Nowadays, I rent a house in St.Giles which I share with Charles Turton. Charles plans to become a surgeon eventually while I decided to follow in my grandfather's footsteps and become a general practitioner.

Charles left to go to war and was lucky enough to return in one piece, unlike poor Uncle Dan.

I didn't go to war. After passing the medical, they informed me during training I had a weak right arm. It seemed strong enough to me in daily life, but a break I had as a child left me without enough strength to hold a rifle for any length of time. I returned with my tail between my legs and volunteered excessively to make amends for not being on the frontline. I even had a spell as an air raid warden, the unform helping to assuage my guilt a little. I didn't let the power go to my ~~though~~ head like some.

The expression on Elise's face was disapproving before she flounced out the door this morning. She had high hopes of being a doctor's wife once upon a time.

"You need to take a long hard look at yourself, Bertie, if you're to stand a chance with me. I don't recognise you some days."

She's referring to this morning.

We didn't discuss her staying the night, so she must have slid into bed beside me at some point. But if you insist on taking somebody by surprise, you risk being surprised yourself.

It was too early in the day for conversation, never mind theatrics. Knife in hand, I carefully study the butter seeping its way into my warm toast, allowing the mundanity to be my only thought. Just for second, just until the others slowly wedel their way back in.

I'm not sure what Elise wants from me. Yes, I may have a few too many brandies after my evening meal some nights or a few more beers if I frequent the *Bird & Baby* but I'm always up by mid-morning. I have eggs for breakfast, soft-boiled as they remind me of breakfasts at home as a child. If Mrs Pawson isn't coming in, I take the rubbish out, bang the cushions, wipe the tops. I have my routine and I did incredibly well in my final placement at Moulsford Surgery. Now I'm winding down to crank up again to be a fully-fledged general practitioner.

I was always going to be a doctor since I helped grandpa sterilise his instruments of torture as grandma laughingly referred to them. I miss them both, I miss their easiness.

Since the end of my placement, I've had a little too much time on my hands. Hence the amount of alcohol I'm consuming being tipped slightly towards copious on the scale. I'm not sure how I can stop the train.

Charles too is becoming a little tetchy of late. We've grown up so much since the war but even before then we were both old heads on young shoulders. He lost his father to Spanish influenza.

And I lost you.

Elise keeps giving me one more chance, yet she keeps renewing it. The memory of VE day is slightly hazy due to being a little inebriated, but in the middle of flag-waving and raucous frivolity there were men down on one knee all around us on the street. She disappeared at teatime, and I didn't see her for over a week. I know now she was expecting me to pop the question.

Charles has been a constant support, ever cheerful until recently, a person who always looks for the silver lining in the darkest cloud. I was supposed to be going up to meet his mother in Northumberland when we graduated but I doubt this will be on the cards any longer. They live in a small town with an isolated beach on their doorstep. Many a time I pictured us walking along the sand, windswept, discussing our future animatedly. I hear Charles on the phone to his mother every Sunday in the hallway. He speaks quietly into the receiver, yet there's still no mistaking how much he loves her.

Those telephone calls home, I'm sure they tipped the scale, I'm sure they made me start to look back to a different time. The end of my current situation is nigh, but although I'm clear-minded on the professional front, I'm somehow unable to fathom my next personal step. Much less take it.

I've had plenty of warnings. Each new day is a chance to start again. Then as the morning slips to the afternoon, Charles and Elise are no longer my main priority. By evening I'm not worried in the least about getting them back onside, in fact, I'm not worried about anything whatsoever. I like that part of the day best.

Charles isn't being so tactful today; tact wasn't getting to the heart of the matter.

"I don't like you when you're pie-eyed, B," he says, "you scare me. You're a loose cannon, almost like a ticking bomb. I have a constant knot in my stomach waiting to see what will happen next."

I get the picture. It's late morning and I'm nursing my cup of tea and a pounding headache.

Elise flounced out before Charles returned with the papers.

To my mind I slept like a top last night, but Charles is enlightening me. He looks tired in the cold light from the tall sash windows, and I may be the culprit. I haven't noticed anything in the real world for a long time. He says I had him up until the small hours ranting incoherently until he persuaded me to go to bed.

"I've run out of options," he says, "I have no idea what to try next to stop it happening. You must know by now you're going to lose Elise too if you're not careful. You need to speak to someone soon."

He pauses to think how to go on.

"Please," he says, with a half-smile.

Why can't I remember? I used to be able to, and Charles isn't one for hyperbole so it must be bad.

His eyes are upon me as I process his words. Something in my expression satisfies him the timing is right, so he leans over and passes me a small card. I read it to discover the card is for university pastoral support. I stare at it a moment, realising I didn't like mention of the word 'too' in the middle of our little chat. This puts a different complexion on things, Elise is one thing, Charles quite another.

Lifting my head, I look straight into his eyes. I haven't done this in a while, and I can't hold his gaze for long. His smile is gone.

"This is the last time I'll keep you up, you have my word," I promise him.

I look out of the window at the hustle and bustle of a busy university town, heads flurrying past at regular intervals.

People will be going about their lives with worries far greater than mine yet not in need of a coping mechanism.

I intend to keep my promise as I've been too wrapped up in myself. Maudlin, that's the word for someone who's full of woe when they're drunk, a good word to describe my behaviour.

Dropping my head, I stare at the dog-eared contact card in my hand which Charles went to the trouble of getting for me. It must have been lurking in his pocket for some time waiting for the right moment.

"I've been thinking you would benefit from talking to someone and a clear, concise plan now you're qualified will be a good start."

I wouldn't dream of telling him, of course, but I think the world of Charles. He calls me 'B' and I call him 'C', and in my mind this means the same. I don't want him to grow to detest the sight of me for being a millstone around his neck. I want us to laugh until our stomachs ache again, laugh like I never laughed with anyone before, not even papa.

I haven't seen enough of papa. I could just talk to him. I've been avoiding him, and this must be painful. So many people are hurting because of me, people who haven't done anything to deserve it.

The tears are burning. I'm not a crier but I'm shocked as one tear trickles down my face, and I wipe it quickly away with the back of my hand. Charles's eyes widen and he has no idea what to do. I tell him I'm sorry and stem the flow because I don't want the poor man to feel guilty for simply telling the truth.

I see papa in my mind smiling at me, making me see sense without judgement, without hammering home his point. Charles has been a fine substitute and I'll miss his quiet presence I'm sure of it.

But I can't mistake this feeling, though I still take a moment to process my thoughts. This morning is full of surprises though to most the feeling would be rudimentary enough.

  I want to go home.

Chapter 47

I check my train ticket is in my jacket pocket. Curling my fingers around it a moment later I check again.

The ticket is there of course, but I'm somehow unable to stop my heart pounding unless I've put my hands on the little piece of card.

I decided to think of two weeks at home as a little holiday. It will do Charles good to have a break from worrying about me. I'm glad to finally be out of the way as we've been avoiding each other after my display of emotion, both of us awkward about it.

"I'm not saying it because I want rid of you, I think it will do you good to go home and have a change of scenery," he said when I told him my plan.

His light had gone out. I remember Frances saying that about papa once and we never really worked out how to turn it back on. It's more than worn out and weary, it's like someone has tipped you upside down and shook you, emptied you out. In Charles's case I'm the someone. He still cares about me, and this is the one thing keeping me in check.

I nodded unable to speak because I know he really does want rid of me.

I think of Elise. I've no idea why she's so keen because as far as I'm aware I've never led her on to think I would be suitable as her husband or anyone else's. Oddly, she's onboard with me taking my little holiday when I expected to have to fight my corner. She was nodding along before I'd even finished my defence speech, making me think Charles had already told her.

"Good idea. You'll feel better when you've been home," she said, "I can't understand why you've never been back before. The last year at university is always such a pressure, everybody knows that."

It sounded like she was reassuring herself as much as me. That moment would have been my chance to tell her I wasn't coming back, that she could do so much better for herself. I looked at her, sitting on the edge of the bed while I packed, with circle eyes and pink cheeks. Her blonde hair is cut to her chin in the style of the actresses she admires at the pictures, and it really suits her.

I couldn't do it.

I also couldn't stop her reaching out to cup her hand around the back of my neck to pull me gently towards her. She uncrossed her legs, then shuffled to place them either side of me on the bed. She leaned forward to kiss me, her tongue appearing in my mouth before she pulled the towel around my waist with her forefinger.

"Mmm, look at that, and all for me," she said, making what was on offer sit up and take notice. She does have a smutty, earthy edge to her sometimes, especially in temper.

I laid back to enjoy her worryingly expert moves but not for too long as I didn't want to peak too soon. I pulled her dress off and she stood to take off the rest of her clothes very slowly. She then laid down beside me and waited.

She raised her arms above her head in a 'come and get me' sort of way and I rolled over onto her warm body. Her nipple hardened between my thumb and forefinger then she spread her legs so I could slip inside and hear her small gasp of surprise as if she wasn't expecting it. It wasn't long before she was moaning loudly into my neck, telling me she was ready. So was I, but I controlled myself enough to pull out just in time. I was the last thing a baby needed in their life.

Afterwards I laid quietly, listening to her tell me her plans for the coming week then she pulled my arm from around her back and got up to dress. I was surprised to be in this position after our last row, but it can't be termed a row because two parties need to involve themselves in the debate. She was ready to leave quicker than usual making me think I might have been on the receiving end of her pity.

I thought yet again how breath-taking she is as I watched her dress and redo the line down the back of her lower thigh and calf with a brown eyebrow pencil. Smudged or otherwise, she has the best legs in Oxford. I should be proud she even has eyes for me, never mind she wants to devote her life to me. I know a queue of men are waiting to catch her attention, including Charles who tells me often I'm a lucky man and skating on thin ice.

Consequently, my relationship with Elise is now floating around my mind as unfinished business.

I'm glad when the train arrives at the platform spurring me to gather my things together for the long journey home to Yorkshire. I packed one case, and the porter lifts it into the compartment for me. Once settled in my seat, I watch the rush of bodies piling into the other carriages. Book in hand, I'm all set to pretend to read should I be joined by others in the compartment. I'm not keen on being drawn into a conversation with a stranger.

There is something which would stop me feeling this terrible. I've found it very difficult to push it to the back of my mind for two days.

Alone and staring out of the window I watch town turn to country. It seems so long ago since I've been part of the world, I may have become institutionalised.

I need to work out a new way to prop myself up now. I know I'll be forever at risk of slipping back, of replacing one crutch with another. I've read plenty about addictive personality traits recently.

To have such a need to go home, so I'd wake up crying for it would have been unthinkable only days ago. I was glad to see the back of the house when I left, and I'd been staying at Oscar's whenever I got the chance before then. I wasn't keen on Highbrook even when I was old enough to get over my vivid imagination. I remember the trouble I had getting to sleep when I was small, finding every excuse to go down to Frances's apartment. Her floor didn't have the same atmosphere though it was only down one flight of stairs. Odd when I think about it.

Oscar—I wonder what happened to him. Frances agreed to me staying away in the end because by then she was agreeing to anything. After St Edmond's Oscar was heading to Cambridge to do Economics. We had many a conversation with his father, Jonathan after dinner about investments and how he'd made his money. It held a fascination for them which eluded me. Papa had made plenty of money, but we never spoke about how he made it. Frances said money was Jonathan's god or something along those lines.

I've decided to surprise papa. He's never one to venture far so the longest I'll need to wait is until he gets home from work. I've only spoken to them very occasionally over the telephone as invariably I was working over the holidays for the war effort. Papa suggested coming to see me once or twice, but nothing came of it. Taking the lead from each other meant we never arranged anything, we're both as bad. Papa's a homebird preferring not to stray too far from the peace and quiet of Highbrook.

All he's ever wanted is for me to be happy. Often parents say this but then offer confusing caveats and provisos so it can seem a little hollow; Oscar's parents were like that. They were supportive, but only to a point until you disagreed with what they wanted you to do. Papa means it. University, the war, they've been a diversion, but I miss him I've realised and not before time. I should have rung him each week and chatted about the mundane, small things like Charles and his mother. I should have written at least, but shamefully it didn't occur to me.

I must change twice, once in Birmingham and again at Leeds but finally, the train slows, and I see signs of familiarity as we pull into Horton station. I remember the times we came here, spending hours on a weekend watching the trains, timing them, drawing them and chatting for hours in between. I had a special book I used to record these vital facts. I can vividly recall the day the great *Flying Scotsman* came through, diverted from the main line north for some reason and we just happened to be there. It was all over in seconds as the locomotive gushing smoke sped through the tiny station, Papa waving wildly. I picture myself, legs dangling from the platform seats, waiting patiently for the next train to arrive wearing my little leather winter boots and coat with the scarf and hat grandma knitted me. I lived in those boots. Papa said he couldn't bear to throw them away when he'd finally given in to the fact that I'd grown out of them. He planted ivy in them then put them in the shelter of the top step of the house. He had a bronze plaque on a stick engraved especially which he placed amongst the ivy that read, "*These Boots Belonged to a Special Little Bear*." I smile at the memory and lay odds they're still there. I hope so.

We found the trainspotting activity after you'd gone. That's when we started a new routine and fun activities were a large part of it. We were never at home, driving here there and everywhere most days to do something to keep ourselves occupied. We didn't go far before and I know now that was odd. There are too many odd things to remember about growing up in that house, disturbing things which only make sense when you're older. I had the strangest childhood, but it wasn't a bad one. It's wrong to think that.

I suppose coming home is bound to rake over old coals.

The only person I spoke to about what happened to you was Charles. I think about how I found out the full facts that Christmas, how I discovered the full extent of what you did. I'm winded and quickly drop the nasty little memory like a hot coal and kick it away only for it to roll back to sit at my feet. It stares up at me so long, leaving me with no alternative but to pick it up and carry it again.

My breathing sounds too loud for comfort in my own head. I pull my ticket from my pocket and hold it all the way to Horton and when the stationmaster asks for it, I struggle to let go.

I was drunk when I told Charles about what happened, but not drunk enough to forget I told him.

That was a mistake.

Chapter 48

I fasten my Mackintosh to the wind, staring down the track as I wait for my taxi. Frances will be over the moon to see me. I've spoken to her a little more than papa whilst I've been away but not much, often forgetting to call her back if she left a message. She can be persistent, so I would crack eventually.

I imagine her asking Crawford to serve tea but without all the trimmings these days due to rationing. I close my eyes at the thought and sigh. I'll just have to go along with the charade for papa's sake. She will have a million and one questions, and he will listen carefully to the answers and try to gauge how I really am. Whatever happens I'm not saying anything tonight, I'm completely bushed and don't want to put a dampener on my homecoming.

Frances will see through the pretence because she's always had the ability to see right through me somehow, picking up on everything I said or didn't say. How I hated sharing her with anyone when I was young.

I look down at my hands noticing they're clammy and shaking slightly. Is it because I'm thinking of Frances or the effects of sobriety? I don't know the answer.

I'm pleased when I hear the taxi horn. Taking one last look down the track before leaving I pick up my case. I can still back out, nobody is expecting me. I could get the next train back to London.

I set off because it's no use, my papa is calling me back to Highbrook.

He's calling me back there, whether I like it or not.

*

I choose the back seat of the taxi hoping it will limit conversation. But I've run out of luck.

Ray the taxi driver has moved up from London as his house was destroyed in the blitz and he was retired anyway. He has a wife, three children and two grandchildren whom he misses but he just loves living in the countryside so much he wished he'd made the move years ago.

His house is on the outskirts of Horton, and he can afford to rent a much bigger house. He's quick to point out he doesn't need to drive a taxi, but he likes the beer money, and, most importantly, it keeps him from under his wife's feet ….

After five minutes I drop my head back on the seat and let my mind wander when I realise that he doesn't need me to join in the conversation.

I look at the moors like I've never seen them before and I haven't, not really. The isolation and the silence unsettled me so much when I was young because it made me sense something was watching me. Something unknown. I still feel it now, but I'm not bothered by it any longer.

I spot the gates to the house from the road. Nerves appear from nowhere and I feel sick from the rickety car journey.

Ray seems taken aback when I ask him to stop.

"You live here?" he asks, glancing between me and the vicinity of the house.

We can't see it.

"I do, but I haven't been home since before the war."

"Ah, right. Well, I've heard the stories about this place since I moved up. Are any of them true?"

"If you're asking if it's haunted, then definitely not," I say, handing over my money.

"Nah, not haunted, I've just heard tales about the people …"

He suddenly stops talking when he realises the people who he's referring to will be my relatives, friends at least.

259

Intrigued, I'd like to find out what he thinks he knows about them or if this is merely hearsay.

Ray is suddenly less forthcoming.

"Oh, you know, what small towns can be like, rife with gossip. Old washerwomen most of them. They've little else to do if you ask me."

I watch as he grabs his leather bag for my change. The silence is uncomfortable after the barrage of conversation he's subjected me to all the way here.

He offers me the money, but I shake my head and hold my hand up to protest.

"Thank you kindly, sir, it will stand us a round at the *Crown* tonight," He sniffs, adding, "Good luck with the homecoming."

Opening the car door, he removes my case from the boot, and sets off before I've even opened the gate. I stand staring after him a moment, pondering why luck should need to come into it.

As I head up the long driveway of Highbrook I remember how my friends at school told me it's known around these parts as 'The House'. Of course, I paid no heed then but now I think I'm very lucky to live in a house which is special enough to be given a pet name.

I stop and look around to see a change in the garden. I'm used to it being well-kept, more orderly. I wait at the bottom of the steps and spot my boots. The ivy is now spilling over the stairs and suckering itself to the house. It's good to see them though it prompts my emotions to start bubbling too near the surface. I clear my throat and open the front door.

Dropping my case in the hall I look down the darkish corridor towards Frances's parlour. It used to be my most favourite room in the world, a port in a storm. In comparison, today I'm struggling to put one foot in front of the other to head towards it. Where's Crawford; surely, she heard the bell?

Frances appears in the doorway, tidying her hair.

She comes to a halt and her mouth drops. I will be the last person she's expecting to see.

"Well today has suddenly taken an about turn," she says quietly.

She looks different. I suppose she would after so long, but I'm thrown by her looking younger rather than the reverse. Her hair is a little longer, curled from her face in waves. Her clothes, her skirt and silk blouse make her look less austere.

"Frances," I say, removing my hat but staying glued to the spot.

She does a little half-run down the corridor, her house shoes tip tapping on the tiles between the runners. When she pulls me into her arms, I imagine it seems to her like I have a ramrod up my pullover. She smells like Frances adding to my confusion.

She steps back to study me closely as I expected. Her brow slightly furrows before she smiles and I lower my eyes, uncomfortable from the scrutiny and nearness of her.

"Well, you're a sight for sore eyes, I must say. It's been too long," she says.

Her smile doesn't stop her words sounding pointed.

"I know, I'm sorry," I tell her.

She was the person who could make everything better for me once, I remember. I miss that.

"How long are you back?"

I sigh inwardly because I really don't want to commit, I'm taking it day by day for now. I'd rather not be standing here under the spotlight; all I really want is to see papa.

"I'm not entirely sure but at least two weeks as things stand."

This isn't a lie at least.

"Where's Crawford?" I ask.

She sets off walking and I follow.

"Well, the potted version is she became ill, and went to stay with her sister. It was a shock when two weeks later she sadly died of a longstanding heart condition. We were both unaware of it. I didn't want to tell you over the telephone. I know you were fond of each other."

I don't why I would find this so shocking considering the age she would have been, but I do. She's always been in the house from the moment I could remember. I wish Frances had told me because I would have come to the funeral.

But would I … really? I'd like to have been given the opportunity at least.

We stop at the end of the corridor, and I see Frances now has a new kitchen installed. I'm disoriented as she points to a table under the window. So much has changed, yet I suppose this is what happens in life when you're not paying attention.

Sitting down I stare out at the kitchen garden. It's much larger than before the war but then it would need to be.

"I'm so sorry about Crawford, you must miss her."

She glances at me and nods as she sets a tea tray.

"Do you have a replacement?" I ask.

"I've had many, but they weren't up to scratch for one reason or another. As you know, I have mixed feelings about servants and since the war, well, everything has changed. I've had this kitchen installed and I can manage with some outside help for household chores and of course the garden. A Mr & Mrs Warren from the village come twice a week."

This explains the slightly unkempt grounds. Twice a week is nowhere near enough time to devote to them.

I fold out the paper, pretending to read and I can see her in my peripheral turning every so often to look at me. She will be thrilled to have me back in the fold. I'm hot and uncomfortable wiping my forehead when she's not looking on the corner of the tablecloth.

"What time is papa due home?" I ask.

"It varies. He's working too hard but usually no later than half past six."

The kitchen clock says ten minutes to six, so I have a while to wait. I steal a look at the new kitchen; this part of the house was a boot room if I recall. Frances's apartment never felt like a separation to me, not then, only another floor of the house.

She's always had impeccable taste. I've never known how old she is because she says a gentleman should never ask a lady her age and a lady should never divulge it. There's nothing no surer than change as grandma once told me and my, there seem to have been some changes.

Frances motions with her head for us to go into the parlour. I just want to climb into bed, but she disapproves of daytime naps. She leaves the room, telling me she's getting the best biscuits out for the occasion.

This room hasn't changed, I see. The fire's ready to be lit as it gets cold in the evenings around here unless we're in the middle of a heatwave. Picking my usual spot on the settee opposite the fire, I notice the blanket I always used to snuggle down in is still hanging over the arm. I swallow and sit down on my shaking hands, a peculiar position to sit in which Frances spots at once.

She sits down opposite me and scoots back in her chair. I hold my breath waiting for her to speak; the start of the interrogation is looming.

"So, I won't ask how you are because I can see for myself. It's nice enough but no haircut will be enough to pull the wool over my eyes."

She smiles softly, and I throw her a token one back because I haven't the strength or the words to go over it. She knows.

Sipping her tea to stall, it looks like she's considering the best way to tackle things. I admit to not being very forthcoming.

Suddenly she puts her cup down on the side table and sits forward, making me jump.

"We haven't much time, Albert but I simply must warn you about your papa before he gets here."

My stomach muscles clench and I don't know if I'm in a fit state to handle a revelation so stay silent. Things have taken an unexpected turn, pushing me and my troubles to one side.

"Well, I'll just have to get to the point. It hasn't been easy since you left. Your papa wants you to have your own life, of course he does, but it's been hard for him," she pauses, "A little too hard. I've been trying to support him, but it hasn't been easy."

She pushes the hair back from her face, slightly flushed.

"He seemed fine when we spoke."

When was that exactly? It eludes me. She's being over dramatic. He's at work so he can't be so bad surely.

"Really, do you think so?"

I ponder the odd conversation we've had. He seemed the same papa of old, I'm almost sure he did. The guilt is getting a cold grip again.

"What's been going on?" I ask.

I hear the crunch of the gravel as dad's car approaches the house. Frances looks more startled than I do at the sound. She's flustered, jumping up from her seat.

"Don't tell him I've been talking about him," she says quietly as though he can hear.

I nod a confirmation her secret is safe with me. Rushing down the hallway, I don't care about anything else anymore, I only want to see my papa.

He's taking his things out of the boot by the time I get to the front door. I stand on the top step and wait for him to appear. The wind has got up making me feel chilly.

I don't understand why but my heart is hammering so madly. This isn't adrenaline, it's almost a dread or even a fear. I'm hopping about from foot to foot like a child with impatience.

Slamming the boot shut he steps from behind the car. I watch his face hang, thinking Frances really wasn't being overdramatic. He looks as bad as I do, worse perhaps.

He drops the briefcase you bought him long ago on the gravel and almost falls over it in his rush to get to me. Our arms go around each other, and I just sink into him. Burying my face into his neck, I can't seem to let him go. I don't want him to look like a stranger. Everything is wrong.

I let out a long breath to get control of myself, stepping back but keeping a hold of his shoulders.

"You're getting too old for shocks by the look of it," I tease, hoping to lighten the mood.

He ruffles my hair just the way I remember.

"Cheeky pup, I can still give you a run for your money."

That will have to do for now. It's all so forced and surreal, nothing like our usual easy banter when we're around each other. But that was when I was a child.

He stoops to pick his briefcase off the ground. You bought it from a leather shop in Horton for Christmas for him once. It will have been one of the very few trips you made alone, and I remember his face when he opened it. I want to have a briefcase of my own just like it one day.

"Come on, Bertie Bear, let's get you in," papa says, putting a stop to my reminiscing.

I stare at the back of his head as he goes up the steps and think of Ray the chirpy taxi driver.

It seems I do need that dose of luck after all.

Chapter 49

This homecoming is a complete disaster.

When we join Frances in the parlour her smile is taut, and papa's smile is a mirror image. I'd like to run away from my once favourite room and fly up the stairs, the exact opposite of how I felt growing up here. It seems my life has flipped on its head.

"Well, this isn't the evening we expected, is it William? I'll warm us some supper while you chat."

They both widen their smile in my direction. I feel a chill down my spine.

Papa loosens his tie and rolls up his sleeves before putting a match to the fire.

His drawn expression makes me think about the day he told me you were gone. I've thought about that day so many times since. It must have been the hardest thing he's ever had to do, and he couldn't possibly have predicted my lack of emotion. How ashamed I am now.

He doesn't ask how I am because he will need to work up to it.

"It's so good to see you, son," he says, "I think we need a plan now you're back home for a while."

I snort though I tried for a laugh.

"Well, you've always loved a plan," I say.

He made so many plans for us to keep busy after our lives changed. It was as though he had to keep moving so his mind didn't catch up.

"I was thinking of staying a couple of weeks, but I might stay longer if that's alright with you?"

I must stay longer; my priorities have suddenly changed.

"Of course, it's more than alright."

We're being very polite.

Frances calls us into the dining room, and we troop in together to see hot pie and vegetables steaming on the table, courtesy of Mrs Warren I imagine.

Sitting in our usual places, papa raises his glass of red wine to give a welcome home toast. Frances joins him and I raise my water. They don't ask why I refused a glass of wine as this wouldn't be unusual to them.

"Well, your grandma and Uncle Daniel will want to see you when they know you're back so we'll give it a day or two, shall we?"

He winks conspiratorially at me and I'm thankful we're thinking along the same lines.

The omission of grandma and grandpa from the list hits home. They fell ill and died within a couple of years of each other when I was at boarding school. Frances said grandad just gave up. He was always a simple soul, fun to be around and pulling all the usual grandad style stunts to make me laugh. Grandma was his rock, solid and strong and it doesn't surprise me now that he didn't last long without her. I'm sure he would be proud of my career choice.

The stilted conversation is painful, and I can't help noticing papa and Frances haven't looked at each other once. My food is sticking in great lumps at the back of my throat. I sip my water and talk about my degree and placement, going into ludicrous detail to fill the unbearable silence.

I'm relieved when Frances puts her cutlery down neatly on top of her half-eaten food. It looks the same as the rest of our plates.

I can't stand it any longer.

"Papa I'm so tired, do you mind if I go up?"

As I smile inanely at them the blood drains from his face. Frances jumps up from the table, and clatters about piling up the plates.

"I thought you'd want to stay down here tonight, you usually do."

Not for years have I wanted to stay down here. I'm frustrated but try to keep the mood light.

"Let's go up so I can sleep, I need my bed ... please."

He stands and tells me it needs a bit of a tidy as he's been busy working lately.

"I really don't care; I can clean up tomorrow. Come on, old man."

I pull his arm, play-acting like a little child to cover my growing exasperation but he doesn't budge.

Good grief, I've had enough faffing about for one evening.

Grabbing my suitcase, I head from the room. I don't look at either of them, but I sense them looking at me. I thank Frances for supper and charge from the room just as Papa's arm extends to pull me back. He's too slow.

My hands are shaking as I try to get my key in the lock but this time most definitely not from lack of alcohol. I glance over my shoulder, relieved to see I'm alone. He's given up and nowhere to be seen.

Pushing the door open I step back. I take in the scene, my mouth wide then wretch from the smell.

Oh no papa, this peculiar homecoming has suddenly turned so much more peculiar.

*

My watch says seventeen minutes past ten.

Will papa have gone into work today? Part of me expected to wake up to him calling me for breakfast like nothing had happened. But even he can't bluff his way out of this one.

I was sick in the night, bringing up all the supper Frances warmed me. I didn't want to eat, and it would have been acceptable once for me to refuse supper given the state of me. It would have been fine once, and I wouldn't have needed to be polite at the risk of bringing back my food.

268

It was the terrible foisty smell that hit me first. It slowly dawned on me the windows must have been bolted all the years I've been away. One by one I inspected each room, covering my mouth with the sleeve of my pullover.

The sight was disturbing, like a still life with macabre connotations. Each room I went into looked the same as the day I left to go to boarding school. Every ornament, every pen, every book was positioned as though I'd stepped out of the room ten minutes before. Even the calendar on the wall displayed the same month and year—September 1931

Steeling myself to look in the room you and papa shared I prepared myself to see it from the fresh perspective of an adult. It was perfect— eerily so. I'd stepped into a kind of mausoleum, a shrine to a time or more appropriately to a person. That person being you.

Papa has clearly been living elsewhere. How did he know I had come home? I remembered Frances nipping for biscuits in the scullery, she must have rung him from the telephone extension there. So, his genuine shock was at the sight of me, not my homecoming.

Surely, he wouldn't have been living with grandma all this time, she's been well for years. I never thought he'd left Highbrook permanently, but they could have told me absolutely anything, any tall story.

Any barefaced lie.

There was no chance of falling into bed as my head was too full of questions for papa. I wanted to speak to him alone. I headed back to the living room of our apartment and saw the welcome sight of the settee. Kicking off my shoes I laid full length to wait for him to come upstairs and talk to me.

What a relief to finally rest my pounding head after the longest, strangest day.

The next thing I remember was waking up perspiring, with the hot tingling at the back of my mouth letting me know it was time to make a run for the bathroom.

Papa didn't appear. He may have been waiting for me to go downstairs to talk to him; never the twain shall meet.

Now I don't want to face the situation or papa. I've lost the impetus I had in the night, lying awake for hours after being ill. I've reverted to form, and I can't face having the awkward conversation.

But I don't like the thought of papa being ashamed of his strange behaviour. I know I must get to the heart of the problem and that won't happen whilst I'm hiding up here.

After splashing my face with water and combing my hair I stare at myself in the mirror. I'm still in the crumpled clothes from yesterday.

My serious face looks back at me. I look different, more mature. Perhaps it's because I've suddenly discovered there's nothing more sobering than the thought of a beloved father who is on the brink of losing his mind.

Chapter 50

Frances is talking to someone outside. The voice isn't papa's, it's male but unfamiliar.

We've never had visitors other than family before I think standing on the top of the stone steps at the front door. At least we haven't to my knowledge, but then I'm clearly out of the picture. Frances has her back to me, so the man spots me first then waves as though he knows me well. He's smiling, and I instantly smile back at the stranger from my innate sense of politeness.

I stroll over to speak to them as I've been seen.

"Albert, this is Mr Carr, papa's business partner. I don't think you've ever met before."

We haven't. I remember Frances telling me papa's thoughts on mixing business with pleasure before I left and how he worked so well with Harry because they knew better than to do it. I don't understand why he's here without him. My stomach flips.

He holds out his hand and I shake it. He has a confident, firm handshake they tell you to use at interviews.

"We meet at last, Albert," he says.

He's a handsome man. Standing next to his smart car with his fair hair and big smile, he looks a little out of place. Frances is staring up at him as he speaks. I imagine people stare up at him often and he's used to it.

"Yes, nice to meet you, sir," I respond.

"Harry, please."

I can't help myself. I turn quickly to Frances to ask her if papa has gone to work.

I'm brimming with questions for Frances too, but we have an intruder in the house.

I catch them glancing at each other, almost speaking without words. They know so much I don't and that's not fair.

"Come inside, we need to tell you more, you must be terribly worried after last night," Frances says, ushering us in the house.

Harry follows behind us and I'd like to slam the door in his face. If I can't talk to papa, I must speak to Frances on her own about the goings on at Highbrook.

He sits down without an invitation and lounges back in one of the chairs by the fire. This is far from his first visit.

She looks across at Harry, who gives a small smile of encouragement.

"I want to start by saying how upset we are you've found out about papa this way. Obviously, you can see he's not himself and you're an adult now, so owe you an explanation."

She glances in Harry's direction yet again. It's like he's her puppeteer working her strings. Come on Frances, this isn't you.

"He hasn't been himself for a very long time, but along with your grandma, Harry and I have been doing our best to look after him between us."

They've all been looking after papa, even grandma and Harry. If he's been in such a bad way, why have they kept me in the dark? I've been an adult for quite some time.

"No doubt you won't have wanted to worry me, but I would have come home if you'd told me. I could have helped too. He might not have deteriorated so much if I'd been here."

"That's the last thing your father wanted," Harry says, "You have your own life."

I run my hands through my hair, my foot tapping the floor manically. This man, is he deliberately trying to bring out the worst in me?

"Yes, and he's part of it," I say, "Are you and my father friends rather than business partners nowadays?"

Harry appears to be unaffected by my tone.

272

"Well, I admit I was more concerned about the business in the beginning and we're not exactly friends per se, but we're in a very different place to where we were. I only want him to get better, we both do."

He leans over to pat Frances's hand, only once but I want to do something drastic. I've never wanted to do something drastic before. I thought Harry was married, I thought Frances was happy not to be in a relationship. They look far too cosy for comfort, and it's all so unexpected.

They're both staring at me, waiting for a response.

"Do you have a plan?" I ask, addressing Frances.

I'm not happy but I'm not sure what she would expect under the circumstances. It would be better if we were having this conversation alone, she must be aware, though she does seem extremely comfortable with him.

"Well, we're hoping now you're back even for a while, you might be the tonic he needs. He won't want you seeing him like this so it might trigger a new start for him, for all of us," she says in a voice intended to soothe me, "No secrets, it's as simple as that. It's been sprung on you, but we weren't expecting you back yet so we're having to ride the situation. Things change Albert, it's a long time since you left to board. Even without a war, so much can change in days never mind years."

I sigh and drop forward, placing my head in my hands. Frances is right of course, I've no right to be rude. I decide to adjust my attitude to the problem.

I look up as Harry stands to make a move.

"I'll leave you both to it and get back to the office, but I'll call round again soon," he tells us, "Don't get up Frances, I can see myself out."

He has been coming regularly, it's patently obvious. After bowing in Frances's direction, he nods my way, saying my name and almost swoops out of the room. All very theatrical but she loves it.

"Tea, toast?" she asks as we hear the front door close.

"Yes, please," I say, my mind elsewhere.

"We'll talk about you later," Frances says.

My own problems have disappeared into the mist.

"How long has Harry been coming?" I ask when she hands me my plate.

I'm still getting used to him being here at all.

"It's not what you might think, we're not, how to put it, companions or anything of the sort."

Her cheeks flare like she's been caught out. I'm not sure if I believe her entirely but this is really none of my business. I decide to get back to what's important.

"I think I may know more than you realise," I say, putting my toast back down on the plate.

Sitting up in her chair, I can almost see her studying the implication behind the words.

"What do you know?" she asks, cagily.

Putting my plate on the side table, I give her my full attention.

"Papa wasn't looking after grandma when she was ill, was he? He wouldn't have stayed away from me for so long without at least calling to see me. Not papa."

Her mouth opens and closes, as if she's thinking up a lie. But she thinks better of it.

"How did you manage to work that out when you were so young?"

"To be honest, I didn't until last night. I had other things on my mind. Things such as thinking up every excuse under the sun not to come home."

Her throat moves as she looks down at the rug. I'm suddenly tired of skirting around the important topics.

"Where was he all those months before that Easter holiday?"

She smooths her perfectly straight skirt to delay an answer.

"This isn't my information to share," she says, looking out of the window.

This isn't her information to share she says. How dare she. I'm furious she's denying me the answer to such a crucial question and about my own father no less. I've had to ride far too many new emotions in one morning.

It's all too much.

"That didn't bother you once if you recall," I snap.

She whips her head in my direction, but I don't move a muscle. Frances doesn't frighten me anymore, intimidate me even and we've both just this second found out.

I sit staring at her until she looks away. Wearing her expensive-looking skirt and blouse her hair is soft and shiny like she's just washed it this morning. She's wearing a touch of make-up I notice but not too much. That's why she looks younger, I realise.

My mind wanders to that Christmas long ago when everything changed. I try to veer away from the painful memory, but it makes its way back as it often does. That day when she changed, or she showed me a side of her I didn't know existed.

I can see her face now, like somebody spinning around in a horrifying mask, the one's that terrify small children. I'm certain I was being a little annoying, but I was a child, a young boy and Frances always encouraged me to be myself.

I remember pulling away at first when she grabbed my arm, thinking it would be easy, but it wasn't. She had plenty to get off her chest, plenty of dreadful facts to share with me, facts no child should have to listen to about his late mother. I couldn't take my eyes off the hand on my arm, wondering where her strength was coming from and where she was taking me. Up to our apartment we went, down the corridor until we came to a stop at the huge green door at the bottom of the attic stairs. Still, she continued shouting, spittle flying from her mouth to land everywhere, mostly on me. From nowhere she changed tack.

"You only have yourself to blame, Joshua. You're a spoilt little brat, you always have been, I should have listened to your father when he told me, he might still be here if I'd listened."

I was shocked, I was confused but somehow, I realised it would be best if I spoke up, though I was petrified to do it.

"I'm not Joshua, Frances, I'm Albert," is all I said.

It was as if I'd thrown a bucket of ice water over her.

Her eyes grew wide, and her mouth flew open like she'd made an horrific discovery. I watched the darkness in her eyes disappear at the realisation. The Frances I knew returned almost at once and I stepped back as she dropped to her knees in front of me. Crawling like an animal then to cling to my legs, I wanted to run away but I couldn't. I listened to her apologise over and over, say my name over and over as though reminding herself who I was.

The whole scene played out in around four or five minutes, such a minuscule amount of time. It took only a few minutes to change me for good.

We've never spoken of that Christmas until today. We've never mentioned how she took great satisfaction in enlightening me about what happened to you. The facts have done their best to wrestle their way to the forefront of my mind at some point each day or night since.

She gets up from her chair now but doesn't speak, look my way again even. I hear the front door open and close, and I head over to the window to watch as she goes down the front steps and around the back of the house. She's no doubt on her way to the summerhouse she had built before I left. She's still in her slippers.

Deep in thought I move away from the window but don't sit down. I'm thinking about the name from the past I'd completely forgotten about which somehow or other saved my bacon that day:

Joshua.

I head back upstairs to bathe and to clean our apartment but also to ensure I'm nowhere to be seen if Frances decides to return indoors.

Opening each window in turn, I let the birdsong into the silence with two questions preying on my mind.

What went on here alone with her son, the son I've never set eyes on, but more importantly …

Where the hell is Joshua?

William

Chapter 51

I don't have to close my eyes to picture that room.

White walls, white bedspread, oak flooring that different anonymous people wearing the same style of green overall mopped every morning. There was a suitcase case at the end of the bed which my mother had brought in at some point. I noticed a desk but no chair. They may have thought I would throw a chair. If this was the case, they knew nothing about me as I'm not a chair throwing type of person.

It was exceptionally clean, and the smell swung between hot food and cleaning fluid like in hospital. But then this is where I was—in a hospital for the broken mind. The Jack and Jill nursery rhyme popped into my thoughts sometimes when the doctor was talking, the part which went, "He went to bed to mend his head with vinegar and brown paper."

Vinegar and brown paper would have done just as good a job because my head wasn't for mending. Not then.

Thank heavens they took me to a private institution in Harrogate. I had no idea where I was, but I wasn't particularly fearful. I opened my eyes to hazy memories of Frances's face and my mother's haunted with concern, wondering I imagine what kind of horror story they'd walked into. My memories rolled on to me passing out and falling in a heap on the floor of your cold little cottage. They'd found us out. They'd found out our heinous lie.

My chest tightened at the thought. Then after what seemed an age, a doctor with a weary expression he was doing his best to hide came to give me a little sedative. I was free of pain within seconds.

The next time, I awoke to my mother's face, but not looking herself at all with hair slightly askew and no rouge or powder making her look like a stranger. Only one person could visit it transpired, and there was a man's face appearing rhythmically on the far side of the tiny window in the door. He walked back and forth outside the room endlessly as though on sentry duty. Was he there to protect my mother in case I suddenly lashed out? It was more than likely just protocol.

My mother was pensive and out of her depth. I doubt she'd even heard of a breakdown let alone understood how her son could have been the victim of one.

Her hand came out and I recoiled. I wouldn't have meant to, but I was unused to physical contact from my mother so I will have been alarmed. She pulled her hand back to rest on her handbag, her face drained of all colour to almost disappear into the walls.

"You gave us an awful fright, William," she said with a tired smile, trying her hand at a light jovial tone.

It still sounded like a ticking off, but I wasn't worried as I didn't feel anything enough to worry about a ticking off.

"I'm thirsty, mother," I said, my voice cracking.

Reaching for some water, she beat me to it, handing me the cup. It seemed at first, she was going to hold it to my lips, but she reconsidered. I took a gulp and laid back down to stare at the man swinging like a pendulum outside the door.

I remember so much but it was as if I was watching it all unfold from afar in a swirl of mist. A mist which swirled around the entire time they incarcerated me in that room.

The Pastures was a better class of mental institution, but your environment I discovered is insignificant during such times. I had my own room, somewhere to relax and unwind in theory. For me, I think my pills were doing just as good a job.

After an indeterminate amount of time passed with regular one-to-one sessions, a diagnosis was made – a diagnosis of depression caused by a delayed reaction in coming to terms with the death of my wife. They had no idea what caused the delay. They would never have been unable to deduce why unless I explained, because the reason was so very bizarre and obscure. I understand this now.

There's nothing much to reminisce about during my time at *The Pastures*, no excitement, no chair throwing, histrionics, wailing and flailing, just the daily grind of psychiatry sessions, medicine and mealtimes, all best forgotten.

Finally, after many meetings behind closed doors, it was decided they were unable to take me any further, but they weren't casting me adrift. They could see with regular out-patient appointments and medication I would recover. But I had a better chance of a full recovery if I wasn't living alone, they said.

My mother was my only visitor the entire time. She sat and read to me from a book or from a newspaper, and I came to look forward to her visits every day. Eventually, I realised it was December when the usual routine altered slightly to accommodate Christmas.

"Merry Christmas, William," she said on Christmas Day, "Next year will be a better one."

My final assessment was due on Thursday 3rd January, and they "recommended" I stay at *The Pastures* until such time. Christmas wouldn't be Christmas anywhere for me, I wasn't feeling festive or very much at all, but I was doing and saying all the correct things to be discharged.

What sounded like merriment if only from the staff, was happening in the dining room, the distant sound of a tinny piano being played by somebody drifting down the corridor. We were set to join the fuddle for a while but at the last moment, I couldn't take the walk. I asked my mother if we could eat in my room instead as I didn't like it in the dining room, surrounded by people who reminded me what state of mind I was in.

"Of course, wherever you're comfortable eating is fine by me."

She'd started to be more attentive, more motherly. She made small gestures which I'd hardly noticed at the time like smoothing my hair, folding clothes, light forehead kisses. Those were no small gestures from my mother.

She settled herself in the other chair waiting for the staff to serve her Christmas lunch on a tray. How positively grim it must have been but to her credit, she took it on the chin.

"Now, I think we need to discuss the week after next. I'm sure you'll be glad to see the back of this place. I've been having a think and I know Highbrook is your home and Frances a good friend, but I'd like it very much if you came to stay with me. Just until you're … better."

She played with the tartan cotton napkin, running the fabric through her fingers, expecting a rebuke, I should imagine. Her hair and make-up were perfection again because after all it was Christmas. Her red woollen cardigan complimented her light brown hair I remember in the swirling mist of recollection.

"I would like a chance to look after you for a while. Of course, I know it will be strange at first, but it would mean so much to me."

Her eyes swept up from the napkin, and she looked at me coyly.

"I know we've never lived in each other's pocket, but I'd like the opportunity to mother you for a little while … if of course you'll let me."

She needn't have been so uncertain of my intentions. I could never have returned to Highbrook and being alone at the cottage would have been more insufferable. Her offer was a lifeline. I must remember to tell her if the right moment presents itself.

When I began to feel better, I was overwrought with guilt. Some may say I shouldn't have been so hard on myself because I was in an awful place mentally. I was recovering from a mental breakdown.

But all I could think was, deplorably, I hadn't thought about Albert for weeks, not even at Christmastime.

When it dawned on me the shame caught in a net which coiled itself so tightly, I was unable to break free no matter how I thrashed.

That Christmas night, after my mother left, I stared out of my window of my room at *The Pastures* knowing I'd be back out in the cold in days.

I sat in the silence of my room, fascinated by the circle of light in the blackness of the night. I hadn't noticed it in years.

Oh, Nell, I'd like to just sit and stare at the moon with you again. I'd settle for that.

But by then the mist which shrouded my thoughts did nothing to diminish the sickening reality.

You are dead.

Chapter 52

Harry has been ready to leave since he arrived.

Unused to visiting the sick or frail of mind, his right foot crossed over his left leg is twitching, his smart argyle socks on full view.

"Nice place your mother has here," he remarks, looking around the tasteful sunroom filled with lush ferns and wicker furniture.

"Indeed, she keeps a nice house, or Franks does," I quip knowing my mother is well out of earshot.

My small attempt at humour is meant to put him at ease and I succeed, with him raising the small chuckle it deserves.

He straightens his tie, saying, "I know you mentioned returning to work after Spring Bank but there's no rush. Everything is in hand so don't return before you're ready."

He's not quite so sunburned at the moment as holidays to the coast will have been put on the backburner whilst I've been absent; whilst I've been pulling myself together.

Am I together? Enough to nip back to Frances's once over the Easter holidays to see Albert at Highbrook. It wasn't so bad, better than I expected, and Frances kept us distracted, fussing, offering cake, dishing out all the usual comforts we both enjoy.

Albert was a little quieter than usual, but he will have been feeling bored and missing Oscar. He'd only come for a weekend as we'd agreed to him going to Cornwall with Oscar's family. We will have to meet. If he comes back for longer in the summer, I could arrange some trips for the boys to keep them occupied. I have doubt for the first time within our relationship. Has he moved along from spending time with his old papa, was this why he was quiet?

I would like him to see a little more of his grandma. My mother's been an absolute marvel, credit where it's due. We've reached a comfortable living arrangement. Not chatty or delving into our innermost thoughts and feelings but comfortable, nonetheless. How odd I should think of Highbrook as Frances's house rather than my home now. The pills are certainly helping, but they're not a resolution. Albert is my resolve.

Harry's been calling around once or twice to see me and I've seen a different side to him. He seems more human, endearing even, much like my mother. I've been deeply touched by his concern for my welfare.

"Well, I can't lie, my life of Riley is at stake here so get your skates on and get back to work," he said, the first time he came but even then, his expression gave him away. He was worried, I could see it all over his face.

My mother asked Bailey to serve gin and tonics for them and iced tea for me. Sitting down opposite me she looks beautiful in her new grey two-piece and pale lemon blouse.

I can't help thinking my father has provided well for her though his name is still never mentioned.

"So, William tells me your wife has been unwell," she says to Harry, taking a sip of her drink.

The pleasant tinkling of ice gives us an evocative sound of summer. It's nice I should notice.

"I do apologise, I've forgotten your wife's name."

She doesn't know her name because I've never talked much about Harry, let alone his wife.

"Catherine. Yes, she hasn't been herself of late, but then she's at a difficult age for a woman, I imagine."

I watch my mother's face drop at such a crude diagnosis. A difficult age has connotations of the menopause, and this is certainly not a subject one brings up in polite society. I see a glimpse of my old mother but find myself wanting to ease her discomfort.

"A trip to the coast will be just what you need," I say, "Organise a trip, Harry, you're long overdue a holiday."

He leans forward in his chair, and I wonder what he's about to disclose.

"To be honest, I'm not sure either of us are bothered about going much nowadays. Her parents are thinking of selling up."

He looks over at my mother.

"Fancy a holiday home at the seaside, Mrs Hudson?"

"Sylvia, please," she laughs gently, then turns her face to me, raising her eyebrows.

"How about it, William, might it be just what the doctor ordered?"

I return her warm smile and think about how far we've come to interact in such way. I can't stay here forever but this is the perfect arrangement for now.

After Harry's visit today, I sit awhile which I do too much, and this will have to change. My mother bustles in with my medication right on the dot. She hides it somewhere unfindable, not wanting to involve the staff. Believe me I tried to find it in the early days but I'm glad I didn't. Albert is back at the forefront of my mind, though he's away at boarding school. I think of Frances at Highbrook on her own. We must visit.

I take my pills and reach for my book. Restless, I'm distracted and must re-read the passage more than once.

Placing the book back on the table I know the reason I'm unable to focus, and for once it's rather a pleasant realisation; completely unforeseen.

The realisation that finally, just when I was beginning to think they had deserted me, my friend has come calling.

*

It's the time of year where the moors lift one's spirits after a hard winter, my real rehabilitation if only I'd been sound of mind enough to know it.

The heather is tufting for mile upon mile, touching the sky in all its late spring purplish tones. I should have come sooner but you can't force these matters. I'm still unsure if heather and cloudless skies will be sufficient to salve my wounds, but they certainly won't do them any harm.

I feel you, Nell. I feel you beside me, walking a path of togetherness. I don't want to cry, and I don't, I want to remember it all … properly. I want the pain to hit me and crush me, having felt so little for so long. If I don't face it head on, I can't move forward, I'll be stuck in my own mind and Albert will have lost both parents. I can't let that happen. You must help me now to not let it happen.

How could you leave us?

I've never thought this before but then for long enough I didn't think you'd gone anywhere. I tear my walking bag from my shoulder and throw it on the ground. It fails to make a satisfying sound on the cushion of heather, but now I realise I'm angry at you for leaving us and in such a way. A way which would warp my sense of loss and bereavement and I'm forced to live with the extra burden of remorse.

You didn't have to do it. You had it all worked out, it was doable, and I was doing it. It was the lesser of two evils, but it was working, your plan was working. I had you, I had Albert, he had Frances and he had me. Albert leaving home meant the guilt could start to lessen to a dull ache. I would have had the world in the palm of my hand again, even it was in the strangest of ways. Happiness much like love is in the eye of the beholder, different for everyone.

I had it, but you took it away.

I look up at the sky, then hang my head.

Except I never had it. I thought I was living a lie when all along you were never even there, you'd left us long ago. I wasn't enough in the end for you to stay.

So many questions plague me. Can I go to the cottage, is it too soon? Can I keep plodding on for miles until I reach the path, then the door, then can I find it in me to open the door again?

One thing I've learned the hard way is monsters only grow bigger and nastier the longer they're left to skulk about your headspace, so it won't be any easier to do it next week. I sling my walking bag over my shoulder again and take the hardest yet all-important first step.

I learned so much at *The Pastures* about retraining your mind to live in the present to seek reassurance from the here and now. How you should focus your senses on what's happening in each moment rather than looking ahead or worse in my case, behind. I try it now. I think of the watery sun steadily soaking its way into the back of my pullover then my shirt, I listen to the sound of my footsteps on the bracken, tuning into each rhythmical step until it slowly soothes me. I think of you holding my hand loosely, fingers clinging together. I pray you will never let go.

If I look up now, I'll be able to see it. Closing my eyes, I raise my head then open them slowly, fearing the unknown. Not the unknown place, the unknown reaction to the place.

But when I see it, I find my footsteps quickening to get inside. The trees behind are still swamping, the whitewash a little dulled but somehow, it's beckoning me, and anxiety is no longer a stumbling block. I don't even need to wait at the back door as I pull out my key and unlock it to find it's still sticking.

Nothing has changed here.

Nothing has changed that is … except everything.

Frances

Chapter 53

I had the summerhouse built as a haven, somewhere to go to inspire one's imagination, connect with the great outdoors.

Today it cannot inspire me.

One would think I'd be angry but I'm not. It's as though Albert has delivered a stinging slap, albeit verbal which was long overdue. I deserved it.

Of course, I've relived that Christmas enough times without Albert's bleak reminder, but the problem I find myself with is that I'm unable to recall exactly what I said to him. I'm unable to piece together the puzzle. This may be for the best; the mind is a wonderful thing.

I must remind myself it's a rare occurrence to lose my temper; I must have been tested and tested beyond reason.

But, like Joshua he was just a little boy.

I thought Albert turning up yesterday meant we'd turned a corner. Of course, he'd come back in the three long holidays they had each year at boarding school, but Oscar's parents had him well and truly ensnared with their frivolous plans and holidays.

After the clinic I expected you to go back to the cottage not to your mother's. When you eventually came to see Albert, I had to listen to how you'd reached an understanding and he really should see more of his grandmother.

It was all a ruse for Albert of course. You'd been living at the cottage for quite a while by then but moved back to your mother's when Albert came home.

"I don't feel ready to take Albert to the cottage, Frances. Not yet at least, it needs a little more exorcising," you told me when you called one time.

I knew the real reason. If Albert discovered you lived at the cottage, you'd have to explain why you left Highbrook. You made me think living at the cottage was a temporary arrangement, but of course I'd read the letter. I knew better.

You were visiting more regularly by then, keen to look after me even in your fragile state of mind. How I loved you for it.

We were sitting together on our favourite bench seat overlooking the moors. You rarely went indoors, and I'd come full circle, snatching moments of your time. Except now your mother was the other woman.

You looked thinner, still handsome but dreadfully pale even under the shade your hat. You took it off a moment and I spotted the smattering of grey in your hair. It made me think of Ben, but I shook it off quickly.

"How on earth do you keep him occupied at your mother's?" I asked.

You laughed. You didn't notice my tone but then you noticed very little.

"To be honest, it would be just the same if he was here because teenagers are very insular as I'm sure you'll remember with Joshua. He reads his grandfather's series of medical books cover to cover, engrossed by the diagrams and out of date treatments. Although we do take ourselves off every day to get from under my mother's feet. We've enjoyed a few little chats."

I tensed unnecessarily. Albert clearly hadn't said anything to you. He was cordial when we were alone and more engaged when you were around. Albert was only too happy to be free of Highbrook and free me.

He was good at pretending but then we're pretending all the time and I get tired of it. All because of you, William, my dear sweet boy.

I just can't picture Sylvia with two men in the house. She's so regimented, her days so structured, but then people change.

"How are things with your mother these days?"

I just had to ask.

"Same old Frances," you said pleasantly, "Playing your favourite little game of twenty questions."

I threw him a tight smile.

"I'm only teasing. Every cloud has a silver lining and the kindling of a relationship with my mother is just that in the situation we find ourselves in. She told me she's been taking lessons from you Frances as you've always been a rock. But of course, she could never be you," you quickly added.

My face must have given something away to make you add that little proviso. I have always been your rock, for all the good this has done me now. Sylvia has been over to see me on a few occasions, but it's been quite some time since her last visit. I imagine she's too busy playing her own little game of happy families to spare time for me. Is it any wonder I find myself at breaking point on occasion? The situation we find ourselves in, indeed.

Thank goodness for Harry, is all I have to say.

After your little episode as I now think of it, Harry called at the house in January. I looked out of the window to see his impressive car and wondered who would be coming out here to see me. I'm always ready for visitors, so I fluffed my hair in the mirror and sat by the fire.

Crawford came running upstairs.

"Madam, a Mr Carr is here. He tells me he's Mr Hudson's business partner."

How very unexpected.

"Show him in and organise refreshments if you will please, Crawford," I told her as she hurried away.

Blonde and dashing, is how I describe Harry, a golden version of you and Ben in looks at least.

"Good morning, Mrs Cundall," he said, sauntering confidently over to meet me.

"Mr Carr, a pleasure to finally meet you."

He kissed my extended hand, and I asked him to take a seat.

Heavens, he had what they might call sex appeal, in an obvious way if you're taken with that kind of thing. I thought I wasn't.

"I hope Mrs Hudson rang ahead. I asked her if I could help in any way, and she said Will could do with a few things fetching. By the look on your face, I take it you weren't forewarned."

Clearly Sylvia was far too busy to keep me in the frame but that had become a well-woven pattern by then.

It might have been my imagination, but I'm sure his eyes were roaming me head to toe as he spoke. I was hot but quite comfortable under his gaze. He was the kind of man who would judge a woman by her appearance. Obvious is another word I'd use to describe Harry. But obvious meant you would always know where you stood. Men with depth are hard to read, unpredictable.

He was easy to talk to and someone to talk to was exactly what I needed. Other than a trip to Leeds to buy clothes, which had lessened since the war, I could go days without company. I missed you; I missed Albert, I even missed your mother.

I took Harry upstairs, and he collected a few more personal belongings as I wondered why she hadn't sent someone else to do it. He read my mind.

"I thought I would see the result of Will's hard labour and I've been keen to meet you too, Mrs Cundall."

He flashed a broad grin my way.

He promised to call again but I didn't see him for a few months after our initial introduction. Now he calls quite often and even with you sometimes. Our interaction is amiable, nothing more, though I must admit I wouldn't be opposed to testing the water just for the mischief of it. His wife is older than me and the odd comment he makes doesn't paint her in a particularly flattering light.

The summerhouse darkens now with the gathering clouds. I don't want to go back inside, but it's getting chilly. I've never called on you at the cottage because I know you wouldn't appreciate me turning up unannounced. You've been on a steady decline since Albert went to university and just didn't come home. The situation is harder to bear as we thought you'd made a moderate recovery when he was at St Edmond's.

I rang you at the office when Albert arrived yesterday but said to act surprised of course. You didn't have to feign surprise in the end because the sorry state of him knocked you for six. I doubt I'll get to the bottom of why he looks so wretched now. What a pair you make.

Harry's been coming more because he too has new concerns, even though he says your work is as exemplary as ever. He asked me to try and find out about your decline, saying if anyone could find out, it would be me.

Did I imagine the twinkle in his eye as he said it? I can't deny I revel in the harmless fun of it all.

I did a little digging, mentioning to you how you'd lost a little weight when I really meant far too much. I suggested seeing a doctor. You told me then you've had a stomach full of doctors and in any case, pills make you swap one kind of madness for another. This explained so much—you've stopped taking the medication. Terrible idea.

I think I might take the opportunity to call in on your mother to see if she can shed any light on things. Encouragement to seek help from all sides might just do the trick.

I look down and notice I'm still in my slippers. I head to the hallway to grab my outdoor clothes from the cupboard, opening the doors silently. So, I'm lowered to skulking around in my own home to avoid running into Albert now I see.

On the drive over, I decide on the best course of action with Albert. I think I'll just knock and breezily pretend nothing has happened when I get back. We can do cordial again for the time being. If he's home for a while I still have chance to get him back on side.

Pulling up at your mother's I spot her car in the open garage. The curtains are back in the house, but for one room I notice. She does have a lovely house, the lodge being very modern in comparison to Highbrook, and very, I search for the right description. Sterile, very sterile. It's double-fronted with a pleasant garden and it's set well away from the other houses on the avenue. I spot another car at the side of the house. Now, what's he doing here at this time of day?

I see a small shaft of light shimmering from the centre of the drawn curtains. Somehow, I'm pulled towards it and glance over my shoulder to check I'm alone before I decide to take a peek. I enjoy a tiny frisson of excitement in doing something a little risky and can't help but think about the last time I peered in a window years ago.

I spot Harry first, his trousers around his ankles then my eyes grow wide at the sight of Sylvia in a very 'un-Sylvia like' position.

I should have learned my lesson. I saw far more than I bargained for years ago and today is just the same.

So, not content with taking two of my men, now she's greedily helping herself to a third.

As I head back to the car, I'm unable to stop my wicked thoughts. I just can't help wishing it was me who had been caught sprawling over the dining table, or any table, having some mischief with Harry, or, or … I don't know if I dare even let my mind go there.

Sylvia knows much the same as I that age is no deterrent to wanting and wishing.

How I wish I was the one who'd been caught in flagrante delicto.

Albert

Chapter 54

They finally put me through to papa in his office after they told me he was in a meeting all morning.

Last night, I saw Frances disappear in her car, so I ran downstairs to take food to decamp in our apartment.

My first task then was making it more habitable.

The simple act of opening the windows had made all the difference and I gave it a spruce, cleaning not really being my forte. I had to find some way of getting rid of the unpleasant smell. My bed airing, I played my radio which I brought home from Oxford. It felt better, not right but better. All the while I was busy, I thought I shan't be spending time with Frances unless I'm forced. I heard her come home about an hour after she left, slamming the car door and then the front door. Not surprisingly she hasn't ventured upstairs but I don't regret tackling the subject even now I've calmed down.

I avoid the subject of last evening and ask papa if he's free for lunch.

There's a pause where my stomach dips.

"Well, how about I take the afternoon off, and we head to the coast? We haven't done that in a while."

"Even better. See you here about what time, half past twelve?"

"Perfect."

I saw papa pulling into the drive and ran downstairs not a moment before.

Frances wished me a good afternoon as I came down the stairs and I returned the greeting even waving her goodbye as ever. I'm not giving papa another reason to worry, and I know Frances will be thinking the same. Whatever else she might be, she does love him.

"You should have seen their faces at work when I told them I was heading off and wouldn't be back for the rest of the day," he tells me as I get in the car, "I understand you met Harry yesterday."

Papa looks smart and business-like, quite kempt. Where did he stay last night?

"He was different to what I imagined but I try not to make snap judgements about people."

"Oh, so wise for one so young," he says, "He's better for knowing is Harry."

He's mistaken if he thinks I'm making small talk for the hours journey. I draw breath to speak but he beats me to it.

"I'm sorry you didn't get the welcome you deserved, son."

I glance at him, his face focused on the road ahead. He looks tired, like he hasn't had a restful night's sleep in forever. I've been hiding from Frances, but I've shot myself in the foot by not seeing him. He needn't have been missing from my life for years. More importantly under the circumstances, I shouldn't have been missing from his life.

"It might have been better to give you notice I was coming back, but in a way I'm glad I didn't. I wouldn't have known then about how things are."

I avoid saying how bad things are.

He sighs, taking a hand from the steering wheel to rub the back of his neck. He looks red-faced and awkward, but as tempted as I am to break the silence, I wait.

"Shielding your children from the harsh realities of life is so important to a parent. I've tried to shield you from the realities I could control, I know you've had to face up to some of them."

He means you of course, but he doesn't know I know just how harsh the reality is.

"It looks as though we're both struggling a little," he says, "How about we struggle through together?"

He briefly glances my way, but I stay quiet. It's paining me, I want to console him and tell him everything will be fine but then the train will come to a screeching halt and might never start up again. I hope he knows what I'm trying to say with my silence.

I hear him sigh.

"I suppose I just couldn't be bothered, Bertie, that's the top and bottom of it. Work is just that, I need it for the focus, and I've come to realise Harry and I are the bones of the business. I don't want it to fail for your financial future more than mine. But Highbrook doesn't feel like home anymore."

This is hard for him to tell me. It's the first deep conversation we've ever had. Perhaps he talked openly to you or to Frances—I hope so.

Now though he has little choice in the matter. I've seen it. I've seen what he didn't want me to see.

The newness of being frank and open is unnerving. I don't know yet how to be a man with my father. I left him when I was still a child.

"Well, it won't be home, will it, I'm not there," I say, trying to defuse the tension with humour as I'm prone to do. I'm told I'm like my grandpa in more ways than one.

Papa smiles without looking at me. The smile is a little weak like he can't quite muster the energy but genuine enough.

"Anyway, let's just relax and have a good day. I've missed you, Bertie."

"Bear," I respond quick as a flash with a grin. We both laugh together at our silly old joke. All the madness can wait for now.

I just want to spend the day with my papa.

*

Before I left, we searched for a different beach to create new father and son times, and eventually found Silverdale. I suspect neither of us like it quite as much but for me at least this is a close second. It stopped us having to retrace the journey to Whitby, dragging up old memories on route. The last time we came, was late summer before I headed off to boarding school. I remember Frances joined us. It was our last special day together as a threesome.

Although today isn't sunny the day is warm enough, so papa leaves his jacket in the car, loosens his tie and rolls up his sleeves. He looks odd and out of place. We perch on a wall next to the huts on the beach to eat our fish and chips out of the newspaper with tiny wooden forks.

The sea's choppy and we watch a fisherman, legs dangling from the lonely pier. I'd like to join him; it would be nice to lose myself so much in the task in hand nothing else matters. With little to occupy families here it remains a sleepy fishing village.

The fish and chips always taste better eaten from newspaper just as tea tastes better from a porcelain cup. Frances told me that. I'm annoyed with myself for spoiling the moment in allowing my mind to wander to her.

My minds so far away Papa's voice seems to roll in from the sea when he speaks.

"Well son, you've heard my story, do you think you're up to sharing yours?" he asks me, fixed face looking towards the sea.

I watch his hair flying around madly in the wind having given up on his hat.

I can't help feeling I've only been told the loose version of his story. As for me, I must be careful how much I disclose, and this is a fine line to tread because he's not a fool. I scrunch my empty chip paper into a ball and choose my words.

"To be honest," I say, "I started drinking a little too much. I wanted to nip it in the bud."

He studies my expression and nods once eventually when he's convinced that I'm telling the truth.

"It was easy to slip into the drinking culture. At first it was a novelty but lately it's become part of my day. It got out of hand a time or two, nothing too dramatic, but I found myself wanting to come home to see you."

I hang my head, ashamed to be making the admission.

"I wish now I'd visited you," he confesses, "I thought you were loving life in Oxford."

"I was to begin with. I suppose I thought I'd replaced you with Oscar then with Charles, but you've always been my best pal."

He pushes me from the side. I push him back.

"Charles is one of the reasons I'm back earlier. I've been making life difficult for him on occasion, and he's reached the end of his tether. For now, but not for good I hope."

The fisherman heads away from the pier and waves our way. We wave back. We're alone together for now on endless sand, back together again on our very own beach.

"What was it made you start drinking more heavily, do you think?"

I'm thrown by him asking the question, as I thought he would just assume it was part of university life. I watch the fisherman sauntering home for his tea.

I know exactly what it was that tipped the balance if only I was able to discuss it with him.

Frances and grandma discussed you so much when I was young that now, I think they were obsessed. One afternoon when I was about eight, I heard them talking about you never being happy.

Why weren't you happy? I thought back to my own behaviour remembering I couldn't wait to run downstairs to Frances, to head off for the day with Frances. I treat her as though she was my mother and at the time, it was like she was.

I confessed my feelings to Frances once and she used my guilt against me that Christmas. She was happy to blame my behaviour, all the while knowing I was battling with guilt about my involvement. That was also the day she told me about how you died.

I just can't forgive her for it.

The first time I heard Charles talking to his mother on the phone I could sense their bond, I could feel it and it reignited the spark of regret. But this time as an adult.

All this is irrelevant, a moot point I realise. It isn't about me anymore, this is about shielding papa, making him well again.

Instead, I think of what Elise said to console me before I left and use this as a decoy.

"Oh, you know, the last year of university is always the hardest, everybody knows that."

The irony Elise should be the one to come to my rescue isn't lost on me.

We have a walk on the beach then, saying very little just enjoying each other's company.

But by the time we've had an ice-cream and head back to the car the upset yesterday has pushed its way to the front of my mind again.

As we drove home together, tired but mainly because of the healthy sea air, I had no idea the next day would be such a pivotal day in my life. I had no idea a higher power was at work with sole charge of the wheel.

And it had me on course to meet the absolute love of my life.

It turned out to be a bitter-sweet love story.

Chapter 55

I've yet to discover where papa's been living.

Finally, after I ask the question half a mile away from home, he tells me he'd rather show me.

"I'll pick you up at ten in the morning. I've already decided to take another day off as I'm long overdue a break."

I'm intrigued, but this means I must return to Highbrook and spend another night without him.

Frances's shadowy figure is waiting at the window as we approach the house. As if this place doesn't unsettle me enough, an ethereal entity staring out from the window doesn't help.

"Good day, boys?" she asks, as if time has stood still and we're coming home to her like years ago. I just can't help missing it for a second.

"We've had a lovely day, thank you, Frances," papa says, "I'm picking Albert up tomorrow to show him where I've been staying. The time has come to move life along a little."

She throws him a glance, her expression full of questions. He looks more himself after only one day, with a coastal glow about him that's clear for her to see.

"Yes, good idea," she says levelly, no doubt wondering what moving life along entails, "I'll see you tomorrow then."

Papa kisses her cheek then pulls her into his arms. Their love is plain enough to see, but not enough it seems to keep him under her roof.

As he heads off, we're left alone with only the drone of the radio in the background. I decide it might be better to play the long game with Frances. Speaking over each other, I can tell we're both uneasy at our first encounter since the fallout.

"I was just going to say, there's some suet pudding to take up if you'd like some. I've kept it warm, just in case."

"Great, my favourite, yes please, Frances," I say as though reading from a script.

I know she isn't fooled. But then papa is our priority so, this little dance will just have to suffice.

For now.

*

"I never had you down as a man of mystery," I tell papa.

The sun is soaking the moors and it makes me think I must be getting old for noticing. Either that or absence is making me appreciate what I've always taken for granted.

"I wish I could say I was so exciting, it's just I think you'll like what you see, and it's as much yours as mine anyway."

"The plot thickens," I say, popping a pear drop in my mouth. He knows I love pear drops.

The car slows soon after.

"Well, we're nearly here. Kindly indulge me if you will and close your eyes."

I glance at him then do what he asks, happy he's being playful.

I had the first decent night's sleep in months last night. I wrote to Charles to tell him about my day at the coast then wrote much the same letter to Elise. I wasn't sure if it was leading her down the garden path but decided she deserved a letter at least. Turning off the lamp I lay in my childhood bed and slept like a top for the first time in years. I worked out how many. Five years at boarding school, eight years at Oxford including an extra year for the delayed timetable due to the war—thirteen years of my life.

It was like laying down to sleep in the deathly silence of an underground coffin for a moment, but then the very same silence meant I slept solidly and woke around nine.

I woke ready to make plans for my future. Elise would be proud of me.

"You can open your eyes now," papa says, switching off the car engine.

I do as I'm asked and then blink. I blink again. Where on earth are we? This is like the land time forgot with a tiny cottage sitting in front of a giant woodland. We haven't been driving very long but it's as though we've come to the ends of the earth.

"This was your great grandmother's cottage. Can you believe your grandma Ann grew up here with her mother and father? He was a woodsman.

In truth, I can't believe it because the cottage doesn't quite look real. So, this is where papa's been hiding. No wonder he likes it here; I like it too already.

I jump out of the car to get a better look. The quiet here is peaceful, a different quiet to Highbrook.

"I love it," I say, glancing between papa and the beautiful cottage, and back again. His face is a picture of joy which makes him look youthful. Joining me at the end of the gate, he looks like a weight has been lifted from his shoulders. What would be so troubling he couldn't tell me about a little cottage?

"You haven't seen inside yet, it's not grand, like home."

Home. I haven't had a home since I was eleven years old, when Frances's apartment was home. I brush the thought off, annoyed with myself yet again I'm allowing her to spoil every happy moment. Well, I suppose getting yourself back on track doesn't happen after just one good night's sleep.

Papa takes me around the back to explore the woods which seem part of the garden. Then he shows me inside, the tour of the tiny rooms taking all of two minutes.

I heave a deep breath, choking back tears as I look at the formal photographs of you with your parents and Uncle Daniel, you with papa, with me, with both of us. I have pushed your image further and further to the back of my mind, struggling sometimes to remember your face. I wish I had looked at your beautiful face more, I wish I had devoured every detail of it. The house is bursting at the seams with something wonderful.

The faintest noise escapes me. Papa puts a hand on my shoulder, and it stops the noise progressing.

"Sit down, son, I'll make some tea," he says quietly, "Well, it's compact and bijoux as they say but it has so much character, so much atmosphere. I prefer being here to Highbrook at the moment.

Thirteen years is a long moment, but then I suppose he was looking after grandma for a while.

If only we'd lived in this little house when I was growing up everything would have been different. It would just have been the three of us, no interlopers. I shake my head at the thought.

"Well, now you've seen it, I didn't know if you fancied a trip to Horton for lunch. We could pick up some provisions afterwards."

I sit in the chair, all the while wondering if this is your chair. How I hope so.

After tea, we head to papa's gentlemen's club, and I join him as a guest. He tells me that soon he'll make me a member. He's so humble, so unassuming I forget sometimes how wealthy he is. After a hearty lunch and a read of the papers by the fireside we head to the centre.

Turning onto Market Street, I pop my letters in the post box then see a man and a woman heading towards us. It takes a moment to register the man is Uncle Daniel. He looks so different, but then he would having lost a hand in the war. I can't quite put my finger on why he's so changed, but then the war has done terrible things to people. Terrible things which are rarely if ever mentioned. Charles told me some it.

The woman turns her head to look at me. She's wearing a green two-piece costume and a light brown velvet pillbox hat with a veil over her eyes. They complement her copper hair falling from under her hat to her shoulders. Her green eyes try their utmost to hold mine.

Daniel shakes our hands, and I'm thankful at least his right hand is untouched.

"You've met Ava before, William, haven't you? Ava this is Albert; Albert, Ava."

The familiarity of the introduction by first name is a sign they know each other well, but Daniel doesn't elaborate.

"Albert, so nice to meet you. Your uncle has only good things to say about you."

"The pleasure is mine" I say lifting my hat, then find myself at a loss for words.

She smiles a beautiful smile, but it isn't only her beauty which entrances me. It's the way she moves, so graceful and ladylike. Like you, I suddenly recall.

I'm grateful she has plenty of questions and she's listening intently to my very brief and succinct answers, her eyes roaming around my face and to my hair as I talk. A heat creeps up my back and I look away.

"How long are you home?"

For once the question doesn't irritate me and after the last couple of days, I've gained a little more clarity. The cottage would make a fine retreat.

"I'm back for the foreseeable future perhaps for good," I say, looking at papa.

His overjoyed expression takes me back to my father of old.

"That will be wonderful for your father, I imagine," Ava says smiling at him.

Now her face turns towards me and this time I'm unable to look away.

"Well, we must dash, I have a meeting in Leeds in a couple of hours. Ready?" Daniel asks Ava.

I'm taken aback at his sudden retreat from our conversation, I think we were all expecting to arrange another meeting.

As we say our farewells and walk away, I'm unable to resist the urge to look over my shoulder.

Nobody was a surprised as I to see Ava had the very same urge.

Chapter 56

I'm parked at the Falls in papa's spot as I think of it now.

He's at work and not due back for hours. I'm finding the fact he lives like clockwork is working to my advantage, especially of late.

So much has happened since my twenty-fourth birthday, not least of which is that I am now Dr Albert William Hudson. Alongside passing my driving test and working at Leeds Infirmary until I can secure a position as a general practitioner nearby, means there have been plenty of reasons to celebrate recently.

I've been able to celebrate properly, having more than one pint of beer, but I haven't moved onto the hard stuff at papa calls it because I haven't felt the need. I might not have the addictive personality I thought after all.

I saw Charles and Elise at our graduations in Oxford. Charles was shocked when he saw me.

"Gosh, you look like a new man, or perhaps you're back to the old Bertie," he exclaimed when he saw me, "Country life suits you by the look of it."

Continuing his studies to be a surgeon his plan is to land a job in Harley Street eventually. It might be a long shot for some, but Charles's father is well connected.

His mother will have been expecting to meet a different person I imagine. Charles looks like her; they have the same warm smile. She will have found out so much about me, and I was a little ashamed.

They met papa and Frances under the spires of the impressive university I'd taken very little notice of during my time there. Papa was in awe of the architecture, the quads, the shops in the cobbled streets, and I tried again not to think about the fact it was the first time he'd seen them. We've come so far, he and I and living in the cottage was nothing short of idyllic at first.

Elise joined us briefly on the day though she may have wished she'd refused the invitation from Charles. I couldn't really blame her. I telephoned her to have the difficult conversation eventually. Life had moved on so much and she deserved to hear it from me, not read it in a letter.

"So, finally, you have the gumption to come clean. Our relationship was always one-sided I realise now you've given me plenty of time to mull it over, thank you for that. To think I put so much effort into trying to get you back on your feet. Charles too."

I heard her tut and imagined her raising her eyes to heaven with irritation. I saw that expression many times.

"I know and I'll never forget it," I said, "You were always too good for me. I'm sorry, Elise."

She sighed.

"Well, I suppose we were young, but I really was prepared to wait until you got your life together."

Her candidness touched me, and I was surprised she was letting her guard down.

"I know it would have been better all round if I'd just told you how I felt. I was a coward, avoiding the conversation. If it's any consolation I feel awful I didn't take the opportunity before I came home. I had so much in my head, things I didn't tell you about and I should have."

"We all have worries, Albert," she said, and I considered elaborating for a second.

I couldn't even if I wanted to.

She will have been sitting in the shop between customers, starting the wait all over again for life to present her with a better opportunity.

"See you at the graduation, then," she said, her voice sullen.

"I'd like that," I said, not really knowing if I would, "Cheerio for now, Elise."

The line went dead, and I sat looking at the telephone feeling like a grown-up. I'm living in a grown-up world now, for so many reasons.

And even stranger, considering it was one of the more taxing conversations of her life, Elise never swore—not once.

*

She's late.

I'm getting restless so get out of the car to sit on the bonnet, sliding my hands into my pockets. Ears pricked, I'm like a rabbit listening for a fox.

Finally, I see a person darting in and out of view through the trees, and my heart hurtles upwards with a rush of adrenalin. This is the way I feel regularly at present.

She's wearing her tweed skirt and heavy boots under a warm brown hat and coat, which could make her look frumpy, matronly even. But this could never be the case. The age gap is less of a concern for me than her but then she casually informs me I've been searching for a mother-figure. To be honest, sensible clothes or not, she doesn't look in the least bit motherly.

I slide off the car and walk over to meet her, no doubt appearing calmer and more in control than I am.

"Sorry, sorry," she says, looking a little flushed, "I couldn't get away.

From work or from Daniel I wonder.

"I'm just glad you're here, I was getting worried."

Her shoulders rise then fall as she heaves a sigh.

"He's been round again," she says.

I don't need to enquire who 'he' is. He won't take no for an answer and he's becoming a concern.

I've run out of suggestions about how to handle the situation. I curl my arms around her, and she nestles into my chest underneath my coat. We listen to the waterfall while I try and think of another approach. The weather is too cold to be out here, I'm thinking, we should go back to the cottage.

"I could just tell papa, then he can have a quiet word with Daniel. He'll be on our side when I explain how we feel."

She pops her face up.

"Are you mad? Your papa would never do that. You've told me he's not one to interfere and he's fond of Daniel. It's all such a horrible mess."

I agree but I want to make her feel better.

"Good job I'm worth it then," I say, quick as a flash, making her smile and give me peck on the lips.

I love those kisses, reliving how they make me feel so much of the time we're apart.

"Look, it's absolutely freezing out here. Why don't we go to the cottage, papa won't be home for hours? We can talk, try and come up with a plan of action."

She hesitates, then nods.

"Alright, if your papa arrives home early, I can hide out in the woods until you come find me."

We laughed at the thought.

Back at the cottage, the fire only needs a little broddling to have it glowing again and I throw some more logs on to keep it blazing a while.

Papa and I talk about you so much more now. He tells me little things in passing, like how you took your tea—milky, no sugar or how the wind was your favourite sound, which was just as well here, and how you couldn't live without books. Every detail is so significant, helping me build a picture of my mother. Somehow it doesn't sadden us any longer.

It's just right for us to be here. We still visit Frances regularly, I can't escape it, but at least we're never alone and I've been playing the game so long, I'm quite the expert.

309

Ava's sitting on the small sofa, waiting for me to join her and I grab my tea from the side table to settle down.

"You know, I can understand why Daniel can't accept it's over. You were together so long from what you tell me, and now after losing his hand he'll be vulnerable," I tell her.

"I'm a nurse, that's the least of my concerns in terms of appearance. It's the man who's changed beyond recognition. Losing your mother affected him in many ways and then the war just fuelled his bitterness towards life. He became unrecognisable."

We're solid enough as a couple, but I still have a nasty little worry they might get back together. I wake up in the night thinking about it and how I would struggle to get over it if they did.

I lift her legs up to warm her feet under her stockings. This is the first time we've been alone together here or anywhere other than the car. It makes me happy when she relaxes under my touch.

Sitting together and gazing into the fire it's as though we've been married for years. Like she's come home from a shift, and we've had tea and all we need to think about is what will be on the radio tonight. I like it. I like it very much.

Her face turns my way, and I stare into those green eyes trying to gauge what's afoot.

"How is it I talk to you as though you understand. How can a twenty-four-year-old understand?"

I could be offended but I'm not.

"This is no run of the mill twenty-four-year-old you're dealing with here, you know."

I pause wondering whether to speak the words aloud for a second time. Should I? Well, she's the right one to hear it if I do. She's watching me as I swallow.

"This particular one has hidden depths and they're far too deep if truth be told. He even worries he might have had a hand in what happened to his mother."

I'm not prepared for her reaction, the look on her face. She jumps off the sofa to land at my feet. She holds my hands; strokes my face and I want to cry so I close my eyes. I didn't mean to cause her such distress, yet how foolish to think there could be any other reaction to such an admission. I don't want any secrets from Ava, she deserves to know who she's dealing with … warts and all.

"Oh, my darling boy," she says, "How could a child have a hand in that? Daniel told me your mother loved you and your father so very much. It would be impossible to hide a love like that, but she was troubled he said. Apparently, she was the same when they were growing up, peace somehow eluding her. Some people are just prone to melancholia. I can't bear it that you've carried such a burden and for so long, I just can't."

Raising from her knees, she kisses me so gently I feel a tear slip down my cheek. I don't want to cry because this is a profound moment in my life, like papa described his first meeting with you when I asked him.

Her lips pull away and she runs her thumbs gently under my eyes to dry my tears, her own eyes moist. Her lips come back for more, the kiss intensifying, taking us to a dangerous place. I feel her fingers undoing the zip of my trousers, her soft hand slipping inside. I'm overcome with passion, and she can feel it.

Lifting her skirt, she climbs astride me, her lips searching for mine again. When she slides her way down me and stops, I have a sensation I could only dream about. Unbuttoning her blouse, I slip the thin straps of her camisole down her arms slowly, so she groans, pushing her hands into my hair to pull my face towards her nipple. She groans louder when I roll my tongue over it gently. A tear wets my face when I kiss her again. I don't want her to cry I want her to drown in me, think of nothing else but me. Thrusting my hips upwards, she cries out, dropping her head backwards and thrusting downwards to meet me.

I think now of nothing else but her. All I want is her ... just here, just now.

All I want is this. This love.

Papa never came home early. I saw him pass from the cover of the trees by the Falls as we said our farewells and kissed properly like the lovers we are. She no longer thought of me as a flash in the pan, a young boy with a silly little crush on an older woman. She saw me as a man.

After she left me, I got back in the car, and I thought how in one short afternoon I'd come to understand my father so much more.

Poor man, I thought, staring out of the windscreen, tears rolling down my face.

Poor, poor man.

Joshua

Chapter 57

You have become a cause for concern.

Once or twice a year was disconcerting, but now you're coming six, even seven times. Something must have altered in your own life for you to increase the pressure and I'm beginning to worry I might crack and play right into your hands. I mustn't allow you the power.

Of course, I've played out the scenario of challenging you. I've imagined telling you to leave us alone many times, but I know I won't because I could never risk getting too close. I would run the risk of looking into your eyes.

Playing into your hands could trigger a conversation or even a row. Either would suit you better because this indifference as you see it, will be hurting far more. I would love to be indifferent; I dream of it.

Thankfully, Kate's more rational than you but then this is one of the many reasons I chose her. I was careful who I chose and very relieved when she chose me back.

If I want to pretend my mother's not there, then this is what we'll do, Kate tells me. The same as if I ever want to go outside and tell you exactly what I think of you, then we will. I often imagine the look on your face if I were to confront you. Except that was never our relationship.

Carving my own path without you makes me incredibly proud. It took many years of slowly gaining self-confidence, but landscape gardening pays well, especially now I've managed to secure wealthy clients. These clients have even begun recommending me to lords, judges, members of parliament and the waiting list is growing. Employing a team of staff means Kate no longer needs to work, and we have help in the house. It was always going to be important to me to balance my time at home and at work, and even more so now I'm a father. I don't want to repeat the mistakes of my own father who, had he lived, would have been tussling with regret. But he was avoiding you, so I shouldn't really compare us.

Emily and George ran in from school just as I was peering out into the winter dusk. I saw you. Wearing your heavy coat and hat you were sitting almost out of sight but sadly I could still spot you in the thicket. It's like some instinct.

Our home is at the end of a row of Victorian houses and only a stone's throw from the station. When you discovered our new address, we considered moving, but I've decided I will not let you drive us out of our family home. I have no doubt you would discover us wherever we go, except if we moved abroad and this seems ludicrous, as though there's a threat to our lives.

Kate told me once a person is unable to control you unless you hand them the power. I understood perfectly, but if you've already handed them the power it can be so much more difficult to take it back.

You live in hope of a reconciliation—hope is all you have—and it looks as though you won't be giving up on it.

George is in his room for now but he's often out with his friends playing in the street. A twelve-year-old boy is a mystery to me because I can't relate to prepubescent surliness and hostility, and I look on him as a kind of scientific case study. His behaviour fascinates me. Kate is not so fascinated, but she still knows how to deal with him without any unpleasantness. I can't abide unpleasantness.

Emily is sitting on the rug by the fire plaiting the hair of her new doll, Mary carefully swirling the strands of blonde hair around each other. Her own plait is coming undone and she's forever tucking her falling hair behind her ear, a habit she shares with her mother. I usually like this time of day, I liked it more when George was playing with us, but you can't have everything, and this phase won't last forever Kate says.

I have a spot where I can look out discreetly from the dining room window and I head over more regularly than I should to assess the situation outside.

Twilight is coming quicker now October is here, and the ground is shimmering with frost. A train is due, so I hope you have plans to return on it. You look an otherworldly figure, sitting in shadow on the embankment. Losing sunlight means you'll be freezing cold, further confirmation you're more desperate.

For God's sake, mother, go home before Kate gets back, I think every time I look out and you're still there.

Heading back into the snug kitchen, I put the kettle on before joining Emily. The pie for tea is ready and waiting to go in the oven when Kate gets home. She's such a good wife, a good mother. A good woman.

I jump as I hear a knock at the door. Every hair on the back of my neck alerts themself to the ominous sound and I sit transfixed. Oh, surely not.

Emily looks my way.

"There's somebody at the door, daddy," she says, assuming I haven't heard as I'm sitting straight as a bolt in my seat. Her voice spurs me into action.

Getting to my feet I ask Emily to stay where she is as I head to the hallway, throwing a reassuring smile over my shoulder at her as I leave the room. I can see the outline of someone through the glass under the streetlamp, but I can't tell who it is or even if the person is a woman. I consider not answering but they knock again. I walk on, accepting my fate.

Placing the chain in its cradle, I open the door to peer around.

My relief is palpable.

"Yes, may I help you?" I ask, stomach churning, mind elsewhere.

"Good evening, I'm very sorry to bother you, but by any chance are you Mr Joshua Cundall?"

I would prefer not to be having this conversation, but I find myself intrigued. Regardless, politeness will always be my steer in life.

"May I ask your name, sir and the purpose of your visit?"

"My name is Albert Hudson," he pauses, "I lived for many years at Highbrook with your mother. I would be most grateful if you could spare the time for a chat."

As I stare at him through the gap in the door, he can see enough of my face to read my expression.

"Please don't concern yourself, she's gone. My purpose is not to cause trouble, I can assure you. I followed her here, something I should probably have done years ago.

My eyes grow at the frankness of his statement. After a moment's reflection there's something about his expression which makes me open the door to this curly-haired stranger.

A stranger who I know already is anything but.

Frances

Chapter 58

I let myself back into the cold, empty house.

Switching the lamps on and lighting the fire does so little to warm it up.

Knowing I would be out, I had some leftover stew waiting. I put a match to the stove thinking if ever there was a symbol of loneliness, it was warming a meagre portion of leftovers.

The same loneliness draws me to visit Joshua more nowadays like a moth to a flame or more aptly perhaps, a sinner to confession. At times l can think of nothing else until I've given it another try. Of late the draw has been more powerful than usual and I imagine it will be bothering him. If I crank up the pressure, it will do the trick, has been my thinking. This is all I can think to do.

All these years I've only ever wanted us to have a moment alone so he could look into my eyes, and I could explain it was an accident. I could tell him I didn't kill his father and he could see the truth for himself. The eyes never lie.

But he must come to me. I doubt he would open the door to me, and I can't flag down his car or plead with him on the street. I'm not fool enough to think that ploy would work.

The dead house is scorning me again. With Harry calling less often I even considered selling, until I came to my senses. I can settle better when I at least have a plan of some sort, but a plan has been eluding me for a while. Thankfully, I've come up with a way forward.

The next person to get on side is Albert. His little outburst when he came home from university took me by surprise, but this silliness has gone on long enough. I'm going to the cottage this week to clear the air because he's been very adept at avoiding me and this has got to stop. It shouldn't be impossible to redeem a semblance of a relationship. Surely one mistake shouldn't wipe out nearly twenty-five years of devotion.

I blow out my cheeks wondering if it depends on the gravity of the mistake.

So, I let the ground settle for four days. Four days used to pass in a blur but now time seems limitless. I've been to-ing and froing in my mind, but today might be the day to head to the cottage. I'm still mulling it over as I'm putting my linen away and hear the chime of the front doorbell. Good heavens, I nearly drop the basket, I'm so shocked by the sound of it after all this time.

Pulling open the door with more than a tinge of anticipation about who might be visiting it wanes when I see its Sylvia. Flowers in hand her smile is as big and bright as the crescent moon. I spot her driver waiting in the car reading his paper.

What an infernal cheek. I'm aware Harry hasn't entirely betrayed me, but he did show signs of leading me down the garden path with his flirtatious behaviour. When all the while he was busy doing unmentionables with her ladyship.

What do I have in the pantry to offer her? Butter scones, they will suffice.

"Sylvia, how perfectly lovely to see you."

Settling myself by the fireside, I notice she's made herself at home already, reading a book from the table as she waits for me to join her. She's always seemed extremely comfortable at Highbrook, but then it was home from home for her for long enough. I've placed the flowers on the windowsill—sweet Williams, how very apt.

"You know, Frances," she says, helping herself to my homemade raspberry jam without a care in the world, "I realise I've been somewhat neglectful, though this was never my intention. I've missed our little chats."

"Oh, I understand, you've had a lot on your plate, Sylvia."

My cheeks are stiff from a fake smile already.

"Yes, well the boys are doing well now, thank goodness, so you and I can spend more time together. You know, like we used to. I was never away then and you must have been sick of the sight of me some days."

She smiles to herself at the memory, convinced I wasn't sick of the sight of her because she's perfectly correct, I wasn't.

The boys; the boys! I nearly choke on my tea, listening to her weak explanation for dropping me like a hot brick once fostering and nursemaid duties were surplus to requirements. If she thinks she can waltz in here and pick up where we left off, well, she takes the biscuit for sheer brass neck, she really does.

"How's Harry?"

I drop his informal name so sharply into the conversation she can't think quickly enough. This is satisfying, watching her redden and glow suddenly like she has a fever. I know the kind of fever she has.

"Harry? Mr Carr? I haven't really seen him since William's been more himself. He called a time or two in the early days like he did here, he told me."

I can't exactly say what I spotted when I was peering through a crack in the curtains a while ago, so I tell her I've seen his car at the house a few times when I'd tried to call. His visits could well have been innocent but we both know they weren't. We're far too long in the tooth to dance that silly dance.

Sighing, she drops her scone on her plate, apparently suddenly lacking an appetite.

Harry's visits to Highbrook now long gone, the festering bitterness has become a boil fit to burst.

And burst it does.

"Might I just say something, Sylvia if you would indulge me?" I ask rhetorically as she raises her eyebrows, "I thought you had more respect for me than this. I'm not a blithering idiot. It appears you're far too busy and important to bother with me nowadays. If you remember it was me who befriended you when you couldn't stand the sight of your daughter-in-law, when you pretended your family didn't exist, when you offloaded your secrets. Now I'm expected to understand you forgot about me when it suited you and pretend it didn't happen."

She places her cup and saucer back on the tray, dabbing her mouth with a napkin, nails buffed to the colour of a pearlized shell from the bottom of the ocean. Always the lady.

Am I going to get short shrift or humble pie?

"You mean when you showed me the light and I stepped up to look after my family when they needed me?"

Damn this woman, she may just have served me up an equal portion of both.

"It doesn't bother you that Harry's married?" I ask, wide-eyed with sarcasm.

I watch a shadow drift across her face as she daintily clears her throat. I've clearly angered her.

"Frances, I don't have to explain myself to you or anyone else for that matter, but his wife left him a few months ago for someone she knew before they were married. A common occurrence now from what I gather: since the war people are less afraid to seize the day it seems. However, it was no less of a shock. Harry had his suspicions for a long time beforehand, but I suppose he thought she loved him too much, or even that she would never do such a thing. How wrong we can be about people sometimes."

Yes, very wrong. I would never have had you down as a bending over the dining table kind of gal, Sylvia or even an earth mother once upon a time.

Well, well, well, this is a turn up. I wonder if William knows.

Sylvia gets up from her seat suddenly and heads to the coatrack in the hall to put on her things. Watching her sashaying along with her crocodile skin bag and fox fur, I don't think I've ever seen her looking so youthful before. Her hair is a shade lighter too and she has that spring in her step, the one I can barely remember.

Buttoning her coat, she says, "I never understood why you let your staff go, Frances if I'm honest. Life must be very domesticated for you nowadays. I shall look back fondly on our time together. We may have served a purpose for each other at the time, but sadly friendships sometimes run their course. I've been feeling a little guilty of late about not seeing you enough but thankfully you've removed this little burden of pressure for me."

So much hidden malice, but she was always the coldest fish in the river.

I'm seething. I'm jealous Harry has chosen her over me, jealous William and Albert have chosen her over me and I must not allow her the satisfaction of getting the upper hand.

Would I have done something untoward at that moment? Would I really?

I'll never know the answer.

Just then I caught sight of a car trundling down the drive through the glass in the front door over Sylvia's shoulder. She whipped her head around when she saw the look on my face as it dawned on me what kind of car it was. It was a car which only meant trouble was afoot. I thought they had come to inform me something had happened to you, or Albert… or Joshua. How foolish of me, why would they have done such a thing? I'm not the next of kin or even emergency contact for any of you.

Every one of you has far more important people in your life.

You all have far bigger fish to fry than little old me.

321

Albert

Chapter 59

I'm still surprised I was allowed into Joshua's home so quickly.

I could have been anyone, even with mention of his mother, but then a person who has darkness lurking, and I'm certain already he does, is probably more open to persuasion. I understand.

He doesn't look like Frances. From portraits, he looks like his father.

He asks me to wait in the dining room a moment, and nods to a chair. He pulls the door but doesn't close it and I hear him say something I can't quite hear. A tap of light footsteps tells me they are making their way down the hallway and up the stairs.

"My daughter," he tells me, gesticulating with his head for me to follow him into the parlour. I knew he had a son but not a daughter.

As I'm sitting down, I'm startled by the slam of the front door and a woman's voice calling, "Only me, love."

I return to standing as Joshua rushes past me to explain who I am but he's too slow to stop her being surprised by a stranger in her home.

"Kate, this is Mr Hudson," Joshua says quickly, "He's just arrived so I know as much as you but apparently his family lived with my mother for years."

I walk forward to introduce myself wanting to put her mind at rest.

"Most people call me Albert. We lived in a converted apartment above Frances at Highbrook for a long time; since I was born in fact."

"I see," she says, her expression saying otherwise, "Why have you come here today? You can be truthful. My husband and I have no secrets, I know all about his life… his childhood."

She looks at her husband but doesn't smile. His expression is fixed waiting for an answer. She's understandably protective.

"As I explained to Mr Cundall, I certainly don't wish to cause trouble, I swear, I only want to ask a few questions. I think I might have an idea about the kind of childhood your husband may have lived."

I almost see them reading each other's thoughts.

"Please, sit down," Kate says, putting her basket down and hanging her coat over the back of the chair. They both sit down together whilst I'm thinking if I could get a foot in the door, I was only expecting to talk to Joshua.

I join them around their fireside, very uncertain how to continue the conversation. Does she really know everything? Surely everyone has things their spouse is unaware of intentional or otherwise.

Kate slides her hand over Joshua's as they sit side by side on the settee.

"Where are my manners?" he suddenly asks, "May we get you anything to drink?"

He too has impeccable manners I see, a trait passed on by his mother, just like she passed it on to me. We could be related, I notice now. We look so alike, act so alike, it's almost too unsettling for words.

Raising my hand I tell him, "No, but thank you, I'm fine, I don't wish to take up too much of your time this evening."

They're both looking at me as I turn my hat on my knee with nerves.

"Well, now I'm actually sitting here you can imagine I'm finding it difficult to know where to begin."

"Perhaps the beginning would be a good place. You've clearly got something on your mind and I'm guessing it has a lot to do with my mother and her more disturbing side."

Joshua has unexpectedly come to my rescue, and his words hang ominously in the air between us. The purpose of my visit must have been obvious, I suppose. Why else would I be here without his mother? I let out a huge tidal wave of a breath.

I see Kate's knuckles whiten as her grip tightens around his hand. I think of Ava, and I wish she was here with me doing the same.

After a long pause I start: "Yes, that's right though it was only one terrible time, which was enough. I somehow managed to avoid another incident but I've worked awfully hard at avoidance.

He opens his mouth to speak but before he can I press on, unable now to contain what is within: "I couldn't stand not knowing any longer, I had to find out the truth. Why you never visited, telephoned, wrote even as far as I know, it was all too strange. I had to find out what you knew. There was a trigger I'd forgotten about—she called me your name at the end of the outburst when I was eleven—I recalled this when I relived the experience a while ago. We were standing at the bottom of the attic stairs at the time. Now I think this may be significant."

I pause to look at them both.

"Outburst seems such an inadequate word to describe her behaviour, don't you think?"

"Oh, believe me I know it's inadequate," Joshua says, "Indulge me if you will: You try and bury the trauma, but it rekindles itself without warning. Filled with resentment you still can't help wondering what it was that you did to deserve it. You want to hate her, but this is too prosaic. Is this ringing any bells?"

Kate takes her hand away to rub the top of his arm gently to ease his distress. I'd almost forgotten she was there for a second as I processed what he was keen to spell out in black and white. I'm astonished someone has summed up so succinctly how I've felt for over half my life.

My leg bent at the knee is twitching rapidly with nerves.

"It would be best to mention my mother committed suicide when I was seven. Before then and even afterwards for a time your mother was like a mother to me. I almost think she may have planned it now, though to be fair, my own mother had mental health issues from what I gather. I was very young.

"I'm so sorry to hear that, Albert," Kate says with genuine sympathy.

Inclining my head slightly I acknowledge her kind words.

"I wasn't helped by your mother telling me she could understand why she would do what she did with a son like me."

I hear Kate gasp and her misted eyes fill with compassion.

"She knew no limits, no boundaries, I can imagine her saying such as terrible thing," Joshua says.

This is a very personal conversation to be having with somebody you've only just met. Even so, I sense they're both relieved to finally be having the discussion.

"I must check on the children," she says, "If you don't mind, I shall leave you both alone to talk."

Joshua nods as she leans to kiss his forehead before heading upstairs. He wasn't drawn to a mother-figure, rather the opposite.

I see a room strewn with family photographs displayed in gilt frames and they have embroidered cushions on the seats, all signs of a home which they care about and fill with love.

Joshua follows my gaze, his eyes glazed with memories I'm sure he tries to swallow but keeps coughing back up like a nasty phlegm. We have that in common.

"What a wicked thing for her to say," he says eventually, "But she knows not what she says when the devil is at her shoulder. Just because she said it does not mean it's the truth, you must remember that."

I hesitate to ask my next question, we barely know each other, but somehow it doesn't seem that way. He's watching me intently, wanting to delve around my own thoughts I suspect, yet waiting patiently until I'm ready.

"May I ask, what was the final straw?"

Leaning back in his chair, he runs his hands down his face, but I know already he's going to tell me the answer.

"Well, the memories of that day are clear as yesterday but when I say it aloud it seems implausible.

He gets up to walk to the window.

"I'd suffered many years of mental abuse by then, but the reason I left that day is because, well, because I've never been certain if she had a hand in my father's death."

It wasn't what I was expecting to hear. I never thought the reason for him cutting ties would be so dramatic. "Yes, I'm aware of how it sounds but I've genuinely never been able to decide whether she pushed him from the terrace in a rage. My father had seen her true colours and he wanted me to stay with my grandmother whilst he sought help. She was enraged, I'm sure you can picture the scene. I only knew I couldn't stay at Highbrook living under such a cloud of suspicion."

Once I would have shrugged off such an admission. We were talking about Frances, who alongside papa was my entire world for the early part of my life.

"I'd like to say I can't believe it," I tell him quietly, "But I've seen the devil at work with my own eyes."

We sit with our thoughts for a moment, processing the shared information.

"Would you care for a brandy?" he asks me, "I think we could both do with one."

I smile and as our eyes meet, I know our bond is cemented.

By the time I'm on the train home my world has shifted . We've both made a decision which should have been far harder to make than it was.

Kate as a partially neutral party is in complete agreement, the only problem I have now is papa, but he's at risk just the same as anyone. Love is no protection. Joshua offered to be present when I explain because we agree such a situation seems very far-fetched. We've lived with the broader picture for many years whilst he's been in the dark.

The broader picture is that his father's 'accident' should have been an isolated incident, but something Frances said that Christmas is flying around my head. It was something she hissed as she enlightened me about the events which ended your life.

"I tried to grab her, I did," she said, "But she just wanted out of her sorry little life and who the hell could blame her?"

There was only one reason she would say such a thing. Frances must have been on the pier if she tried to grab you before you fell into the sea. We can't think of any other plausible reason. So, now it transpires there are two incidents. Can you have two isolated accidents?

Thank God I went to see him to help piece together the jigsaw in my mind. It seems so clear to me now.

Chapter 60

I stare at the sky through the branches of the tree.

I've had far too much drama of late, so this is just what the doctor ordered. Or the nurse. Nurse Ava's head is resting on my chest, her hair falling across my chin. Our pulse rates are steadily declining after all the exertion. There's something wonderful about making love in the isolation of the woods we decided. We've made a habit out of it since the weather turned warmer.

"One day I'll wear my uniform and nothing else," she teases.

I groan, "Promise?"

She laughs, raising my hand to kiss it.

"You're easily pleased. I promise."

My mind quickly goes to Daniel who is always hovering around my thoughts. I haven't seen him at all, but should I be the one to talk to him instead of Ava? How and when would be the best time to tell him and should we tell him first or papa? I groan inwardly this time, tired of asking myself the same questions.

I've answered one question satisfactorily though; the one where I asked myself if I'd like to marry Ava. I love her like a man loves a woman not a mother figure, how Daniel will have loved her. How papa will have loved you. She is a mother figure but I'm comfortable now this is only part of it.

Nobody was more surprised than I when Ava told me that she had ended her relationship with Daniel months before we met. He was struggling to come to terms with her decision, hounding her, he was taking advantage of her kindly nature. We bumped into each other at the hospital in Leeds only days later. I'd no idea of course she was a nurse before then, but she was a sight for sore eyes walking towards me down the corridor that day. We were surely meant to be.

Before our first time at the cottage, we met on a few occasions for a walk and the irony of that isn't lost on me, knowing from papa how the two of you met.

Daniel had taken it hard, but he wasn't the same man who had come into her life years before she said. Also, if she was being perfectly honest, she wanted a family. She may have been pushing him away without realising because he didn't. I at once asked myself if I wanted children. Undoubtedly, was the resounding response. I must have subconsciously decided years ago to respond so naturally.

At the memory, my mind goes to you and then to Frances. It swings from you to her every time, like you're a pair. Except you're not.

Ava cuts into the silence, knowing me all too well by now.

"Are you thinking about her?"

I don't know if she's referring to you or her, but the answer is the same.

"I'm trying not to but it's difficult when I've upset the applecart so much for papa."

"I've been thinking," she says, lifting her head, "Please don't dismiss it immediately. You should consider talking to someone."

I would laugh if I didn't know she was being deadly serious.

"By someone I presume you mean a psychiatrist. My mother tried that tack, so I found out. On the slight chance she wasn't pushed, she jumped into the sea, you're not at the end of a pier in the middle of the night in winter if you haven't got the idea in your head to start with."

"Albert, you're not your mother, when are you going to realise? You have plenty of your father in there too," she says, in her gentle but firm way, tapping my forehead to make the point.

This would have been a major source of comfort once, but he's proved himself to be fragile, some might even say unstable. I wonder sometimes if your love drove you both to a kind of madness out here in the wilderness.

"A psychiatrist can't possibly help me any more than you, my love," I say.

I don't want to dampen the mood.

"Anyway, I think you just need to take my mind off it, as only you know how."

"Oh, you and your distraction techniques, Dr Hudson."

She laughs and I kiss her to try and bring a smile back to her face. I must sort myself out before too long, this isn't fair.

The soft kiss grows to something far more passionate, and I just can't get enough of her. She's beautiful of course, but more than that. Her energy is powerful, positive and I understand why she became a nurse. I'm young not stupid, I know a good thing when I see it. I know when it's right.

As she reaches the heights, I join her.

I don't want to go back to the drama, I just want to be here in the woods with my girl.

*

Ava has fallen asleep, and I'm pleased because she needs it. What with night shifts and broken sleep, she's worn out.

I like the feel of her in the crook of my arm, fitting like a glove. The peace returns and it's not long before I'm gazing at the clouds scuttling through the trees once more.

Did you have a mind you couldn't switch off I wonder. I suppose you did, or you wouldn't have got to the place you arrived at. That requires so much thought.

The police have opened a fresh investigation but both cases a very cold and the only new evidence they have is our accusations. None of it can be corroborated so it's just our word against hers.

Frances is at Highbrook with the investigation still not officially closed, but I can't see they have much to investigate. Joshua said the police will have raked over the details from the two inquests, but the verdicts were very conclusive. The police think we may have an axe to grind. Of course, we do but we think it's solid enough to cut through her excuses, enough to bring about her downfall. They aren't seeing the broader picture and some of this will be because Frances is a master of disguising her true self. Papa hasn't seen it in almost three decades, so it's hardly surprising when a chat with police over tea and cake didn't raise any alarm bells.

Six months have passed now.

We had waited at the cottage for papa to come home from work before we went to the police station in Leeds to report our suspicions. That was the first time I had doubts when I heard those words said aloud. It sounded so unbelievable, so absurd.

Though papa was with us I was too concerned with justice and protecting him, and I didn't give enough thought to the consequences for him after such an accusation. I regret that.

The day before I'd gone outside to pave the way with papa for an unexpected discussion with Joshua. I would have liked to have done it alone, but I doubt I could have presented a cast iron case without his story.

Papa shook Joshua's hand politely and sat down after the introductions. Never one to make a scene he appeared composed.

"I know to say this is a shock would be an understatement," Joshua began, "It's still sinking in for me too, believe me. But I know my mother well."

Hesitating to vocalise his thoughts, he decided he must.

"I suffered periods of mental cruelty throughout my childhood. The worst part is I always had my doubts about what happened to my father—did he fall or was he pushed. I now find it all too much of a coincidence after Albert's tale."

Papa dropped his eyes, taking off his jacket and loosening his tie like the day at the seaside. I wanted to be back there. He was stalling for time to consider his next move with an audience.

He swung around suddenly in his seat to face me.

"Why didn't you tell me, son? I had no idea what Frances is apparently capable of, I've never seen it. Why didn't you speak up? I didn't even know you'd discovered what happened to your mother."

His face was frantic, but only I could see it as he delivered his words in his usual calm way. I wished then more than ever that we were alone.

The word 'apparently' jumped out at me with all its connotations. I understand his reservations because like so many things, you really must see it to believe it. The whole point of involving the police was I wasn't going to take a chance papa did see it.

I explained I wouldn't have told him at all if I hadn't discovered what happened to Ben, but now I had, surely, we must at least try and stop her from being at the heart of yet another supposed accident.

He got up from the settee to lean on the mantle and stare into the fire.

"So, you think your mother pushed your father from the terrace?"

He raises his head to look in Joshua's direction. Joshua nods only once but doesn't speak.

Papa couldn't continue. We'd never spoken about the manner of your death, not once. He looked back down into the fire.

Staring at each other for the longest time, neither Joshua nor I knew what to do next. I had to think of something.

"Papa, I think you need some time."

I walked over and put my hand on his back. The slight tremor of his body made my throat tighten.

"I'll see myself out," Joshua whispered as he collected his things from the chair back.

Coming out of his stupor papa clicked quietly back into polite mode, holding out his hand.

"Joshua, I'm very glad to finally make your acquaintance, I only wish it was under different circumstances."

"Likewise, I'm sure, Mr Hudson" Joshua said, shaking his hand then turning to leave.

I followed behind, looking at papa over my shoulder.

He had already left us in spirit. How thoroughly naive and immature of me not to realise the extent of what he would be feeling. The pursuit of justice had clouded my vision.

Pressing my lips to the top of Ava's head, she doesn't stir from her deep, peaceful sleep.

The sky is darkening.

I close my eyes and see papa's face on that day.

When I realised too late that well intentioned or not, I had been reckless enough to reopen a grievous wound for my own father.

Frances

Chapter 61

My hand hovers over the bell.

An adage of my own springs to mind where one should be careful what one wishes for as my wish has finally come true. This was always one of my favourite sayings. I have many.

Before I have chance to ring the bell the door swings back, and here he is. Here's my son waiting to greet me finally.

Oh, how I wish this were the case. How I wish my dream really had come true.

Sadly, this is more a case of my son bundling me inside the house before the neighbours see. The two other significant men in my life are standing behind him in the hallway, like a pair of soldiers on guard.

They have summoned me. Not to the cottage, which would have been preferable, but to Joshua's terraced home. I know I've been waiting patiently to be allowed access to this house for years, but not in these circumstances .

I received an invitation by post from Albert with the date, time, and venue, and here I am. Here I am, in line for more questioning, as if I hadn't had enough.

Joshua steps to one side.

"Thank you for coming," he says.

You and Albert incline your heads in unison by way of greeting. Such polite boys, I'm immensely proud.

We all follow Joshua like ducklings, myself in the middle and I watch my son stride ahead. The slight hunch of his shoulders is the only sign he's not as confident as he appears. Only I as his mother would know, of course.

He extends a hand to a seat under the window of the cosy parlour. You and Albert sit either end of a leather button-backed settee and Joshua takes the other chair. I'm far more nervous than when the detectives called round for some gentle interrogation. If such a thing could exist.

It was quite easy in the end to bat away questions about two incidents without witnesses where inquests had already been held. I suspect the boys came across like they are simply trying to settle a score with a mother who may not have been perfect. I wasn't too concerned after they left.

The betrayal however is a different matter, nothing less than a kick in the teeth. Why hadn't they come to talk to me, challenge me even before they went to the police? I found myself most disappointed of all in William for not extending me the courtesy of fair warning.

It wasn't a surprise I didn't see anybody over the Christmas period, though there was a tiny part of me thought William might just be the one to post a card through the door. The fact that he didn't will have hurt him as much as me.

January was a terribly long month, and the others haven't been must better though I've tried to keep occupied. I realise it's come to something when this hostile meeting, one which has been a cause of dread since I received the invitation, is preferable to being at home. I notice the photographs of Joshua and his family, a beautiful blonde wife and two beautiful blonde children. Will they remain strangers after today? I'd like to pull a master stroke and convince them I'm not the face of evil.

Joshua opens the conversation—this is his home, and I am his mother after all.

"We only have one aim today. We would be so relieved to finally hear the truth from your own mouth after so many years," he says.

He doesn't refer to me by any title and he's unable to look my way. I'm not angry with him, I haven't been angry since the day he left, not even after he involved the police. I still only wish to be part of his life again.

Albert catches and holds my eye when I look over, brazening it out, and you're pretending you're simply not here at all. I'm becoming more uncomfortable by the minute, and I drop my eyes from Albert's gaze first.

I clear my throat.

"I'm pleased to have the opportunity to talk to you all today though I fear you have already convicted me without a trial. The police haven't found a shred of evidence to support these wild and unwarranted accusations and to continue an investigation. I was hoping you would accept by now your suspicions are unfounded and apologise for the distress you've caused."

That's it. Just the right amount of indignation.

"Yes, the police informed us of their decision, hence the invitation. You need to understand it was less about a conviction and more about some degree of justice and hearing it from you directly," Joshua says.

You go over to look out of the window. I peer beyond you, through a gap in the pattern of the heavy nets and see the spot where I watch from the embankment. It seems such a silly thing to do when I think about it now, but it was my only link with my son. Something is always better than nothing, especially when it comes to one's children.

Finally, William speaks. "Frances, the boys, or rather we must hear from your own lips, what really happened. Did you have any involvement in the… the…"

Oh, William, you really haven't planned what you wanted to say. I think yet again how that damn woman managed to reduce a strong fine man to a broken shell.

"The accidents," Albert says, sitting back in his seat, "Papa, are you alright?"

It irritates me he's speaking to you like a child, but you don't answer. I'm sorry you've been put in this position as it must be making you want to wither within.

Joshua and Albert are waiting on the edge of their seats.

"To be perfectly frank, I suspect we may be wasting each other's time. I don't see how I can convince you both events were accidental. You have memories which are no doubt very vivid, but at the end of the day, you were both children with overactive imaginations."

You spin around from the window so suddenly I think my heart will fail me.

"Precisely, Frances, you make the valid point yourself. They were both children. Neither of them is a liar; if I know nothing else, I know that . Discounting every other accusation even, how could you be so vicious and cruel to what were effectively your own sons? You made Nell feel a failure as a mother, then, after she left, I trusted you as a mother to my beloved child. I trusted you and you spat it all back in my face!"

My jaw hangs. Oh, I think I'm going to be sick. I swallow numerous times to be sure I have myself under control and stare at you. Your face is a contortion of anger. I've never seen it before, not even when I told you what I'd seen that day when I followed Nell. You were still relatively calm and collected when I'd pulled the rug from under you. I stand corrected; she didn't manage to smother every ember in your belly it appears.

The boys' expressions no doubt mirror my own look of incredulity.

You stride out of the room then out of the house in seconds. I hear the slam of the front door and the car door quickly afterwards. I want to run after you. You're right, of course you are, William. Your condemnation of me is far more powerful than any judge and jury.

"I couldn't have put it better myself," Joshua says now, "Albert and I know you're more than capable of being so out of control with rage, jealousy, whatever else, that you could take someone's life. You might not mean to, and you might even be remorseful but at that moment, at that very moment, you could do it. I've seen what you become, so has Albert," he nods in his direction, "You can't sit here and deny it to both of us."

A tear rolls down my face. Did I start crying after your outburst, or after hearing the harsh words my son spoke to me? I'm unsure, but my face crumples. I must stop. I try to remember when the last time I cried. I remember now it was the day lying on your bed, choking with emotion and memories of Nell.

Albert is staring at me like he hates me. Joshua's face is more benign, his hatred has faded to cold indifference. I know which is worse.

"I'd like to go home," I say quietly, through my tears.

I don't want to go home but I don't want to be here anymore, there is a clear distinction.

"Did you do it, did you kill Joshua's father and my mother? There are only us here now. All we really want from you is to know, Frances."

They stare at me, waiting for a response, eyes pleading.

"Please. Just tell us," Joshua says now looking directly into my eyes, something he's been unable to do since he was a boy.

I scramble for a handkerchief in my handbag. Two sets of eyes burn the top of my head as I dab my nose and stare at my shoes.

"Would you believe me if I said I really don't know the answer?" I ask.

I watch them both look at each other as though I've just confessed to murder. Perhaps I have.

"Yes," They both say simultaneously.

I watch Albert drop forward, elbows on knees and Josh jump off his seat to kneel at his feet and check he's alright like a true big brother. As Albert raises his head they share a gentle knowing smile together, forgetting I'm in the room already.

Surplus to requirements once more.

I breathe out and make to stand up, knowing if nothing else has come from this traumatic afternoon and whatever lies ahead for all of us ...

I have in some perverse way managed to make my boys happy.

Albert

Chapter 62

I'm calling at Joshua's for tea on Saturday. I still find it odd when he rings me, but I really like it when I hear his voice on the telephone. In just over a year, we've become like an extended family, papa and grandma joining us from time to time. I hope Ava can join us soon.

Grandma and Harry are indeed an unusual combination. Unusual but strangely a good fit for each other. I thought she was content to live on her own forever, like she'd tried marriage and didn't like it very much. They've become engaged after Harry's wife admitted adultery and they divorced.

Papa and I called around one night, and she almost blurted out they were courting, wanting to break the news to us on our own.

"I'm aware this isn't ideal, William," she said, "But I've been on my own for a long time. I more than just like Harry, he makes life light, carefree, which reminds me of someone I knew a long time ago when I was young."

She didn't enlighten us about who the person was, and we didn't ask. She stared at papa a moment and looked like she might be worried about his thoughts on the matter. If I'm honest, I thought Harry was sweet on Frances but clearly not. I'm not sure yet what to make of him, but then I remind myself I will soon be hoping everybody is happy for me when my big secret is revealed.

I may not have cared for grandma very much growing up but then as Ava says, she had the devil whispering in her ear.

"Well, I refuse to call him grandpa," I said, to give papa more time to digest the revelation.

He looked over at me.

"No, and I'm certainly not calling him father," he chuckled.

Grandma looked relieved and I was touched she cared so much about our opinion. We all still seek approval whatever our age it seems.

"Well, I know I'm a little older," she said, as I thought of Ava again, "But I'm very taken with him is all I can say."

"Whoa there, mother, I don't care to hear the ins and outs of it all," papa said, with a twinkle in his eye, "Give me time to get used to the idea first if you don't mind."

I just hope he'll receive my news as agreeably, but I had better give him chance to come to terms with grandma's new situation first. Yet another delay.

None of us has seen Frances. I imagine her barricaded in at Highbrook, licking her wounds. She will be living out a life sentence there because we certainly won't be popping in for tea and cake.

I see Ava walking down the track towards the cottage. Checking myself in the mirror over the mantle I notice I could do with a haircut. She loves my curls, finding it hard to believe my hair was straight until puberty. I glance at your photograph and back at myself. I must be around the same age you were when you met papa. He will no doubt see you every day in me because there's no denying that I'm your son.

The snow isn't settling as yet but it won't be long. I hope Ava isn't snowed-in before papa returns from work as he may well decide to come home early. I'll just have to say we met by chance and then tell him the truth later.

I check the fire is blazing and go out to meet her.

She's grinning from ear to ear, and I know my face will be the same. Oh, how I love this girl.

"Hello, handsome," she calls as she's heading down the path. She's wearing the brown boots I bought her for her birthday and a dark green coat, her beautiful hair peeping out from under a cream woollen hat. Her smile drops when we're stood before each other, and her eyes roam my face. She wraps her arms around my neck drawing my head down for a kiss as the snowflakes fall on our shoulders.

Our shift patterns have kept us apart for too much recently.

"I won't stop long. I nearly turned back when the snow started but you were like a wizard, drawing me to your mystical cottage in the magical woodland," she laughs, nuzzling my neck.

"So, just to confirm, you're with me because of my property and land. And here was I thinking I had so much more to offer."

"Oh, but you do Dr Hudson, believe me."

A stirring appears as our mouths clash, tongues tangling this time with sheer unbridled lust.

I hear a voice making our lips pull apart abruptly. I lift my head up as she swings around. Papa has caught us; our luck has finally run out. I'm briefly grateful I don't have to pretend any longer, but the feeling quickly disappears.

The voice doesn't belong to papa.

Daniel is bounding down the track, his expression warning me we're both in terrible trouble. I've imagined this expression many times.

I tell Ava to go inside but she stays rooted, her hands still on my arms. I tell her again more firmly, thankful when she makes a move.

"My own nephew!" Daniel shouts, "Apparently, I should have followed you sooner. Don't tell me this … this… little boy is the reason you wanted to end our relationship."

Ava stops walking and turns around to face him. I keep myself planted firmly in between them both. Her face flushed, the snow is melting into her hair, her clothes but she's oblivious.

I put my arm out to stop him going any further, but Daniel slaps it away.

"Get your hands off him," she spits, running forward so I grab and hold her, "I wanted to leave you long before Albert and I became a couple if you must know. Not that it's any concern of yours any longer, Daniel, you can't manipulate me anymore."

I turn from Ava to stop him putting his hands on her. Is this how their relationship was, I wonder as a fist comes hurtling my way, knocking me clean off my feet and into the snow.

"You can have the first one, Daniel, but don't even think about another," I tell him, getting up from the ground and rubbing my jaw to see Ava is already pounding on his chest, yelling at him to keep his hands to himself. My gentle little nurse is now like a woman possessed.

"Stop it, for heaven's sake!" I yell, pushing myself in between them again and spreading my arms wide.

Suddenly a silence descends as Daniel steps away. I hear a sob and turn a startled face towards him. He drops to crouch in the snow, arms locking around his knees, all the time crying softly to himself. I just can't bear it, neither of us can, we both rush towards him and sit in the snow beside him.

"Daniel, I'm so sorry you've found out in such a way, we were trying to protect you. Daniel looks up briefly and his eyes flash a dart of anger at us.

"Oh, that's very noble of you," he spits.

"I'm sorry, Albert was going to speak to you soon, I promise," Ava tells him, rubbing the back of his hair.

"Ava is telling the truth, I really was."

Dropping my head back now at the thought of what is unfolding guilt floods me like a tidal wave. This is my uncle who I love very much.

He lifts his head, his watery red eyes paining me.

"Albert, I loved you, how could you do this to me?"

We sit staring at each other, his expression now one of sadness rather than anger.

"I'm so sorry, Daniel, believe me. We tried to ignore our feelings, but I suppose we weren't strong enough."

He takes his handkerchief from his pocket, wiping his face then staring at Ava. She's now watching over us yet keeping a discreet distance. She always knows the right thing to do.

As he gets to his feet, he stands red-nosed, a sense of defeat rounding his shoulders. Oh, Daniel. I make a move towards him, but he steps away his eyes narrowed.

"Your father will be disappointed in you," he says, walking backwards to retreat from the debacle.

I try to swallow down my shame.

Of all the parting shots he could have made, this one is the most effective.

Chapter 63

I don't even raise my head when I hear the car outside.
I don't find myself rushing to the window, thinking of an alibi, running outside; nothing.
Ava jumps into action on my behalf.
"Albert, it's your papa, what are we to say?"
Her eyes are wide and frantic like mine should be, only my papa finding out was inevitable and long overdue. I must stand and face the music.
"Albert, are you listening to me? Your papa is here…"
The back door opens, and papa comes into view, briefcase in hand, boots ankle deep in snow. I feel in a trance as I rise from the chair to greet him and take his belongings.
"Hello, you two," he says cheerfully, handing me the briefcase so he can stomp the snow from his boots on the outside step, "I'm glad you're taking shelter from the weather."
I wonder why he's not asking questions then remember this is my father. Glancing over my shoulder, Ava's face is drained of colour as though the blood ran away to hide, much as I'd like to. I busy myself hanging papa's coat as she fills the kettle.
We're in for a long night, I might have to sleep on that little bed of grandmas.
"So, I take it you're here to tell me you're together finally," papa says, reaching for a towel from the over rail to rub over his damp hair.
Ava and I stare at each other then back at him.
"I think I saw you on the moors about a year ago, and then I've spotted you both a couple of times since. This alone wasn't enough for an open and shut case of course, but something told me you were courting."

Ava sits down in the chair by the fire but doesn't speak. I'm sure she thinks the ball is very much in my court.

"Why didn't you say anything?" I ask.

"I thought you didn't want me to know at that point and I was in no rush to be told. You were still deciding about each other. Tonight, is obviously the night to tell me, and I wasn't going to watch you both squirm after my unexpected appearance. I'm nothing if not a patient man."

He goes to smile but stops himself midway. I stare at my father at a loss for words.

"Ava, would you mind terribly if I took my son for a twilight walk in the snow like we used to do when he was a boy? We won't be long and then when we get back, we can have tea. I hope you won't be offended by my indulgence."

His eyes never stray from my face.

"Not at all," she says, from the other room, her tone of voice unfamiliar, "I'll read for a while by the fire."

I'm unable to look her way as we put on our coats and boots, I don't know how to act or what to do.

The snowy night-time walks we had when I was a child were never like this, I think as we head into the darkness of the woodland. The only light is from the sparkling snow and a lantern, but papa tells me he knows a sheltered spot. We walk in silence for a few minutes until he finds the fallen tree under the fir. We're not completely sheltered but enough to take the brunt of the weather.

I don't want to talk but I don't want to stay in the house either, so other than running away in the snow I'm trapped.

"So, what is it, Bertie," he says, brushing the snow from the tree trunk and gesturing for me to sit down, "Is it because Daniel doesn't know yet?"

"He knows," I say, pushing my hands in my pockets, resembling a little boy no doubt. I remember Daniel's cutting words.

"I see. When did he find out?"

"About an hour before you."

"Ah," he says, one word saying it all.

I look down at our boots side by side and think of my little boots on the step at Highbrook.

"So, you've had quite a day by the sound of it," he says, leaning into me from the side. I lean back.

I'm glad we're side by side rather than facing each other. I remember the day at the seaside when we sat in the same way for our chat on the wall. I want to tell him more but I'm not certain how much.

I take a deep breath.

"I don't know if I can live with the guilt, papa. He's devastated and I'm responsible".

He takes his time to respond as usual but I'm not uncomfortable.

"Our heart sometimes takes decisions out of our hands I think."

He sounds very profound and incisive, but words won't make everything better. I run a hand through my wet hair unsure how to go on.

Bending at the waist, he rests his forearms on his thighs. He'll be uncomfortable as these conversations are a trial for him.

"You know, there are times when I wish your mother was here to have these talks. You and she are so alike, at least the person she was before she became ... unwell."

I don't speak because I want to hear what he has to say so very much. A person who speaks the least often has the most to say, Frances said that once, and she was talking about papa.

"You know, if we are a person of good character, every one of us has at least one crisis of conscience at some point in our lives. Only good people have a conscience. We then have decisions to make which may be painful to someone else. We're just human beings, trying to fathom life out as we muddle along, batting balls away for much of the time, and sometimes we don't hit the net. Then we're ashamed because we don't want others to look at us unfavourably and worst of all, we don't want to look at ourselves in that way."

He's right but how dearly I would love life to go back to how it was less than two hours ago. But it can't, not ever and I must accept it.

"You need to establish if the loss of Ava is too high a price to pay. Only you know if you can live without her. I can't tell you how to feel but I suspect she might be worth trying to overcome your guilt at least."

Ava's beloved face floats into my mind. I know papa would have made such a sacrifice for you. He's clearly a man of hidden depths and I wonder if he has secrets and if I would like to know them. I decide quickly that I wouldn't.

What a terrible mess.

We sit looking at the snowy woodland, like a dark, atmospheric painting which is ours for the taking on the doorstep.

"I'm glad we did this, papa," I say, eventually, "You've lived more of a life than you let on by the sound of it."

He turns his head to look at me and I look back at him with a frail smile. He's so handsome but I'm beginning to finally believe he will always choose to be alone.

"I don't know but I am a flawed human being the same as everyone else," he says, standing and holding out his hand to pull me up.

Tramping through the snow back to the cottage I have no idea what to do when I get inside. I open the back door and papa says he just needs to get something out of the car. I know this is only an excuse to leave us alone.

Ava's looking out of the front window, only a few short steps away when I enter the kitchen. She turns to give me a terrible haunted look, a look which makes me gulp huge clumps of air and then burst into tears at the sight.

Walking towards each other, we meet halfway, the warmth of her body and the fire bringing me a kind of comfort I've never had before.

Will I still overcome the guilt tomorrow, the day after—who can possibly know?

But for today, at least, I know one thing for certain:

I have come home.

William

Chapter 64

I pay no heed to the seat ripping a hair's breadth more than last time as I settle into the chair. It's not a statement of style, the purpose of this old chair is pure comfort. I nudge the volume on the radio letting Mahler's symphony wash over me like an ocean wave. Nothing else matters at this moment.

Too soon the melody is gone, melting to the banal, monotone voice of the host.

Opening my eyes is like a key unlocking my mind to memories, restarting the cogs which somehow refuse to rust and stick fast. I often think it would be better if they could.

Albert and Ava are on their way home from Charles's wedding in London. He married Elise but only after seeking Albert's blessing.

They became a couple after Charles invited Elise to London for the weekend. He'd long held a candle for her apparently, and she decided she felt the same once they'd spent some time together again. Albert is delighted for them both and they had a wonderful time at the wedding he said when he rang.

"Elise was just a dalliance, papa, she was never the one for me," he told me, and I'm inclined to agree.

Ava is his girl, even I can see it.

I met Daniel a couple of months after I officially found out about Albert and Ava. We met at the pub where you and I went that first day we reunited on the moors. I chose it deliberately, unsure how it would affect me yet knowing I must find out.

I went early, ordering a pint of Taylor's and I sat at the table by the fire. I was fine, drinking my beer, watching the flames. Removed is the best description and pensive about the meeting with Daniel.

He arrived about half an hour later to join me by the fire. He looked tense but not nearly the wreck of a man I was expecting.

"Good to see you, William," he said, holding out his hand.

We shook hands, careful to hold eye contact then I ordered him a glass of the same beer. We made small talk about my mother of all people because we'd little to talk about, but it helped.

I braved it first.

"I'm sorry how things have turned out, Daniel," I said.

It was a start.

He blew out and took a swig of his beer.

"So, we're really going to talk about it then, are we?" he said, smiling and looking exactly as I would if I were in his shoes. Like he'd prefer to be having a tooth pulled.

"She was the one, Will, that's all I can think to say."

I was foolish in thinking I had it all under control, that I knew how to tackle the situation. It was your brother sitting opposite me and I understood more than anyone what he was telling me.

"I can't deceive you, of course I think it would have been better if Albert had met somebody else in some other way, but I can't ignore the fact he's my son and a good man. However, if there's one person who knows how it feels to lose a love like you describe, admittedly under different circumstances, well, you're looking at him."

Picking up a beer mat, he rotated it on its edge between his thumb and forefinger distractedly.

"You do indeed, but this way I know Ava's still waking up with someone else, sharing a life, a love," he pauses to swallow, "More than likely having children and not just with someone else, with my nephew."

He was right of course he was, and whatever I said I wouldn't be able to make him feel better. We both knew it and I think we both knew it would be the last time we'd ever meet again.

Once, the thought of losing that familial link with you would have left me panic stricken. I had that panic when I saw Albert and Ava by the Falls - it was obvious they were in love, and equally obvious to me that I would have to lose Daniel. I had to lose Daniel because I couldn't lose Albert. One always has a choice to make under these circumstances.

"Fair point," I said, "I think we both know nothing I can say will put it right or resolve the situation. But I do wish you happiness when the time is right to move on."

He slapped the beermat down and leant over the table.

"Like you did, you mean."

We stared at each other, his face far too close to mine and I reminded myself I hadn't done anything wrong to Daniel. His tone was less admonishing and more menacing, and I thought about you as a child and then Ava. Not everyone is who they appear, in fact most people aren't.

"I'm glad we've had this chat, Daniel, truly. We needed to meet and now we have."

I didn't move for a long moment.

Then he swigged the last of his beer in one giant gulp and banged his glass down hard so other people looked our way startled. I was startled but I'm not scared of Daniel, and he knew it.

"I won't insult you by lying and saying it has been a pleasure, but I wish you all the best, William," he said.

I stood up to shake his hand, forever bound by good manners but he was putting his coat and hat on. He left my hand hanging in mid-air when he'd finished.

"I see," I said, dropping my hand to my side, "Well, I'll just say one last thing before you go on your sister's behalf: Albert and Ava are sorry, we all are, but we intend to get on with our lives and live them as best we can, and we genuinely hope you will too. You owe it yourself to live your best life for you, or if not for Nell."

There was a pause and, in his eyes, a momentary cessation of hostilities, perhaps the beginnings of acceptance. Then it was gone. His lip curled.

"Forgive me if I'd rather not take life advice from you or my sister if you don't mind."

I watched him leave and storm towards his car from the window. You idolised him but I see a streak in that man. It's hard and unpleasant.

Ava clearly saw something to make her leave him even before Albert came back from university. I remember how he was set on finding his birth mother and not coming clean about it whether he left you living a lie or not.

Watching him drive away I couldn't help being relieved to see the back of him. He was a link to you, but he wasn't you.

And Ava for all her guilt and remorse may well have had a lucky escape.

Chapter 65

How I've enjoyed this evening trying out various titles for size.

Grandfather, grandad, grandpa, I considered them all.

Grandpa is the one which fits me best.

I'm ready for retirement. Harry is a little disappointed because he isn't yet, but I'd like to be at home every day. I want to await the arrival of my grandchild and devote myself to them for the years I have left. I'll never be stuck for something to keep myself occupied because Highbrook is a perpetual work in progress.

And now I will never be lonely.

I sip my tea keen to head back upstairs but I've still a few items to store away. Harry was bragging about his shed being far better than mine, last week. His competitive streak is comical. His shed is impressive, everything to hand on custom-made oak shelving but this shed knocks Harry's into a cocked hat. This shed is brimming with history and character.

There was mention once of him and my mother moving into the apartment downstairs.

"I think it would be the perfect living arrangement, don't you think, Sylvia? You will be able to look after your mother and I in our dotage, Will, especially as it's at ground level."

My mother's face remained as deadpan as Harry's, and I looked between the two of them as we were eating dinner.

Harry cracked first, laughing inanely, then my mother joined in with a ladylike titter I often hear now, quite the double act.

"Admit it, I had you there for a moment. Your face, dear me, you're far too polite, Hudson," Harry said.

They mentioned it only to scare the living daylights out of me, of course. Who wouldn't love their mother to find happiness, even with the force of nature who is Harry?

I turn off the radio and let the silence drift in.

Oh, Frances, it's strange but I miss you, I do. But I'm so glad you're gone.

It was terrible the first time I returned to Highbrook after our … intervention. I knocked on her door like a stranger, months having passed. She looked older, frailer even. The house and garden were unrecognisable, and she was more so. I would have walked by her on the street.

I shouldn't be here, I thought, but somehow, I had an urge to see how she was. The urge increased over time. Albert would never have understood because he's young, living his life in black or white, not the varying shades of grey maturity brings. Frances had nothing, nobody and I wouldn't wish that on a dog, never mind a fellow human being.

"William!" she exclaimed when she saw me standing on her doorstep.

She staggered backwards to sit on the step as tear upon tear disappeared into the collar of her housecoat.

Once this would have seen me running to comfort her, soothe her distress in any way I could. I'd never seen her weep. Instead, I had a numbness which concerned me, and I didn't recognise myself. What had this woman done to me?

Any conversation would have been a mere platitude. I made her tea and heated some soup she didn't touch. She wasn't dirty, more unkempt, but I ran her a bath like an invalid and waited until she came out in her grubby housecoat to sit by the fire. She sank into the chair as though exhausted. She was exhausted but not physically; mentally she had been put through the wringer.

I asked about the Warrens, but she said they'd retired although she thought it was just an excuse.

"The police at your door starts rumours which can get out of hand," she said.

I wondered if the rumours were true. But still, she is the only one who can answer that.

"Does Albert know you're here?" she asked.

I shook my head.

"Does anyone know?"

"No, Frances, nobody knows I'm here and I'm not even sure I should be."

She looked like I'd slapped her face.

"Then go," she said acidly, running her hand through her damp hair which was too grey and too long, "I didn't ask for your pity and I certainly didn't ask you to come."

"Of course, you didn't but you need my help. You're sinking, I know how that feels. You helped me once."

She twisted the cord of her robe around her finger and back again in a repetitive motion.

"You know, William, I think it's this house. In the end Highbrook has brought nothing but misery to everybody who's lived here."

She was wrong. Everybody was perfectly happy at Highbrook until she interfered.

I was too slow to dampen my anger.

"Then sell up," I snapped.

Her head turned to look me in the eye, and I held my breath, startled. She didn't look quite so frail.

"I live in hope I can convince you and the boys eventually that I didn't do it, that I didn't do any of it."

I was choking with fury.

"I'm not certain how you can do that if you can't convince yourself.

Her eyes averted back to the fire.

"I thank you for taking the time to visit but I'm not fit for company. I'd prefer to be left alone."

I stared at the pitiful sight of the lady who took me under her wing years ago when I desperately needed a wing to nestle under. But it was under false pretences, taking advantage of a lonely man and then sabotaging his happiness in manipulating the love of his life, terrorising his motherless son.

There would be no peace for me, for any of us, until someone held this woman to account.

The responsibility laid at my door.

And I am nothing if not a man who faces up to his responsibilities.

*

Albert's eyes widened as he fell onto the settee.
"A full confession?"
I nodded.
"Absolute."
"But why would she do such a thing after all this time, after all the self-doubt?" he asked.
"She just wanted to do the right thing in the end, son, for you and for Joshua. That's what I like to think."

We sat a while in silence.
"I must tell Joshua."
Frances cast a shadow over their young lives, preventing them from ever finding contentment let alone happiness. Her shadow followed me around for long enough but she's steadily becoming nothing more than a memory, a ghostly folklore of Highbrook.

Albert looked so young or is it that a father never sees his son as a man, not truly. I sat down beside my son and drew him into my arms, his heart pounding against mine. I rocked him as you would have done. It was the most natural thing in the world because this man is my boy, I thought letting my tears flow freely without shame.

Chapter 66

I've been living at Highbrook over a year without Frances.

I'm now the sole owner having bought her apartment from Joshua who discovered his mother held it in his name. During the process I found out from her birth certificate Frances was never even her real name. She was plain, old Joyce Baxter—yet another untruth to poison the mix.

Much like Joshua, Albert would never live here again. He and Ava love living in their little cottage.

Perhaps if you and I had …

I push the regret aside.

No matter, privacy is the key to my contentment as old age creeps in, privacy and solitude.

I have almost restored Highbrook to its glory days. I've been working from room to room, forcing myself to relive the memories. All of them. This house needed far more exorcising for me than the cottage.

I've always had a yen for the simple life. Now finally I have it.

It was a while ago when I found them.

Decorating the bathroom, I finally cleared the cabinet and came across their whiteness staring from the innocuous brown bottle. And I remembered all their bittersweetness. Holding one pill between my thumb and forefinger I turned it this way and that studying it with renewed intrigue. I popped one in my mouth on a whim and swallowed. It was gone and I waited for something to happen. Nothing happened, so I took one the next night and slept like a baby so when they ran out, I replenished my supply with Dr Ratcliffe. He was very understanding of my long-term battle with sleep deprivation.

In the silence of Highbrook, I have been thinking yawning, cavernous thoughts. They've taken me down twisting, turning paths of an unfathomable maze.

My doubts slowly returned. How could you ever have left us to live our lives without your love? It would have been like throwing us to the wolves.

I looked for your note. It was waiting patiently, tucked inside the front cover of *Little Sunbeams* on the bottom of the bookshelf, exactly where I left it.

The note was so evocative I could barely breathe as I read it and wept. Eventually collapsing on the bed, I slept with the neatly folded sheets of paper clutched in my hands, waking in the same position as when I fell asleep. I read the note the next night, weeping less but it served to propel the circling of my mind with recollections which had no beginning and no end. I was going mad.

Then one long night something happened, something made me sit up to turn and throw my hands across the bed. My face was wet with tears and perspiration, fresh from a dream in which you slid between the sheets next to me, moulding your body around mine. You were warm just as though you'd been sitting by the dying fire in our bedroom for a while watching me sleep.

You whispered in the darkness, "I'm here now, William, I have come home. I've missed you, my darling. I've been waiting, observing. I've been waiting for the right time and now that time has come. Our son is happy so you and I can love each other from this night, until the end and beyond. You will never be lonely again, my love, you have my solemn promise … never again."

Closing my eyes, I allow my thoughts to run at will. Thoughts of your curls brushing my chin as you laid on my heart, of your breath caressing the downy hairs of my chest. Your soft breath only confirming to me your lifeblood.

I spend the following day in the garden pottering, the memory like a warm cloak around my shoulders. It saved me.

Locking Stanley's shed for the day, I bound towards the house, towards the wonder that is Highbrook, tapping the bench with the view then spotting Albert's boots on the step, crumbling but still held together.

Much like me.

My eyes stray upwards then further still to the very top, coming to settle on the terrace.

Shielding my eyes from the dying sun's rays I raise my arm from the shoulder and wave left to right, right to left, left right, over and over. My mouth stretches wide into a smile which becomes a low laugh. I quicken my pace in time to the calling, the glorious, the magical call of the dream.

The dream which has finally, absolutely become my best life.

Printed in Great Britain
by Amazon